When the Vow Breaks

A novel

by

Cynthia L. Berry
Sheila A. Taylor-Downer

Professional Prodigy, Inc.

Published in Hillside, Illinois by Professional Prodigy, Inc.
P. O. Box 641, Hillside, IL 60162

www.professionalprodigy.com

ISBN: 0-9702909-2-6

Authors Note:

This book is a fictionalized work. Any references to actual events, real people, living or dead, or to real locales are coincidental.

Song excerpts by:

A Long Walk (Groove), Jill Scott, Hidden Beach Recordings (2001)

Sweet Love, Anita Baker, Louis A. Johnson & Gary Bias, Elektra (1986)

You Brought the Sunshine (Into My Life) The Clark Sisters, composed by Elbernita Clark, Elektra (1983)

I Want to Thank You, Alicia Myers and Kevin McCord, MCA records (1981)

A Street Life, Cynthia L. Berry, lyrics & music © 2005 HPM Productions

Publicist: *Janet Thomas*
Cover design: *Barron Steward*
Cover design: *Karen Knight*
Editor: *Donya T. Hooks*
Proofreader: *Beverly McKinley*

the

will to survive

is greater than

any journey

we travel

it carries us through

challenging our spirit

to rise above

and live . . .

c. berry

Acknowledgements

With ***God****, all things are possible. I give all praise and honor to God, who is the inspiration for all that I do.*

For my rock, the love of my life, ***Anthony****. You once said that I am "the strongest woman you know." I love you more than you'll ever know.*

My children, ***Isaiah, Bethani, Mariah, Joshua****. To each of you, I give my self, for you to live and be free. You are my legacy. Dream in color. . . I love you.*

To my parents, ***James*** *and* ***Jenny****. Thank you for "raising me right" and for always giving more of yourself than I deserved. Love conquers all.*

To my birth mother, ***Gail*** *(Ruby), Robin. Without you, I would not be. I thank God for you and the family.*

To my parents in law, ***Barbara*** *(Joe), Rick. For the strength and love you've always given, I thank you from the bottom of my heart.*

*To "the grands" (****Hildur*** *and* ***Amelia****). Two strong survivors. . . Love survives. Love you!*

To my husband's grandfather, ***Edward****, who passed early this year, I wish you could have been here to see this. It is simply "MARVELOUS." We miss you.*

To my brother-in-law, ***Chris****. Thank you for always listening and encouraging me.*

To all my Aunts, Uncles, cousins too numerous to capture in this book alone. I love you!

To my lovely lady friends and you seven know who you are. Thank you for loving me, as I am... You are always with me. I love you dearly. Stay strong. . .

Special thanks to my editor and dearest friend, ***Donya T. Hooks****, author and editor extraordinaire. You are one of the seven. Time has made us stronger. Love you girl!*

To ***Dawn Schofield*** *&* ***Annette Wilson****- two spiritual sisters who spoke life to this book. May God continue to bless you richly. Thanks for speaking the vision.*

To ***Sandra Bejar****, for countless days of listening to me dream. To* ***Cheryl Gardener*** *for confirming, "It is so . . ." For* ***Ruth Zulfiqar****, It's time to sell!!!!!!*

Pastor Rich*,* ***Pastor Russ****- I thank God for your leadership and unwavering faith.*

To ***Sheila Taylor-Downer****, my business partner and friend. It's been a tremendous journey, but we've made it. We've been through so much in such a short time, but faith has kept us strong. Thank you for always pushing us forward. You're one of the seven.*

To those I have not mentioned by name or relation, please charge it to my head not my heart. To educators, professional acquaintances, friends, family, and readership, enjoy the life God has given you. Thank you for believing in me. . .

Cynthia L. Berry

I want to dedicate this book to the many authors who have helped shape my mind and somehow made me think that I, too, could write.

*To my mother, **Beatrice Taylor** for being my earliest model of an avid reader and for instilling a love of books in me. She is my rock to stand on. If not for her where would I be?*

*To my twin daughters, **BreAnna and Brittany,** who keep me young and spark my imagination - they are our future leaders.*

*To my siblings, **Eugene, Sandra, Sharon** and **James**; these are the people who were around in the early years when I was becoming me. Without the strength I got from these people, I could never have written this book.*

*To my Pastor, **Tracy Jennings and First Lady, Cynthia Jennings** of Total Christian Life Ministry for helping me to get in the right mindset while I finished this book.*

*To my friends, **Carla Campbell, Pamela McClay**, **Christine Finley, Susan Lee, Sherita Taylor**, and **Schleria Taylor**, who have encouraged me, stood by me -they are my greatest critics and supporters.*

*To my friend and mentor, **Robyn Williams**, author of Preconceived Notions and A Twist of Fate, who simply told me to write.*

*To my business partner **Cynthia Berry** for her vast knowledge of life, language and grammar. Thank you for believing, encouraging, understanding and tolerating me through the whole process. You gave my words new life.*

*To my cousin, **Chandra Taylor** (Twiggy), who always supports my efforts. To my friend, Beverly McKinley and Carolyn Curse, who encouraged me to continue on even when I am tired.*

*To my colleagues, **Margarita Gonzalez**, **Jo-Lynn Marshall**, **Nilsa Steigelman**, and **Joyce Evans** for their support and letting me sleep when necessary ☺.*

*To three very strong women; **Ravinia, Sapphire** and **Jade**. Thanks for your incredible journey.*

*And last but not least, to **God**, I thank You. You are my muse, my inspiration and my life. Because of You – all things are possible. For your endless Blessings – I dedicate my soul.*

If I left anyone out, please charge it to my head, not to my heart.

Sheila Taylor-Downer

Special Acknowledgments

***Barron Steward**, awesome cover. Thanks for taking the vision and making it real. **Earl Sewell**, you came through just in the nick of time. Thank you. Special thanks to **Karen Knight**- you are a Godsend! Thank you for your special touches. **Ron Childs, Nikki Woods**, **Lissa Woodson** and countless others in the "biz"—thank you for nudging us on.*

Cynthia & Sheila

TABLE OF CONTENTS

To my sister, **Miranda Richardson***, who through her own life challenges, taught me countless lessons. I'll never forget you holding my hand and never giving up on me, despite the prognosis. You carried me in your silent prayers, whispering in the stillness of uncertainty. Your ever-giving spirit has renewed and inspired me beyond measure. We are both survivors and that miracle from God keeps us alive. My love for you will always be thicker than blood. I dedicate this book to you.*

Love Always,

Cynthia

I would like to dedicate this book to all of the cancer survivors and survivors of abuse, rape, and domestic violence. We must fight together if we want to win this deadly war.

Love Always

Sheila

When the Vow Breaks

Chapter 1

FIRST BAPTIST

She could feel what he was thinking as he briskly walked past her down the center aisle. His cool, Drakkar Noir-scented breeze caressed her face, a gentle tinge on the cheek. She turned her head as not to notice, but his aroma was too intense. The pew on which she was sitting, seemed even closer to the altar than a few minutes ago, and Ravinia realized that she was disclosing more than was appropriate for a proper Christian lady. Wrestling to make sure that the church mothers sitting alongside the base of the massive Plexiglas altar stretch could not see up or down her Chanel suit, she managed to tuck her 18 inch black skirt just beneath her right thigh, so that when she crossed her long, lean legs, the lacy edging of her girdle wouldn't peek through.

Reverend Wright was looking mighty fine today. A sturdy man of the cloth, he stood a towering 6 foot 8 inches tall. Compared to Ravinia's, 5 foot 7 inch medium frame, he was Goliath. The right Reverend seemed even taller when standing in the pulpit/choir stand. He was the Cary Grant of preachers, and he knew it. His rich, ruddy, nutmeg skin, smoothed by years of cocoa and shea butter, glistened under the coliseum-type lights. The "brotha" was just fine. Women of all nationalities, creeds, and colors flocked to the First Baptist Full Gospel Evangelical Assembly "mega" church, just to get on the front row or grab an aisle seat so that they could look up at him and display their wares. And here was Ravinia, falling into the same pitiful trap.

As she reached for the church program, which was more like a mini souvenir guide because it was ten glossy, full-color pages choc full of coupons and ads galore, Ravinia noticed there was a post card inside. "Men's Fashion Show--$25," the header read, "Ladies only!!! Lots of **SINGLE** men." The bolded, underlined word **"single"** jumped out at her.

Ravinia could feel her upper lip curl up as she sneered. She quickly checked her facial expression because, by sitting on the front row, she was on public display. One never knew when the TV camera, filming the service, would focus on one of the church members, so it was best to make sure the expression one wore was appropriate for viewing purposes. Inspecting the men clad in outlandish three piece suits with matching felt brimmed hats and walking canes, Ravinia flipped the laminated 4" x 6" card back into the program booklet. *This is easy.* Ravinia muttered to herself. *I simply couldn't go gallivanting around like a single woman, even if it is for the church. I'm married, for heaven's sake. I can't go. Or can I?*

Ravinia felt like a single woman, although she said "I do" over 10 years ago. *Huh,* she thought quietly to herself. The words "married with children" stung sweetly in her mind. She loved her kids; it was the married part that stung. *If it weren't for this pale, washed out mark on my finger, I wouldn't even remember I was married.* Looking around to see if anyone could hear the pounding thoughts in her pretty tousled head, she traced the circle over and over again. The humidity had started her hair to rise and form little ringlets on the nape of her neck. *No romance, no excitement, no joy. None of that in years. I wouldn't even be thinking about parties or the good preacher if I had anything that even resembled a marriage at home. Oh wait, did I say good?*

Distracted by thoughts of self-pity and demise, Ravinia barely noticed that Reverend Wright had been looking intently at her this whole time. Still oblivious to his apparent interest in her confused state, Ravinia teetered between whether she should go to the show, which she found utterly over-the-top, or go home after church. Ravinia crossed her freshly waxed, mahogany legs with lustful thoughts brewing. Rebuking the unholy concept being whispered in her ear by the tempter himself, condemnation mixed with the pure heat of passion made her start to perspire. Starting to fan herself briskly, it was then that she noticed the Reverend rise up to sing the sermonic solo. She thought sarcastically to herself. *It's his Sunday again? Oh no...* She casually tried to scoot down in her pew, but that looked foolish. Instead she busied herself to keep her eyes averted by flipping through her Bible. She was looking for a good scolding scripture that would help her purge her mind.

Just then, the lower half of Ravinia's body went numb and a cold chill ran down her spine. As she slowly took her eyes away from her Bible, she found that the Reverend's eyes were focused intently on her. It was like he was looking right through her when he was in the pulpit. She could feel his piercing eyes seeming to undress her, but she would look away in shameful disregard. Reaching to habitually twist the 3-carat diamond and platinum band on her ring finger, which served as a convenient reminder of her husband, she realized she had left it on the bathroom counter when she ran into the shower that morning.

Forced to face her temptation head on, Ravinia nervously crossed and uncrossed her legs, as the scratching, scuffling sound of her Leda pantyhose seemed louder than they really were. Yet, no matter how hard she tried to ignore it, she was somehow drawn into the rich, spiritual intonation of his second tenor voice. Perhaps it was how he held the *"s"* when he sang *Yes* with such vocal control that only the finest formally trained Gospel artists could do. Or was it the way his vibrato allowed him to croon in such a way that made the ladies sit on the edge of the pew and jump up and down waving their lacy scarves like they were trying to hail down a cab saying, "Sing that, Rev. Sing that!" Some folks said he sounded like Luther Vandross and Be-Be Winans wrapped up in one. Whatever it was, Ravinia, being an accomplished musician and soloist herself, could fully appreciate the Reverend's vocal abilities.

Wishing however that the Reverend was more focused on his ministry of song than his personal conquest, Ravinia looked up to find some healing for her sin-sick soul. Instead she found him looking right at her. She wondered how he could sing with such power and authority with lust trampling through his mind. Or was it just Ravinia's mind playing dirty tricks on her? Maybe she was imagining that he was looking just at her. After all, the entire front row of the auditorium was filled with beautiful women. Why would he single *her* out?

Anxiety crawling up her legs and into her uttermost being, Ravinia began to feel as if everyone could read her thoughts. She worried, clasping her dainty French manicured fingers together as if she was really pious. Pulling out a little pink tissue, Ravinia started wiping the beads of sweat forming along the length of her nose. *Lord,* she searched her mind desperately, *how can I have these feelings here in this place of all places, when I am supposed to be thinking holy thoughts?* Just then her mother's voice stomped through her mind saying, "Vinia, you know you ain't right. You just ain't right. You're going straight to hell."

Having the fear of God attack her consciousness, Ravinia began to quake at the very thought that had just warmed her soul and body. Tears of spiritual remorse began to flood her soul and leak from her eyes. Not realizing she was standing with her arms lifted towards heaven, she knew she needed some help from on high and looked up for that strength. Of course, the rest of the congregation thought she was being intensely moved by the Reverend's rendition of "He Looked Beyond" and started shouting and rejoicing around her. But, Ravinia couldn't perpetrate. She was not moved by the Reverend's song. Instead, she was contrite in the guilt that she had carried with her to church.

Yet what she felt was more than mere figments of her vivid, unbridled imagination. It would take more than Ravinia's resistance to overcome this type of temptation. Reverend Wright was looking at her, and not just because she was in the front row, either. He had intentions.

Chapter 2.

AFTER CHURCH

Carefully folding the church bulletin in half, Ravinia tucked it into her Bible. She gingerly picked up her purse and started to inconspicuously, or so she thought, make her way out of the church building to the parking lot. Anxiously wishing the crowd of ushers blocking the exit would move their conversation out the door, Ravinia sighed loudly. She knew they heard her when one of them glared back at her, but kept right on talking like she didn't hear her. Finally acknowledging her presence, Sister White, one of the ushers, said "Aight, Sista Hamilton. We'll be moving out of your way," she remarked while donning her 1949 press-n-curl do. You could smell the pungent scent of Sulfur 8 as you passed by her. Her hair didn't move and each glistening strand seemed to hold droplets of sweat like a blade of grass holds the morning dew. "Thanks," Ravinia replied abruptly, picking up her pace within the pew she seemed to be trapped in. It was obvious that Ravinia still needed deliverance because every little thing still upset her and her patience was wearing thin.

Gleaming from a recent scalp oiling, the lights shone brightly on the observant usher's deep middle part, which divided her hair into two equal sides. Sister White had two silver bobby pins neatly placed on each side, just above her ear lobes to secure the frizzy graying edges from popping out. She was head of the usher board and so she smiled a saintly smile as she fiddled habitually with her white usher gloves. You could see the worn marks on the tips of her fingers. She took her position seriously. Sister White could be counted on to be at her post every blessed Sunday morning and through the week, too. She never missed a service and believed that church attendance was next to Godliness. Reverend Wright would brag about how she would always beat him to church, as she was the first one there on Sunday. She would already be sorting out the bulletins she had picked up from Kinko's on Saturday, making sure each one had an offering envelope. If there was something going on after church, she knew exactly where the pastor would be or the location of the event.

Standing about 4' 6", the tiny woman looked up at Ravinia, who was anxiously trying to maneuver herself around the crowd that had collected at the sanctuary door. Sensing Ravinia's urgency, and in an attempt to give closure to her own personal conversation, the seasoned usher gently hugged her daughter Jade, who was visiting that particular Sunday and whispered loudly, "You have a blessed day, baby. I'll give you a call when I get home." Her rich, charismatic voice echoed sweetly, in the near-empty sanctuary. It was the kind of voice that made you self-conscious of your sins and aware of every cruel thought you ever harbored. Ravinia sensed the ushers were ending their lengthy conversation but still was very anxious to leave. She thought to herself. *Why did I have to sit all the way up front in the first place? If I had of gotten a seat near the back, I could have been one of the first ones out.* She apparently had forgotten that she was late to service that morning and the only seats available were in the front row.

Ravinia wanted to get out of the church without being noticed, let alone stopped by anyone, namely Reverend Wright. But being at a church with so many members, she would have to walk two whole blocks just to get back to her car. She knew the best course of action would be to go straight home, even with the forlorn knowing of what would be waiting there. She dreaded going home and thought about stopping at the shopping mall beforehand. Just then, the crowd of cackling ushers finally parted their group like the Red Sea. Ravinia gratuitously thanked them and made a run for it in her three-inch black and white spectator sling backs.

Just one more hallway, Ravinia thought, as she neared the end of the corridor *and I'm home free*. "Tha-nk ya, Je-sus," she uttered under her sporadic breaths. *Lord, Jesus, please let me make it to the door, please, Father God*, her thoughts becoming prayers under her panting. Ravinia had become a Christian about two and a half years ago by watching T.D. Jakes on television. He was ministering at a conference called, "Woman Thou Art Loosed 2" and spoke to the core of Ravinia's very soul. While accompanying her newly appointed partner husband at a citywide fundraiser for Mayor Daley's re-election, she met Reverend Dr. William Wright III. There, she talked to him about her newfound love, Jesus! Ravinia had such jubilance after she got saved that she attracted people to her like bees are to honey. Her sweet demeanor was very desirable and people wanted to know what she was all about. She, in turn, wanted everyone to know about her life-changing experience and shared the good news with whoever would listen. Excited to talk to such a beautiful new convert and possibly get her to come to his church, the mega-church pastor gave her one of his business cards. On the back inside a voice bubble it read, "I'll see you at CHURCH next Sunday!" with a black and white caricature of the Reverend. Next to the image was a tiny, hand-drawn map with the main cross streets labeled. The very next Sunday, Ravinia started attending First Baptist regularly, and Reverend Wright was very pleased.

Almost breaking a sweat, Ravinia neared the corner adjacent to the outdoor exit. Just then, a deep baritone sounding voice echoed behind her. "*Sistah Raveeeen-yah*!" he crooned. Stopping dead in her tracks, she realized her desperate prayers had not been answered. *I could just keep on walking*, she thought, *but that would make him think I'm anti-social or something crazy like that. God, why didn't you just let me get to my car!!?* Ravinia questioned silently, but there was no audible answer.

Hesitating to turn around, Ravinia lost the seconds it took for the good Reverend to catch up to her. Before she realized it, he was standing right behind her. His presence made her warm, anxious and sick to her stomach, all at the same time.

"That is a beautiful suit you are wearing this mornin' *Sisss-taaahhh*," the good Reverend commented in his deep, preacha-man voice. He had an exaggerated way of overemphasizing certain syllables that annoyed Ravinia to no end. "You sho'll did catch my eye from the pulpit," he winked.

Ravinia shyly twisted herself around to look him directly in the eye; eyes that made her melt every time she met them. "I did, did I?" she retorted, sighing as she stressed the second "did" as if to pique his interest. She liked playing the cat and mouse game, but sometimes didn't know when to stop or when it was appropriate. Being married certainly warranted not playing those kinds of games except with her husband. Crossing her thin arms in front of her, she braced herself and prayed that God would give her the strength not to succumb. Reverend Wright's hazel-green eyes lit up and he began to smile, revealing recently whitened teeth. His hair had sleek, basketball waves that lay obediently on his perfectly-rounded head. They had been delicately created by years of vigorous brushing with a dab of Royal Crown, mixed with a sprinkling of water and a tight stocking cap. His professionally-groomed mustache connected to the fine hairs of his goatee and sideburns with a thin, well-defined line around the perimeter of his jaw. She smiled back, realizing she broke the first rule of going cold turkey. Ravinia struggled with some very tumultuous temptations in her life and had decided that enough was enough. But facing the temptation head on was not her best strength. Yet as long as she attended First Baptist, she would have to see the man that led her astray.

"Abstain from the very appearance of evil," the *Chastity Book for Temperate Christian Women* warned. One of the church mothers had given it to her when she confessed her sins at the altar on a Sunday night in March. And as a diligent new convert serious about her commitment, she read it cover to cover, memorizing the scriptures that were given for each step. Of course the Reverend didn't appear evil, but the temptations he posed certainly weren't holy either. These temptations were completely antithetical to her new belief system, yet somehow she felt like she was the cause of it all. She couldn't understand how the man she looked up to for moral guidance and spiritual teaching could be so double-edged. It was as if when it came to infidelity, he somehow thought that the Word didn't apply to him.

Lord, why did I do that?!! I didn't want to do that. Help me God! Ravinia subconsciously pleaded, wrestling with her inner being for merely smiling at the man of cloth that was chasing her down, yet another Sunday. *God, I just can't do this again . . .*

"So, Vinia, are you coming to the fashion show this afternoon? Down home lunch and entertainment. Only $25. You can't beat that with a stick," the cunning Reverend inquired with a playful grin. He had a cute, little dimple set deep in the right hemisphere of his cheek that kept jumping in and out at will.

"Can't you go with Sister Reynolds?" Ravinia asked pointedly, trying to divert his attention to more wholesome options in companionship. Mattie Reynolds was engaged to the Reverend, but had not been attending the church lately. The word around church was that she caught him with another woman and was reconsidering their commitment.

"Uh, well, no. Mattie isn't feeling well, so she didn't come to church today," he quickly explained, lowering his voice a couple of octaves. "Besides, I didn't ask you to go with me. I was just wonderin' *if* you were going."

"Well, I really do need to get home, Reverend. You know how Xavier is and everything. . ." Ravinia's voice trailed off, thinking about her husband sitting back watching the game in her spotless living room.

"Ravinia, come to my office. We need to talk," requested the Reverend in a familiar, slightly yearning voice, while taking a firm grasp of her arms.

"But I got to get home, get the kids ready for school and everything," Ravinia choppily continued in her weak excuses to the man she called "Pastor." Her eyes shifted nervously as she desperately tried not to look directly at him. Whatever she did, she had to stay in control, but historically, this was not any easy task for Ravinia.

"Tomorrow is Labor Day," the Reverend reminded. "Is there something wrong? You seem so—distant," he asked, stilling his voice so passers-by would not suspect. He waited for the last person to pass, waving dutifully and smiling like the Cheshire cat in *Alice in Wonderland* while stretching out his arms to her as if to coax her into a loving embrace. The Bible said to greet one another with a holy kiss, but Ravinia was sure this is not what God intended. Unnerved by the friendly gesture, Ravinia looked up and caught amber and olive motes seemingly chasing each other in his almond shaped eyes. It was just something about those eyes of his that made her weak. They read her mind, they mesmerized her, and the Reverend knew this. In fact, he knew at a very early age that his eyes could capture any girl's desire, and he not so innocently used this to his advantage. Every emotion could be read through his eyes, and Ravinia's secret passion for him was reflected back at her.

"Come on Vinia. Let's *pray* about it," he begged. Ravinia knew that she shouldn't go, but could not resist his wiles. Finding her feet lighten as she moved forward, she walked numbly with the Reverend to his office. Each step made her heart pound even faster and Ravinia knew what she was doing would lead to trouble. Closing the heavy door behind them, Ravinia walked around looking at the pictures on the wall of his office. The room was dimly lit and mildly cool. It smelled like fresh lavender and eucalyptus with a hint of peppermint oil. You could tell he was a single man, but still looking. Nearing the couch, the cleansing scent of cedar and pine tantalized her nose and she started to sneeze.

"Bless, you. I won't be long Vinia- I just want to change out of these wet clothes." The words became powerless as they faded from the room. Reverend Wright excused himself and went into his private bathroom.

"Did you enjoy the service?" he asked over his shoulder, in a tone that seemed to imply that the only answer he expected was "yes."

"Well, yes," Ravinia responded, acquiescing to his inflated ego. Their passive-aggressive conversations always seemed to make her out to be the weaker of the two. "It was good," she continued, however looking slightly puzzled. If there was one thing Ravinia wasn't, it was stupid. She knew why she was in the office and she knew Reverend Wright's intentions, yet she could not understand how he could combine talking about things of a spiritual nature with what they did behind closed doors. Or maybe she was just jumping the gun again. Maybe he just wanted to talk.

But in her spirit, it just did not seem right. She felt so conflicted and torn finding that the nature of man, or rather some men, was very inconsistent with what they taught, especially in the church. Law officials, police officers, and politicians alike all seemed to have this perpetual weakness when it came to matters of the heart and what was lawful and true. This bothered Ravinia and didn't help her sense of wanting to do the right thing. It was confusing and simply immoral, and like her mother had vividly reminded her not more than three hours ago before she left for church that morning, it just wasn't right. But unfortunately, the very man she trusted to lead her on the straight and narrow path of righteousness was personally escorting her down the broad path that leads to destruction and eternal damnation.

"Just good?" the Reverend questioned in a higher-than-normal pitched voice. Ravinia began to cringe, realizing this was truly a mistake. If only she had kept on walking.

"Ok," she slowly replied with a voice that cracked as she muttered under her breath. Looking around a bit, Ravinia tried to figure out a way to get out of the mess she was about to create. Regretting she let him talk her into his office in the first place, she hesitantly replied, "Uh Willie, I thought we were gonna talk. I-I-I really got to be going," she said while nervously jumping at every stray noise.

"You know he ain't no good," the Reverend pointed out in a muffled voice, as he walked out of the bathroom in dark khaki shorts and a short-sleeved red shirt. The definition in his calves diverted Ravinia's attention from his alluring eyes briefly as she remembered it was the Lord's Day and she was breaking at least three of the 10 commandments. Fixing his collar in the mirror outside of the bathroom, he continued, "I don't know why you still run home to his sorry behind."

Ravinia agreed blindly, "Yeah, I know but..." All the while she was thinking, b*ut you ain't no better. After all, it takes one to know one*.

"But what?" challenged the Reverend. "I think you're scared of what would happen to you if you left him. You don't think you can do it on your own, do you?"

"Stop, Willie. Just stop it. Do you really think I am *that* stupid? That I don't know what is *really* going on? I mean, for that matter are you really that much different than him?" Ravinia screamed at him, thinking of his fiancée and that she, herself may be the other woman that Mattie Reynolds was so suspicious of.

Breathing heavily and obviously realizing he was not achieving his initial goal of seduction, the Reverend softly said, trying to regain his composure, "I see that you're upset, baby. Come here," he coaxed, in his moment of weakness, reaching out to Ravinia.

"Don't *baby* me. You know, you think that because you are a powerful preacher with 10,000 members in your congregation every Sunday that you can do just about anything you want, with anyone you want, and are somehow exempt. You think that no one would even dare cross you because of what you think you possess!" Ravinia exposed tearfully. Stepping into the Reverend's space, she sternly curved her full caramel lips and pointed her slender finger at the preacher. "Willie, I just can't do this anymore. It ain't right. There comes a time when it's not about what I can get from you, but what is really best for me."

The Reverend grabbed her shoulders and drew her into the comfort of his strong arms. He obviously ignored everything she had just said. To him, it was like she said, "Take me Willie, take me now." There was that intoxicating smell of Drakkar and sweat again that permeated his neckline that was so irresistible. Slowly rolling her eyes, Ravinia's long, silky eyelashes flipped up. Her burnt-orange colored eyes, reminiscent of a Caribbean sunset, glimmered in the afternoon sun peeking through the skylight in the ceiling of his office. They revealed the not-so-innocent fire that drew men into her.

"Vinia," the Reverend breathed, inhaling the crisp White Linen fragrance lingering on her blouse, "you know when you get like this."

"Like what?" Ravinia whispered coyly, still teary-eyed, but also giving in to the emotions that made her notorious for bringing men to their knees. She didn't even stop to think at this point because she was too far into that carnal place she prayed she would never go again. The conscious voice in her head kept saying, *Just say no. Just say it,* over and over again, but she ignored it. Why couldn't she resist? Why couldn't she say no? The question why, however, was not one of the many things that were trampling through her little mind at the time. The anxiety of getting caught was though. Any one of those busy-body secretaries of his could just walk in on them at any time. They had keys and weren't afraid to use them. Nervously, Ravinia glanced over at the door and noticed it was locked and the clasp was secured. She sighed gently, and felt her face draw a slightly puzzled look on it. She hadn't even remembered him locking the door in her rush of mixed emotions. Perhaps she, in her fumbled imagination saw, but didn't really see.

Her guilty conscience had her heart choking up in her throat. She felt powerless in the situation she had helped create. She had heard an evangelist once say, that when you are in trouble, you should call out, "Jesus!" But again, she didn't have enough spiritual know-how to rebuke this man who claimed to know the Savior. And despite her apparent uncomfortable demeanor, the Reverend didn't seem to care that he was playing church with a congregation that revered him. Starting to cough, Ravinia moved away from the Reverend abruptly. This could have been a sign for her to make her getaway. But, even with a way out provided, she didn't make her escape. Not seeming to notice or care, the tempter just came closer and closer.

"Girl, you just . . . you just . . ." dropped sensually off the Reverend's lips as he drew closer into her space. Kissing was just the beginning of their indecent afternoon activities. At this point, Ravinia forgot about the door and the people who could be listening on the other side. She didn't care that her kids were at her mom's, waiting for her to pick them up from a long weekend. She didn't even struggle anymore with the conviction that wretched her, despite her previous tear-jerking cleansing experience at the altar that morning, where she had promised God she would never, ever sleep with another man that wasn't her husband. She had in a matter of seconds wrestled the urge to resist down to the floor along with the articles of clothing that had begun to collect around her feet.

ꕥꕥꕥꕥꕥꕥ

"So then what happened?" asked Dr. Sykes.

"Isn't our time about up?" retorted Ravinia, bucking her dreamy eyes out of her steamy recount of the events that so easily beset her. She slammed her journal soundly and tucked it in her upscale leather carryall. Peering at her watch, Dr. Sykes, reluctant to admit that she had gotten sucked into the recollection rendered so exquisitely by her patient's writing assignment, sighed deeply and uttered, "Why, I guess it is. I'll see you next week at 11 a.m. Okay?"

"All right," Ravinia unwillingly mumbled. "I'll be here."

Chapter 3.

SAPPHIRE SYKES

Born in a small, rigid town in Southern California of about three thousand lost souls, I came to be. My father was an authoritative, obsessively religious man and my mother, well, we'll just call her troubled. Every kid with even a hint of a defiant soul thinks his family is a little weird. But the difference between other families and ours was that insanity around here was very, very real. When I was about 8, my mother was taken away, kicking and screaming in the middle of that endless night. Later, I learned that my father did the unthinkable and had her committed to an asylum. Her abrupt absence left me with a deep, dark emptiness that only loneliness filled.

Because of my father's pervasive need to keep control, I lived as a prisoner in my own home. From grade school through high school, I was required to go to school during the week, church on Sunday, Monday night prayer, Wednesday night Bible Study, Holy Ghost Friday, and don't forget choir rehearsal on Saturday. No time to just be a kid. I knew that some how, some way when I was finally free from the powers that be, I would never again darken the doors of another church. I think my father's narrow-minded thinking is what drove my mother into her bizarre world. It took everything I had to not give in to the voices that haunted me—to keep my sanity. The spirits that taunted my mother had somehow been left behind, chasing me around my bed at night. I would grow tired of their larking about and would stop, look through the evil apparitions, and say, "She is not here any more. They took her away. Now, just let me be." To this day I don't know if they were real or imagined, but for a little girl without her mother, it was terrifying.

Life without my mother left me bland. I barely remember my elementary and high school days except for the fact that I was forced to go, no matter how I felt. My father was a tyrant and never gave in to my antics. Suffering from endometriosis, a painful condition that wouldn't cease until I would have my first child, my monthly cycles became more than I could bear alone. I began exhibiting destructive bulimic behaviors by the age of 13, winding down into a cycle of purging and starvation to the point of chronic fainting at church and school. The school nurse would call my father and tell him what she suspected but he denied her claims that I was troubled and in need of medical attention. He forced me to eat everything off my plate in an attempt to make me submit to his command. And if I didn't, he'd beat me until I ate. But what he didn't understand was he perpetuated this illness in me. The very thing he tried to destroy rose up in me and I was too young to know what it was. This generational curse refused to allow me to properly nourish myself though I had every desire to. I couldn't get free, as much as I tried on my own. What my father didn't realize was that this behavior was characteristically symptomatic of the severe trauma I had experienced from losing my mother at such an early age.

Evil had taken up residence in my empty soul and I begged to be free. I had never figured out that what I was doing was because mentally I was afraid to grow up. Subconsciously, I did not want to have a menstrual cycle every month. In my mind, that would lead to me becoming a woman, and I couldn't let that happen. I couldn't face looking in the mirror and seeing "her" stare back at me. I had read somewhere that if my body weight was insufficient, my period wouldn't come. My father never really acknowledged that I had an abnormal attitude towards my body. He just knew that I needed 'deliverance'.

One night at a tent revival service that had come to our town, my father led me down for prayer. A powerful, traveling evangelist prayed for me. As he laid his anointed hands on me, I felt a release of my stomach and my insides started to churn. That night I ate and didn't gag for the first time in years. I knew I was healed. And that was good enough for me because I finally desired to eat again.

I kept that healing inside of me along with every other emotion I had ever felt, holding onto the hope that one day I could really be free. I internalized my life, still wrought by the constant ridicule I received at school. Buried in my studies, I became a scorned outcast, despised by my classmates. I refused to go to my graduation because I knew that only hatred would find me there. My father scorned and whipped me for bringing shame to his name. Taking my mother away from me though was worse than any persecution he could put me through. But something inside me persevered so that I'd soon be able to stand on my two feet one day and find a way to leave this wretched place I once called home.

At age 17, I set off for a small, private college in Boston to major in Psychology. I guess you could say that taking the Psych courses served as an attempt to understand the challenges I faced, and to provide self-help. I can remember the bus pulling up to the school around noon. The ivy circled what appeared to be the library building. The climbing vines barely revealed a clock striking 12:00 p.m. that late August morning. Waking up, I felt half-confused, hot, and downright miserable. The long ride on the hard seat from the airport was almost unbearable but it was worth it. I was finally free from the unrelenting clutches of my father and all that he represented.

To my surprise, college turned out to be much different than I had imagined. Everything seemed cold, lonely and detached. It was easy to feed my antisocial outlook on life. The only good time I seemed to have in college was when I was drinking. Getting drunk and the behaviors that accompanied my drunkenness seemed to be a major extra-curricular activity around campus. Just about everyone seemed to do it. Perhaps being an only child played an important part in my alcoholism. Maybe the ravages of losing my mother added to the obsessive behaviors that followed me day and night. But this one thing I do know: that tragic life event left my diluted psyche constantly searching for security. Sadly I found nothing but an obsessive, compulsiveness as a surrogate.

On March 24, 1979, the Kappa's decided to host an old school step show to raise money for their scholarship fund. The music was jammin'. Liquid jazz filled the air as guests gliding to Miles, sipped from their wine coolers and Long Island iced tea (which contained no iced tea), and imported beer. It was the jam of the year.

To be honest I really didn't expect to meet anyone interesting or attractive. But that night, a friend of mine introduced me to William Wright. He was a junior seminary student. William had translucent, dreamy eyes and warm, honey colored skin. His height put him head and shoulders above the other men in the room. He drew me in with his captivating eyes, deep voice and easy smile. We talked for hours that night about everything under the sky. There was something that I just naturally liked about him. We started hanging out and studying together. By the end of the semester; a strong closeness had formed between us. We were like old friends, and indeed, I felt that we were just that. My ability to go from playing the dozens in my smart-alecky, sistah-girl way to eloquently imitating the King's English, amazed him. He admired my quick wit and surprising shyness. Rolling the name my father gave me off his tongue like he was Rico Suave, he made me dizzy taking my name in vain. We would pick up jerk chicken at the Jamaican restaurant on Massachusetts Avenue, and while my throat burned from the spicy tang of the extra sauce I had to have, he would go on and on about my forward thinking and how tight my 'fro was. Being with him just felt right.

After meeting William, I could really see how free I could be. There was a strong part of him that truly believed without any doubt that all things were possible with God. He had strong conviction and charisma to match, and I believed that he really wanted to do the right thing in life. He didn't push religion on me like my father did; and yet he explained the Word in ways in which I could completely relate. With all the wrongs that had already happened in my life, with him things felt right. Of course, it was to no one's surprise that we became a couple. We were always together. I actually enjoyed talking about the various translations of the Bible that he was studying for interpretation. I even said the Sinner's Prayer at a campus church service I attended with William.

On our way home from a party one night, the inexplicable happened. Nothing that had ever happened to me before that day could compare to what he did to me. Not the many whippings with the cut-off plastic clothesline by my father. Not the hateful things that the kids in high school would say to me as I walked home from school numb to their bantering. Not even the self-inflicted wounds I made in my youth all the nights I yearned for my mother's touch. To this day, I cannot fathom why William would do this to me, the way that he did this to me.

He raped me. Just as simple as that. I can't say it any less blunt because it happened just that way. Abrupt and cruel. No warning. No signs or writing on the wall. I kept asking myself, *How could this happen? He came from a good Christian family; a long line of ministers.* Baffled with the question that still rips through my insides just like he ripped through my tender layers of innocent trust, I asked myself over and over. *Why did he choose me?*

When the man I trusted my life and my heart to realized it was actually a heinous crime he had committed *against* me, and not willing sex, he dropped to his knees before me and begged for my forgiveness. *My* forgiveness? How dare he. What even gave him the right to even ask? To even sit at my feet. To even look at the scorn he had left encircled around my bedside.

I couldn't find any suitable words to spit at him that would fit the transgression he had committed against me. How do you face a man when he was the only one you had ever trusted to love you and he betrays all of that in one night? At that moment, I was engorged with all the hurt he had left inside of me. I didn't even know if I could have forgiven him. How could he do this to me? He marred me in so many unspeakable ways. Confusion flooded me and I drowned in his maddening stares of helplessness. If I hadn't of been in shock, I would have closed my eyes. But still I couldn't bear to look at him or find tears to wash away his shame. He stole more than just my innocence. He took what I thought remained of my existence.

I don't even remember when he left my room. For days, I laid on my bed, frozen. My throat was dry, my mouth sour, and the pit of my stomach raw. I was cold and nothing felt right. I didn't leave my apartment for anything or anyone for about 3 weeks. I could not bear to see any human, face to face. I cried and cried until my anguish dried my tears. Out of guilt and pity, he called and called, leaving word even with my neighbors trying to explain away the pain he had inflicted upon me. His fruitless efforts left me with even more thoughts to constantly remind me of him, while the bruises he left had me swollen on the inside--physically, emotionally, and spiritually. I was broken.

What could I say? I had once truly loved William. I had envisioned us together like every young, Black woman sees herself--with a strong, powerful man. I saw our future, conquering the world with my newly released carefree spirit and his conviction for humanity. I even saw Jesus in his eyes. He had brought me to the crossroads and I wanted to believe, but in his haste, he even took that away.

When we were together, I thought back to how William was so passionate about having an intimate relationship with God. He lived it as much as a student could live it and I wanted that closeness to God, too. I guess God can use people even if they aren't the image of perfection to do His will. Seeing what has become of William now, a pastor of one of the largest Baptist churches on the south side of Chicago, perhaps he has allowed God to heal him. Certainly, a lot of people have found God at William's services. You don't get that many members for nothing. But, for me, it is going to take a lot more than years of tears to get me to believe that the Reverend is a changed man. I can't put my trust in men anymore, especially men in religious positions of authority. I just won't. There is so much more temptation for those who rise to power.

My dreams were shattered by this man's futile attempt to control and tame a spirit that was only borrowed to him, never promised. I wanted nothing more than to make this horrible, unbearable thing go away; to put this gut-wrenching experience behind me and go on with my life. To stay would keep me as his prisoner, and I vowed the day I left my father's rigid, abusive rule, that I would never, ever let another man enslave me again, especially one I loved.

It was hard to forgive him, and sometimes I question if I really have. The relationship, of course, was severed and dissolved. Trying to escape the humiliation, I left school and Boston. That is when I landed in the Midwest. Still on the verge of self-destruction at the age of 20, it seemed as though I was only managing to get more and more confused about what I should be doing with my life. I had to get a hold of my life. School seemed to be the perfect place to refocus my anger into constructive energy. Although, I got the grades, I yet thirsted for more. Having a relentless desire to succeed, I continued my education and received my doctorate, *summa cum laude*, from the University of Chicago. I still had the nagging feeling that something important and indefinable was missing in my life. To stop feeling pity for all the wrongs in my life, I decided to help people with their problems.

Embarking on a successful career as a psychotherapist, I opened my own little practice on Michigan Avenue. Highly recommended by several high profile therapists with whom I had done research during my college career, my clientele began to grow. Soon, I was able to move from my Hyde Park apartment to a gorgeous penthouse on Lake Shore Drive, a few minutes from the office. My friends thought I had "arrived," but my life was yet shapeless and void. I had never been with anyone in a romantic way or held a significant relationship. How could I? Every man I had ever trusted betrayed me. The events, which had taken place, were still very vivid in my mind, and the terrible thing about them was the fact that they seemed to rewind over and over again in my head. How could I ever trust another man? I couldn't think straight. I had so much anger inside of me until now.

Chapter 4.

APPEGIO's

"You're late again," the voice from her past echoed. Dr. Sykes peered over her copper, wire-rimmed glasses that rested on the slightly flattened bridge of her otherwise keen nose. Smoothing her fitted suit jacket from the waist down, Sapphire looked down at her lunch date. The crisply dressed therapist thought, *why am I even here?* With pursed cinnamon lips, Sapphire mustered up a heavy hearted, "So I am," and rolled her lightly shadowed eyes abruptly. Her lashes twittered nervously when she was put on the spot.

With a hearty chuckle that made her remember he was a preacher, Reverend Wright replied sheepishly, "Sapphire Sykes, or should I say Dr. Sapphire Sykes, since you're a doctor and all now. I'm so glad you could join me for lunch." It had been over 20 years since she had seen William but his voice still gave her chills. He stood up to honor her presence and sat down again, admiring the feminine way she maneuvered her backside into the narrow space between the table and her chair. The Reverend was just full of lust from sun up to sun down, and there was nothing anyone could do about it.

"Willie, you don't have to be so professional with me. You know we go way back," the doctor reminded. Sucking in her breath, she worked at remaining poised and calm. This was going to take a bit more patience than she had brought with her that afternoon.

"Bluelight. But you know, I just want to do this the right way, you understand," the Reverend explained gingerly. He clumsily used his extra large hands to describe his words. Sapphire noticed that not much had changed about him. There was a little graying at his temples and a few crow's feet around his eyes. But those eyes were still as lucid as Sapphire remembered.

"Well, until you become my patient, all that just isn't necessary," the 43 year old therapist replied knowingly, raising her left arched eyebrow for emphasis, as she carefully unfolded and placed the white linen napkin over her lap.

"Girl, you always trying to get somebody to come see you and tell you all about their issues. And you must charge $150 an hour to listen! My congregation and I can get counseling for free and get a direct connect to the Almighty!" Lifting his hypocritical hands, he waved in an upward motion. Then he took a sip of the ice water sitting on the table. The condensation forming on the glass made messy, wet concentric circles as it melted down and collected on the white linen table cloth. It reminded her of the leak in her ceiling of her student apartment back in Boston. Sapphire focused her attention on the spot until she realized that the Reverend was trying to poke fun at her occupation, and somehow compare it to what he did for a living.

"Willie, at least I don't sleep with my counselees!" Sapphire snapped. Just then, realizing she went somewhere she really shouldn't have, she slapped her left hand over her mouth. What she had just uttered was hearsay. But with his reputation and their past on the line, she didn't put anything past the Reverend.

"I'm sorry, Willie," promptly apologized the doctor for her unbridled tongue, realizing her verbal jab really didn't make her much better than him. No matter how low-down he was, she couldn't break the patient-doctor confidentiality policy she had with Ravinia, not even to slam the man who had caused her the most pain. "I guess sometimes I just can't restrain myself."

"Uh huh, yeah. I guess I deserved that and a lot more." The Reverend replied remorsefully, thinking back to the last time that he saw her. Convicting thoughts swirled around in his head, making him question whether he was even worthy enough to make her acquaintance for an early dinner.

"So," Sapphire continued in a crisp, firm voice, trying to move the night along. Regaining her focus she requested, dripping with liquid sarcasm, "Let's just not go there because it still makes me disgusted just thinking about how you did me. It took me years just to even swallow your name without gagging." The therapist hesitated before continuing on. Taking a sip of the ice water, she blurted out, "Why am I here anyway?"

"Well, as you probably already know, the church has really grown," the mega-pastor explained, dismissing the guilt-filled thought that he just had.

"Yeah, what do you have, like 10,000 or something like that? I think I read an article or something in the *Tribune* or was it *The Defender*?" Sapphire commented knowledgeably, cooling down quickly to a slow simmer. She was still upset, but was also determined not to let a man from her past give her an aneurism.

"Something like that," Willie said responding in a hesitant voice, trying to keep her on track, "and, well, we really need to have some professional counselors on staff, and I- I was just wonderin' if you would consider starting a ministry in my . . ."

"NO!" Cutting him off mid-sentence, Sapphire emphatically voiced a loud declination. Her long, black eyelashes flickered angrily, making her deep blue-violet eyes appear almost animated. The thick density of her luscious, dark lashes naturally lined the length of the therapist's eyes, making them appear well defined without eyeliner or mascara. Sapphire always wondered where she had gotten her eye color from since no one in her immediate family had eyes even remotely close to blue, let alone any other hue except brown. Her mother told her the mysterious eye color came from a distant uncle. But when Sapphire asked her father, he would just look at her as if she had stolen money from him. Wherever she got them from, they served her well now. The iciness of her heart began to seep through them, making her wintry eyes seem almost glazed; absorbing any warmth she had shown previously from her usually glowing countenance. Angrily Sapphire pierced him with the very same eyes that had enraptured the Reverend many years ago. He felt them aim for his heart just like the night he had robbed her of her sanctity from within. Her characteristically high Cherokee cheekbones pronounced themselves on her face, as her nostrils flared. Apparently, needing to re-emphasize her position, she stopped her flippant reaction and reiterated her answer with a bellowing, "As God as my witness, NO!!!"

"Girl, watch yo' mouth up in here!" the Reverend shushed loudly, adjusting his clerical collar, trying not to draw too much attention to their conversation. He was a well-respected pastor and community activist. The last thing he needed right now was more negative publicity. The write-up he got in *The Chicago Defender* made him seem larger than life and somehow, that had an adverse affect on how people were viewing him lately.

"Now Willie, you know good and well I cannot work for, with, or around you. I know *too* much about you. And I wouldn't recommend anyone of my associates to work with or for you, either," churned Sapphire in a low, hushed voice without a single blink or stutter.

Realizing he had put her in a position he couldn't easily walk out of, the Reverend quickly dismissed the question and said, "Man, ev'ry body acting crazy this week," rolling the thought of Ravinia in his shaking head. No sooner than the word "crazy" had dropped off his lips, Sapphire snapped her neck and cocked her head 45 degrees while giving him a look that would make Mike Tyson quiver. "Now I *know* you ain't going there. Who *you* calling crazy?" Sapphire blasted while unsnapping the flap of her purse to reach for her cell phone.

"Bluelight, you know I can't win with you. Never could, never will. You got to know I didn't mean it like that," putting the other foot in his open mouth.

"Whatever, Willie," Sapphire sighed, flipping the little phone up to check her voice mail. The phone was almost half the size of her credit card when closed. She was somehow slightly eased by the Reverend's reference to her nickname in their college days. She reluctantly mulled over the concept that perhaps she over-exaggerated the intensity of the rape almost 20 years ago, but didn't dwell on the thought long enough for it to take root in her mind. She considered the fact that perhaps he could have had a hard week and was dealing with other issues, including coming to terms with his past with her. So maybe his “crazy” reference was not meant to drudge up her past issues with her mother’s illness, but intended for some other mysterious delusion.

Just then, Sapphire’s stomach growled loudly, making her already flushed face turn the apples of her cheeks deep crimson. "So, do I still get lunch or what?" Sapphire asked exhaustingly, tucking her silver cell phone back into her pink, suede hounds tooth Coach bag. The mixed media bag complemented her pointed-toe, pencil-heeled mules.

"Yeah, we still cool," the Reverend replied, rubbing the oils deeply into his head that were collecting in the thinning part. You could tell he was thinking about something from his past. Whatever it was, it was certainly troubling him enough to cause deep frowns in his forehead. Making sure his waves reached over it sufficiently, he asked Sapphire, forcing himself out of his thoughts, "You still like shrimp alfredo with the grated Romano and Parmesan cheese, right?”

Sapphire, attempting to lighten up the afternoon, said, half smiling, "And, you know this!" realizing too that she was feeling slightly relieved after standing up to the Reverend. In fact, she had built up a hearty appetite and her stomach showed its boldness by sounding a soulful growl. Sapphire looked down at her abdomen, as if she could somehow stifle the obnoxious sound with just a simple stare. But, as she looked up slightly embarrassed, the Reverend started to laugh. And to her surprise she did, too.

Chapter 5.

REVELATIONS 3:17

"Ooh! This is my song!" chimed a light-hearted Sapphire as *A Long Walk* by Jill Scott trembled through the restaurant's amplifier. Sapphire, caught up in the soulful rasp of Jill's trumpeting force against the cymballic percussion, closed her violet-lined eyes and snapped her long, slender fingers to the beat. Against the songstress' vocals she blissfully reminisced about nights at home in her cozy penthouse on Lake Shore Drive, sipping sparkling white grape juice, listening to Wynton Marsalis and just 'chilling' in her own sanctuary. To her, that was living. And she didn't mind letting people know that she enjoyed her alone time. Before Sapphire realized it, she was singing with the track, resurrecting that sultry, alto voice that had won her a spot at the Regal Theater many years ago.

Looking up, she realized Willie was looking right in her wide-open mouth, just like Ravinia described in her journal. However it didn't seem to faze her. So she continued to amuse herself and at times, even him and started singing to the Reverend with her cavernous, azure-like eyes gazing into his olive-green eyes as if she was on stage. Expressing the almost spoken lyrics with her hands, Sapphire appeared to drown out every care she had in the world.

Before jumping into the chorus, Sapphire opened her eyes that had closed when she began the line, "I can feel. . ." Continuing her jazzy ballad, she actually could feel warning eyes from the corners of the room gaze at her. But she didn't care if they liked her interlude or not, or if they even failed to understand the freedom a caged bird has when it sings. She learned that some things you just have to do alone, and never is there more strength when you have to stand by yourself, standing for what you believe. *Let them look, enjoy or hate. This is my time*, she thought proudly to herself. In a slightly restrained alto voice she cried, signifying to the air,

Conversation, verbal elation, stimulation
Share our situations, temptations, education, relaxations
Elevations, maybe we can talk Revelation 3:17 . . .

"Who you think you is girl, Jill Scott?" snickered a cynical Reverend Wright, interrupting her vocal melody with his eyebrow hiked up like Jack Nicholson himself. He took great pride in piercing the bubble she had just blown up. "You need to just stop," he added like he was embarrassed by her singing with the track. "Carrying on like that. Ev'ry body jus' lookin' at you! I bet you don't even know what Revelation 3:17 says," he jeered, trying to belittle her in his pompous, self-justifying way. Since the doctor had clearly turned down his business offer, he had little use for her. His interest in her diminished by the minute and he was notably less careful about his tone and word choices towards her.

"Yeah, well maybe I did get a little beyond myself, but I *can* flow with a lil' sumthin'- sumthin'," answered Sapphire confidently, smiling for the first time that evening on her own. Pulling back a lock of her shoulder length, freshly coiffed feathered hair; she inspected her ends noticing that two of the 100 plus ends in her clutch were split. "You know, there was a time I could. . ." Sapphire almost uttered the unthinkable. Luckily the Reverend cut her off. She was getting a little too casual with him; much too casual for someone who had endured what seemed like hours of pain and suffering at his hands. Considering leaving before she finished her shrimp, Sapphire grew restless. *This was a mistake*, she thought regrettably to herself.

"Could what?!!" fired off Reverend Wright, finding a prime opportunity to lash back at her. He apparently forgot he was in a posh little restaurant and lost his composure. "Girl, you so, so—what you psychoanalytical folks call, uh—uh, rigid, yeah rigid. Now, back in the day, well that was a . . ."

"Are you trying to say *FRIGID*? Me, frigid?? Willie, please!" interrupted Sapphire, half laughing at his ignorance, knowing though, that he was half right in his speculation. It took all she had within her being not to let out a full belly laugh. He was trying to psychoanalyze her without any formalized training. *Folks think they know, but they don't,* she thought loudly to herself. And for the life of her, Sapphire couldn't understand why this simple man would even perpetrate that he did. Softening her tone, she realized she was now drawing attention to herself, yet again.

Sapphire sternly enunciated every syllable as she looked him in the eye, pointing her finger and saying, "Don't you even try to analyze me, Willie. You simply aren't qualified," forcing the Reverend to follow the outline of her lips in verbatim syncopation.

"Like I was saying," Reverend Wright said, persistently and casually ignoring her last remark. "Maybe back in the day. I miss those times, you and me." Sapphire couldn't believe her ears. *No he wasn't going back there.* Her thoughts began to cloud and clash with each other. She needed to end this lunch and with a quickness.

Suddenly, Sapphire began to feel a warm sensation move over her. She looked at her glass and remembered. It was a familiar feeling, but she did not welcome it. She couldn't and she wouldn't. And no, she was not getting tipsy. She specifically decided before she came to meet the Reverend that she would not order any wine because she was determined not to let anything, including the Reverend, intoxicate her into any after dinner extracurricular activities.

Convinced that it was the Reverend trying to take her back to a place she refused to go again, Sapphire, pressed her full spice-colored lips against the white linen napkin, folded it squarely, and placed it on the table next to her lipstick-stained fork. Unclasping her little pink purse, she realized she only had enough cash to take a cab home, and since he was "bringing" it, he needed to pay for it. In an irritated voice she asked, "You got this, Willie? I really do need to go. I got to review my notes for tomorrow's sessions. And, I have court first thing." Sapphire snapped her purse soundly, causing the Reverend to jerk at its abrupt sound.

Looking offended at her bold announcement, and at the fact that "she just was not acting right," the Reverend brushed her off and waved her on, stuffing another jumbo shrimp, laden with rich, creamy Alfredo sauce, drizzling down the thickness of the spinach fettuccine, into his big, mustached mouth. No “see you,” no “good-bye,” no "lata, baby."

Satisfied with his cool acknowledgment of her leaving, Sapphire quickly got up to leave and turned around to face him. She wanted him to see exactly what he could never have again. Her long voluptuous body eased itself back into the fit of her little, off-the-shoulder black dress while she tucked her purse under her arm. The cold clasp sent a chill through her as it hit her bare armpit, but she was able to play it off. Sapphire added coolly, "Oh, uh one last thing, Willie," adjusting her wire-rimmed glasses habitually, while holding the last syllable of his name just long enough to grab his interest.

"What's that?" looking up as if there was a chance that she might have reconsidered dessert. Sapphire put her right forefinger on her lips and then quoted just loudly enough for the Reverend to hear and maybe the adjoining table. Stressing each verb phonetically, she quoted:

> *“You say, 'I’m rich; I have acquired wealth and do not need a thing. But you do not realize that you are wretched, pitiful, poor, blind and naked. Oh yes, the address, Revelations 3 and 17. The King James Version."*

Realizing his self-righteousness, presumptuous thinking and overall lack of etiquette had messed up his game yet again, the Reverend apologized, "Sapphire, wait. I was wrong." Sapphire, satisfied that she had just one-upped him sufficiently, did a security check for her purse, and twirled her 24-inch waist around a full 90 degrees, making her well-proportioned, but considerably thick hips and shapely legs follow in a harmony that would put a runway model to shame. She knew he was watching her shift her weight with each stride, but she didn't give him a second thought.

Already half way out of the restaurant, Sapphire begged her legs not to fail her. Her body was strong and cut. She still did Tae-bo faithfully each morning, although the rest of the world had moved on to Pilates. Using her rock-hard calves to maneuver around the dinner crowd, she made lean, swift strides to ensure he would not follow her. Careful not to misstep or stumble, she took one last look at the first man she had ever loved before shouting, "Taxi!"

Chapter 6.

THE RAPE

Sapphire clutched the white cotton percale sheets tighter as she squirmed fiercely. The inner part in her thigh was now raw and bumpy. She prayed that this ordeal would end, but it was like he was a madman. What had gotten into him? They hadn't even had sex before and here he was, forcing himself into her. Screaming a blood-curdling, painfully throaty utterance as each pound of his uncircumcised flesh devoured her coveted innocence, Sapphire prayed in her spirit that he would stop.

Remnants of her spirit-man floated above her looking down on the room from the protruding pebbles of the whitewashed stucco ceiling. They lay wait to descend in an effort to comfort her, to help her eventually repress the worst of that God-forsaken day. Sapphire held on for dear life and had thrown her emotions into oblivion so that she could feel nothing. She would eventually block out these horrific scenes only for them to resurface later in life, in case of a recurrence or incident that was equally tragic in nature. She traced the yellowed-brown, water-stained cracks that had etched an intricate pattern against the otherwise-perfect ceiling with her eyes. Anything to distract her from the 285-pound man that was raping her. When it rained, there was a tiny leak that dripped full, round droplets of water right on her head. It was all she could do to distract herself from what was brutally being done to her.

She pleaded with him to stop, but her attempts were futile. Her cries fell upon deaf ears. Sapphire felt powerless in her shocked state, planted to her own bed with his large, calloused hands clamped down on her tiny wrists in a completely submissive position. Apparently this was his idea of sex; brutally unbridled and unrelentingly violent. The pain in her ovaries and uterus was intrinsically unbearable as the pitted, little knot in her abdomen grew tighter and more intense. He kept pushing himself further and further up in what remained of her virginity until the constant pressure from his weight temporarily paralyzed her lower limbs and pelvis. She was sure her tailbone would snap off at each blow, but she didn't realize how resilient her less-than-average frame was.

The tremendous feeling of nausea taunted her but also tended to interrupt her scattered attention from the thrashing of her tender vaginal layers. Delicate membranes within her labia were shredded and lay loose around the deepness he had carved out from his vastness. In her mind, the piercing of her hymen was the worst part, having never been touched by a man. She had to emotionally detach herself from what was happening to her in order to survive it. The sickening taste of root beer mingled with sauerkraut and Vienna beef escaped from her palate as she vomited her dinner all over Willie. Only then did he stop his spastic exploit to see that Sapphire was not enjoying their entanglement, and in fact, was writhing in pain.

With a confused look on his sweat-laden forehead, he said in an out-of-breath, yet annoyed voice, "What's wrong?" He seemingly was only concerned at the fact that the contents of her stomach had just erupted all over his chest and right arm. Sapphire, shocked that he could not distinguish between consensual sex and rape, passed out. Could he not see what was wrong? Her body grew limp and was drenched in blood, unlike seconds ago when every muscle of her formerly taut body was unnaturally contracted and so rigid that she looked like she was frozen in time. The pain was beyond compare. She would have rather been gang raped than to see the man she loved hovering over her in blatant disregard not noticing the horrific expression on her face.

Being a virgin, Willie realized that there would be some blood on the sheets, but was not prepared for what he saw. The white cotton sheets were saturated profusely with bright, red blood. At first, he thought maybe she got her period. But, somehow he knew, despite his infinite male ignorance, that she didn't. It was only then that he actually looked at her and noticed he could only see the whites of her eyes. Starting to panic at the thought that maybe he went a little too far in his attempt to coax Sapphire into sex, he tried to resuscitate her. He ran to the kitchen to get some ice and water. Opening the door of the maize-colored Frigidaire with the silver cursive 1950's logo, he pulled out an old-fashioned metal ice tray and pulled the lever up to release the ice from the metal separators. Walking over to the scratched up, white porcelain sink, he found a relatively clean bowl in the drainer and dumped the ice into it. He turned on the faucet and put just enough water to cover the ice cubes in the bowl. Running as fast as he could, balancing the bowl, he stopped in the little pink bathroom for a plush olive-colored towel. He hoped that the blood wouldn't show so much on a dark one. He was wrong. Trying to stop the bleeding from her vagina, he held the icy, saturated towel between her legs for 5 minutes. It wasn't long before he found condemnation staring him in the eye.

Why won't she wake up? He pondered guiltily to himself. *Did I kill her? How could I kill her? We were having . . .* his wandering mind rapidly recycled the legion of questions flooding his brain, trying to rationalize the disastrous situation that lay before him. Willie quickly found out Sapphire wasn't dead because her body was very warm. *God, please let this girl wake up! I didn't mean to hurt her, honestly, Lord,* he pleaded with his Master. If there was ever a time the frightened seminary student wanted a prayer to get through, it was now.

From Willie's lips to God's ears, Sapphire's toes began to move. *Thank you, Lord.* She was alive, but not awake. Removing the packing he had created, Willie saw that the bleeding had finally stopped. He was relieved because he could not take her to a hospital. They would think he did this to her, which he did, but they would not understand his intent. He thought to himself in a self-serving way, *maybe I was just too big for her?* Still trying in his weak attempt to somehow overcome this mishap, his trifling soul reveled in its attempt to justify the blood, the trauma to her femininity, the fainting.

He didn't understand that what he had done in his drunkenness was simply unforgivable, nor did he realize that the crime he had committed against this woman was unlawful, despicable and loathsome. He had taken the one thing in her life she wasn't willing to give up yet—her most prized possession, and stomped all over it with his selfish pride. He couldn't control his libido. Not this time. He was out of control. He felt that if Sapphire was half as interested as she led on, she would want him sexually. After all, most of the women who say "no" really mean yes. Right? Willie was confused and distraught. He thought Sapphire shared the same feelings and wanted the same things he did. From time to time, they had jokingly hinted around about getting "freaky" and he thought she was cool with it. Never once did he even fathom in his thinking that she would have reacted the way she did that night. Over and over in his head he reviewed the events of the evening, and yes, the signs were there. Why hadn't he picked up on her uneasiness when he ripped off her blouse? Couldn't he see all the goose bumps that had popped up on her arms when she covered her small, firm breasts from being exposed?

Sapphire could not rid herself of the ghastly thoughts that plagued her for years after the rape. *Did he really think I was getting excited? What part of 'NO" did he just not understand? Why didn't he just stop and leave me alone. What made him just keep on pushing himself on me when it was more than clear that I did not want him that way?* Even through all the rape counseling and support group meetings that she attended, she never answered every question that taunted her pretty little head. And for many years, that troubled Sapphire, intensely. She had been recently asked to teach an evening class at Northwestern University on Rape and the Psyche. Always hoping to deal openly with the thorn in her side, Sapphire wrestled with the idea of teaching that particular class. She knew that she could do it, but she didn't know how much of herself she could put into it. Everything Sapphire did was with heart and soul. And this was something she couldn't allow herself to be a part of. Not yet.

Chapter 7.

1727 SHERIDAN ROAD

"The car needs an oil change. When you gonna take it to Jiffy Lube, or does the Prima Donna expect me to do it?" asked Xavier, standing there looking at Ravinia all puffed up like a peacock. Half smiling, half smirking, Xavier's hands were casually placed in the pockets of his khaki Dockers as he stood by the edge of the pebble stone walkway.

Closing the door on the S500, Ravinia softly responded, "Honey, I'll take it Tuesday. You know, it's Ladies Day." Quickly scooping up her purse and Bible through the opened window, she noticed her skirt was caught in the door. Opening the door quickly so her perceptive husband wouldn't notice her blunder, she realized her blouse was still unbuttoned from her earlier activities.

"So, how was church?" Xavier inquired in a less than interested voice making a mental note of her appearance. "You spend more time at that place than in your own home. How much of my money did you give away *this* Sunday?" he grunted. Seemingly perturbed by her newly found devotion and that she had spent the better part of day away from home, Xavier continued, "And that Reverend Wright," he muttered under his breath, but certainly loud enough for Ravinia to hear, "more like Reverend Wrong, if you ask me. I hope you didn't get in the $100 line this Sunday!"

Ravinia, riddled with guilt and anxiety, swirled the exchange between her and the Reverend around in her mind so fast she started feeling dizzy. Losing her calm demure, she put her hands on her head as if to hold in her brain. Trying to even her temper, she moved her fingers to her temples, attempting to massage away the guilt that pounded in her head. She decided the best course of action would be to ignore Xavier's question altogether and avoid the topic of money.

"So, uh, did you play today with Dr. Schroeder? Weren't you supposed to do a round of golf or something?" Ravinia averted, untucking her blouse from her skirt, trying to find the missing button from her placket. It was crinkled and moist from the sweat she lost running back to her car when she was leaving church.

As if looking for a random thought on the one and a half acre concourse, Xavier pondered and proudly boasted, "Yes, we did 18 holes! That Bill, he knows I am so much better than him, but he constantly challenges me," the third year partner chuckled proudly, acting almost surprised. Xavier had made the partnership at Omicron Consulting and had started playing golf with various big shots in and around the North Shore area.

Ravinia rolled her eyes at the pompous attitude her husband exuded. Sometimes he was even too much for her. Xavier enjoyed listening to himself brag about himself, and this irked Ravinia to no end. However this time she figured she would just let him rant and rave about his wonderful self to ease her way out of confrontation. She thought it would take the pressure off her and he wouldn't be so concerned about her church experience, or so she thought.

Stepping up the limestone steps to the deck, Xavier stopped and took a hard look at Ravinia, remembering why he had come outside in the first place. He realized that it was 4 p.m. and Ravinia had not gotten back from morning service. With church ending around noon, he determined that it would have been more than enough time to drive from the South side of Chicago up Lake Shore Drive, and Sheridan all the way north to Highland Park. She should have been home no later than 2 p.m. Of course, knowing Ravinia, she might have taken I-94 and stopped off at Old Orchard for a quick Sunday afternoon shopping excursion. Or maybe she stopped for a bite at the Cheesecake Factory. But Ravinia didn't have a leftover box with her and there was not a Macy's bag in sight. Something was not right.

Searching even further back into his memory, Xavier inquired gallantly, "So uh, Vinia, what took you so long?" Unfastening her white-piped black peplum jacket, Ravinia slipped off her sling back heels and slung them on her middle finger behind her left shoulder. Grasping the deck railing, Ravinia bit nervously on her bottom lip and faced her husband.

"There was a fashion show and I—"

"And you donated my hard-earned money to the good ole Reverent Wrong, didn't you?" finishing her sentence with his assumption. As he accused her, he stressed the "t" for emphasis. Xavier's voice was a conversation mix between a serious Tiger Woods and the character, Carlton from *The Fresh Prince show,* with the depth and distinction of Chip Caray, the sports announcer. There was just not enough feeling to actually connect one to him or the words he tried to relate. Xavier's over exaggerated way of talking unnerved his wife who grew up with considerably less than him. Although she believed in speaking distinctly, sometimes Xavier was so over the top, it made him sound just as arrogant as he looked. She wondered how he even could consider himself truly African-American the way he carried on. He certainly seemed to forget where he came from when it was convenient. There was nothing sincere about Xavier and this contributed to Ravinia's searching heart for the truth in love and ultimately life.

It frustrated Ravinia that Xavier was so particular about how she spent their money. He could spend thousands of dollars on golf equipment and fundraisers for the firm, but when it came to church and sacrificial giving, he couldn't understand the significance of tithes and offerings. If folks knew just how much he had to pay to buy into the partnership, they'd know how much of an Uncle Tom sell-out Xavier really was.

"Not exactly," Ravinia tried to spit out, but Xavier, with his two-edged sword-like tongue, lashed back line for line.

"Then what *exactly,*" enunciating his words in perfect diction as if to undermine Ravinia. "I mean, what exactly does that mean?"

Trying her best to skirt past the pointed question, Ravinia used her feminine charm to weasel her way out of answering truthfully. Lord knows, she couldn't afford to tell him now. She was still building her case against him at the same time and needed more evidence.

"Reverend Wright asked about you," Ravinia brought up in a sweet, saint-like voice meant to make him think about the destination of his soul. "He was wondering when you were going to come to service again."

If he even gave Ravinia's guilt trip a second thought, it was not apparent. "I bet he did, old joker," Xavier mocked with an audible detestable laugh as if he was talking more to himself than to her.

Successfully deterring her suspicious husband yet another time, Ravinia climbed up to the top step on the deck. Reaching up, she began to stroke Xavier's brownish-black Creole waves that lapped around the nape of his neck. Letting her manicured nails slightly scratch over his scalp, she found the place on his head that would release his mind from more speculation and massaged it deeply. She placed a quick peck on his slightly flushed cheek and sauntered past him in bare feet, inspecting the state of the flowering red and white pansy basket since the first frost of the year.

Ravinia had left the house wearing pantyhose but didn't think even Xavier would notice that level of detail. His café au lait complexion revealed deep, permanently etched lines that had formed on his high forehead, gently browned by the sun. His face had grown quite serious, and that began to worry Ravinia.

Just then, he began to look down at his wife's face. To him, she was ageless with her naturally bronzed skin and beautifully full crimson lips. Xavier still looked puzzled and distant, but somewhat satisfied with Ravinia's response. He put his hand around Ravinia's little waist and nudged her towards the screen door and loudly growled, "I'm starved. Do we have any brie?"

Chapter 8.

LOW DOWN DIRTY SHAME

The twilight passed through the slats of the bathroom window as Ravinia was finishing her evening shower. Scrubbing feverishly with her loofah, she couldn't seem to get the scent of the Reverend off her quickly enough. The aromatic cucumber-melon body wash tantalized her nose and with her third full-body scrubbing, her senses began to calm. Tonight was the last night Xavier would be home before he had to leave for his semi-monthly business trip to Manila and she knew that she would have to take care of some wifely duties lest he suspect something.

Ravinia, however, was growing tired of the torrid escapades of her secret meetings with the Reverend. The conviction of having an affair with a man of God just went against every sanctified bone in her body. Her mother had raised her in a Pentecostal church and although any type of adultery was undoubtedly a sin, the stigma associated with what she did seemed to hold much more deception and accountability than any other sin she could commit. This was especially true for her mother, who Ravinia revered and to her accomplice's followers, who Ravinia feared.

It was almost 9 p.m. and Ravinia could hear the thundering of the surround sound blaring though the house. With the kids still at her mother's house, Xavier took advantage of the opportunity to watch movies to his liking. And so, thinking she could run to the bedroom without Xavier noticing, Ravinia sprinted her naked cinnamon body down the hallway, feeling the coolness of the air hit the tiny hairs lining the small of her back. She rarely used the master bathroom that Xavier had designed. Ravinia preferred the 2nd floor bathroom that she had redone last summer after her trip to Rome. When she got into her room and flicked on the light, she saw Xavier standing there, with nothing but a towel wrapped around him.

Oh man, Ravinia thought. Her heart dropped almost as fast as her breasts. She dreaded when Xavier saw her naked. She always seemed to feel as if she were in competition with all the newer models that arrived every fall at Omicron Consulting. Xavier always got a new crop of interns and for some odd reason they were always female and very attractive, as least in Ravinia's mind. And like a popsicle, she stood there frozen in front of the man she had married almost a decade ago. It was the most awkward moment she had experienced in years. *He's gonna see them. I know he is going to see them,* Ravinia thought to herself frantically, referring to the multitude of stretch marks lining her abdomen and stomach area like strands of tangled DNA. She had gotten them while pregnant with the twins during her first marriage. The dark, raised lines seemed to be drawn on her stomach like that of a shrunken-in globe. The intricate pattern probably made sense when she was eight months pregnant but now they were ugly and disfiguring. Reminiscing back to when she was pregnant, she remembered tracing the outline of the broken veins into what almost appeared to be the shapes of the continents of the world. Her then husband, Markus, used to smile as he talked to her belly calling her semi-permanent scars "history-lines" saying they were beautiful and told the story of the two of them. Now, all the unsightly scars did were puckle with the rest of her skin that had loss its elasticity after she had turned 40.

Xavier looked at his wife and his restless eyes showed no mercy. He seemed distant and his disposition sought release from Ravinia for the night. It was clear that intercourse was the furthest thing from his mind. He said a quick, "Hey" to break the ice between them and tightly secured his towel around his size 34 waist. Xavier was very fit for his age. He worked out constantly and his skin was always clear and taut with a slight ruddy glow. His upper body was robust and his chest muscles held great definition. Although his slightly bowed legs were on the scrawny side, he wore them well. Ravinia was also in pretty good shape, but some early signs of aging had begun to show and in her vanity, this made her very insecure. Xavier had barely scanned over Ravinia's naked body before he quickly walked towards his closet to select his clothes for his business trip. Ravinia noticed his Louis Vuitton duffle bag and suitcase were already set out next to the dresser. Feeling slightly conflicted by his reaction, she realized that she actually did want him to look at her, if only admiringly.

Grabbing her black silk robe from behind the bedroom door hook, she quickly turned her back to the door of the closet and slipped it on. Walking over to her dresser, she reached in and pulled out a long, black satin gown. No matter how he made her feel, she was certain that any part of her that he touched in the middle of that night would be smooth. Still faced in the opposite direction of Xavier's closet, she took off the robe, laying it on the earth-toned, Mediterranean-inspired chaise lounge at the foot of their bed. Slipping the gown over her head, she wiggled it down the length of her body until it landed on her hips. Noticing that Xavier had apparently fallen in his walk-in closet, she decided she could take a little risk with getting dressed. However, she was starting to have a slight dilemma. *These annoying hips,* she scowled in her head. Ravinia had more-than-ample hips for an average sized, medium-framed woman and every time she put on a slip, a gown or a dress, the article of clothing would collect and drape where her hips were the widest. She pulled the remaining part of her gown down, smoothing the lace insets that were strategically placed at the waist. As she gently flattened the wrinkles, the stretchy black lace brushed the stretch marks that reached from under her breasts to above her bikini line.

Catching a glimpse of herself in the full-length whitewashed oval mirror, she noticed how beautiful she really was. In all her slender fullness, she realized that she was a woman, wholly. The span of her childbearing hips chortled at the narrow-minded thought that she should change her appearance just to please her husband. Just earlier that year, she caught Xavier reading an article about breast augmentation. He had casually left the magazine open to that particular page when he left for work that morning. Ravinia knew it was suppose to be a hint but she took it as a stab in the back. Although she was only one year his senior, she at times felt like she was 10 years older than him. And the way he treated her at times confirmed that.

Turning to the side, she found just enough perk in her bosom to know that her body was still an eye-turner and that she just needed to understand the value of herself to really appreciate all that she was. But guilt became her enemy when she glanced hesitantly at her face. Her complexion read words she didn't want to see. Truth looked at her and the scripture she was trying to remember in church that morning was trying to find its way into her heart. Troubled by the slight wrinkles that had formed in her face, she knew it was time to stop the affair with the Reverend. She couldn't afford to keep living that way. Stress was starting to show on her face and that alone was too much for Ravinia. Even though she was sure Xavier was involved with someone at work, she knew that two wrongs could never make a right. She had to call it quits and the sooner, the better.

Ravinia was so riddled with remorse that she didn't even realize that Xavier had come out of the closet. Standing there behind her, her husband encircled his arms around her distinct waist, pulling her back into his chest. She could feel his definition behind her and began to slightly resist. Thinking about the Reverend, she knew she just couldn't be intimate with her husband that night. And although she had scrubbed down to a new layer of skin, when Xavier held her, condemnation would not let her feel clean. She needed to be purged and it just wouldn't be right. Wondering how she would get out of making love to him, Ravinia knew that she had to think quickly.

"Baby, I'm not feeling well," Ravinia lied. She knew it wasn't exactly the truth, but her conscience would not allow her to sleep with two men in one day. Plus the feelings she had made her stomach sour and she felt like she needed to lie down. Besides, seeing Xavier behind her made her feel insecure. She didn't even know if she wanted to sleep in the same bed with him, but decided that she had made her bed and had better lie in it.

"Ok, but you know I am going to be gone this time for a week," Xavier said blandly. *A week?* Ravinia was puzzled. *I thought it was only for 5 days. Why would he have to stay the weekend?*

"I thought you were only going for 5 days and you would be home Friday night?" Ravinia questioned, wondering what was really going on. The fiscal year had ended last week so he couldn't be trying to use up the surplus in the budget.

"Well, I have to meet with clients Friday night and my partner thought it would be nice to stay the weekend. They've never been to Manila, before." Xavier's voice trailed. He began to sound worn-out.

Ravinia numbly walked over to the bed where she had spent countless nights crying her self to sleep.

Uh huh. Ravinia's thoughts began to get the best of her. She knew that the Tuesday after Labor Day was the day when the new interns started their 6-month stint at Omicron each year. Only the best of the best would be selected to stay to finish the 3rd and 4th quarter. Xavier was leaving on Labor Day so maybe he had already met with his group the week before. However Ravinia couldn't help but wonder? *Could Xavier be going to Manila with one of his interns already? Or was this 'partner' someone new to Omicron?*

Ravinia was beginning to get angry but couldn't let on to Xavier. The tension in the room began to rise, but that didn't stop Xavier from climbing into the bed where Ravinia was sitting. She was still stunned at how calmly her husband had told her that he would be gone for 7 whole days doing God-knows-what with whomever he wanted. Ravinia could almost kick herself when she realized that she would be staying at home keeping his home and their children clean while he went gallivanting abroad with someone she didn't know.

Then she realized why she had started seeing the Reverend in the first place. Xavier was always very secretive about his affairs, but his silence gave consent. Ravinia let her heavy eyelids fall, closing her tired eyes. She didn't care that she still had eyeliner and mascara on. The events of the day had been a bit overwhelming for her and she wished she could rewind back to 7:05 a.m. when she awoke. Regret was settling in and Ravinia's spirit was contrite. However, the issues that had troubled her during the day began to inundate her dreams. Scenes, from countless private counseling sessions where she had poured out her deepest thoughts and sins to her Pastor, clicked in her mind like a child's View Master toy. It was times like these, when she felt worthless, used and pushed aside by her husband. Ravinia knew that Xavier only married her because she represented what he couldn't be on his own. The night would not end as her dreams turned into bizarre nightmares. The tempter had come yet again into her space. But this time, he was not manifested as a man, but a spirit taunting her in her sleep. *If only I could wake up,* Ravinia dreamed. *If only I could just wake up. . .*

Chapter 9.

THE DRYER

The Indian summer nights were long and hot without him. The air conditioner was up as high as it could go, yet she was in desperate desire for her husband. Even though he had brushed off her weak excuses just a few nights ago, Ravinia had quickly forgotten the reasons why she deferred the advances of her husband. Ravinia ached for Xavier for the first time in years. And of course, when she desired to have him more than a pint of Ben and Jerry's butter pecan, he was on a business trip in Manila. It seemed like his trips to the Philippines were becoming more and more frequent since Labor Day and that made Ravinia uneasy. Tossing and turning, she decided to get up and walk around the house. It seemed so much bigger when he wasn't there. The twins were spending the weekend at her ex-husband's house, and their adopted daughter, Randella, was fast asleep in her room.

Ravinia wasn't really hungry, but she did want some fresh ice water. Her throat was parched. The air conditioner, which had run all summer, needed to be serviced and didn't really cool things off on the second floor of their 4,200 square foot English Tudor any more. Ravinia never wanted a house that large, but Xavier insisted. He was all about "dressing to impress" and that included all material possessions from the diamond Rolex he wore on his wrist to the gold fixtures and green marble he demanded for the master bathroom.

The carafe of ice water she had brought up earlier had perspired all over the ledge she had set it on, forming a wet ring that made it slide a fraction on its own. Just looking at the dripping condensation made Ravinia think about how much she desired Xavier. There had been many nights where Xavier had poured a glass of water, sliding the icy glass against the length of her bare back as she lay with her backside facing the door of their bedroom. Jerking from the chill in her spine, Ravinia would try and play possum but was rarely successful. Then he would close the door behind him and tease her with little, icy sprinkles until she awoke just conscious enough to make love.

Xavier should have called by now, she thought as she walked out on the balcony wanting a cool breeze to sweep over her. Her hot flashes seemed to intensify when Xavier was away and even though fall had found its way on her calendar, Ravinia still preferred the house to be a cool 68 degrees at all times. Looking out on the multitude of autumn leaves rustling around in the October twilight, she felt the beauty of the eve envelop her. The golden bronze, brassy copper and fading emerald leaves reflected back the encapsulated light of the moon. Caught within the wind's breath beneath their flimsy dry stems, the carefree leaves seemed to be holding onto what little life remained in them, taking a circular skip on the wind around the back of Ravinia's patio. Autumn was her favorite season in Chicago because it was just cool enough to wear suede and just warm enough, at times, to go bare-armed and barelegged until mid-October. Of course, living in the North Shore meant cooler temperatures closer to the lake and Ravinia didn't care too much for the cold. One could always depend on the air to be cooler by Lake Michigan and that was one of the disadvantages of North Shore life.

Once again, Ravinia felt the loneliness of Xavier's absence. She knew that she couldn't keep up this charade much longer. Thinking made her restless. She grew tired of the constant lies and deceit. Twirling around the platinum band, her thoughts wandered back to her childhood. As the prongs of the high setting on her stone ring kept hitting her bent pinky finger, the princess-cut, three-carat diamond gleamed in the recessed lighting of the hallway leading to the bathroom. Xavier had given Ravinia the upgraded ring when he made partner. As she looked around her sienna marble, Tuscany-inspired bathroom, she began to think about taking a bath in the Jacuzzi with Xavier. *Wouldn't that be nice?* Ravinia thought, going back in her mind to their early years together. They hadn't done anything like that in a while. Why wasn't he ever home when she felt this way?

Running her pampered fingers along the Italian tiles, she thought to herself that she had certainly come a long way from rust-covered commodes that barely flushed unless you plunged them before and after using. She recalled the sewer-scented tiles that reeked with mildew and mold stains from years of water damage. They were a far cry from the luxuries Ravinia now possessed. She was glad her mother had gotten her and Nate out of the Cabrini Green projects when she did. She had read somewhere that they had moved most of the remaining people out of the near North ghetto recently to the far reaches of the poorer South suburbs and some parts of Gary, Indiana, too. And Ravinia knew it was probably for the better that they had escaped before the mass exodus.

The gold fixtures with perfectly aligned towels hung over each emerald-cobalt-amber mosaic glass basin. Ravinia had just remodeled the second floor bathroom, day room and kitchen, based on the movie, *Under the Tuscan Sun*, so there were extravagant Italian influences throughout the house. Catching a glimpse of herself in the gold-encrusted oval mirror, she noticed the wear and tear of life creeping upon her. Leaning in to get a closer view, she saw tiny little wrinkle lines forming around her eyes and in the corner of her lips. She turned on the light to make sure she saw what she thought she saw. Burning the candle at both ends apparently was catching up with her. Tightening her silk robe around her proportioned waistline, she stepped on the scale. One hundred forty-two pounds the digital panel read. She had put on 12 pounds since she had stopped working at Omicron Consulting. Scowling at herself for not continuing to work out once she left the firm, she went back to the mirror and loosened the robe, allowing it to drop to the floor.

Xavier wasn't home so she didn't have to worry about him walking in on her. Looking at herself naked in the mirror, she noticed that her almost C-cup breasts had a slight droop. Raising her arms above her head, she looked for any changes and did a quick circular lump check on each of them. Placing her hands on her waist, she faced the truth display, and saw that her hips were spreading. Unlike a month ago when she had her gown to mask the intricate details of her body, she could not hide from the sight she was revealed. There was some interesting cellulite puckering along the outside of her thighs. Rubbing her legs, as if the cottage cheese-looking fat deposits would suddenly disappear, she felt like she had let herself go. Ravinia knew that if she was going to keep Xavier interested, she had better start to work out again. Being without the Reverend, she felt abandoned intimately. But she was determined not to go back into the infidelity she had once known with her pastor. However, she quickly realized that she missed the relationship she had with her husband and wanted to make amends with him.

Ravinia knew she wasn't exactly Xavier's type. He preferred waif-looking women with tiny breasts, long, fine blonde hair stemming from dark roots and washboard abs. At least, those were the kinds of co-eds he dated in college at Dartmouth. He probably didn't realize he even had a "type," but Ravinia knew that type all too well. She was at every business function and trade show he attended. She was on every televised broadcast and had snuck her way into the sports broadcasting world, too. She graced talk shows, had both leading and supporting roles in movies and music videos, and was becoming the icon sought after for pageants all over the world. And, of all places, she was the one that did not have to have experience to come in two salary grades higher than the existing seasoned consultants in Corporate America. If she even smiled or flipped her hair behind her ear, she seemed to warrant a 20% merit increase.

She appeared to be everywhere and was not satisfied that society had embraced her as beautiful. It was because of "her" that Ravinia's teenaged daughter, Jamila, wanted to dye her naturally brown hair, ash blonde, relaxing it straighter than the law allowed. It was because of "her" that she had to caution her teenaged son, Justin, that there might be heartbreaks, if this "type" did not accept his proposal to go out on a date. And if they did, the consequences and mere controversy of interracial dating, ridicule, hatred from other races, and background differences may be difficult to overcome. But, "no's" would never discourage her son's bold teen spirit, because society said "she" was what was hot. And how could Ravinia influence her cautious views on her own children, when her own former husband was engaged to his own version of a flesh and blood Barbie doll?

Certainly, like a bloodhound, the "type" that Ravinia had identified as competition for her own sensual brownness, still sought after every high-powered successful African-American man. And "she" had no trouble finding many that found her attractive, although they were already married to beautiful African-American women. Ravinia knew this woman and fought tooth and nail to prove to her gawking husband and the entire consulting world that she, a prominent woman of color, had a place in society, in corporate America, in his life, and as his soul mate.

Knowing this, she realized that Xavier had dated many Caucasian and Asian women in college and those thoughts were a constant concern for her when he spent long nights at the firm. Already suspicious that he might be dabbling in interracial infidelity, Ravinia followed a thought that supported her own insecurity and severely breached her faith in him. She went into his closet and inspected his clothes. A wife can always find evidence if it is meant to be revealed. Sliding the mirrored closet doors, she peered inside the oversized walk-in closet, as if the boogieman was in there about to lunge out at her. She felt like she was snooping, but didn't stop to acknowledge those feelings. Justified that her suspicions could be real, Ravinia started searching through his Armani suit jackets, the ones he wore to after-hour events. She looked for scraps of paper, old business cards, or used tissue with traces of lipstick; anything to prove he was lying about not having an affair.

Finding nothing of significance, Ravinia went downstairs frustrated. She was a little dizzy from leaning over and poking through his pockets. Upset at her inability to obtain proof, she wandered down to the laundry room, a place she seldom visited. The maid came in every other day to take care of household-type things like washing clothes, ironing, and thoroughly cleaning the bathrooms and kitchen. Ravinia, mysteriously led to the dryer, opened its door and started pulling out the towels. She thought she might take a swim to cool herself down, and began folding the fluffy white pool towels. Noticing that something other than a towel had fallen to the floor, she saw a white on white string bikini. Reaching down to pick it up, Ravinia carefully picked up one of the loose strings and looked at the article of clothing as if it were diseased. She knew it was not hers or her daughter's. Neither one of them could ever fit all their thickness into a string bikini. A little disgusted by the thought of some other woman's dirty swimwear mingled with her laundry, she shuddered at the thought and gathered all the towels and tossed them into the garbage. As far as the bikini was concerned, her first impulse was to throw it away, too. But, she couldn't do that because it was evidence that she could fling at Xavier when he returned. She had finally found the evidence she knew was around.

Tucking the little, floss-like panty into the pocket of her black silk robe, she seemed very pleased that she had found it, and in an odd sort of way was somewhat relieved by the encounter. However, Ravinia started feeling undesired and somewhat defeated in her attempt to make her marriage work. Suddenly the urges she had for Xavier were gone, as well as her desire to cool off in the pool. Frustrated at her discovery, she realized this is what she wanted to know. But did she want to know so she could be with the Reverend? No—that part of her life was certainly over. Or was it just that she sought company for her own wretched misery? Perhaps she thought it would be easier to tell Xavier about her own affair, if she knew for certain he was party to one, as well. She knew that it was not her fault entirely for the infidelity, but she still felt that perhaps she should have been the wiser of the two of them and not given into the temptation.

Xavier would be coming home tomorrow and Ravinia wondered if she could face him. She struggled with whether she would tell him about what she had found in the dryer or just let him wonder why she would be so distant. Taking a quick surveillance of her own soul, she knew that whatever she did, she needed to get away from the Reverend and his church. She thought long and hard about her next steps as the evening slipped into night. Growing tired, she decided to go back to bed. Remembering what she had come downstairs for in the first place, she started wondering about the "other" woman. Who was she? It made her mad because here she was, all ready to rekindle things with her husband and there was someone already in her place.

Ravinia started thinking long and hard about the irresponsible decisions she had made with the Reverend. Letting the guilt of her conscience sink in, she knew that somehow she would not be able to get out as easily as she thought. She wanted a clean break from the Reverend, but she knew he really did have a thing for her. Her mind then wandered back to Xavier. *It only serves me right,* her thoughts pounding so loudly in her head she could almost hear them echoing off the dank basement walls. *How could I think he wouldn't do the same thing? He was already suspicious, always asking about the Reverend in a derogatory tone.* And then she started calculating all the possibilities he could have chosen from at Omicron. Thinking about all her former female co-workers from the firm, she scanned through their names like a card catalog in her mind. After narrowing down the choices by comparing the size of the bikini with the hip size of the ladies she knew were vying for him, she realized that it was a hopeless attempt to try and rack her brain to figure out who was sleeping with her husband. The only thing Ravinia could really do was just wait. But for how long?

Chapter 10.

GOOD TIMES

Cabrini O'Green, (at least that's what the sign said on the front of the building), used to be my home. Dark stairwells, cement-block walls and steel bars on the windows sealed in the dread and hunger of some of the poorest people in Chicago. I remember many days of running home from school, dodging bullets from the Disciples and Vice Lord gang rumblings. Coolie High was filmed just blocks from where I earned my first set of street smarts and learned how to hustle for a pack of watermelon Now-and-Laters. Just about everybody was on welfare, at least where we lived. Food stamps could buy a lot more than just food. That's for sure.

The late 60s, early 70s were a turbulent time in Chicago. The night my baby brother, Nate was born at Cook County Hospital, gunshots popped and crackled through the streets. We were supposed to be back in school, but folks kept their kids at home in case the riots started back up again. People didn't need half an excuse to start breaking windows and pulling out their pistols, sticking up business owners for a 19 inch black and white television set. There were more boarded up buildings in 1969 than I had ever seen, and some of them never recovered from that turbulent era.

Momma risked her life everyday going to work up North. She kept house for this well-off Jewish family that lived in Highland Park. Mr. Jacob Weiss was a very successful real estate broker who owned several apartment buildings in downtown Chicago, and a few parking lots in the Wrigleyville area. With a couple of wise investments, before long, he became a multi-millionaire in real estate.

Before I started school, Momma would take me with her to work at the Weiss's. Judy Weiss, a wonderfully gorgeous Bulgarian, reminiscent of Eva Gabor, was very active in the community. She was a second shift nurse at Highland Park Hospital and her husky, yet sultry voice, and deep midnight blue eyes, captivated me. Mrs. Weiss was always so glamorous; I thought she could have been a movie star. I admired her ever-changing hair color and styles, switching between golden blonde and ruby auburn, wearing anything from a bob to an upsweep, almost as often as the seasons changed. She would laugh at me when I would stare at her dark roots and say, "Ravinia, my darling, you aren't the only one with dark roots." Being just a child, I didn't realize the double meaning of her words. But they strike me now, truthfully.

It was because of Mrs. Weiss that I got my name. When Momma was pregnant with me, the Weiss's took her to the *Ravinia Festival,* to see a classical performance. Momma closed her eyes and dreamed of a time when her life could not be so different from the people she worked for. She dreamed that her children could go to the best schools and not have to worry about gangs and violence. The eloquent, soothing music gave her hope. As she listened, she felt me leap in her belly and she knew that I could hear the sounds envelope me with their warm, melodic rhapsody. She fell in love with the name R-A-V-I-N-I-A. She knew that if she ever had a girl, she would name her Ravinia *(pronounced Ra-ven-ya)*, in hopes that she too would live as free as she felt when she was there.

Momma and I took the El train from Sedgwick to Belmont and changed for the train going to Evanston on the days I would go to work with her. I looked forward to having days off from school because I could escape from the dreariness of the ghetto, if only for a few hours. At the Howard Street stop, we would wait for the Evanston train that took us to Linden. Mr. Weiss would pick us up in his new 1965 Canary-yellow Cadillac Sedan de Ville and I would slide across the maize-colored back seat, feeling the butter-soft leather on the back of my four year old thighs. The station wagon my daddy drove had this rough, scratchy maroon and navy plaid material covering the seats, unlike the smooth glove-like leather of the Weiss's car. The vinyl parts of the seat of our car were cracked, torn and so worn; you could see the dark yellowed foam underneath. Sometimes, Nate would pick at it and Daddy would get mad and yell at us, saying he couldn't have anything for us. Nate was very sensitive. He would start to cry and Daddy would call him a "sissy" and a "momma's boy," saying he would never have a pot to pee in. I would sit there and just stare out of the window, looking back at Nate who would wet on himself every time Daddy said the word "pee." Back then, Nate had a weak bladder and couldn't help himself.

Nate loved Momma, more than anything in this world. He never wanted to be away from her. Most of the time, she would take him out to the Weiss's with her to work. But when she worked late for them, with formal dinner parties and various evening gatherings, Daddy would have to watch Nate and that seemed to make our father extra belligerent.

Nate was a momma's boy. He was scared of Daddy and had a right to be. Born a preemie, at four pounds two ounces, Daddy never gave him a fighting chance. Thinking he would die before reaching six months old, Daddy never held him, claiming he was too small and fragile, "a weakling." Momma and Ma-Dear, my granny, would hold him and feed him Pet-Milk, along with Momma's breast milk. Ma-Dear said that would fatten him up, and sure enough it did. Nate actually got to be quite a chubby little boy, and that made Daddy mad too. Nate would eat the best food at the Weiss's, unlike the rest of us, and that upset Daddy. He couldn't put the kind of food they did on his table. When Momma and Nate would get home, Nate would boast in his four year old little voice and say, "Vinia, we had the biggest pork chops today. They were juuuuicccyyyy!!! An' they was falling off the bone. Mmmm—mmmm! Momma the best cook in the whole world!" Stretching his chubby little arms out to demonstrate just how big "the whole world" was, Nate was just happy to get away when he could. But our father had to always find fault with something or somebody. Daddy would mutter something about how Nate's fat behind didn't need any pork chops and how he was spoiled enough already. Nate would start to turn beet-red with his high-yellow complexion and start crying until beads of sweat would form around his hairline. He'd run to Momma and she would give Daddy this seething look where her brow would almost touch her right eyelid. Daddy would look at her and get the hint, but would keep muttering under his breath. Momma would almost have to stop fixing our dinner to tend to Nate. Sometimes, I would come and get Nate and drag him into the bedroom and try to console him. But I was even jealous at times of the food he got at the Weiss's. Momma didn't bring much food home because she didn't believe in taking handouts. And she would never take anything that wasn't hers.

But from time to time, when the Weiss's had a dinner party, Momma stayed to prepare the food and serve the guests. There would be so many leftovers that Ms. Judy would beg Momma to take some food home to us. We would be so happy to see all the fancy food from the party. Filet mignon, twice-baked potatoes with chives, little finger sandwiches, and lemon chiffon cheesecake with cherries. It was like Christmas time because we never had that kind of food at our house. We simply couldn't afford it. Plus, Daddy didn't like "fancy" food. Momma would try new recipes, like scalloped potatoes and Daddy would complain. "Woman, what is this mess? Why can't you just make plain ole mashed potatoes? We ain't rich Katie Mae. Don't be trying to switch things up on me. I like things plain and simple, see? Plain and simple." Then, he would slam his fist on the table like a spoiled little child who didn't get their way. Momma would just look at him, like she was thinking, "Why in the world did I marry this man?" She too had been raised with things plain and simple in Louisiana, but had come to Chicago to find a better life. If it weren't for her ability to think big, she would have never survived her first winter here.

Judy Weiss, on the other end of the spectrum, was a high-society type. She had all the latest fashions and magazines. When Momma would take a lunch break, she would flip through the magazines. She liked the *Good Housekeeping* magazine most of all because of all the different recipes it had in it. From perfect Jell-O molds to 30-minute hamburger casseroles, she found new and exciting ways to turn traditional meals into new ones. The Weiss's loved it and would pay her generous bonuses when she came up with a new recipe that was Kosher and delicious. Working at the Weiss's was a great escape for her. She dreaded coming home each night to Cabrini and prayed for a way to get her and her children out of the misery she had crawled into.

Chapter 11.

CHI-TOWN DRAMA

In June of 1989, my girlfriend Jade asked if I would go with her to *The Cotton Club*, a small dance club in Chicago, just south of the Loop. She wanted to introduce me to this gorgeous sax player named Jake Devine. I really wasn't in the mood to meet another starving artist, but in my predicament, what else could I do? When we arrived at the club, the music was bumpin'. We could feel the bass thumping, vibrating against the heels of our shoes as we walked up the sidewalk to the little whitewashed club. I never understood how they could fit so many people in that place, but they did. *The Cotton Club* was always packed. Jade got us seated near the front of the stage; the best seats in the house.

I had always felt guilty about going to clubs. Memories of my father's strict rules about secular music still rang clear in my head. "You can't get away from it," trailed his stern, scruffy baritone voice, reminding me of long Saturday night choir rehearsals. After rehearsal, some of the kids would get in their cars and go to the McDonald's down the street from the church. As soon as they got in the car and cleared the church parking lot, you could hear the stereo pump up a remix of Gloria Gaynor's *I Will Survive* or some other late night disco track.

Daddy would start pointing his finger at the wayward teens and say, "Look at them heathens. Now they know better than that. I know they parents raised them better than that. See 'em, popping they fingers to the devil's music!" Then he would look at me starting to get into the music myself and begin to chastise me as if I needed a personalized Bible thrashing. "All of you young folk going to split Hell wide open! You wearing nail polish, Sapphire? Loose yo' hold Satan!" he'd say, shaking his tattered Bible at me. "Sapphire, you got a Jezebel spirit just like your mammy, as sure as my name is Leonard!" Then he would spend the rest of night rebuking me as he dodged the cars on the freeway. There was no use in replying. I wouldn't be able to get a word in edgewise. And if I did reply, I would end up paying for it with a backhand lick to the jaw. Daddy didn't believe in young folks back talking grown folks. I wondered many nights why he compared me and my mom to Jezebel. Mom did like to look good and she kept herself up—hair and nails done. A little makeup or "hamburger helper" as she liked to call it. That was her code word for makeup around Dad since he was against everything even remotely liberal.

In all the years of attending church, Bible study, choir rehearsal, every midnight musical, revival and tent deliverance service, I never understood why something that was supposed to be so free and liberating as salvation could be so restricting and punitive. My father made it seem like God wanted a perfect man, one that was born without sin. But I knew in all of his self-righteousness, my dad was also a born-again sinner. Perhaps he had forgotten what it was like to be free from sin, to love and forgive like the Bible says. Maybe he thought that just being in church all the time was enough to save him and that somehow he would make it to the pearly gates by having perfect attendance on his permanent record. But that never made sense to me. How did sitting on a church pew each Sunday morning and every other day the doors were open, make a bit of difference in your life if your heart wasn't right?

Growing up with my father, I always felt like I could never be good enough to be truly saved. I mean, I had lost the closest person in my life, my mother, the one I loved the most in my entire little life. I couldn't understand why that would happen to me. Sometimes I felt like he wasn't even my father the way he treated me. Calling my mother a jezebel made me wonder what my mother had done that could be considered so hideous. What sin did she commit that would make him such a madman?

How could this be God's love allowing my father to be the tyrant he was, separating us at the heart, soul and mind? And in my heart, I knew the answer to that age-old question. I think that is what turned me off from just going through the motions in my life. I was not going to just go to church and be the big pretender. No, there was something more to God than just a church building and rituals. There had to be a closeness that told me He was there; keeping me alive in the midst of all the tribulations I had been through. Little did I know, I would be calling out for Him sooner than I thought . . .

Despite the stern voice of my father bellowing in my ears, the smooth and silky vibes from inside the club were calling me from deep inside this hip Chicago legend. My girlfriend squealed when the doorman let us in. After waiting about ten minutes, I was soooo glad when we went inside. Jade had been singing off-key. Jade is my girl and everything, but Lord knows she was as tone deaf as a love-sick mule that night. It was between sets and the DJ was spinning some deep house tracks. Back then I loved house music. The track changed and a wonderful alto voice came through singing, “I wanna thank you Heavenly Father . . .” I was shocked. I hadn’t been to a club in a long time, but I had never heard anything close to Gospel being played in one since Al Green was putting out hits in the early seventies.

I want to thank You, heavenly Father
For shinin’ Your light on me
You sent me someone who really loves me
And not just my body

This woman was speaking to me. I felt the words she sang penetrate and hit my soul like a dagger. I did need someone in my life. Someone that would truly love me. After Willie, I thought I’d never love again, but after years of coming to terms with myself, I realized that I would not limit my perception of love to the heinous act of one man. Truly, there must be someone out there who could love me on my terms. And after ten years, I was ready to find out.

Just then, another set of inspiring female voices was spun into the mix. They sung in rhythmic harmony.

You brought the sunshine
In my life
Threw out the life-line
Saved my life

Jade leaned over and looked at me, stirring the ice cubes mingling in her Diet Coke and lime wedge. Neither one of us drank. We knew we both didn't have any business sitting up in a club but we were there to meet Jake, right? After what happened to me in college, I vowed to never let myself be intoxicated again. Seeing my perplexed look, she said, "I didn't know the Clark Sisters had crossed over! Girl, if my Auntie heard this, she would roll over in her grave. You know she sang with Mattie Moss Clark, bless her soul," she lamented, waving her hand and going on like she was in church.

That's the Clark Sisters? Playin' in a club? Oh wow, what has this world come to? On the one hand, the music was lively and uplifting. It was a pleasant change from all the begging and sexual undertones most of the secular music of that time carried. But on the other hand, it was a bit unusual. When some of the older folks realized that the Clark Sisters were in the mix, they got off the dance floor and sat down or went to the bar. The younger crowd didn't know the difference and kept on dancing. My mother had an extensive collection of albums with Mattie Moss Clark and the Detroit Mass choir on the cover. Every sanctified, Pentecostal church choir knew at least five songs written by Mattie Moss Clark and they were careful to sing them right. My mother had sung with the State Mass Choir under the direction of Dr. Clark as a youth growing up in Detroit. Dr. Clark used to say that you had to get the note right. And Momma would say, "Sapphire, you got to get the note right." I missed Momma so much. I wanted to go home and call her later that night just to tell her I had heard the Clark Sisters and all, but I couldn't. The Clark Sisters were the daughters of the famous choir director. In my solitude, the voice of strength came forth. Out of my sorrow, I found my voice and just like my mother told me, I always got the note right. But still, after all these years, I felt so alone, though there were people everywhere.

Jade reminded me that we had been there over an hour and hadn't met Jake, yet. She took a less than subtle scan around the club, waving to a couple of folks she apparently knew from around the way and sighed, "Girl, I don't see him anywhere. Maybe we need to leave. You know I got to go to Sunday school in the morning." I just looked at Jade. I started to think, *oh great. I got all dressed up for nothing. And who is she—at a club tonight and gonna be sitting up in church tomorrow morning*. I just shook my head. "Let just wait a few more minutes." Jade nodded and started looking for one of her buddies to run her mouth with. *Oh well, I might as well order something to drink,* I thought to myself. Just as I lifted my hand to signal for a waitress, the smoke-filled room became like a silent movie in slow motion. It was Jake. Boy, did that man know how to make a dramatic entrance. He was dressed in all black from head to toe. Standing about 5'10", his body, sleek and slender. His black dress pants were neatly pleated with a matching black leather Coach belt with the little Coach embossed tag hanging neatly off its brass buckle. His Stacy Adams were also shining as the spotlight dimmed. All you could see was the focus on the alto sax in his slender hands. The brass horn gleamed in the vanilla light as he raised it to his slightly parted lips and began to slowly blow out silky, fluid notes that enraptured me. Each skillful, melodic run was even more graceful than the first, blending rich, jazzy undertones and blue notes that I hadn't even heard Miles Davis play. I couldn't keep my eyes off of him. Playing that brass horn was like eating pie to him. Sweet and effortless. You could tell he enjoyed playing every note. Gliding up and down scales so fluidly, you could barely see him inhale. He was just that smooth.

I would catch myself every so often staring at his rich chocolate complexion. We were so close to the stage, I could see that his skin was so even-toned that I was certain that a razor had never touched his face. His bald head shone moderately in the spotlight. I didn't care. He was like a melted dark Hershey bar and I could imagine what it would be like to kiss his full, dark mahogany lips. He was tall, lean and beyond handsome. Every note he played seemed to sit on my lap and tickle my knees. I was smitten already, and he hadn't even gotten to the second set. He seemed to notice me, tucked away in the corner of our table, but I wanted to be sure.

Trying to hide my thick body behind Jade, I was a bit self-conscious about gaining a few extra pounds. No matter how I tried to inch closer to Jade, to not seem too obvious, the more conspicuous I became. There was a strong, undeniable attraction between us. He kept following me with his horn, as I tried to move around to look at other things in the club. But nothing would distract me long enough. My focus subconsciously drew me right back to that smooth operator on stage. His dark, penetrating eyes were deep-set and slightly slanted, a young Nat King Cole. Eyes so lively and invitingly warm, they seemed to intensify with each passing moment, catching the light, kissing it and releasing it back into the room.

During the middle of the last song in the set, *Sweet Love* by Anita Baker, he came over to the edge of the stage and jumped off. Landing only a few feet from our table, I was pleasantly startled. I glanced over at Jade, whom I had almost forgotten was there; she looked stunned. He grabbed my hand, looked into my eyes and smiled. I had forgotten the lure of my own eyes and how easily a guy could fall into them. They were bluer than any ocean, with just as much depth. When I thought the night couldn't get any better, this gorgeous man started serenading me. The words blurred in my head. I was falling . . .

Before I realized it, I was lip-syncing back to him. He played as I mouthed the words right back to him. It was so intense. His presence captivated me. I wanted to be on stage with him, but I wasn't bold enough to just climb up there on my own. I knew I could sing. There was no doubt about that. I just wasn't a singer and that held me back. He leaned down and reached for me. I couldn't believe he was motioning for me to join him! I felt like a nervous co-ed. He took the microphone and the half-drunken crowd nudged me on with their, "Gon' girl, do yo' thang. You know you can sing, girl!" knowing they didn't know me from Adam or Eve. Jade wasn't much help, either. She literally pushed me off my stool, not letting me hide my weight behind her or anything else for that matter. Pulling out my dress where it had gotten wedged from sitting so long, I smoothed the wrinkles out of my blue velvet chemise and climbed up the stairs.

Taking the mic, I looked at him for guidance. He gave me a key of $F^{\#}$ and I was off and running. It didn't take me long to find a place in the song I could join into. I opened my mouth and a voice I had never heard before came out and grabbed the crowd.

With all my heart I love you, baby
Stay with me and you will see
My arms will hold you, baby
Never leave, 'cause I believe

Jade looked at me and smiled. She was my strength throughout my entire ordeal with Willie, and she knew that I needed this release. I knew I was hitting all the right notes but that wasn't as important as the fact that I was standing right next to such a fine-looking man, creating harmony for the first time ever. I had lost my inhibition just that quickly and began to feel the attraction of a possible new love.

Jake stopped playing and put his sax down so the lead guitarist could do his solo. Taking the opportunity to lean down and whisper to me, he gave me some line about how intrigued he was by my voice. He wanted me to meet him backstage after the show. I looked back at him, as wide eyed as a baby doe, and tried to play it off. But even my conservative side found a nook and cranny to hide in that night. Well, to say the least, I went wild! Jade and I looked at each other, and she cupped her hands around her lips, as if nobody knew what she was doing. She mouthed, "I told you he was fine!" I nodded in complete agreement, trying to keep my composure but I was so excited that Jake was interested in me. I closed my eyes to savor the moment. Mixed feelings of joy and anxiety shot through my body like I had never experienced before, as I walked to the back of the stage.

As I stepped behind the curtain, I felt an amazing sensation that scared and excited me all at the same time. I was falling hard for him. And that notion excited me. I didn't know if I was coming or going. It was all so surreal. I couldn't believe this was happening to me.

After the set was over, Jake came back and just started looking into my eyes. He said that he had never seen a woman with eyes so captivating. When he asked me from where I got my eyes from, I got a bit defensive. He sounded like he thought I had I bought them from a store. I thought well enough of the man looking down at me to believe he wasn't trying to insult me, so I mentioned to him that my mother told me that her uncle had grayish-blue eyes like the sky—almost cerulean in color. I never met that uncle or saw pictures of him. But my eyes translated into a deep, almost indigo blue with hints of violet. My mother named me Sapphire because at birth my father said, "That child's eyes look just like blue sapphires." It was odd to see a brown child with striking blue-violet eyes, but here I was. I remember my mother mentioning that the nurse kept saying that my eyes would change some day, looking into my mom's amber eyes and my father's dark brown eyes. But they never did.

That night Jake and I went out for a late dinner at The Parthenon in Greek Town. As the night waned into the early morning hours, we went to the North Avenue beach and walked along the shoreline under the moon and stars. The moon was bursting with ambient light, inviting us to stay and keep her company. Its almost eggshell hue gently danced its luminance upon the deep night of Lake Michigan to entertain us. Even the lake participated in the performance; a fitting partner to the smiling moon.

We found a bench and just sat there talking endlessly for hours. He held me, kissing my eyes and face, talking about the places he had traveled and his plans for the future with his band. He wanted to go on tour and was really excited that everyone's schedule was finally free. There was a deep satisfaction in being embraced by a man with a sensitive side, who enjoyed me and listened to my thoughts and dreams. I had reservations, but suppressed them because I knew it was time for me to love again. Something about Jake just felt so right. I didn't want the night to end.

We were having so much fun it surprised us to see daylight inching its way on the horizon. Where had all the time gone? Would my fantastic dream end by the light of day? As I climbed down back to earth, things began to settle. When we had exhausted the night, we exchanged telephone numbers. He walked me back to his car, and that's when the feelings of doubt rushed in. I began doubting myself and the possibility of having a viable relationship with a musician. But the surge of emotions that flowed through the night outweighed the doubt remaining strong and powerful within me.

Before I could get into the car, Jake put his arms around me and gave me a full-bodied hug. I felt the heat from our bodies permeating, one into the other. It felt so wonderful to be touched. It had been a long time since I welcomed the arms of a real man around me. It was beyond words.

Our date was a unique and unforgettable experience. And, it wasn't before long that Jake and I knew we were meant for each other. We jumped the broom in a simple, intimate ceremony that same November. Jake and I would still have a few months together before the band would begin on tour that following March. That's when love's true test would begin.

Chapter 12.

UP IN SMOKE

Those first few months were blissful. Being newlyweds, Jake and I spent days and nights wrapped in each other's arms, finding our love stronger than the urge to eat or even sleep. But, as all marriages find out soon enough, the honeymoon would come to an inexplicable halt. We were hopeful though, and wanted to make things work. I was so happy to finally be married that sometimes I think I worked too hard at trying to keep Jake happy. Ever since the rape, I had been very self-conscious about the ugly scars that had not disappeared from my skin. When we were on the cruise, I tried to cover the ones on my arms. I didn't expect Jake to return so soon to our cabin, and he caught me spreading the opaque paste over the marks. He took me in his arms, and said, "Sapphire, don't worry about the scars. That time in your life is over. It's just us now. I mean, you'll have to live with the scars he left, on the inside and out, but you can't hide them. You have to learn how to accept them. So does everyone else. I love you the way you are. Just as you are." Then he would kiss every scar inflicted by another man on my body, telling me how beautiful I was and that he would never hurt me. Tears of unspeakable joy started to flow down my face as he made love to me. I couldn't help it. This man who I called "husband", had me by the heart and soul and I was finally free to love. After the rape, I didn't think I could ever love again and feel that I could submit myself sexually to a man, even married. But Jake showed me such compassion that I wanted to love him back. He brought desire back into my days and passion back into my nights.

The way Jake played his sax was the way he loved me. Tender and gentle, yet strong and powerful. The boldness he spoke when he blew perfect notes was how he called my name, *Sapphire*. It made me shiver. Holding me in the strength of his arms, Jake often embraced me and in him I found my safe place. The way he caressed my face spoke to his experience in life, but also of pain. He too had been hurt deeply and found that our love was healing.

Jake and I had a deep, abiding commitment to our marriage. I trusted him as much as I could trust any man at this point in my life. He taught me things about myself I never knew. He saw things that no one else could see in me. This man, unlike most men, could bring out the best in me. He could also bring out the worst. And It didn't take long to see that there was a secret side to Jake, a dark side that I wish would have never reared its ugly head.

On one occasion, Jake came home from a tri-state tour after only two months. The ticket sales were low, and his band was falling apart. They decided to cancel the rest of the tour. Jazz was just not taking off. Jake got depressed. He seemed to look at this as his personal failure, and further compared it to my own success. Every little thing I did seemed to upset him. At first, I was too involved with building my clientele that I didn't see the signs. But time gave way to make it all too clear; we had some serious marital issues brewing. Not only did he criticize my cooking, but he also refused to eat meals with me. Only six months prior, the man couldn't get enough of my famous red beans and rice. Whenever I came home with a couple of shopping bags from Marshall Fields, he would give me a strange, pouty look, as if to say, "You've got a lot of nerve." It was like he found fault in any and everything I did. He grew more and more distant, moody and withdrawn, to the point of almost shutting me out completely from his life. It was then that I actually saw he had a drinking problem. Before I knew what hit me, the cycle of verbal abuse began.

"Sapphire, where you going?" Jake called out. *Why is he always trippin' on where I'm going. What does he think?* Sapphire thought angrily to herself. She was getting sick and tired of the constant badgering. They had only been married 6 months and Jake was acting like he was her daddy.

"Honey, I'm going to a conference, remember?" Sapphire replied loudly, so Jake could hear her over the shower.

"Seem like every time I turn around you're going somewhere."

"Baby, you knew when we got married that I was a professional woman. This is part of what I do. Besides, I only go a few times a year to these events. I've actually slowed down how many I attend."

"Uh-huh. You sure there isn't someone else you're going to see at that conference of yours? Some doctor-friend or psychologist or whatever y'all call yourselves." Stepping out of the shower, Sapphire couldn't believe her ears. Was he accusing her of cheating? *What is wrong with him?* Sapphire thought, contemplating whether she would make that thought vocal.

"Did you hear me, woman?" Jake's voice roared. Sapphire was sure the neighbors could hear. *He must be drinking again,* Sapphire thought.

"SAPPHIRE!" Sapphire was livid. *Oh no, he didn't. See now he is going too far. Just wait 'til I get downstairs. He's gonna wish he never opened his big, drunk mouth. Just don't say anything,* Sapphire coached herself. *There's no reason for both of you to be running around the house yelling at each other like you are fools,* her common sense told her.

I knew that all he needed was to work again, to help him feel like he was contributing to our home financially. Jake needed to feel like a man. I knew he felt defeated and challenged because I was supporting the both of us. But, in all my degrees and case studies, I couldn't reach my own man. In the hundreds of relationships I had salvaged and helped put back together, I was helpless in fixing ours. There was nothing I could say that could make him feel like a man again. He had to be defined by the ability within himself to pick his behind up off the couch and go out and get a job. Then and only then would he begin to realize his worth again. But that never happened. Instead he'd rather call me outside of my name, words reserved for creatures that walked on all fours.

It seemed like he was drunk and angry all the time. To deal with his insecurity, he would find anything to argue about; my education, my status, my beliefs were all targets. Our marriage was deteriorating and, while I continued to look for affection, conversation, honesty, openness, and career support, Jake was seeking satisfaction in his exertion of dominance, sexual control and domestic violence. Things were getting worse. I couldn't go anywhere without him calling me every half hour, asking me where I was like I was his teenage child. The scales were tipped, and even though I was the most secure in the relationship, I couldn't help but find failure in my own ability to sustain a viable relationship. It came to a point where I just couldn't take it anymore.

One evening, I remember Jake coming home so drunk that he stumbled down the stairs, crashing through the banister and breaking it off its posts. I was so mad at his blatant disregard and disrespect; I got my keys and went out for the night. Now he was physically tearing things up and I was at my wits end. Since he was barely working, any money I gave him was used to purchase liquor; feeding an addiction I had overcome in my own life. Things would settle down from time to time. He would have bouts of sobriety. I would try to help him, giving him support without nagging. Things would look up for a while, but soon I would find myself living in the same abusive world I had escaped from twice before. However, this time I was in a commitment, for better or for worse. And this certainly was worse. When we exchanged our wedding vows, the promise to stay together seemed simple enough to do. On the contrary, the real life version turned out a lot different than the fairy-tale one. What we hadn't counted on was unemployment, alcoholism and neglect, which ultimately resulted in an endless cycle of verbal abuse, physical violence and mental turmoil. Of course, it was easy to love this man when he was sober and things were going just fine. But it takes a special kind of person to live through cycles of rage and abuse while supporting a man that cannot support you.

I would think to myself as I lie in bed next to him, looking at him all passed out, his pores reeking of brandy or whatever cheap corner-store liquor he could manage to buy. I kept wondering *when are things going to get better?* There were hard liquor bottles all over our house—under the bed, lying on the counter, even hidden behind the shelving in the garage. It got to the point where I had to take drastic measures. I had to pour his liquor down the sink, add tea or water to the bottles and leave nasty notes behind letting him know that I found another hiding place. But that would only make him more and more angry. I finally told him that if he did not get some help immediately that I would leave him. Jake agreed and said he would get some intervention.

Later that month we learned that I was pregnant. My heart sank. How could I have this baby? I had to decide if I wanted to live up to that standard or be real and draw the line. Did I really want or need my husband to be my patient, too? Could I really be responsible for two people totally dependent upon me? In a strange sort of way, I held a small glimmer of hope. I guess all those surging hormones made me imagine incredible things, because I was really fooling myself. Hormones, love, victim fantasy—whatever it was, wouldn't let me give up on Jake though. Not at first. I knew that this wasn't the right time but I hopelessly believed that this pregnancy would complete our family, and maybe bring Jake back from his drunken stupor.

Another evening, after a long day at work, I drove home about nine. In the distance, in what appeared to be our home, I could see what I thought was a steamy mist coming through the 2nd floor bathroom windows. When I got closer to the driveway, I realized that it was smoke billowing through the windows. Then, I thought about Roslyn, Jake's five-year old niece whom he was babysitting for his sister. *That's not right*, I thought to myself. Things just weren't adding up. I began to panic. Although I could not see it, I suspected the worst. Suddenly, I saw bright orange-red and yellow flames jet out of the window, lapping black soot against the white frosted windowpanes. Pulling into the driveway, I jumped out of the car with my six-month pregnant belly leading. I bounded across the lawn to the front door of the burning house. Once inside, I began running through the house. I thoughtlessly did not take into consideration that I was risking my and my unborn child's life to find him. Over and over again, I kept breathing into my lungs the thick, black smoke that was now coming down the stairs from the bathroom. Gasping for air and the chance to survive, I looked for ways to escape. I had to get out of this inferno of smoke and fire, if not for myself, for my unborn baby.

Screaming his name, I finally found him passed out on the bed in the guest room. Begging him to wake up, I realized it was hopeless. He was so drunk, his eyes were bloodshot and his sweat saturated with liquor. He could not awaken. I was terrified at the thought that Jake would die in this fire. If I didn't rescue him, he would surely die. There would be no time for him to be rescued because the fire engines had not even arrived yet. Reluctant to leave him behind, I realized that I would have to drag him out. Pulling him with strength I didn't know I had, I managed to make it back to the front door. Grabbing my swollen belly, I screamed until my throat got hoarse and dry from the toxicity of the fumes. The life inside me kicked frantically, as if trying to escape. Little Roslyn had gotten out of the house and was running around the front lawn aimlessly. I dialed 911 and relayed my address. Aching from shooting pains in my belly, I felt woozy. Then I fell to the ground. That was the last thing I remembered.

By the time I had awakened, the doctors were standing over me. They were explaining to my husband that I had lost the baby. I felt worthless and empty. I felt defeated in all that I had lost. Somehow, every positive thing that I had done in my life was seemingly drowning in the despair of losing my unborn daughter. All the life that was thriving in me just hours before was snatched from me in a matter of minutes. Destructive thoughts filled my mind, as my feet lay exposed on the cold, metal stirrups. Chills ran up my spine and I felt raw and sterile. All the white and steel of the room made my legs quiver uncontrollably. I had lost the one thing that seemed to love me back. The more I thought about my baby girl, the more I realized how much I would miss her.

When they were finished, they took me to my room. There was only one bed. I knew something was terribly wrong. Sitting up in the bed, the I.V. reminded me of all the pain that was connected to my life. As I reached for the box of tissue on the bedside table, I began to weep loudly. My soul cried out in deep mourning. This was the death of many things in my life. The desperation in my raspy, searching voice revealed the depth of sorrow I had endured from years of emotional, physical and mental abuse. At the vocal rendering of my grief, doctors and nurses came running to my side. No one had come to tell me anything. I had already heard about losing my child secondhand. What a paradox! The one whose life I had saved caused me to lose the one life I needed most.

The helpless look on their faces retold the grieving story that had just played while I was unconscious. I read more than a thousand words that night in their confused expressions, and more than a million spoken words could have never lifted me beyond the intensity of hopelessness I felt at that time. Their unrelenting stares—mixed with compassion and sorrow—made me feel useless and pitied. I didn't want their pity. I wanted my baby girl, the one good thing that would come of Jake and me. And yet, it was not meant to be. I felt robbed and in my heart I held him personally responsible for the miscarriage. Our child could not survive his selfishness, and neither could our marriage. It would take me a long time to understand how to forgive him of his crime.

That was the day our lives went from worse to dreadful. That was when I knew that the vow we took on our wedding day -- for better or worse -- only accounted for the former. We would not survive worse. We were way beyond that and it was time for us to go our separate ways. Another failed relationship to add to my portfolio. Now I had a pair.

My heart was shattered in pieces . . . What started as a beautiful love affair was crumbling before my eyes. It hadn't even been a year and thoughts of divorce had become part of my daily routine. When we finally came home from the hospital, I went up to our bedroom. As I dazed though my occasional streams of consciousness that the sedatives would allow, I decided, however rashly, that we needed to dissolve our marriage. So in my dreams, interspersed with hysterical grieving, I tried to resolve how I would tell him. He came into our sitting room to find me laying on the chaise lounge in deep thought. The air between us was thick; a muggy Louisiana Bayou on a mid-August evening. I can't recall exactly what I said, but my thoughts still linger on the last words I must have muttered: "Jake, I'm leaving you."

I found myself wondering what went wrong in our marriage. How was it that I could provide counseling to others on marriages, bring couples back together—even post divorce, but was unable to make my relationship work? Sometimes I blamed myself for what took place. I kept thinking, *I can't save him—I can't even save us*. I wasn't as brave as the women I knew who just dwindled their lives away, constantly trying to change their man. In later years, I would learn that these women would find me the brave one. They didn't feel brave or bold, but paralyzed, vulnerable, and powerless. Those women had men who couldn't resolve to do anything but blame themselves constantly for not being able to stand on their own feet and be responsible for themselves and their family. I was not the kind of woman who could stand by and allow herself to drown in another man's poison. I just couldn't do it. But for whatever it was worth, I still loved him. I still do.

The choice was hard to make, but I had to leave to save myself. I had to give myself a fighting chance to live again. I absolutely could not be epitomized by the guilt that Jake could not overcome. Before I could even pull my entire luggage out of the closet to pack my things, I still felt like something was happening that was out of my control. A strange sense of loneliness came over me and I began to wonder where Jake had gone. As I went into the bathroom, I discovered that he had not been able to deal with the consequences of his actions. He left a note on the mirror. It read:

Sapphire-

You're the love of my life. I don't know how things went so wrong but we both know it is over. I can't face the guilt of what I did to you and our baby. Every time I look in your eyes, I see myself and I can't bear the reflection. I am so sorry for hurting you and the baby. I can't go on like this, but I'm sure your life will be better without me. I don't know what is going to happen to me, but don't worry. Please know that this is not your fault. I'll always love you.

Jake

The dissolution of our marriage was imminent. But, that did not keep me from once again breaking into a million pieces. I was distraught. The losses of my life were compounded once again and the emotional scarring lay open and fresh once again, torn just as jaggedly as the times before. Although he had destroyed my life, I didn't want him to leave like this. I wanted him to fight for me and figure out a way to survive this, not just for me, but for himself, as well. He needed serious help, more than I could afford to give him. Taking the easy way out was just not fair. How selfish of him. I went down the stairs and held onto the place where the banister had been replaced a few months ago. The stain was slightly lighter than the opposite side. The reminder of Jake's drunken mishap made my blood begin to boil. Where did he go? I scanned over the dining room and then the living room, but there was no sign of him. Roslyn had left her Barbie doll on the couch, so I made a mental note to call Jake's sister, Lynn, to come by and get it. Thinking back to the night of the fire, I thanked God that He had preserved that little girl's life.

Looking in the garage, our car was gone. I didn't know what to do. I was still healing from the surgery I had just a few days ago and couldn't go far. Turning back to the front door, I sat down on the porch and started to cry uncontrollably. This man was not going to just let me be. He was going to do something stupid and self-serving, making me feel and remember his pain for the rest of my life. Although he had said it was over, with Jake it was never over.

I negotiated with myself not to worry about him or think up all the unimaginable things he was capable of doing. However insane it seemed, in my gut I felt like I was responsible for whatever it was he was thinking about doing. Months of conditioning and cleaning up his messes had taught me to prepare for the worst. Maybe he just drove away toward a new life. He could go to Gary to stay with his mother. No. That was too easy. So I tried to lie down, but inwardly, I braced myself.

When the sedatives completely wore off, I had a deep pain in the pit of my stomach. I retraced my thoughts and remembered that I was alone. Jake had gone out but the events were still kind of hazy. I felt so empty without the baby, but was coming to terms with the idea of her being gone.

I got a call later that night; the kind of call you answer, no matter what. Jake had gotten into a horrible car accident. He was driving to Indiana on I-94 and had been drinking. The officer said he had spun out of control and struck the median. His car had jumped over the median and hit a semi head on. The truck driver was okay, a few bruises and scrapes, but Jake died instantly. He had not been wearing his seatbelt and flew through the windshield. They wanted me to come and identify his body, but I couldn't. I had been through so much in the past three days that I just couldn't bear to see another person without life. First burying my unborn child, now this. I called Jake's mother and told her what had happened. I couldn't stop crying. I just couldn't.

Chapter 13.

SESSION II

"I learned to distrust men at an early age. My dad was not the unfaithful type. He was just how shall I say disengaged." Ravinia took a deep pause, looking distant and detached as she reflected on her depiction of her father.

"How intriguing," expressed Sapphire, attempting to draw more out of Ravinia. She adjusted her glasses while holding a thick Cross pen in her right hand. Fiddling with her seat, she uncrossed her legs and crossed them again, putting her right knee over her left. Reaching for her cup of Starbucks coffee, the therapist continued her interview with her patient. In an interested voice, Sapphire asked, "So, when did you first notice this in him?"

"Looking back, maybe it was just the very early stages of Alzheimer's, or maybe it was just the demands of life taking a toll on him," Ravinia recalled, tucking a strand of her copper-streaked hair behind her right ear. "Either way, I knew early on that men could take your heart, wrench it and crush it between their strong hands." Sapphire resisting the instinct to flinch, nodded, thinking quietly to herself, *So true, so true!* Remnants of Willie and Jake still lingered in her subconscious mind, though a decade had passed since she had dated anyone.

Beginning to recollect images of her father, Ravinia's eyes glazed over and set like a mannequin, as she relived certain events from her past. She began to speak almost mechanically as her melancholy emotions had seemingly disconnected from her formerly repressed memories.

"From time to time, he would do disheartening things, like put the pastor's kids before us or use 'church work' as an excuse to not be at home. Being a deacon was his life-long achievement and he didn't let you forget his status in the church," Ravinia said, nodding in affirmation.

Mimicking her patient's response, Sapphire nodded and wrote in her notebook, careful not to interrupt. She found this revelation about Ravinia's father interesting, thinking this may be related to her various issues with men and betrayal. It was fascinating, though not in a psychotherapeutic sort of way. Instead, her heart was pierced with sympathy for her patient. Sapphire wanted to reach out and hug Ravinia and tell her that she could overcome this, just like she herself had time and again. But she knew that was inappropriate. The right time would come. *What was that scripture in Revelations again?* Sapphire's mind searched until it came back paraphrased. *We overcome through the words of our testimony.*

Ravinia continued, emotionally bland, staring blankly out the window. She added, "My father convinced us that he had to be at church when the doors opened and would enforce this ritual upon us as much as my mother would allow." Ravinia ended, as if the story was over. Sapphire began to feel Ravinia's apathy and grew concerned. She didn't want to lose her, especially at what seemed to be a breaking point, but knew she couldn't be more than just a therapist to her. There was something about Ravinia that screamed out to Sapphire. It was as if Ravinia was intended to be in the doctor's life somehow, and in more ways than just this limited patient-therapist relationship that kept them at arms length. Sapphire struggled with this unethical series of ideas. She knew better than to contemplate a friendship with Ravinia. It simply could not happen.

Just then, a breakthrough seemed to come through with Ravinia. One stray tear meandered down the length of her cheek. She was starting to break her emotional strike and Sapphire knew that Ravinia was trying hard to be tough. But if they were going to get anywhere today, Ravinia would have to give in just long enough to begin to release some of her anger, either through tears or words. Holding back the tears wouldn't help unless she began to talk. Either way, Sapphire had to get her going and she needed to be prepared to do so.

Wanting her desperately to continue, Sapphire snapped herself back into a counseling mindset, reached over to the box of Kleenex conveniently located on her desk and handed Ravinia a tissue, careful not to look at her too sentimentally. As much as this tore Sapphire up inside, she could not deny Ravinia the chance to heal through this therapy. She had to remain as detached as possible for Ravinia's sake and this was hard for her. Taking off her Gucci wire-rimmed glasses, Dr. Sykes put one of the ear rests in her mouth and bit hard on it. Her empty stomach growled loudly and angrily as she excused herself. She was famished and this session was running over into her lunch break. However, Sapphire was determined she was not going to stop until her patient was ready.

Blowing her nose, Ravinia clinched the dampened, white tissue in her hand. Pushing her dignity aside, she cleared her throat of the salty-mucousy film that had pooled in the back of her throat and spoke up defensively. "Now, don't get me wrong. I love going to church and all that, you know, but I-I-I just don't understand how you can forsake your wife and kids just to say you got there first? That's just a little obsessive, don't you think?" She looked Sapphire directly in the eye, wanting the therapist to co-sign her opinion.

Not waiting for the therapist to respond, Ravinia added, "To make matters worse, my mother was a bit peculiar, too. Whenever my father was in one of his church-going moods, she would generally give in to his antics, just to keep peace. "Let's go, let's go, let's go! Time to go to church." Daddy would yell through the house *every* Sunday morning. I truly dreaded Sundays as a child, because I never had any time to get fully dressed and pull myself together before his ranting began. We always seemed to forget something at home—a Bible, a Sunday school book, a wallet, you name it. To be observing the Lord's Day and keep it holy, we had so much resentment around going on Sundays it was almost sacrilegious." Ravinia shook her head slowly side to side, punctuating her recount with her own actions. Her mother's words, *"That's a sin and a shame"*, rang in her head. She wanted to cry but resisted yet again.

Caught up in her patient's story of her childhood church going experience with her parents, Sapphire had to snap herself out of a daze. She found herself daydreaming about the last time she had seen her own father alive. It was the day she left for Boston. She didn't even say goodbye. She briefly wondered how he was doing. Remembering the last look she saw on his face when she was 17, she shuddered at the thought of what he did to her mother and how she missed her. She abruptly jolted herself out of her own reverie.

"Anyway, I can remember Momma and Daddy getting into a fight about his clothes or tie, something petty like socks not matching or something like that. That back and forth mess would continue into the car where their voices would get louder and louder until they literally bounced off the closed windows of our beat up, 1959 olive-green station wagon. I always faced the back so I didn't have to see their faces when they argued. Then something would set my father off and he would start speeding as though the devil himself was chasing him. I always thought he did this to scare Momma. We never crashed, though. But we came close a couple of times. Being annoyed and a little frightened by his attempt to gain control of the argument and her fears, Momma would demand for him to pull over and let her out. Yes, literally let her out. And he did. Wherever she asked to get out, he would just leave her there to make it home the best way she could. And Momma would do just that, ending up walking miles home on the side of the road."

Resisting the attempt to interrupt, Sapphire thought to her self, *What a despicable man. No wonder she's so messed up.* Vigorously writing notes about her suspected diagnoses, Sapphire noticed Ravinia's eyes left their gaze from their expansive view of Lake Michigan and the breathtaking Chicago skyline from Dr. Sykes 47th floor office, on to her black notebook. Her patient's nervous eyes quickly scanned over the handwritten pages. Hoping that Ravinia had not fallen into an insecure state and become too concerned with the notes that she was taking, Sapphire set the notebook on the floor and looked at Ravinia. She clasped her hands together and bent her shoulders in slightly to lean in closer to Ravinia, giving her, her undivided attention. Seemingly unnerved, Ravinia continued, flicking her eyes back to the silvery view of Millennium Park in the distance.

"I remember once, my father let her off and us kids too, on the West Side of Chicago, near Madison and Ashland. Back in the day, it was pretty bad over there. No Harpo Studios. No renovated United Center. No new housing development. You know, I-I-I- uh," Ravinia stuttered, beginning to make sobbing sounds. "I kept on thinkin' he would come back for us. 'Daddy's coming back,' I told my mother, in my confident six-year old innocence, as we walked and walked to the El. 'He has gotta come back.' I will never forget that placid look in her eyes when I looked up at her. It was a knowing. She knew her man. But all she said to me was, 'Okay, baby.'" Ravinia paused, and swallowed audibly. Trying to force back the tears that were pushing themselves out, she looked around the room and then at her therapist. Then in a mouse-like voice, the shaking patient squeaked out, "But, he never did. . ."

And then she stopped speaking all together and stared intently out of the window again. Sapphire just let her be in case she needed to talk some more. It was evident this was the revelation that needed to be told. Then after about 3 minutes of complete silence, Ravinia just got up and walked right out the door. Picking up her notebook, Sapphire jotted down the remaining thoughts she had about their session. Walking around her office with a plethora of anger and mixed emotions, Dr. Sykes, tried to separate Ravinia's experience from her own, but found herself entangled in a fury of raw feelings. Reaching for a fuchsia Post-It Note, Sapphire scribbled a note to call Ravinia the next day. Feeling her stomach growl, she thought, *I should have never let Ravinia leave in such a distraught state*. As a therapist, Sapphire wondered if her patient would ever return. As a member of the sisterhood, in her spirit she knew that she wouldn't.

Chapter 14.

STREET LIFE

Ravinia ran as quickly as her the length of her legs would take her. She wasn't ready to deal with the feelings she had just dredged up about her father. She had gone to Dr. Sykes to figure out why she couldn't be faithful to her husband, her past relationships, and most of all, herself. Feeling helpless and alone, she walked and walked down Washington Street until she saw the sign for the redline train going Northbound. Blinded by the stinging mascara smear that had found its way into the wells of her eyes, she click-clacked down the uneven stairs to the vending area. It had been over 25 years since she had taken public transportation in Chicago and things looked a little strange.

Mingled with the scent of rancid French fries left by a rushing commuter, three-day-old urine and other varied sewer scents, Ravinia found a Pepsi vending machine and inserted a dollar bill. She figured if she watched a few people, she could figure out how to pay the fare. There was no attendant, so she had to wait a few moments for someone to show up. Ravinia wiped the can off with the corner of her navy suit jacket, making a mental note to definitely put this one in the cleaners. Not exactly sure which direction she was going, she decided to take whatever train took her back up North.

Just then, an interesting couple came up through the turnstile. With each one's hand neatly tucked into the other's rear jeans pocket, they gave Ravinia the once over, with her Prada bag, vintage, high-heeled Gucci boots, and her tailored pin-striped pantsuit and just looked away, as if disgusted by her expensive taste.

"Excuse me, I am sorry to bother you," Ravinia inquired. The couple stopped and looked at her as if to say, what could you *possibly* want from us?

"How do I get on the train?"

The smart-alecky guy peered at her over his Ben Franklin-type shades and noted in a low-pitched drawl, "Well you have to pay a fare," and kept on walking. It was apparent he thought the conversation was over and that he had done his good deed for the day. You could tell he was either an IT geek or a perpetual student by his laid back, unbuckled, rumpled up style. Ravinia, becoming frustrated in her failed attempt to quickly flee from her sorrow, looked at the rear view of the young dreadlocked co-ed couple and snapped. "Yes, of course," she yelled after their departing backs, "But *how* do I pay for it? There is no attendant, here!" Ravinia was clearly irritated. The guy stopped and looked back at the angry Black woman yelling at him with a half-cocky expression on his face. Pursing his lips like he was perturbed by her question, the young man hesitated for the sheer joy of it.

It was at that moment, Ravinia had to brace herself. He was intentionally being difficult and it was striking a nerve with her. Then, when he seemed fully amused at the fact she was showing physical signs of frustration, he nudged his friend forward and they started walking back to Ravinia, now standing with her arms tightly folded in front of her. She wanted to snatch the red bead right out of his ash-blonde, scruffy-looking, half-braided goatee, but she thought that might be too brutal a gesture. Besides, all of his various body piercings made her cringe. They just looked nasty and unsanitary, and that made Ravinia step back when he approached her.

"Oh, well, uh, you put the money in the machine over there. See?" He pointed in the direction of the vending area. "And it gives you a card. Then, you put the same card in the turnstile." He demonstrated with his hand moving in a downward motion. "Then it lets you through," he retorted knowingly, still attached at the hip to his Bohemian-styled brown-eyed companion.

"Really?" queried, Ravinia. "It sure would seem simpler just to have an attendant."

"Yeah," agreed the female counterpart of the hippie-wannabee couple. Showing a silver ball and chain tongue piercing, the girlfriend laughed, twirling her finger around a curly tangle hanging out from her dishwater blonde hair. "See what happens when Republicans get in office." She and her boyfriend laughed a knowing laugh and then waved to Ravinia as they went on their way.

Ravinia recounted back to herself. *They weren't even born in the 70s. . . God help 'em.*

"Thanks," Ravinia expressed audibly, but they were already on their way up the slanted stairs to the street. Quickly mastering how to get a fare card, Ravinia inserted a $10 bill into the feeder. She had already blown the last single she had on a can of diet Pepsi. Bolting through the turnstile, she met some folks that had just gotten off the train. Most of the people didn't even look at her or take notice of her presence. They walked right on by, minding their own business. Those that did look were either businessmen, who tried to get her eye, or indigent ones who wanted some spare change. Making her way down to the subway platform, Ravinia spotted a red painted bench about three-quarters of the way down the length of the platform. She hurried to claim her spot on the free-for-all seat.

In the distance, she spotted a street performer getting set up to play again. He was an interesting fellow, almost a one-man band with his guitar, harmonica stand slung around his neck and mini amplifier. Doing a quick mic check, he greeted her with a friendly wave. Taking off his black White Sox baseball cap, he smiled at her. Ravinia felt a little uneasy as she sat down on the bench, scooting to the farthest corner away from the strange, almost too friendly man. The street performer kept adjusting his harmonica holder around his neck until his Hohner 1501, "bluesman special" mouth organ fit snugly between the fasteners. Tightening his yellow bandana around his clean-shaven, smooth, brown head, he took out a green pick from his black jeans, set it between his straight, almost unnoticeably gapped, ivory teeth. "Here's a little song I wrote. I hope you'll like it, pretty lady," he said looking at her, winking, and then pivoted around to greet his non-existent crowd. It was apparent that his quality of playing didn't depend on the number of people in the audience, because he played just as grandly for fifty on-lookers as he did for one.

Not waiting for a response, the bald, bearded man began to strum on his blue acoustic guitar a mellisonant tune that reminded Ravinia of the days she played strings. He then began to sing a poignant song that struck the very essence of his only listener.

You spend your life

One day at a time

Draining your love

Without reason or rhyme

I can't find myself in you

The words I need elude me

Where's your heart in all you do

Your soul can't rest, why can't you be?

About midway through the song, she realized the song oddly described her. Curious that she could receive revelation by a song played by a street performer, she busied herself as not to notice the affect the lyrics were having on her. But the melody was too soul stirring; it called to her. Cupping her chin in her hands, she rested her elbows on her knees and dreamily let the musician minister truth to her.

If life was a song

You'd just hum the lines

Never livin' the words

This 'ole world defines

Endless trembling—you try & run away

You can't hide from life

It always reads what your lips won't say. . .

When the encompassing rumbling noise of the oncoming El train drowned the resonating sound of the harmonica, Ravinia opened her bag and pulled out a twenty from her wallet. She wished she had more to give, but knowing that morning she was coming to the city, she had intentionally only brought a few bills, the $20 being the largest. In five minutes, this stranger had told her more about herself than all the preachers and shrinks put together. Careful to place his "offering" in his guitar case, she looked up at the man she had brushed off before. He was no longer just a street performer. He was the bringer of truth. And for once in her life, Ravinia understood what it was that she was running from.

Chapter 15.

THE TRUTH

Staring intently out of the dingy, shaded window of the train, Ravinia caught a glimpse of something that would change her life forever. Almost breaking her neck to see if what she saw was real, she cupped her hands around her tear-streaked eyes to get a better view in the dimmed car. The passengers facing her pretended not to notice her odd behavior, but she knew they were watching her. She tried to ignore them and leaned in as close to the pane as she could. A couple of fleas flew up from the ventilator and almost into her nose as she waved them away, trying to clear her nostrils and see out of the window at the same time.

It was him. Rather, her husband. He was on the southbound Belmont Avenue platform lip-locked with some bleach-blonde young girl, clearly half the age and size of Ravinia. With his arms wrapped around her bare waistline, her thin hand was conveniently tucked in his left back pocket. *That little hussy.* Ravinia fumed in her head as she began to see red through the dark pane of the train. The bright orange lights made it difficult to distinguish faces, but she knew it was Xavier without a wavering thought. She'd recognize that receding hairline anywhere.

Stopping to think with her head and not her heart, Ravinia reached into her purse and grabbed the little camera phone Xavier had given her for Christmas. *What a gift.* She pondered to herself, snapping a couple of pictures of them sharing a long, intimate kiss. *This man is going to hang himself with his own rope.* Those were the very words her mother had said about Ravinia's father just days before he left them.

Just then, a salty film began to well in her mouth as she could feel her cheeks burn crimson. With all that she had gone through today, first with Dr. Sykes drudging up unwanted memories, and now this? Of course, this was the conclusive evidence she was seeking, but it was so blatant. Ravinia sat back in her seat and sulked loudly, drawing unwanted attention to herself. In a fit of rage, she let violent thoughts seep out of her pores depicting how she could walk up on him sleeping and pour hot grease over his naked body. Folks sitting by her started moving to the seats on the opposite side of the train from her, probably thinking Ravinia was insane. She vaguely remembered her grandmother telling her a story about how she did that to her third husband for stepping out on her, and how he never tried that stunt again after that vengeful day. Ravinia's Creole blood boiled.

Catching herself before the murderous thoughts actualized and became vindictive intentions, Ravinia realized he just wasn't worth the salt it took to season his food. To sit there and be consumed with him and what he was doing to her was a waste of time. After all, she was just as guilty. But, Ravinia found that although she had suspected Xavier was having an affair, it still hurt to see him with someone else.

It all made perfect sense now. This explained why there was a size zero, white bikini bottom in her dryer with her white Ralph Lauren pool towels and whom it apparently belonged to. This explained why she found fine, over-processed blonde hairs on the headrest in Xavier's Mazerati. This explained why he smelled so strange when they made love and why she had a never-ending yeast infection for the last 3 months.

But a white woman?? That hurt worse than anything. Or so she thought. Ravinia wondered why it even mattered. She knew that if it would be anyone, she would probably be Caucasian or Asian because she was the type of woman that seemed to be especially drawn to Xavier's brand—African American, successful, and rich. But there was just something that was deeply rooted in her being that made her skin burn when she thought of the sight she had just witnessed. Her seething anger was primal, raw and instinctual, stemming back from a generations-long battle between Whites and Blacks in the South. The fact that the child he was involved with was barely old enough to vote didn't much matter as much to Ravinia as the color of her skin. As much pride as she had in her own beautifully rich nutmeg complexion, she felt defeated and second best to the choice her husband had made. She knew how she felt was unforgivable and perhaps unfounded, but she could not help the feelings she had. Her mind soared uncontrollably. *How could he do this to me and with someone like that? How could he sell out? How could he be so selfish? How could he cross the proverbial color line?*

Before she could finish feeling sorry for herself, guilt poured thickly over her like a hot Cajun roux. *What goes around comes around,* kept swirling around her frantic mind. "You brought this on yourself," she heard in her mother's condemning voice that commingled with her own thoughts. But, it was all true. Ravinia did have it all and she was seeing the evidence of losing it all right before her weary eyes. She didn't know what was worse: losing all her money, leaving her suburban home, marring her reputation or shattering the symbolism of a blissful life. What that myth represented was of greater importance to Ravinia than she had ever thought it would be. She was certain that some day, Xavier and her would end up separating, but she didn't realize the impact it would have on her emotionally.

Invisible tears began to fall as she quickly approached the Howard Street stop. Narrowing her eyes to tiny slits, Ravinia crossed her arms and legs and let the motion of the train rock her back and forth, fueling her fury. She didn't care who saw her. As the train halted to an abrupt stop, she stepped off the train and onto the platform. The cool Lake Michigan air hit her tear-streaked face. Thinking back over the events of the day, Ravinia tried to find a remnant of something good, something to hold on to, and something to keep her from jumping off the platform. She reminisced and searched, finding only a trace vision of that smiling, dark-skinned man she had heard singing in the subway. Ravinia tried to remember his words, but couldn't find them. She knew that something he said made sense and spoke to her, but the events that followed kept flooding her head, drowning the memory. She wanted that back. She wanted truth.

Ten minutes passed before the train to Wilmette came and it took everything Ravinia had to keep herself from completely losing it. For the rest of the ride to her destination, she viewed and reviewed the three pictures she had taken of her husband and his mistress. Why did this woman bother her so much? Never mind the fact that this barely-out-of-braces gold digger wanted Ravinia's life. Just the thought of them kissing together in public irked Ravinia to no end. Judging from the way he held her in his arms, there was no end to the gamut of things they must of have done with each other. This made her more and more disgusted. Thoughts of destruction were overtaking her. Ravinia had to calm her self. Her blood pressure, which was usually low, was at a boiling point. She could feel her temples expand and decrease almost in time. Ravinia knew that if she didn't relax, she would end up feeling worse than she had felt earlier in the day and she didn't want that. Drudging up all those old feelings about her father had given her plenty of reasons not to ever go back to see Dr. Sykes again. She hated feeling like an abandoned little girl again, taunting herself with the questions of why he left them.

Satisfied that she would probably not find a resolution between her and her philandering husband, Ravinia stared out of the stained window. Incidentally, Xavier left a message on her phone that he wouldn't be home tonight until very late and not to wait up. He was supposedly taking clients out for a night on the town. Ravinia listened to the lie rolling off her cheating husband's tongue and began to despise what she once thought was a solid foundation. However, as much as she tried to feel wronged by Xavier's lies and infidelity, she couldn't help but feel that she was not justified due to her own contribution to the mess that was her marriage. She had stopped taking the Reverend's phone calls and had made up her mind that she wasn't going to commit adultery anymore. Something about doing it made her feel so dirty afterwards, that even if she did repent, she still felt like she had let someone down. That someone was herself.

But she couldn't stop the hurt. *Why?* Ravinia pondered deeply, searching the inner crevices of her soul. *Why did this hurt so much? Why did he have to do this to me?* Ravinia questioned her ability to please her husband, and thought silently to herself, feeling the tears well up. *Well, I hope that wasn't it.* Remembering that they had not been quite as intimate as they were when they were first married, she concluded that that was the thing that sent him away. Of course, the signs were there. Late nights, long, unexpected business trips, a white bikini in her dryer. Ravinia looked back at the pictures on her phone and saw the frivolous passion in the young woman's hopeful eyes. Suddenly it struck Ravinia. This is just a thing. A fling. It has got to be. Xavier had just made 45 and with all his newly acquired power as a new partner, perhaps he was feeling that he needed to impress someone. Maybe he was just sowing some of his left over wild oats from his bachelor days. After all, he was a bachelor well into his 30's. Maybe this young thing would satisfy his longing to expand his chest and boost his ego.

Ravinia knew that she couldn't and shouldn't try to justify his actions even though she did try to understand and find some relief in this fragile, desperate explanation. Nearing the Wilmette stop, she dialed Dr. Sykes' number and left a message with her answering service. She had not made an appointment before she left, and although she felt despondent and lost earlier, she knew that she needed to at least give the counseling a try. While she didn't want to continue down the path of her past with the doctor, maybe Dr. Sykes could help her figure out her future and whether or not she should divorce Xavier. Maybe she could help her determine why she felt so bad about Xavier's affair, or explain why she was so torn between the Reverend and her own salvation.

Looking down at her phone, Ravinia saw her mother's name staring back at her. She wanted to talk to someone, but didn't necessarily want to be preached at, either. Her mother would probably side with Xavier anyway, because he couldn't do anything wrong in her eyes. She, too, was blinded by Ravinia's husband's success and the gifts that made him the favorite son-in-law, even though she had only one. "You got a good man, Vinia. Don't mess it up, chile," Katie Mae would often say to Ravinia. "That boy got sense *and* money." Ravinia hesitated and pressed the button to dial her mother's number. The line rang and rang.

"Jesus loves you," a sweet little voice answered. It was Randella, Ravinia's 4-year-old adopted daughter. Tears flooded Ravinia's eyes.

"Hi baby, can I speak to Ma-Dear?"

"Mommy is that you? Are you crying?" the precious voice asked.

"I'm all right," Ravinia lied. She didn't want Randella to think anything was wrong, although her daughter was very perceptive.

"Give the phone to Grandma, ok?"

"I love you, Mommy. Grandma! Mommy's crying on the phone. She wants to talk to you." Ravinia closed her eyes, cringing in her daughter's innocent revelation. The next voice she heard was her mother's.

"So what did he do, baby?" *How did she know I was calling about Xavier?* Ravinia got off the train, her boot heel tripping on a loose board on the platform. She leaned on the rail so she wouldn't fall. Starting to cry heavily, Ravinia sobbed loudly.

"He cheated on me, Momma. W-W-with a White woman," stuttered Ravinia, like a scared little child.

Katie Mae paused and started her lecture right off, not giving Ravinia a chance to explain about what she had just witnessed. "Well, sometimes even the best of 'em won't do right. Well, what you gon' do? I mean, what can you do? Now y'all are even, right?" Ravinia's mouth dropped. She knew that her mother was bound to say something insensitive like that. Ravinia didn't even bother responding to her crude remark. Her mother acted like she had never sinned a day in her life.

"Ravinia, are you there?" Katie Mae asked in a demanding voice. The kind you respond, "Yes ma'am," to. She apparently had not finished giving Ravinia a piece of her sanctified mind. "Sit down, Della, you hear?" she called sternly over her shoulder, muting the receiver with her hand.

"Yes, ma'am. I'm still here. I-I-I've got to go now, though. I need to go home. I'm not feeling well. Can you keep the kids tonight?" Ravinia asked, sniffling and shaking in the chill of the night, hoping to end the conversation quickly. The temperature was cooler by the lake.

"Sure, baby. You sort things out. I'm not trying to be hard on you. You just got to see things as they really are. Your grandmother would say, 'God watches over all babies, drunks and fools.'"

"Uh, huh," Ravinia said shaking her head in despair. Ravinia wondered which one of those helpless ones her mother was comparing her to this time. Pushing aside the new emotions her mother had created, Ravinia whispered into the phone in a slightly, hoarse voice, "I'll call you in the morning before I pick up the kids, okay?"

"That's fine, sugah. Try and get some rest. Though what you really need to do is get on yo' knees and pray. I love you, baby. See you in the morning."

"I love you, too," dropped Ravinia, as she opened the door to her car parked in the train lot. It was dark and her car was only one of three left on a Friday night. She didn't want to go home to an empty house, but she knew it would be the best place to think out her next steps, good or bad. Plus, she needed to print the pictures out, just in case.

Chapter 16.

THE PERFECT PARENT

It was amazing how Ravinia and my life were mirrored. The last session with her really brought back memories of my parents, for better or worse. My thoughts carried me back to many years ago when I was growing up in Southern California. Funny, sunny California: surfer dudes with their boogie boards, and crazies along the coast worshipping the sun as a vacation, or otherwise in hopes of modeling in a used car commercial. We were the perfect-picture of the upper-class family in an established neighborhood in Santa Ana. But pictures lie. My father sold policies for a leading insurance company. He made a good living, as I recall. Financially, at least, I can never remember wanting for much. My mother was a wonderful, but peculiar woman, filled with an enormous, expressive love. I can remember as a child that before going to bed my mother would set the table, putting out the glasses and flatware for breakfast. Then she would wake up at 5:00 a.m. every morning to begin our breakfast. By the time I would awaken, she would be sitting at the breakfast table with her Bible open and her prayer list tucked in the seam, waiting for my father and me to join her. She was such a tender mother and a devoted wife. Why didn't my father see that side of her?

My mother was the talented cornerstone of our dysfunctional family. If something ever needed fixing, she would pull out the tool belt and get it repaired. Looking back at my mother's natural curiosity and zeal for life, I imagine that she could have done anything she wanted--and excelled at it; especially in music. Even without formal training, she had an impeccable sense of pitch and timing. She sounded nothing short of angelic when she sang in the choir. Her soul seemed to stir and would overflow when she sang. Her infinite love of music was innately passed on to me.

Mom was my strength. She was instrumental in establishing my belief system by keeping me in church. My strong sense of values and morals were cut directly from the cloth of lessons she would teach me in a quiet voice. "Baby," she would say barely above a whisper. "Don't do nothing if your heart ain't in it. It dishonors God and compromises your self-respect." She said that to me after she offered to teach me how to plant flowers in the garden along the side of our house. I wanted to get back to reading a new book that was really getting good, so I rushed through the planting and ruined the entire bed. They never did grow that spring. I felt awful.

It was through these powerful, unfaltering teachings that I carved a life for myself. Her spirit is yet alive and well within me. She taught me to trust in myself, despite what others thought, no matter what. Somehow, her instruction never seemed like a lesson; just an invitation to have some fun. We would make dinner, clean the house or do the laundry by making it a contest or an experiment. She was assuring me that I would be able to take care of myself. As a child, I didn't see chores as a way of being close to my mom. In my lifetime, I had seen my mother wear many hats, both successfully and gracefully, and I knew that if I had an ounce of the confidence and strength that she had, I too could accomplish almost anything.

My mother would sacrifice her life to give the very best she could. In my eyes, she was the picture of perfection. But behind the scenes of our picturesque lives dwelled insanity—literally. Rarely seeing eye to eye with my father, there was more bickering than there were kind words, more anxiety than peace, and more shame than pride. Affection, at times, was almost non-existent in our home, except for that expressed between my mother and me. My young spirit had a knowing that things were very wrong in our home. I kept thinking childishly that they would simply get divorced and I would go to live with Mom. Although I loved them both, I clearly did not love them equally. Mom was my very life and breath. I would stay with her. There was nothing that I could do to stop them from fighting; and as they always do, the arguments got worse. I grew very weary, but was too afraid to say anything or even cry. My father was a tyrant and I hated being ridiculed or scowled upon by him. His deep, scratchy voice was reminiscent of Wolfman Jack, and it frightened me. In my memory, it was a rare occasion that I can recall being hugged by him.

Mom was the complete antithesis of my father. She actually thrived on motherhood. Parenting was her passion and you could see in her eyes that it filled her heart with great joy. She especially loved being *my* mother. Over and over she would tell me that I was the best daughter a mother could have. I loved pleasing her because it made her smile; and as the years waned, her smiles were few and far between. I tried to behave and do everything a good girl should do. It made mothering me an ease and joy. Being a wife, on the other hand, was not as fulfilling for her, if her empty expressions and our four walls could tell the story. By the time I was four, their marriage was slowly deteriorating. My father, being unreasonable in his demands on her, began to severely affect her personality. Their relationship, and subsequently their finances would also suffer. Mom would go shopping in an effort to forget her worries, but soon this became obsessive, and her spending grew out of control. When the bills came in, my father would react as to a child, taking her credit cards and cutting them up, scolding and threatening her if she dared to get any more. She seemed to know that, in time, she would no longer be able to shelter me from his rage. He was out of control and most times she seemed to fear for her life. I am convinced that this is what slowly drove her crazy. It broke her spirit; and then finally, it destroyed her mind and resolve.

When I was about five years old, before the spending, before the emptiness came, my mother began to exhibit eccentric behaviors. Once I walked into the kitchen and she was boiling milk still left in the carton. I asked, "What are you doing Mommy?" wondering why she often had such a distant look on her face. Sometimes my father and I would take a walk to the store and leave her staring out of the window. When we returned, she would still be there, talking as though someone was actually there. Perhaps, that was the only way for my mother to cope with the abuse of my father. Perhaps it was just a defense mechanism. If any one were to ever ask me, I would tell them my truth: that he drove her crazy.

One Sunday morning, Mom wondered off into the wooded area behind the back of our church and was gone for what seemed like hours. Everyone in the church was frantic and began searching for her. When they found her, they said she said she felt a bit lightheaded and was rambling on and on about being Queen of the Nile. It wasn't long thereafter that the gossip began. People began to talk and whisper around town about her. I tried to ignore it at first. But children are cruel, and I was not saved from either the teasing, or the ostracism of my playmates. I had no reason to believe all the lies. That was my mom. I knew the truth—my truth and that was all that mattered to me. But what I couldn't do was turn a deaf ear when people started talking to me directly about her.

Mom suffered a long time at the hands of my father, but nobody but me knew the extent of that. All that they could see was the picture perfect upper class family in an established neighborhood in Santa Ana. It was understandable why she could no longer separate reality from fantasy. Some days he would beat her repeatedly. Other days, he would yell and scream at her, calling her worthless and a lot of other words I didn't know the meaning of at the time. I wondered what would kill her first, the beating or the mental abuse. Maybe she overcame the misery in her life by escaping in her head. Maybe her love for me was the only thing that made her not just give in and die. I hoped and prayed she was still alive somewhere. Somehow, she still felt alive in my spirit and my memory of her still rang true in my heart. My hope, however naïve, kept her alive within me.

My father was tyrannical in his discipline of my mother. I felt so sorry for her. I never understood what she could have done to him to make him treat her that way. From where I stood with a counter-height view, she didn't do anything at all. Little did I know that the dictates of a cruel world would require no action on her part at all. My father could breathe pure evil. It was in his blood; perhaps a generational curse that had not yet been broken. Maybe he was repeating a traumatic cycle, a destructive legacy passed down by his father and his father before that. The cycle of spousal abuse would ring true throughout the African-American community, yet be kept quiet by fear. But I was too young to care about other people's families. It was happening in my family and I didn't want people to misrepresent with their gossip the reality of what my mother was desperately trying to endure.

Then the day came when I heard her crying behind the linen closet door. I opened the door to find her crouched next to the vacuum cleaner, trembling. She looked up at me and held my body close to hers and kept saying, "Don't let him break you. Whatever you do, don't let him break you Sapphire." On the day they took her out screaming, all I could hear her say was, "It's not my choice, it' s a matter of choice." Those words stayed with me and I vowed that if I ever saw her again, I would ask her what they meant. I knew my mother wasn't insane on her own volition. The man she married drove her to insanity, and even the strongest therapy couldn't undo the damage.

Years passed and I thought more and more about her. Where memories would have faded in many children, mine stayed crisp, vivid. I was drawn to the mere thought of her. Something within me needed to find her, needed to complete the mental picture with the physical presence of her. Something deep inside yearned for her reassuring touch, her invaluable guidance, her very essence. I needed to know her, and even if she was insane. Perhaps somehow she would get well enough to hold me again.

Chapter 17.

IN SEARCH OF HER

I really didn't know what to expect when I began searching for my long lost mother. Starting with the asylum seemed to be the best option. Besides, it was the only clue I had to her whereabouts. Too young to remember anything about my mother's side of the family, I didn't know anyone who would remember her. My father had once mentioned that she was placed in a home near Santa Ana, but I didn't know if that was the truth or just something he said to throw me off from searching for her one day. When I started searching, I didn't realize how difficult it would be to search out all of the asylums near and around our home in the 1970's. After days spent collecting data on each asylum, I narrowed my search down to four. I contacted each one, and to my dismay, no one had admitted a patient by the name of Marie Sykes. There wasn't even a match under her social security number. I came up empty. What did my father do? Did he commit her under an assumed name? Or worse, did he kill her?

At this point, the only other option was to trample through the California courthouses in search of a death certificate. When there were none on file, I contacted the Social Security Board to determine if my mother was still living. Perhaps she had taken up residence somewhere out of the state of California. Obtaining a dozen social security applications for women named Marie Sykes who had died; I made all of the calls necessary to determine conclusively that they were not my mother's. I ran ads in the local newspaper in Santa Ana. I still came up empty.

Dreading the next step, I tried contacting my father. I had searched many databases for a telephone number, and after many futile attempts, I decided to take a plane back to the town I had grown up in.

To my surprise, the house I was raised in had been destroyed by fire in 1991. The current neighbors told me the tragic news—that my father had also perished in that fire. Why had I waited so long? Why was I so stubborn? The church I went to had also relocated and the neighborhood had changed so much it was almost unrecognizable. At one point things began to feel hopeless. But I wasn't ready to give up. The empathy I felt for my mother gave me the strength to continue searching when every road seemed hopelessly blocked.

As I drove through the little town, I looked up and down every street, searching for someone I knew. In all likelihood, I would probably not recognize anyone. I imagined what it would have been like to grow up with a normal childhood, to hang out in the stores downtown. I looked in vain for a school, park or baseball field, something familiar. The trip through town took fewer than five minutes, but its features remained indelibly inscribed in my mind the remainder of the day. This was my hometown and nothing gave me the familiar feeling of having ever lived there.

With so many roadblocks, I decided to hire a professional investigator. Driving back to the hotel, I looked on the Internet for someone in the area who specialized in reuniting families. I came across an ad for a man named Mike Jensen, and contacted him. I quickly found out that I was really at a loss. All I had to go on was her name. I was hopeful that she had not changed her name. My father being a conservative man deeply rooted in his religion would certainly refuse to divorce her. I was in perfect awe and gratitude when it took the detective less than four hours based off the information I gave him to find background information on my mother: the town my mother grew up in, her maiden name and her mother's name. He called me to say "I believe I have a miracle for you." I immediately left for his office and when I arrived he gave me the woman's telephone number that matched the information he had found. I sat down to take a sip of water and to gather my wits. I was stunned and speechless. He looked at me and questioned, "Aren't you going to *CALL* her?!"

Although I had to gather my courage, I was eager to call. I wanted a moment to think of all of the "right" questions to ask, to determine conclusively whether or not this woman was, indeed, my mother. I didn't want her to deny me. I didn't want to be wrong. Finally, I realized that my courage would not grow by waiting, and that I would have to trust that the right words would come, whatever those words would be.

Will she want to meet me? I kept asking myself. *Perhaps I shouldn't call. If she is still alive, she'd be almost 70 years old. I wonder does she still believe in God?* It was funny how suddenly formal I was beginning to feel as I thought about what my mother would be like now. I certainly didn't mean to feel this way. But in my own struggle to know God, I felt myself trying to see things from her perspective. She may have wondered, "Where was God when they dragged me out of my house, kicking and screaming so many years ago?" I also wondered if my re-introduction into her life would be disruptive - even unwanted at this point? Having lost her at such a young age, many of the questions that I had wanted to know growing up were never answered. I needed to know her so that I could better know myself. More important than all of that, I needed to know my heritage, my culture, my lineage, my people. I just needed to see her face again. There were so many questions to be asked. But that would wait. Right now, I just needed to see her. After that, I would seek order in my life. I would slowly put the pieces back together, with her help. I would be whole again.

That next morning, I was up by 7 a.m. It was 7:30 before I could make my way to a chair by the phone where I sat yet another half hour, struggling with my will to pick up the receiver. What would I say to her after almost 40 years? I practiced aloud. "Hi, this is your daughter?" No, no. That wasn't right. "Hello, this is Sapphire?" Yeah, that was better. But then what? No one answered me back.

Finally, I picked up the phone and dialed the number. Mr. Jensen had found her living in Little Rock, Arkansas. The phone rang and rang, and no one answered. I had probably waited too long. Then to my surprise, someone answered.

"Hello?" A man with a southern accent answered the line. I choked on the fear that had quickly formed and solidified in my throat. Trying hard to swallow, I sputtered out, "Hi. I'm looking for Marie

Sykes." I was pleased that I had gotten out the words in the correct sequence.

Before I could finish thinking about what to say next, the man answered, "Ain't nobody here by 'dat name ma'am. We gots a Marie McCoy here tho'." I eagerly asked, "Are you related to Marie?" "Yes'm, I 'm her husband, Sam."

Clearing my throat, I finally mustered up the courage to say, "Wow. Well, my name is Sapphire. I don't even know if you've ever heard of me, but I am Marie's daughter. Is she in?"

I almost lost my balance when he answered, "Sho' I have. I've heard a lot about you. And yes, she's in. Just a minute, I'll get her." At that moment, I could hear him calling to my mother, "Marie, it's yo' daughter, Sapphire". He said "Sapphie", letting the 'r' go flat so that the second syllable sounded like 'eye'.

The sweet sound of that word "daughter" made my heart do somersaults and dance in my chest. I could not recall what would be said if and when this time came. And as I struggled while holding the line, it soon did not matter. I had barely said "hi" when she took over the conversation.

"I've been hoping and praying a long time for this moment," she said, sobbing and laughing at the same time. "I didn't know if this day would ever come. Lord Jesus, I don't know what to say!"

Just to be in her verbal presence enveloped me in a sweet calm that was at once soothing to my lost soul. To hear her voice brought such a release. Tears flowed without permission and I welcomed them. We would talk for hours that first day; even of the last time that we saw each other. "I wished I could have been there for you, baby." In that sentence, I knew that my healing from losing her as a child would finally begin. She went on to say, "I looked for you years later when I finally was taken off the medication, but nobody would tell me anything, not even your father. But I'm glad you looked for me. There's something I really wanted to tell you. I'm sure your father never told you the truth. Even if you don't ever want to meet me or get to know me, that's all right, but I just want you know that I've never stopped loving you."

Those words chimed over and over in my head and I savored them, because my heart ached to hear them uttered again and again. Even as I had promised myself to not press too hard, the unanswered questions swarmed in my head, a sea of locusts. *What do you look like now? What happened? Why did you leave? Do I have any siblings?* And the biggest question of all that I just couldn't ask, *Are you still insane?*

The next morning as I checked out of the hotel, I could think of nothing else but meeting my mother. We had agreed that I would fly out in the morning to Little Rock, since I was already en route and my bags were packed. Even after all the conversation over the phone, I was still nervous. The reality of seeing her in the flesh after all these years overwhelmed me. I had to prepare myself for what time and her health would make her look like now. I, instead, held fast to my childhood memory of her to propel me forward toward our long-awaited reunion.

When I arrived and the moment of our reunion came, I don't believe either of us gave a second thought to proper protocol. We just rushed into each other's arms and held on for dear life. I finally felt at home in my spirit. We found a quiet place to talk and she gave me her undivided attention. For the longest time, we just looked at each other, touching each other's face and hands. No speaking; just souls meeting. I looked into her eyes and saw looking back at me the woman who was born to mother me. And even without my deep, sea-blue eyes, she would have still known me as her unmistakable firstborn.

I learned that I had a sister, Raquel. I would soon meet her after our private reunion. Sam, my mother's husband, had come along. When I started off my journey, it was to just find my mother. In the end, I found new relatives, old friendships, welcoming arms and that place that I could finally call "Home."

Chapter 18.

AFTER THE REUNION

It had been three months since Sapphire had seen her mother. In the first few weeks, there were daily telephone calls and emails, but as time went by, the calls seemed to lessen. Fearful that the family was losing interest, Sapphire broke down one evening and called her mother to ask if she and Raquel would come to visit. The both of them were very excited about coming to Chicago. There would be so much to show them. Sapphire still found it hard to believe that she had a sister.

For the next few days Sapphire feverishly ran around the city trying to find the perfect gifts for them. Making her rounds to Nordstrom's, Macy's and a few boutiques in the area, Sapphire couldn't decide on what to give them.

On the day of their arrival, Sapphire sat anxiously in her Toyota Highlander. She could barely contain her excitement. As the plane descended, however, anxiety and excitement began to rise. When they announced the arrival of United Airline flight UA2414 from Little Rock, Arkansas, Sapphire sat upright and came out of the depths of her thoughts. One thought would not go fleetingly. Sapphire questioned why her mother didn't fight for her. She had to push it from its place in the forefront of her thoughts, though it resisted stubbornly. That question would just have to wait.

She sat in the arrivals area of O'Hare Airport on a hot, sunny Friday afternoon waiting for yet another dream to unfold. Here Sapphire at 45 years old was waiting in one of the world's busiest airports for the arrival. Just three short months ago she had not even known she existed. This day could have not been more profound if Sapphire was still seven years old, and instead of watching someone take her mother away, she would be waiting anxiously for her father's car to pull up, bringing her mom and new baby sister from the hospital. It would have been one of the most important days in her life, right up there with receiving her Ph.D., getting married, conceiving her child and now seeing her mother again. All of these life events, in fact, were crucial turning points that would mark and shape the terrain of Sapphire's character, and her very existence.

But God did not will it so. Instead there would be great trials and tribulations both of them would have to go through. Years of separation and persecution only would let years of uncertainty fall between them. Seven long years would pass before Marie would find love and life, learning to trust again. That was all behind them now.

Sapphire's mother exited the terminal and threw her arms up to embrace Sapphire, drawing her into a long-awaited hug. Sapphire stood trembling, needing her mother's arms around her again, as they were being watched by lookers-on. Envisioning a beautiful woman with Betty Davis eyes and a Diahann Carroll smile, Sapphire was a little surprised to see that her mother had matured and aged. She was surprised she had not noticed this level of detail on the first visit with her. Her mother's beauty was nonetheless timeless. Even with gray hair and a few extra wrinkles and pounds, she was still her mother. Whispering in her ear, Marie said, "Sapphire, I understand, you were afraid of losing me, but don't be. You will never, ever lose me again."

Raquel apparently took after her father in many ways. She was very tall and lean, with narrow features, almost Ethiopian in nature. Her olive-toned tawny skin was even and it was obvious her exotic looks made people look at her twice to wonder her cultural origins. Her model-like ways coddled her need to be pampered and she often looked at her long, silk-wrapped nails when she was bored with what was going on around her. However, she still was very much Marie's child and donned her smiling eyes and fine-textured hair. It was easy to see that she was very vain, but Sapphire didn't want to think of Raquel as stuck up. She wondered though how difficult it must have been to rear a high-maintenance daughter in Little Rock, Arkansas. And then she felt compassion for her mother and all the love she carried within her.

In that moment, Sapphire began to see Marie, not merely as a mother, but also as a friend. Proceeding to ask Sapphire about the plans she had made, they all expressed how anxious they were to see Chicago. Since there was a busy week planned for them, they returned to Sapphire's condo to get rest for the evening and to get know each other better.

Arriving at the condo, Raquel pulled out of the trunk a large duffle bag she had brought full of family photos. The three of them spread them all over the couch as Sapphire studied them one picture at a time. There was even a picture of her mother, Marie, on her 50th birthday, which took Sapphire's breath away. In just a few more years and a few more gray hairs, Sapphire would be looking the spitting image of her mother. It was like looking at the future snapshot of herself.

The videos were the best. They gave Sapphire the opportunity to see the way her mother moved, talked and even laughed—something she had missed for a long time. Crying and cackling for hours on end, the three stayed up all night sharing stories about their lives. The more they talked, the more they realized how much they all had in common.

That night, the ladies were so engaged in conversation that they never even realized that the sun was coming up over the lake. Sharing the simple pleasure of watching the sunrise with her family was a moment that Sapphire cherished. They were all amused at the idea that they would be going to bed when they should actually be waking up.

Later that day, the ladies took in a baseball game between the Cardinals and the Cubs. The Cubs were victorious over the Cardinals, blowing them out 10-3. This was exciting because Marie had never been to a baseball game. But the day was not the complete paradise as the night before. All Raquel seemed to do was complain. Although Marie enjoyed the game, Raquel complained about how much her back still ached from sitting in the seats that barely held her generous hips. Sapphire would say that it was cold and Raquel would say it was too hot. And when they walked back to the El, Raquel said that she was feeling sick while Sapphire couldn't imagine a time where she felt better. There wasn't much the girls could seem to agree upon.

The next morning, Marie woke up around 8:00 a.m. to make breakfast. Looking out the window she saw it would be a gorgeous day, perfect for going out on the lake. It just so happened that Sapphire had made plans to take her mother and sister sailing on Navy Pier. Hopping out of bed like a kid at Christmas, Sapphire headed to the kitchen. The sound of sizzling bacon and eggs in the skillet made her stomach growl, while the aroma of buttermilk biscuits baking in the oven led her by the nose to the kitchen. It had been a long time since her place smelled this good from breakfast being prepared. Although Sapphire could cook very well, she often didn't eat breakfast at home. It was a pleasant surprise. "Good morning," she chimed.

"Good morning, Sapphire," Marie responded, smiling with a cast iron skillet in her hand, scooping out scrambled eggs with melted Cheddar and Monterey cheese onto a plate.

"It's about time," Raquel muttered ungratefully under her breath.

Sapphire could feel the tension growing between her and her little sister, but decided to ignore it. The food looked delicious, just like she remembered from her childhood and whatever was bugging Raquel would have to wait. Raquel was a little jealous of the relationship that was developing between Sapphire and her mother. Perhaps she saw Sapphire as a threat to her. Whatever it was, it was interfering with the day that was just beginning, and nothing they seemed to do in the hours to come seemed to please Raquel.

That evening, Raquel and Sapphire took a drive to this little coffee shop in the South Loop off of Halsted Street. It was apparent that the sisters needed to talk. Raquel explained to Sapphire that all her life, she had heard every little detail about her that their mother could remember; from her smile to her free spirit. No matter what the situation, Sapphire was larger than life and could do no wrong. Raquel knew that her mother meant no harm but it still hurt.

"Sapphire, at one point in my life, I wished that you didn't exist. I even started to believe that the color of your eyes—even your name, was a lie; something Momma had made up when she was—wasn't in her right mind." Those words hit Sapphire hard, but there was no way for Raquel to take them back. It had been difficult living in the shadow of someone she never thought she would actually meet.

"You know, I always felt like Momma has always loved you more than me. She didn't say it, but then, she didn't have to. All my life, I've had to compete with a ghost, and now that you are here, it is even harder to compete with you in person. You have accomplished so much, and yet you were given so little. How do I compete?"

"Raquel, we are sisters. We shouldn't have to compete with each other." Sapphire felt sorry for Raquel but knew that she was perfectly justified in how she felt. This woman whom Sapphire barely knew was hurting just to keep the favor of her mother. In all that Raquel was feeling, it was difficult for her to empathize with Sapphire's motherless life. Sapphire knew it wouldn't be easy for Raquel to let go of the past. She knew that because she hadn't been able to let go of hers. But one thing she was certain of was that once the past is released, the healing can finally begin. She had to try to help Raquel, because in so doing, she could also help herself.

"Raquel, I know you are hurt by our mother's actions. But I honestly believe she meant no harm. Think of it this way: she was basically mourning the loss of a child. You are a big part of our mother's life. Don't ever doubt that. But don't blame her for missing the other part, the part that was brutally separated from her."

Eventually things started to come around. Raquel started to realize that there was so much she didn't know about Sapphire and that made her rethink her relationship with her mother. As for Sapphire, by the end of the week, she felt overwhelmed with information. While she was very happy, the whole experience was much more emotionally draining than she thought it would be. Moreover, even though Sapphire was excited to know her mother, something else was going on inside of her that just would not relent. Tempted to cut the visit short, Sapphire couldn't bring herself to let her mother and sister know that she was not only exhausted, but also experiencing some strange internal pain that she had not felt before, nor could she easily explain.

On the last night of their visit, Sapphire took them to *Vivaldi*, her favorite Italian restaurant in Oak Park, a near western suburb. It was such a release to know that the week was ending and that the pressure of the visit was coming to an end. Finally, there would be a night where they could laugh, talk and be themselves. It was one of the most memorable nights of that week. Raquel felt like she had found a new best friend in Sapphire. That's when she knew they had finally crossed over into sisterhood. When Sapphire pulled into the alley and backed into the space in front of her garage, she leaned over the back of the seat and handed her sister a little turquoise Tiffany box. Inside was a little, blue sapphire ring, just big enough to fit Raquel's pinky finger. Sapphire lifted up her right pinky finger, showing her identical ring and winked at her sibling. Checking her rear view mirror, she saw Raquel smile radiantly back at her. Her profile was stunning. As she was gazing at the sparkling ring her sister had given her, Sapphire noticed something she hadn't seen before. It was uncanny how much Raquel and Sapphire resembled each other.

The next day, early in the morning, the ladies climbed into the car and headed to the airport. At that moment, Sapphire remembered a question that had taunted her from the day she witnessed her mother being taken away. Smiling at her mother, she asked quietly, "Mom, I know this might bring back bad memories, but the day you left the house, you said: it wasn't my choice, it was a matter of choice. What did you mean?"

"In life, Sapphire, sometimes women make difficult decisions that may cause them to give up their right to choose. Going through what you've been through, you should know that the choices you make are often not the ones you would have chosen if the situation had been in your favor. Although it was never my choice to be sent to the asylum, I knew that if I were to survive the tumultuous relationship I was in, it was my only way out. If I didn't decide to choose to let insanity save me, your father would have surely killed me." Sapphire marveled at the strength in her mother's words. They clasped each other's hands with the strength of understanding, knowing that to choose life meant more than just saving your own.

At the airport Sapphire gave Raquel yet another perfect gift—an open round trip ticket back to Chicago. Smiling, the sisters, separated by 15 years, quietly said their goodbyes. There was nothing that could come between them now. Nothing except a strange pain that scared Sapphire so much she couldn't afford to ignore it anymore.

Chapter 19.

RAVINIA'S FIRST

Orange glaring streetlights blinded my eyes as I looked up into them out of despair. They were the last thing that I remembered, as I fought the tears that kept streaming down my face. I knew that night would hold more than I could ever bear if I had not repressed my memory of it.

Shouting violently at each other, I can't even remember how we got to the bottom of the stairs. I don't know why our nosy neighbors hadn't called the police on us, but perhaps a little intervention would have kept my marriage to my first husband together a bit longer. Words--lascivious and hurtful, but nonetheless true, spewed out of our mouths like molten lava. Something deep inside told me that this would be the end of us, and in my haste to have the last argumentative word, I kept on lashing out at him, like he was the most despicable creature this side of Hades. His verbal abuse had gathered heavy like wet leaves around my feet, and tonight, I was plowing over them and squashing them beneath me.

We had both been guilty of infidelity in our marriage, and saw the hurt it left upon the other. They say two wrongs don't make a right, and that was certain in our case. Our children, small and tender, did not understand why we could not reason with each other, why we could not love each other. It tore me up inside to see them mimic us in their childish bickering. The last thing I wanted was for them to see us like this. But nothing seemed strong enough to keep us from the eminent separation my heart knew would come. Too many layers of distrust had severed our ability to see each other as we did the first time around. Or maybe we were too young to figure out whether it was really worth it.

Markus and I had gotten married while I was a junior at Loyola University. We were just kids and loved just being in each other's company, breathing each other's air, at all times. He was a couple of years older than me and had a studio loft in East Roger's Park near the beach on Jonquil Terrace. Art was his passion and although at times hostile and temperamental, I loved the maddening freedom in his eyes. His curly, ash brown hair with natural golden highlights always looked like it was trying to decide whether it wanted to be curly or straight. Some days, his locks just looked as if they had given up the fight all together. His German heritage, mixed with East Indian and African origins, also fueled interesting discussions of genetics, particularly around the shape of his broad nose and keen nostrils. The simple grayness of his eyes enveloped me in a quiet masquerade, playing the same drama time and time again. Markus was a free spirit, never deferring in to time or tradition. He admired my ability to act impulsively and instinctively, breaking the rules with full intent and no regret. We fell in love quickly, getting married after only a month of dating.

Life was blissful at first, well, until the twins came—Justin and Jamila. Markus couldn't handle the pressure of going to school, working and raising a family. It cramped his artistic, free-spirited style. His art--his first love, suffered and unfortunately, so did his creative spirit. His heart and soul, though, were restored in those lovely babies. And so out of the misery of being absent from the artistic community, he began to create art that included them; tremendous, moving self-portraits with babes in his arms. He would prop himself up in front of the boudoir mirror with nothing more than a pair of jeans on. He would then have me take his picture, holding our naked babies, gazing down at their amazing perfection. The recreation of the photographs onto canvas was the thing that freed him from the trappings of marriage, family, and reality. Interestingly, people loved these paintings more than his previous works and Markus started doing well locally, getting some notoriety and even making enough money to support us on his craft. He had found the ultimate work-from-home gig. I was so happy for him. There he was, taking a deep interest in our children; *and* he was home.

Sadly, I seemed to not be in the picture—not in the literal ones that he sold and certainly not in his mental and emotional space. In all his success, he had somehow left me out. I had to fend for myself in many ways. I struggled alone to finish my senior year at Loyola, and to work, so that we could have health benefits. Markus had made the twins into professional models and spent all his days and nights with them. Venturing out into various studios around town, they were quickly a big hit and were getting calls from top agencies that wanted them for commercials and ad campaigns. I barely saw them anymore. I no longer had a husband to speak of, or the love that had brought us together. I grew estranged from my children, and although I loved them deeply, I painfully missed the life I had before they came.

A man on the first floor of our building started taking notice in me, telling me how fine I was. He told me that my husband wasn't nearly the man I thought he was by leaving me to myself all the time. He always seemed to know when I would be coming home or leaving. My life and routine had unfortunately become predictable. I found myself seeing my loneliness disappear whenever I came up the brownstone steps of our building. Markus and I stayed on the third floor, which was a converted loft. We had access to the roof so it was relaxing to go up there to watch the picturesque shooting stars, and to trace the Big Dipper with our fingers, searching hopefully for the far off skyline of downtown. It also gave me time to reminisce on the many good nights Markus and I had on the roof, just holding each other under the moon, whispering our dreams into the atmosphere. But even as our words dissipated into the night air, without knowing or trying, so had our love for each other.

In the summertime, my neighbor would be faithfully sitting on the stoop, seemingly waiting for me to arrive from school or work. Anticipation would brew inside of me, and by the time I would get to the stairs of my building, I would start to perspire, ever so gently, but just enough to form a layer of sweat between my skin and my clothes. It was just refreshing enough to make me notice the moisture, but warm enough to start challenging my deodorant body spray to step up its game. I didn't look forward to seeing him, because I knew that he was attracted to me and that made me feel uncomfortable. And yet, it was unavoidable. The shortest way to the third floor was through the front door and going through the gangway was not always safe. All I wanted to do was to get home.

Smiling ear to ear, the inquisitive neighbor would often offer me an iced tea or a cold can of Pepsi. I would always decline, knowing that I couldn't start dabbling, even conversationally, with the neighbors. I got married because I wanted a commitment. I was tired of the dating scene in college and Markus seemed to bring out the spark I needed to keep me interested. Today, of all days, was a 98-degree day in the shade. My ankles hurt from being in my high heels all day at the office. I was tempted to take my shoes off and walk barefoot on the sidewalk; but I was more afraid of my soles scorching than my toes pinching. As I neared the loft, I could feel the sweat draining down from my armpits. I prayed to God that our window air conditioner was working, and kept thinking about the cold shower I was going to take as soon as I got home. Like clockwork, there was my neighbor, perched up on the windowsill, like a Cheshire cat. Today, he had a tall glass of lemonade, full of ice and a neat lemon wedge clinging to the rim of the glass. Sugar crystals were still swirling around among the dancing ice cubes.

"Ms. Vinia," he whined longingly, "You sho' look like you need a cool drank. I just made this up for myself, but I'd be glad to let you have it, if you like." Marvin's voice dripped of Southern sweetness, a little too syrupy for my taste. However, I was extremely thirsty that day, and even if he was gay, it didn't seem to matter much now. I knew that he was being nice and that he was lying about having made that just for him. But, as I said, I didn't care. I was too hot and sweaty to just pass up the biggest cool drink I had seen all day long. Plus, this guy was fine with his big brown chocolate eyes and long curly eyelashes. He was definitely a pretty boy and I was sure he had probably pledged Kappa in college.

Reaching out my clammy hand, I grabbed the glass. Water from the melted ice was forming a separate ring at the top of it. I brought the glass up to my parched lips and drew in a long gulp. Forgetting my manners, I stood there wide-legged without shame, enjoying every thirst-quenching swallow. This was a guilty pleasure, but I didn't realize the stakes would be so high. All I could think about was how the tangy lemon was just sour enough to make that rank as the best glass of lemonade that I ever had. The only thing better would have been Momma Tish's

Italian Ice from Taylor Street. I allowed myself the brief indulgence of imagining pouring the flavored slush down my throat and then all over me, to cool me from the inside out. I snapped out of my fantasy when I heard, "Whoa girl, you practically took that in one gulp!"

"I was thirsty. Thank you very much," I sputtered, wiping my lips and pouting slightly from the haste of seeking the cooling relief. "That really hit the spot!"

"You sure you had enough? I mean, I got plenty in the back," he said with a slight wink, getting up off the sill to walk towards the kitchen door.

"No, that's fine. It was really good, though. Here's your glass back," I said, stretching my arm towards the window. He started to shut the window and I retracted as not to get my wrist caught.

"Watch yo'self, baby. I got to shut this to put the air conditioner on. It is too hot up in here. Why don't you just drop that off at my door when you walk up? Okay?"

This man is too gay. Surely, he does not want me. This is safe enough. There's no reason why I can't drop off the glass without causing any problems. Looking up at the curly headed Morris Day look-alike, I said a confident, "Okay," and bounded up the concrete stairs. I rang the bell so that he could buzz me in. We lived on different sides of the building and had separate security doors. It had been a long time since I had been on this side of the building. I pulled the heavy glass door open and walked up the stairs. When I got to his door, he was standing there, half out of breath and fanning.

"Come on in, child. You look hot," Marvin said, sounding like my grandmother.

"Yeah, it is kind of hot outside. You did notice that, right?" I countered, rolling my eyes.

"Girl, you so funny! Honey, please. Can you feel the air? It should be kicking in soon. Gon' and have a seat. I'll bring you some more lemonade." Marvin's apartment was impressive. All his furniture matched. It was cream leather with black trim. His end tables were glass with black and gold horns. It was the latest style. He had some African masks on his shelves and lots of scented candles. I thought to myself, *this guy is definitely sweet.* I tried to keep a blank expression and not show my suspicions. When he came back, I barely heard him re-enter the room because the air conditioner was so loud. While looking at one of his hand-carved elephants, I felt a cold glass on my neck. The hairs on my back began to stand up. *What was going on?* I turned around quickly to find Marvin half naked. I was appalled.

I opened my mouth to say, "I thought you were gay," but nothing came out. He looked at me longingly and said, "You are so fine, girl" putting his arms around my waist. Still in shock, I closed my mouth to find his lips coming closer to mine. Then, I spoke.

"Marvin, you know I am married."

"Yeah girl, I know. He's cute, too. Is he mixed or something? Oh never mind, it doesn't matter. The point is, he don't want you."

I was shocked at his bluntness. He was so confident in his Southern accented arrogance. I didn't know whether to be upset or confused. So I decided to just ask him about *his* sexual orientation. Maybe he was bisexual, but just the thought of him with other men was more than I and my strict Pentecostal upbringing could handle. "So, Marvin, do you like men or what?" I asked directly.

"Mens? Girl please. I *loves* me some women. Oh, wait, snap. You think I am *gay*? Why ev'rybody think I'm gay?" he asked accusatorily, with a wide-eyed glare. He was serious and smiling at the same time. It unnerved me. I was trying to discern if he was joking or serious. In the meantime, the idea that he could be gay or bisexual gave me chills. "For real, are you saying you are *not* gay?" I asked disbelievingly, deciding this was a bad decision.

"Uh, no. I thought I said that. Either you are hard of hearing or I wasn't clear enough," Marvin stated loudly, sounding offended. He took a giant step back, still holding my second glass of lemonade in his hand. "So, do you want this or what?" Stretching the sweaty glass out to me at arms length, it was obvious he was getting perturbed and I felt sorry for him. He was a very beautiful man, but just too effeminate. And besides, I was married with no interest in breaking my vows. I leaned in and took the glass from him and set it down.

Marvin swooped in and recovered my blunder with a cork-padded coaster. He said scoldingly, “Girl, I know you didn’t just put that on my glass end table without a coaster.” He pointed like a primary school teacher to the stack of marble coasters on the bookshelf.

“I’m sorry, Marvin. I didn’t mean to,” Ravinia apologized, picking up the wet glass, trying to rub the wet beads off Marvin’s table, succeeding only in streaking the once clean, smudge-free surface. This made Marvin suck his teeth and roll his eyes. He lunged for the decorative box of tissues next to the sofa arm. In high drama fashion, he labored away at the wet stain, commensurate with cleaning up corn syrup. I was further and henceforth convinced that my first floor neighbor was in denial. I didn’t care *what* he said.

Just then, I leaned in and gave him a quick pat on the back, and thanked him for the lemonade. He started to smile and his baby-fine moustache stretched out over his pink-almost lavender lips. His facial features had a boyish innocence that made me feel all giddy inside. I knew I had to leave at that point. I just couldn’t do to Markus what I knew he was doing to me. It just wasn’t right. But, I knew the women that Markus was stepping out with by name, by face, by voice. Some would call during all hours of the night for him to come to them. They called my house shamelessly, disturbing my precious sleep, haunting my would-be peaceful dreams. The constant, agonizing ringing would awaken my children and me. But it wasn’t just a ringing phone that annoyed me. It was the fact that I didn’t know which of them was on the other line, hanging up when they heard my tired, frustrated voice saying, “Hello, whore. He’s asleep. Don’t call here any more.”

No matter how many times they heard me say that tired old line, they would always call back in a show of brazen disrespect or overall stupidity. I had thought about getting the number changed, but Markus used the line for business, and we definitely needed the money. I don’t know what hurt more, seeing them flaunt themselves around him in the studio right in my view, or being sneaky by calling well into the night.

Either way, I knew that those lonely, trifling home wreckers were aching for my man to come and rescue them from their longing.

I often wondered why the married man with a big shiny wedding band on his finger was always the one that women sought out. I imagined that the married man's appeal lay in the fact that he was some other woman's problem, and that she could just send him home after she finished with him. The other reality is that he represents what she really wants but can't seem to have or keep. Whatever it was, they wanted Markus. And Markus wanted them. Even through out all his blatant whoring, he would still have the audacity to try and sleep with me. But I wasn't having it. I also felt like I was losing my children. The only time I seemed to have with the twins was when I watched them sleep, which was a healthier consolation than laying down with Markus and whatever he had brought home with him to our night.

The desperation in the collective yearnings of the home-wreckers would echo clear in the angry ring tones. I stopped picking up the phone and let it ring, until one night I had enough sense to just unplug it and go sleep in the twins' room. Night after night, I asked him to stop them from calling, but he wouldn't even entertain the discussion. He had the nerve to say that I was overreacting; that they were just clients and to stop interfering with his business. He must of thought I was stupid or something. At one point I chuckled, recalling the comedian telling of a philanderer caught red-handed and retorting: "It wasn't me." He may have been home on those nights, but I knew he was with them just about any other time. After our non-discussions about the calls, he would always stay home the remainder of the night. I told myself that this was at least some form of respect for our household. Still, it was no surprise that the phone seldom rang on those nights. Their strange scent would follow him home, until he just stopped smelling like us all together. I would feverishly wash our bedding and towels, bleach his undergarments until they yellowed, but I just could not rid my home of the stench. That's when we stopped making love completely. I couldn't risk it anymore. I refused to let him give me something of which I would never be able to rid myself. I didn't want the layers of guilt thrust upon me from his conquests. It was just sex for Markus, as it is for a lot of men. The infidelity was just another way to hurt me; a way to get back at me for being with my ex-boyfriend when Markus and I were separated.

There was a time, before the twins came, that I questioned whether I had made the right choice to marry Markus. My ex, Greg, from high school had come to town to visit his mother, and was only home for a weekend. He called me. Things were not going well with Markus and me. I knew I shouldn't go to see Greg, but things were looking pretty bad for us, and I needed a reason to stay with Markus, or to leave him. We got into a huge fight and I packed my suitcase. I told him it was over and I was leaving. I met my ex at Union Station and we spent the weekend at the Palmer House Hotel.

Things seemed much more glamorous and overly romanticized in the auspices of that affair, as is the case of most forbidden things. The heart skips a couple of beats and the blood courses fiercely in the arms of the one to whom there is no devotion. Things happen at the speed of light, momentum and inertia become close allies and the night is forever young. Nothing ever seems to *typically* go wrong, and there is temporary blindness to why it is so wrong. The sheer excitement of the here and now overpower the reality of tomorrow's consequences. When day breaks and the light of judgment shines through the window, we lay among the shards of zero expectations, zero commitments, zero love. It becomes impossible to ignore the face of guilt when the devoted ones unveil themselves in the mind's eye. If you can look at the unsuspecting face of someone who thought you were coming home to him and your kids. If you can look back defiantly saying to yourself, "It was worth it," then your heart is even more deceitful than mine. The cost is always double in affairs of the heart.

It is said that when men step outside of a marriage, it is most often not about having a relationship, or wanting to destroy a marriage, or even loving someone else. Most often, it is the fact that he is blind to the notion that you might still love him or care about him, even though things aren't the way they used to be. It really doesn't have anything to do with the woman either, for that matter. He doesn't *plan* for you to "end up hurt," but you always are. No matter how you brace yourself for the fall, it always hurts. Bitterly.

I've always believed that a man has to resolve to be faithful. He has to be confident, even when he isn't 'getting any,' that he is the most important entity in your life. He has to know undoubtedly that even outside of your *presence*; he can walk in the assurance that no one in the world can shake his faith or turn his head; because that is where the breakdown comes. When a man's faith is shaken, the question becomes: did he have it in the first place?

The separation from Markus was brief, but the soul ties that were made with Greg that weekend were not easily severed. I was pregnant when I had the affair, but I didn't find out until after Markus and I had reunited. Markus was excited to find out about the pregnancy; meanwhile, I still wondered whom I really loved and could not yet move on to celebrating the news. One of the things that drew me to Greg was his ability to talk me through my hurt with reason and understanding. We knew each other very well. And being my first love, I knew I would always love him. Everything was beginning to get complicated. So much so, that I still longed for Greg. I didn't know whom I wanted or if I was ready to give up all that I had worked for with Markus for an old flame.

I tried talking to my mother, and of course, she didn't spare me from name calling, labeling me a "filthy tramp," saying that I couldn't keep my lies from Markus, threatening to tell him that I had slept with another man while pregnant with his babies. She preached lectures of fire and brimstone and questioned the paternity of my babies. I begged her not to tell Markus, because I wanted a father for the twins, their father. He was definitely their father; that I knew for a fact. Momma finally said she wouldn't, but I never really believed her. She loved Markus, and at times, I felt she loved him more than she loved me. She would tell him, "Well I raised her right, so if she acts like a fool, it ain't because of me. She knows better."

In addition to the pain of holding my poisonous secret, I was battling the worthlessness that tore through my insides. Eventually, my mother opened my secret closet and hit my husband over the head with every bone that fell out; calling out my indiscretions by name. Markus took our kids. Even though he stepped out on me shamelessly for over a year, he still felt that what I did was worse and deemed it unforgivable. Although I knew I could never bring myself to have another affair, that vow was not good enough for Markus. I did know better and I had learned my lesson. It would mark the first and last time I would sleep with someone outside of my husband until now. Adultery creates a never-ending cycle that keeps you bound to that lover, unless it is severed. The consequences are even worse than fornication out of wedlock. The stakes are higher than pride or dignity. At least they were for me. I felt hopeless and helpless. I was all alone. And nothing compared to missing my babies. I missed the love I once had with Markus. I missed knowing what it was like to have a home and a family. And I knew my mother was right. Nobody but Jesus could save me from myself.

It often troubled me how I could conclude that marriage would somehow cure me of my promiscuity. It was as if the words, "I do" had a supernatural power that would transform me into the perfect wife and mother. I had convinced myself that the one man I chose to marry as an irrational 21 year old would be able to fill the void left by all the men I had slept with before him. How naïve I had been. In order to truly be delivered and made whole again, I needed to search deep within myself first, and choose to forgive myself for all the times I had yielded my will and surrendered my body and soul to some insignificant man. I vividly remembered each and every one of their faces, and some nights I would spend replaying their faces in my mind like a slide show. I never thought it would bother me so much, but it did. It troubled my very spirit. My spirit needed and wanted its own 'alabaster box'—something that represented a cleansing offering of my worth, so that I could be whole again.

Still I asked in my state of faithlessness, of all my wrongs, who would forgive me? Who would ever want me? What could I possibly do? I had lost everything that I had ever wanted. My husband thought I was a horrible failure as a mother, my mother had no respect for me, and I got kicked out of college for missing too many days of school. How could I forgive myself with all the guilt that had taken up residence inside of me? Little did I know that forgiveness would be the only way to begin to heal the wounds cut so jaggedly and deeply, and left septic over time.

Somehow, I would have to forgive myself in order to move on. I knew there was a life outside of what I had wrecked. I knew that I would someday be able to emerge and find a way to live again. But it would take time, something I didn't want to wait on. The lesson would come slowly that if I didn't forgive myself first, I could not be delivered from all the souls I wanted to be freed from, all the souls I had tied up in my own.

Chapter 20.

GIVING FULL REIGN

Howard Thurman said, "To love is to make of one's heart a swinging door." Ain't that the truth? For Ravinia, her door seemed to have the screen cut out, and at times, to just hang open because the catch needed oiling. She never got over Xavier's affair and knew it had to be more than just the interracial aspect of it. There was so much injustice dripping all over that situation that Johnny Cochran himself would have had to acquit Ravinia. And even though it was wrong on so many levels, Ravinia needed to get over that hump in her life.

Xavier's being with a Caucasian woman made it hurt more than if he had of been with a sistah. At least then, the comparative measure between the two women wouldn't be separated by history and color. The facts were that the woman he was with was at least 20 years younger, 20 pounds lighter and 20 IQ points less than Ravinia. Well, the last part didn't matter so much. But, certainly that was enough to make anyone, including the fine Mrs. Hamilton, look at themselves and ponder their worth. The fact that she was 20 shades lighter just added insult to injury, as far as Ravinia was concerned. Ravinia somehow knew, that what the other woman represented wasn't real. She knew that the young girl wasn't enough for him and that he would eventually grow tired of her. Maybe that was her ego talking. Maybe it was life experience. In any case, she could never bring herself to come to terms with the fact that he did what he did, with "her."

Ravinia had to decide whether to show Xavier the photos from the day on the train. She wondered if she should wait for a couple of days to pass so she could do it without being angry. Ravinia figured that they would somehow gloss over the otherwise gory details quickly and go on about their daily routine. She could simply wait until he showed up the next morning. Either way, it wasn't going to be easy to broach the subject. Xavier was the evasive type and it would anger her even more if he had out and out lied to her. Looking back, Ravinia did somehow regret taking the pictures in the first place. She thought to herself as she had before. *Well, what if it was just a thing? Just something for him to do because he was bored?* Maybe she wasn't providing all the excitement he needed. But then Ravinia thought better of it. Xavier never did anything unless it was at the grandest scale. He had to drive the best cars, live in the best neighborhood, and play golf with the most elite. This would be no exception.

This led Ravinia to wondering why he chose her in the first place. She certainly wasn't the finest female at the firm. The fact that her heels didn't even fit in the back of her shoes was beside the point. Ravinia's beauty was rare, and he knew it. The former Omicron senior manager didn't tell Xavier about her true upbringing until after they were married. After all, he was about to make partner, and she, associate partner. It was unimportant at that moment, on the cusp of such joint success that in her early years she was raised in the projects. It mattered even less that her father had left them to fend for themselves. It was irrelevant that, despite all her suburban education and formal Suzuki violin training, that deep down she was still from the hood.

Ravinia decided that what Xavier didn't know wouldn't hurt him. And she was very much on point in that determination. Their office attraction in the early days was more than mere boy meets girl. He admired her street wit and her ability to think fast on her feet. Ravinia wasn't easily intimidated. She could stand up in a board room of high powered men, three and four levels above her own and tell them straight to their faces that their technology was not suitable for the company, and walk out completely unscathed by their loathing. These high-power professional performances intrigued Xavier. He held Ravinia's command as pure entertainment as he wondered about her virtues as a mate.

Ravinia knew that there were those who hated her at Omicron, but that didn't slow her down. Her mother always told her that when someone is liked by everyone, something is wrong with them. There was no way Ravinia could please everybody, so she didn't even try. She just knew that she was fair, and put her ethics before office politics. Knowing that she could succeed by putting her mind before her feelings, she left her heart at home every morning. That's why it puzzled Ravinia when Xavier started following her around.

Xavier and Ravinia weren't even on the same project. He was working on some Y2K fix and she was working in the Organizational Change department. He was technical and Ravinia was Human Resources. But it seemed that every conference she set up, Xavier was there in attendance. For a man trying to make partner, Ravinia was sure his time would have been better spent brown-nosing the senior partners or finding some solution that would put his name on the map and make him a shoe-in for the next election. She probably wouldn't have even noticed Xavier, except for the fact that he was often the only other African-American in the room. In a company like Omicron, there were always cultural subgroups or interest groups that would network and form a superficial kind of family. Ravinia never had the time or inclination to attend their functions or mingle strictly on the basis of like ethnicity. She was an authentic mover and shaker in her own right. And she made her business contacts the old fashioned way. Knowing her role and doing her job well; identifying the stakeholders and decision makers, and blazing a trail that broke right through the glass ceiling of the good ole' boys clubhouse. In Xavier's case, his rank, not his complexion got her attention and made her follow his career closely. There were still only a few African Americans at Omicron representing the masses and fewer still at their levels. Best practices stated that networking was essential to making life-long connections, and that was Ravinia's impetus for meeting Xavier.

The nasty divorce from Markus caused Ravinia to seldom attend after-work functions. She just wasn't really ready to socialize quite yet. Markus was a bitter man and seemed to try to make life a living hell for her after the divorce. She was forced to see him during visitation with the children and she certainly wasn't going to raise them by herself if she didn't have to. Ravinia stated to him quite a matter-of-factly and before he went traipsing off to Bachelor-land, "I didn't sign up for single parenthood. Which half of the year do you want?" He was not about to just leave them with Ravinia just because they weren't together anymore. They had begotten them together and they were going to raise them together. Just in separate homes. Ravinia was making it easy. He could have his Bohemian life-style back. She had her career, after all. They would both just have to factor the equation of their new lives.

Every time Ravinia saw Markus, he was with a different woman, usually a model or someone extraordinarily exotic. Markus became so stuck on himself because the world he lived in thrived off his creativity. His public literally worshipped him. That fact did not excuse the pompous air he had about himself. He would look down his nose at Ravinia in a way that made him lower than the dirt from which he was made.

Suddenly Ravinia felt the urge to take a shower. She surprised everyone and made an exception by deciding to attend a networking function. This one was exclusively hosted by the Black Engineers Society of Omicron Consulting, LLP, and historically always seemed to be the place to meet and greet other African-American professionals. Being so close to the holidays, it was only appropriate for the function to be held at a five-star hotel downtown. This time it was at the Hotel Nikko. Ravinia had always wanted to see the inside of it. She figured it would be a late night, so she reserved a room with the company's weekend discount and drove downtown from Rogers Park. Taking her dress, shoes and an overnight bag, she figured she could take a nice hot shower, have a pre-dinner refreshment, and get dressed at her leisure. Ravinia had been working so hard these past few months; she needed a little unwinding from her workaholic routine.

As Ravinia checked in, she saw Xavier Hamilton having a Starbucks coffee beverage in the lobby with a couple of other partner wanna-be's. When she had her room assignment, she made her way to the elevator, hoping he didn't see her. Xavier had been trying to make eye contact with Ravinia, but she really didn't want to see anyone before the event, especially since she looked as worn out as she felt and desperately needed a nap.

However, that night proved to be one of the best in Ravinia's life. She got an opportunity to network with a lot of influential people. She had underestimated the brilliance and talent of this notable group of professionals. She certainly would not make that mistake again. She must have left that night with 50 or more business cards. By the time

Xavier and Ravinia actually got a chance to talk, he was down to a few pathetic pick up lines. He failed miserably in his effort to get her to laugh. When finally she did crack a smile and laughed openly, it was because he was so corny, not because he was funny. Ravinia was glad she had avoided him. She wasn't just playing hard to get. She *was* hard to get. And it worked. Letting him pursue her totally fed into Xavier's desire to embark on the quest to divide and conquer. He was definitely the chivalrous type, and that suited Ravinia's need to become self-actualized at that point in her life. She was tired of the rat race that held men who could barely hold a job and who were living paycheck to paycheck. Her ego needed to be pampered. Her spirit needed to be soothed. Xavier was a master at both.

In talking to Xavier about the future of Omicron, she realized that he was unlike any man she had ever known. He was extremely business savvy and confident about what he wanted in life. He was on a fast track to becoming a managing partner and was intent on not letting anything stop him. He was the first man Ravinia had ever talked to seriously in business that had capital ventures on the side that were actually making money for him. Even as the couple talked, Xavier was seeking more venture capital to finance and secure his intellectual property portfolio.

It was also clear that although Xavier talked distinctly, and had next to no rhythm, he was particularly fond of women of darker skin tone. Ravinia took this as a complement; especially since Xavier commented about how smooth and rich her cinnamon complexion appeared. Being extremely fair, it seemed that Xavier was attracted to the opposite of himself.

Graduating from Dartmouth, a very prestigious east coast school, Ravinia found out that Xavier was actually born in England and lived there where his father was stationed. His family moved to the east coast of the United States when Xavier was in high school because his mother grew tired of the strict life in Britain and sought a life free of restrictions. They were extremely well to do. Money came from his mother's side of the family; and their only son was used to the finer things in life. Yet, Xavier was a rebellious soul. Growing up in Europe, his skin color did not affect his world. But he soon found this to be different in the U.S. He needed to know what it was like to be a part of the Black experience.

Although he enjoyed the silver spoon, he wanted to succeed on his own volition. He wanted to realize his dream of becoming high powered on his own terms. He wanted to make his own money. And after receiving his MBA from Northwestern's Kellogg School of Business, Xavier wanted to build his own career. He started working at Omicron Consulting, LLP, as a manager, right out of graduate school. He quickly moved up the ranks and enrolled in the five-year plan of buying into the partnership. That progressiveness made him even more appealing to someone like Ravinia.

Ravinia represented the African-American side of Xavier that he just couldn't seem to voluntarily draw out of himself; so he lived vicariously through her in that regard. She had the experience of living in the ghetto, while pulling herself out with a determination that made her more than just a strong Black woman. Living through the 60's in Cabrini public housing, and then in the seedier parts of Evanston, she knew what it meant to be 'Black in America.' Already accused of not being "Black enough" by his consulting peers, Xavier knew that becoming a partner would distance him even further from the Black experience he sought. He needed something to keep him grounded and to serve as a constant reminder of the things that were important. He promised his friends from Kellogg that once he got to the top; he would keep the issues that were important to them as a people within his focus, doing what he could in his position to raise the bar for his people.

Ravinia had exactly what he needed. He was fascinated by her candid, cultured style. She was a go-getter and knew exactly what she wanted. She was also quite a looker; real easy on the eyes. He could definitely get what he wanted out of the firm with a woman like her in his corner. Ravinia was also a manager for the same prestigious firm; yet she still struggled with money issues. She had two children from a previous marriage whom she needed to support. Her mother had complications from diabetes, and could not work for the Weiss family much longer. Besides, they were getting elderly, too, and would soon move to Orlando to be with their son.

All Ravinia knew was that she needed a break in life, where she could relax and be taken care of. She never thought in her wildest dreams she would end up with someone like Xavier. First, someone more of Denzel Washington's complexion was more her type. She had begun to associate Markus' mulatto-complexion with the torment he had put her through; convincing herself that she simply didn't like light-skinned brothas. Secondly, she was still not completely convinced that Xavier didn't secretly go for the 'other' type. It was instinct, just like figuring her old neighbor, Marvin, for being gay. Everything she knew about the 'Oreo Principle' convinced Ravinia that while Xavier was attracted to white women; they just didn't go for him all the time. That idea made her feel that maybe he was settling. But when the opportunity to hook up with Xavier presented itself, it was almost like a good business deal. She just couldn't pass it up. Weighing the pros and cons of marrying Xavier, Ravinia found that she could live with the fact that he was even more white acting than Markus. She decided that she could live with the fact that he was probably an Uncle Tom and would eventually suck up to almost anyone to make it into the partnership. She even knew that perhaps, she wasn't his preferred type. But none of that mattered. She could see how they both would benefit from the union. So finally, Ravinia relaxed.

Not having to worry about taking care of her mother on her $85,000 salary, which still was under her female Caucasian peers was peace of mind enough. Ravinia knew that no matter how hard she worked, she would never be paid her worth at Omicron. She had learned early on as a consultant that she had to work three times as hard as any one else, just to be compensated on the average. To really shine, she had to be at the top of her game. Years of consistently staying on point still had not put her where she belonged. It was a man's world, a white man's business world--and she really couldn't blame Xavier for wanting a piece of it. He had a dream of becoming a managing partner at a Big Five, and she wanted him to reach it, not just for him, but for the both of them. She knew that if she helped him focus on the projects that would put Xavier Hamilton's name on the map, they would be begging him to buy into the partnership by the end of the following year. With her combination street and book smarts, and her experience with Omicron's culture, she helped cultivate her husband into the shrewd, quick-thinking executive he needed to be in order to survive in pure Corporate America.

It didn't take Ravinia long after marrying Xavier to realize she really didn't have to work. For once in her twenty years of working and going to school, she didn't have to work out of financial necessity. So she quit. Moving to Highland Park from Evanston was quite a culture shock for her. She couldn't get a decent catfish dinner in Highland Park, let alone a bottle of Louisiana hot sauce. But what Highland Park did afford her was the luxury of living the life of a queen, and a chance to start her life all over again without the worry of money or bills. She didn't count on it not making her happy. When her mother worked for the Weiss's, they lived in a huge house only a few blocks away from where Ravinia now lived. She knew the neighborhood well, and as a child she always dreamed of living in a big house on the North Shore. Her dreams had finally come true.

After living thirty years of her life with finances as her biggest issue and debt her greatest companion, Ravinia didn't count on how quickly another issue would move into its place. Xavier's dress and mannerisms were always very elegant, even regal. But this new lifestyle was alien to her. She had seen mostly white folks act the way that Xavier now acted. She assumed that the airs came with the money. She was experiencing what it felt like to make more in one year than some people made in a lifetime; but, of course, it wasn't a dream world. When Ravinia decided to marry Xavier, she also made a commitment to be a good steward of what God blessed them with, so she became the household manager. She put her project and people management skills to work in running Hamilton Manor. Just because they had money didn't mean that they had to squander it. She still negotiated bulk purchases on household items and furnishings, setting up the house as a business account and negotiating purchase prices with head buyers of their favorite stores. Xavier appreciated none of this; not her quarterly savings of household expenses which she documented and debriefed him on. Not the fact that his shirts were always starched, his closet always organized, or his bags always travel-ready. Not even that she, herself, was picturesque and perfect, a willing dinner hostess and lover when he returned from his busy days at the office. Xavier may have had the money of a prince, but he was far from being Prince Charming.

He seemed to be very polite when they met her mother, but Ravinia knew he expected better. Katie Mae, though, was very proud of her new son-in-law and the honor it brought her and her family. She could now talk about Ravinia to her church friends without holding her head down in shame. In fact, Xavier was such a star in her mother's eyes; he could almost do no wrong. This made things difficult for Ravinia. She walked a tightrope to keep her marriage balancing. So much depended on its success. She had finally seemed to redeem herself in her mother's eyes by marrying Xavier.

Without money issues, other gaps and holes began to form in her and Xavier's relationship. Xavier wanted to control Ravinia, something Ravinia was not used to. He wanted her to wear what he thought she should wear, and would get downright angry when she would leave the house without the clothes he had picked out for her. He was overly concerned about her appearance, and with whom she kept company, including her girlfriends from high school and college, saying they were too "ghetto." Soon enough, Ravinia was becoming someone she didn't like. She no longer personified her upbringing, her experiences, or her essence. Something had to be done, but Ravinia was at a loss. If there was something she could not live without, it was her afrocentricity. But in her quest to stay "ever Black," she did find that money could provide her many of the things that she had gone without for so long.

Macy's and Bloomingdale's soon replaced Marshall's and T.J. Maxx. Every other week someone came into her home and provided manicure and pedicure services. The maid service took care of the things she chose not to do around the house, like cleaning the bathrooms, dusting, and other odd jobs she could afford to have someone else manage for her. She, however, did all the meal planning and the cooking; only occasionally getting assistance with prepping. Her mother taught her at a very young age that there was no room in the kitchen for two cooks. Cooking was personal. She added that if you wanted to keep your man, never let another woman cook his food. Ravinia held on to that old-fashioned wisdom like they were pearls of truth.

The one thing that was truly innate for Ravinia was cooking soul food. Xavier secretly loved her down home dishes. Though he would perpetrate annoyance when he saw that she was making a pot of turnip and mustard greens or red beans and rice, some nights she would catch him sneaking in the fridge for a piece of fried chicken so flavorful he'd just eat it cold. Everyone in the neighborhood could smell Ravinia's delectable dishes, but were too polite to stop by and ask for a taste.

Ravinia had to travel down to the heart of Evanston to find some smoked turkey legs, but it was more than worth the twenty-minute trip down Green Bay and Sheridan Road to Howard Street. Besides, it gave her time to stop and see her mother along the way. Xavier didn't admit it, but he liked her cooking because like any other red-blooded male, down home comfort food was the key to his heart. It also did wonders in linking him back into his displaced culture. He did insist on one restriction, however. She could never bring, cook or eat chitterlings in his house. To this, Ravinia agreed. That was a delicacy she too, could live without. Besides, if for some odd reason she ever craved some, she didn't have to go very far to get a mason jar full.

Ravinia hoped that she'd one day fall in love with Xavier. But, she knew deep down that their marriage was not built on love and trust. It was a business deal, an arrangement; at least for her. For Xavier, it was also a means to an end; he needed to create his identity and dispel any rumors that he was a sell-out or an Oreo. In a short time, the nights got long and boring. Ravinia grew tired of being an upgraded housewife with nothing to do. Trying to blend into her community, she filled her days with clubs and philanthropic events to keep her mind busy. But even after joining a North Shore book club through the country club, she found that most of the books "they" read didn't speak to her heart. She wanted to read books by "her" people, but they just were not ready for her. At times, they squashed all of her suggestions of Toni Morrison, Maya Angelou or Zora Neale Hurston, though timeless classics. Ravinia felt alienated in all she *thought* she desired in life. Truth be told, greener the grass, somehow Ravinia began to appreciate that back then, she was just glad they had grass, no matter how brown and dry it was. She was profoundly repressed and tried hard to remember the time she was so poor that she had to make hamburger helper without any meat for the twins and Markus. Exploring her own thoughts and trying to feel the grit of that age past reality, she felt her face smile, realizing that the warm memories of her destitute days made her strangely happy.

In her attempt to refine Ravinia, Katie Mae resolved that Ravinia would always be a little rough around the edges. Learning to play the violin from Mrs. Weiss, Ravinia became a rebel in learning the strings. Always treating her borrowed instrument and bow like it was a toy purchased from a second hand store; she never truly realized the value of her innate talent to play the strings. Making first chair in her freshman year of high school, Ravinia didn't understand that the music she would play would someday release the freedom she sought in her own spirit.

As she threw her purse and coat down on the couch in the living room and walked up the stairs to their room, Ravinia embraced the long-ago feeling that playing an instrument could bring her. Her mind was still in a whirlwind since leaving the El train and making her way home. Each step felt like a five-pound weight on her feet. Trudging down the narrow hall, she stopped in front of her linen closet. Stepping on a tiny wooden step stool that her children had used to wash their hands at the bathroom sink, she reached up into the panel that covered her attic. On tiptoe, she moved the panel to the side and fumbled around for the old case. It took a couple of tries, but she finally felt the leather box and grabbed hold of it to pull it down.

Covered in cobwebs, Ravinia wiped away the layers of dust that had collected over the years. The old case had been carried over to the states from Jewish immigrants from Holland. Before the Weiss's left for Florida to retire, Mrs. Weiss gave Ravinia her Stradivarius violin. It had been brought over by Mr. Weiss's grandmother from Holland as they escaped from the Nazis. The historical significance of this particular violin was more than precious. Ravinia always wanted one of her own, but could never afford to buy one.

Taking the case to her bedroom, she laid it on the chaise lounge and unsnapped it to reveal the gorgeous mahogany instrument. The horsehairs of the bow were still intact and glistened slightly in the dimmed light of her room. Taking out her rosin that was beginning to crack along the sides of its wood encasing, she stroked the length of the bow until the hairs were slightly tacky and powdered. Then, Ravinia carefully took the fine instrument out of its case and lifted it to her nose. As she inhaled its scent, she daydreamed of how many fine musicians must have played it, perhaps before royalty, perhaps before Hitler. The history of the instrument was unknown, but the sound that it would make would be divine.

Ravinia cupped the neck rest, seating it firmly under her chin, and pulled the neck of the violin into position. She found it to be a bit uncomfortable as her arm was not used to being in that position, but she knew that was the only way to get the proper sound. Lifting the bow, she gently stroked the strings and began to play *Canon* in D major. The richness of the lower notes she played was deep and soothing. Ravinia lost herself in the full intonation of her strings and found herself pouring out her heart into its rendering. Years upon years had passed since she had last picked up a violin, but nonetheless the ability to play was still inside of her.

The sharp taut strings hurt her pampered, petite fingers, but she did not mind the pain and embraced the calluses that would come tomorrow. Tonight she would soar, tempting fate to release her from her sorrow. Her fingers ached as they lacked the nimbleness of her youth, but she continued to play from deep within herself, releasing her anguish into the strings, and that made a world of difference in the resonating sound. The beauty that came from the music she played was bittersweet. The injustice of life's challenges found themselves bantering in liquid echoes that bounced off the walls of her bedroom. She knew that in order to bring forth such exquisite, tempestuous reverberation, she had to endure the sorrow. Falling into *Minuet* by J.S. Bach, she found that the intensity of the song became eminent as she poured her heart and soul into every stroke from memory. Over the years, since the last time she had played, she would finger the sequence of it in her head, keeping the melody alive in her heart. But now, her bow trembled as she maintained a steady stroke, as the lack of sufficient curve in the fingerboard caused the middle notes in the range to fade slightly. However, the minor notes were full and dramatic, causing a surge of passion to flow out of her and into her careful strokes. Finally, she came to the end of the last measure and stopped. With a deeply cleansing breath, she knew there was nothing she could do but cry. And cry she did.

Chapter 21

KATIE MAE

As she heard the blaring sound of the Metra train whistle blowing down the street from her house, Ravinia had a vision of her mother. It was due time for a visit. Toying with the decision to trek down to Evanston, Ravinia began to feel the guilt that was disrupting her thought pattern. It had been weeks since she saw Xavier on the El platform and she still wondered how she would confront him. Yet, the shuddering conviction she had just thinking about her mother consumed her. Just the idea of her could do that. Katie Mae Brown, born Katie Mae McGhee, grew up in Monroe, Louisiana. Katie Mae pronounced it Looz'anna. Monroe was a small southern town just south of the Black Bayou Lake. Raised by her grandmother, Katie Mae suffered a hard, abusive childhood. Facing physical and emotional hardships over and above simple chastisement and plain old down home "whippings," the Creole matriarch knew the meaning of a "hard knock life."

Katie Mae by far was *not* the favorite child. She was *not* the child born from love but hate, and so was scorned countless times. Relatives would recount for her the various times she was beaten and left to die when she was as a child. She had to be told because she was beat to the point of unconsciousness, and to remember would cause her seizures. Katie Mae didn't think it odd to be beat that brutally because that was just the way things were back then. In fact, her near death beatings were customary. No one said or did anything, because it just wasn't their place. You just didn't go around telling other grown folk how to run their household; it just wasn't done. If it had not been for the grace of God, Katie would have been dead, sleeping in a child-size grave. However, God blessed and watched over her in her fragile innocence and shielded her from total destruction.

Katie Mae was the product of a horrible crime. Her mother, Bessie, could not separate her vindictive feelings for Katie's paternal donor from the maternal instinct she had for her daughter. Bessie could see the remnant of the white rapist in her daughter's smiling, hazy eyes. When Katie laughed, she bitterly scolded her for the reminder. Bessie could smell his scent in the character of Katie Mae's more-straight-than-kinky, ash blonde hair, when she held a toddling Katie Mae in her arms. So startled by the mere memory of the ill-gotten conception, Bessie dropped Katie Mae on several occasions as a baby. Life was a constant uncertainty for the unwanted ruddy-brown girl from Monroe; yet she emerged. Katie Mae could never remember a time when she was big enough, or Black enough or even smart enough. She constantly lived in the shadow of her brother and sister, who were favorites by design, and treaded aimlessly in their preferred status.

After barely surviving a severe beating with a horse whip for sampling the cream that had risen to the top of a bucket of buttermilk, Katie Mae decided that when she was grown up, she would move up to the North. At the age of 17, she graduated high school. Using the money she had saved from sewing dresses for the ladies at church, she bought a one-way bus ticket to Chicago. Packing a pail lunch of fried chicken necks and backs, two biscuits and a peach, she ran off to find a better life.

Katie didn't have what they called "street smarts." But once she got to Chicago, she did the best she could with what she had. She was a fair child and her lighter skin was always good for a loaf of bread or a free meal at the diner on Western Avenue. Her wide, innocent smile won her many prizes, and she soon figured out that if she grinned at the right time or at the right person, she could get whatever she wanted, within reason of course. Doing various odd jobs just to make it through, she continually found herself helpless and near broke in the big city. Things moved at a much faster pace here. She couldn't just go over to a field or a tree and pick fresh fruit and vegetables any time she wanted. Everything had to be bought at a grocery store and Katie just wasn't used to needing to have money all the time. She needed guidance and sought it from a nearby church on the West Side of Chicago. She was living in a studio apartment near Madison Street when she met a good-looking, blue-collar gentleman by the name of Grady Hansford Brown.

Grady Brown knew what he liked. He saw Katie Mae attending church and knew she wasn't accustomed to the city life. Coming from Mississippi just a couple of years before himself, he was drawn to the gentle reminder that she gave him of the South. He always said, "Dem Looz'ana women sho'll do know how to cook." And he was right. Katie Mae could fix up some buttermilk biscuits and gravy that would make a grown man holler. Wondering from a distance whether or not she was Creole, he admired the ripples of her sandy, almost Georgia clay-red hair when she pinned it up and the way her round near-gray hazel eyes softened her face. Her voluptuous figure defied her modest wardrobe, appearing instead like she had been melted and poured into her clothing.

Katie Mae found Grady to be a little rough around the edges, but he definitely knew his way around Chicago. She also found herself attracted to that dangerous part of him. It made her feel safe in this now big, unfamiliar place. Even more, his smile, wide as the Mississippi River and matching southern drawl, reminded her too, of home. Grady drove a taxi at night, and that was his mode of transportation. He made an honest living working by day at the Fannie Mae factory. On their first date, he brought Katie Mae a large box of pixies. He didn't know pecans were her favorite and she had never had that much chocolate to herself in her life. The man was spoiling her and she secretly hoped it would never stop. If Grady had his way, it wouldn't. He laughed heartily as he bid her goodnight, while she stood doubled over from eating too many pixies.

Their courtship lasted about a year. Grady was anxious to make Katie Mae his wife because she had old-fashioned morals and was going to make him wait until they got married to have relations. It was a good thing that Grady was determined to have Katie Mae, because there were other suitors who were waiting for Grady to mess up so that they would have a chance at the Creole princess. But Katie was sweet on Grady. He was a good, hardworking, church-going man with down home values. She knew that the way to his heart was through her good cooking, and in return for her mouth-watering dishes, he spoiled her with his love.

Finally, Katie Mae had someone who loved her and would take care of her. She didn't mind that he would start fussing when she was late coming out from work. She just chalked it up to his good upbringing.

Grady couldn't stand being late; even if he didn't have anywhere in particular to be. He said it told a lot about a person's character when they were habitually late. "Undependable, that's what they are," he'd grumble. But Katie Mae loved him all the same. She didn't know many men, but all the ones she knew thought and acted the same way: overbearing and bossy, thinking that the woman needed to stay in the kitchen and to have babies. Katie Mae didn't try to change Grady and he liked that she had some independence about her. Besides being determined not to take any mess off of anybody after she got from under her grandmother, she also knew that trying to change Grady wouldn't do any good. They decided to get married.

The first thing Grady demanded was that Katie Mae quit her job at the factory. He said it wasn't women's work, messing with all that heavy equipment. At first Katie Mae looked at him like he was out of his mind. Then she looked a little closer. He wasn't much different from all the other men after all. She braced herself. Soon after they said their vows, things started happening fast. Katie Mae got pregnant right away. Grady worked extra hours at the candy factory to make extra income, but it wasn't enough. Katie Mae found it difficult to scrape enough money together to keep food on the table. In her constant worry that ends would not meet, she lost the baby. Grady blamed himself because he was rarely at home. He was so tired from doing extra shifts with the taxicab; the supervisor at the candy factory caught him sleeping and fired him on the spot. Grady was extremely upset by this, but too tired to complain. He went home feeling beaten down and worn out. He felt like he couldn't get ahead. Katie Mae had overheard some women at the church talking about how they cleaned homes of white women in the suburbs and how the work paid well. Katie Mae came out of her eavesdropping posture to inquire about the lead. The women were more than helpful. It turned out that one housekeeper was fired the previous week. Katie Mae took down the employer's information and stuffed it deep down in her pocketbook.

Katie Mae knew that Grady would probably not approve of her working again, but she also knew that he wanted children badly. With bills piling up from his loss of income and her housewife status, she knew that working was the best way – the only way that they would ever be able to start a family. She asked Grady timidly about getting a job in the suburbs, while he sopped up Alaga syrup and butter with her melt-in-your mouth buttermilk biscuits. "Just for a little while, cleaning houses until you get back on your feet," she persuaded. "No," he stated flat out. "No wife of mine is gon' be cleaning houses less it's mine." But as time went on, he saw that companies were not hiring Black men as readily, and the unemployment lines were growing by the mile. He finally gave in and told Katie Mae if she could find a job, she could work, but she had to make sure nothing suffered at home. That meant she still had to do all the housework, cooking, cleaning, even if he didn't work.

Katie Mae knew that she could live up to his expectations, so she started searching for work. She came across an ad in the Sun-Times daily newspaper. It was a housekeeping job for a wealthy family in Highland Park. She looked at it and thought it would be just too far from home to go way out to the Northern Suburbs. She and Grady lived on the West Side of Chicago. That would mean taking two buses and two trains to get there. Katie Mae felt like it was an impossible task. Continuing her search through the want ads, there were no other positions that she qualified for in the listing. She decided to call about the housekeeping position. She dialed the number and spoke to the lady of the house, Mrs. Judy Weiss. They were so desperate for a housekeeper; she offered to pick Katie Mae up from the Linden Street train station, just to meet her. Katie Mae had a good feeling about the position and agreed to come visit the next day. She didn't tell Grady how far away the job was, because she knew he would immediately say no again.

The Weiss's turned out to be fairly wealthy people who needed an extra hand around the house. They were very involved in their community and often entertained in their home. Offering Katie Mae a very generous salary of $10 an hour and picking her up every day from the train station, Katie Mae eagerly accepted the job.

It wasn't long before the money started pouring in and Katie Mae got pregnant again. Grady was concerned that she wouldn't be able to keep up. He knew that she was strong and a hard worker; but after losing the first baby, he didn't want her taking too many risks. But the Weiss's liked Katie Mae so much, that they made sure she didn't have to work too hard by giving her the simpler, less strenuous tasks. They also gave her days off with pay, taking great care to ensure her return after the baby was born. After nine months, Katie gave birth to a precious baby girl, whom she named, Ravinia.

Chapter 22.

THE LAST JOURNEY

The weight of the heavy guilt trip her mother was sure to lay on her kept Ravinia from going to Evanston. Katie Mae had a way of seeing right to the core of Ravinia. She had a divine gift of premonition that church going folks recognized as being prophetic. Katie Mae would know things before they even happened; and if Ravinia was up to some devilment she would call it out before Ravinia could even devise a plan in her head. The young daughter learned early that she could keep nothing from her mother so when she started down the path of promiscuity, she knew she had better stay away from her all-seeing mother as much as she could to avoid the preaching and revelations that would come once Katie Mae got wind of it. If Ravinia would even think about not completing a chore or errand for her mother, Katie Mae would say, "That's okay. You gon' learn." Ravinia would cringe when she heard this because sure enough, that same day or the next, not long after those words were spoken that scaled her fate, some terrible thing would set itself in motion: a failed grade on a test, a flat tire on her bike, an unexpectant fall. Something shameful or otherwise tragic, just short of death, would befall Ravinia and she knew her mother had to be in the middle of it all.

So, she learned to simply never say 'no' to Katie Mae. God-fearing mothers always seem to know things, and Katie Mae would call and leave fire and brimstone messages on Ravinia's answering machine, warning her to amend her ways or she was going straight "to hell in a hand basket." Ravinia was always taught not to "buck" authority, less risking a swift backhand to the mouth. She would listen to Katie Mae's lectures that echoed, "Hell has enlarged itself for devils like you Vinia. You know you ain't right. You was raised in tha' church! Actin' like you ain't got no sense. If you don't watch it, you gon' split hell wide open. Get right with God, girl. Get right! It's time out for playin' church!"

Then she would start rebuking the whorish spirit trapped inside Ravinia's soul right over the phone until the answering machine tape ran out. Ravinia felt defeated in her relationship with her mother. Katie Mae had this "holier than thou" attitude that Ravinia knew in her spirit that was just not right. She wanted a mother-daughter relationship that was free from judgment and the constant need for validation. Nothing Ravinia ever did was good enough for Katie Mae. Even when she started going to church, her mother criticized her choice, saying that it wasn't the "right" church. Ravinia just could not understand how to receive her mother's unconditional love, and eventually, she decided that she would not waste her life away waiting for it. After all, there was the possibility that her mother was right; maybe she was just a tramp and needed deliverance.

Realizing that it might be better to just call her mother instead of seeing her face to face, she reasoned that any prospective confrontation could be disrupted more quickly over the phone. At times, Ravinia actually believed what her mother would say about her, and that made it difficult to understand why she loved her mother so dearly. It was obvious that Katie Mae did not always deserve or earn Ravinia's unconditional love. Ravinia fought the penetrating, convicting voice in her head that said, *you know, you really need to go see your Momma.* As if a hand had gently pushed her off the bed, Ravinia got up and picked up the phone to dial her mother's number. Her heart started racing and pounding so loudly in her chest that she started to hear thumping in the phone's receiver. No answer.

Feeling her heart rise up into her throat, she swallowed hard. Worry and guilt set themselves squarely, heavily, on her chest and her breathing became labored. She somehow felt responsible for something beyond her reach or control. Ravinia ran and grabbed her cell phone off the green marble kitchen counter and started dialing and redialing her mother's number. Running out the door to the Mercedes, she fumbled to get the key out of her purse and into the ignition slot. She scraped the side of the slot, not being careful in her haste.

Thoughts of doom and death began to crowd her mind. *You should have gone to see her before now. What if something happened to her? You are always so concerned about your own feelings and how she's gonna make you feel. That's not right. You know she's just telling you the truth. You're all she's got, except Nate, and you know he's taking everything she's got.* Ravinia scolded herself. She couldn't stand her own selfishness. Tears started flowing down the apples of her cheeks, streaking her NW600 MAC foundation. Something was terribly wrong and she felt it deeply within her belly. Trying to dismiss the negative thoughts and focus on the positive, the pervasive feelings of dread and uncertainty kept creeping around her. Slamming on the gas pedal, Ravinia drove quickly, barely remembering backing out of the driveway or heading south on Sheridan Road. She sped through Wilmette, thanking God that today wasn't a "racial profiling" day for affluent African-Americans of the North Shore. She cleared the business district in less than three minutes. Not one light or cop had stopped her; not even a bend or twist in the road had intimidated her to cover the brake. The stoplight at Central and Ridge roads was even green. That was a first for Ravinia.

She kept driving until she reached the southbound intersection of Ridge and Dempster in Evanston. Making a sharp right turn onto Dempster, she kept driving until she got to Dodge Street. She parked the car in front of the house. Literally running out of the car, Ravinia didn't notice the tear in her pantyhose from scraping it on the screen door. Knocking on the door, she prayed she would hear her mother shifting down the stairs in her fluffy house shoes, the ones Ravinia had bought her for Christmas, and see her pulling the curtains back just enough to peek through to see who had come calling, saying, "Ain't you got yo' key, Vinia?"

There was no answer. Ravinia's heart sunk even deeper and she could feel her saliva turn thick and mucousy, collecting at the back of her tonsils. She felt like she would vomit. As she thought the worst, she fumbled with her keys trying to find the one to the front door. Finally catching a glimpse of the pale, coppery key her mother had made at the hardware store for her, she wiped away the blinding tears. Ravinia had cried the entire distance from Highland Park to Evanston, and now she felt a stinging in her tear ducts that made her irritated and distraught. They were clogged from the collection of foundation and mascara that was streaked-in by her bare hands. The thin, delicate skin around her bottom lids was now cracked from the dried saline of her tears. They ached from the constant wiping and tugging that she had endured.

As she stepped into the house, a feeling of nostalgia came over her. She quickly dismissed the feeling to focus on locating her mother, starting first toward the living room. The room was neatly vacuumed, with the TV guide sitting on the French provincial antique gold and green furniture arranged like a showroom. Momma's hand-crocheted, off-white doilies were all perfectly aligned on the coffee table and on the walnut hi-fi console. A slight film of dust had collected on top, and that made Ravinia worry. The record player didn't work, but the radio did somehow. Momma said that she had worked a long time to get it out of layaway from Polk Bros. on North Avenue. It was her first stereo, and for sentimental reasons she said she would never get rid of it. Heading towards the kitchen, Ravinia called out, "Momma—you here?" The wary daughter suspected that something was not right, though she could find no evidence of such. She was afraid to think or speak ill will of her mother. Momma's house was sanctified, if you didn't count the basement. That's where Nate lived. Katie Mae kept prayer going in every room and would sprinkle blessed extra virgin olive oil as an added measure. When the pastor of Momma's church had gone to the Holy Land, he had brought back myrrh scented blessed oil and given all the members vials to keep with them, for anointing purposes. Ever since that the day, the home always carried that smell. But this time, there was a strange smell lurking around that Ravinia had never noticed before in the house. Momma's house never smelled foul, unless she was cooking chitterlings, but that wasn't the smell either.

Not finding Momma on the first floor, she bounded up the stairs to her bedroom. Passing her old bedroom, Ravinia glanced in and saw the unthinkable. There Momma lay with her Bible open to Revelations and her reading glasses propped up on the bridge of her Cherokee nose. She looked so peaceful, as if she were in mere sleep. But she was entirely too peaceful. Ravinia knew her mother was dead. Her intuition had told her so as she drove the journey to Evanston from Highland Park in 15 minutes, flat. She wanted to cry, but had lost so many tears to the cool March lakefront breeze on the drive, that her face hurt. The seasons hadn't even fully changed yet, and Momma was gone into the chill of the dawning spring.

Ravinia just looked at her, lying there. The unusual smell of death didn't seem to bother her. As Ravinia sat on the bed, she listened to the voice in her head. Her conscience always sounded like her mother. *"Chile, why you always running that ole tired man down?"* Ravinia continued to listen in her spirit as the familiar voice said, *"That man don't want you, and frankly he ain't worth the salt it take to season his food."* Ravinia almost chuckled. If she didn't know any better, she would have thought her mother was in the room with her. Yeah that was her Momma, all right. The voice in her spirit-man explained, *"Men like him play the game. They prey upon yo' insecurity. They are like foxes that lay wait for someone when they vulnerable and then they lurk in and attack. Bible say it's the little foxes that destroy the vine."*

Ravinia looked around. Momma had not moved. She wondered if this was what her mother would have said to her had she called her yesterday. Ravinia tried desperately to keep her mind silent as she continued to look around. She wanted to see her mother's eyes and look into them one last time. As she was being counseled in the spirit, she looked over at the nightstand and saw a picture of her and her mother on the porch of their house the day they moved in. Momma stood with her right hip on the railing with Ravinia facing her as her arm fastened tightly around her waist. Momma's dress was a traditional button up light blue shirtwaist dress with a slim, fabric covered belt. Ravinia had on a sleeveless pink and white-checkered dress with white fancy socks and black patent leather shoes. Nate was sitting on the steps in his pleated navy-blue short pants and a yellow button up short-sleeved shirt. You could see the scabs on his rusty little knees where he had skinned them up. His buzz cut was so close around the edges, that you could see the sun reflecting off of his scalp. They were on their way to church, and Mr. Weiss had stopped by to bring them to their new home.

She saw joy hidden in her mother's eyes in the picture on the bedside table, so Ravinia set her own eyes upon them to receive more instruction out of respect for the dead. Her mother's eyes were serious, but loving. Ravinia felt like an ill tempered, hardheaded little girl again, except she felt like she had just gotten a whipping. She knew she was a grown woman and that her life was her own choice. But her mother could still influence her, even in death. The motherless child shuddered like a three-year old orphan, feeling just as lonely and afraid. The reality of her mother's death came and went during her discovery. Ravinia could have walked away, but she needed to hear the truth. Something in her wanted to do the right thing. She warred with her convictions, yet again.

Ravinia's mother was the only one who could get through to her, because her mother knew her better than she knew herself. Being the "fast" one, Ravinia's mother always kept an eye on her. Katie Mae knew her daughter and what she was capable of. She must have seen something in her when she was very young to make her know that her baby was vulnerable and insecure. She must have known that she carried a trait that would make her want to seek redemption in every man wearing britches on the South Side of Chicago. But, she never gave up on her, although her strict preaching seemed to fall on deaf ears at times. Ravinia's mother didn't know that Ravinia absorbed every word and that those words of truth kept her from making even more mistakes than she already had. What would she do now that she was gone? Who would protect her from herself? Who would remind her of her worth? Who would cry out for her soul in the wee hours of the night, praying that she would come to Jesus and understand that she didn't need a man to define her, refine her, or re-design her? Who would tell her that she was all right all by herself, that all she needed was to look up and receive the only love that could fill the emptiness carved out by so many unholy conquests. Who would love Ravinia like no man ever could, and like only a mother should? Who would?

Ravinia sat silently, arms clutched as she held herself in the stillness of the cold church. It was so quiet and peaceful as she gazed at the stained glass Stations of the Cross on the arched windowpanes. The little Pentecostal church had once been a Catholic church. The pastor loved the colored glass so much that he refused to have it removed when they moved in. Sitting on the second pew from the front, Ravinia leaned over the pew in front of her, clasped her hands together, and hung her heavy head between her bent elbows, giving in to the solitude of the sanctuary and the emptiness of her loss. If she had of spoken, there would have been an echo. Weeping, they say endures for a night, but for Ravinia, it felt like she had been crying her heart out for weeks. This was her mother's church, and just being in the sanctuary endowed her with an overwhelming sense of serenity before God. Coming here brought back glorious memories of church folk "having church" and "shouting" in the aisles. Ravinia loved to see her mother shout and dance, because she always seemed so free when she was at church. No matter how bad the previous week had been, just getting to church for Momma seemed to lift the heavy burdens of life right off her back. Working all her life, Ravinia's mother never took time for herself. But when she was at church, it was a whole different world, full of people who were like family. Katie Mae would smile when she danced in the spirit, looking up to the heavens like she could see the angels. You could tell she longed to go to the place that they called "Holy." She would spin around and dance jubilantly. That was her life. She would say that she looked forward to every Sunday, because she lived right every day of the week.

Momma's funeral was scheduled for tomorrow, but Ravinia needed to find peace within herself before the service. She looked up at the blonde wooden cross with a crown of thorns lain over the center beam. It hung on the wall above the baptismal pool and the choir stand. She cried out to God to bring her peace and comfort. In the indignation she felt from her mother, Ravinia knew that she depended on her mother to keep her going. She pierced the silence and cried aloud and fiercely, with all she had within her. Ravinia's deep hoarse voice trumpeted as she begged God to give her one more chance. She told God that she needed Him because He was all she had now. Then she walked out from the pew and started down the aisle toward the pulpit. She sprawled out on the floor in front of the altar, prostrate before God. Exposing all of her past, the lies she had covered up, the holy vows she hadn't kept, Ravinia confessed it all, laying it to rest on the altar, giving it all to God and releasing the weight of her yoke from her bent neck and burdened shoulders. She prayed in her spirit that God would have mercy on her and forgive her a lifetime of sins.

As if an answered prayer, Ravinia awoke from her meditation. An old woman cleaning the pews stood over her praying. Smiling at Ravinia, the old woman dressed in a traditional 1960's white nursing uniform, said to her, "Chile, Jesus heard you." Waving towards heaven with her hands lifted up, the little woman uttered softly, "Oh, thank you, Jesus," shaking her salt and pepper head in sacred satisfaction.

"He did?" Ravinia said in amazement, tears blinding her gaze. She looked up at the woman who had a saintly glow on her face. There was something very unusual about her flawless complexion. It was as if she was in a spotlight, but there weren't any lights on in the building except the ones that stayed on by the altar.

The elderly lady smiled, and said, "Oh yes, chile. He heard you, even when you couldn't say a word. Didn't you know you were the apple of His eye?" Ravinia stared in disbelief. For a minute, she wondered how much of her open confessions this woman had witnessed. But Ravinia really didn't care. Her mother was gone and she needed to know that she would be okay. The sweet, old lady leaned in as Ravinia crawled over to the pew from the base of the altar. "Chile, all you need to do is believe that God is."

"God is." That was so simple. "God is." She repeated those two little words over and over again. The little old woman hugged Ravinia and went on humming, an old familiar tune, "The Lord will make a way somehow." She disappeared from Ravinia's vision to finish dusting the pews somewhere in the back of the church. Ravinia knew the melody because that was the song her mother always sang when she was cleaning or doing housework. Ravinia looked around and the woman was gone. But the song wasn't. Its soul-stirring melody rang and sung over and over again in her pain-stricken heart. She felt a sense of peace that she hadn't felt since she was a little girl growing up in the church. She knew now that she could go on; and that although she was devastated by her mother's death, someday time would heal her from the sting.

Chapter 23.

THE REPAST

Nate stumbled in the front door of Momma's house. His eyes were bloodshot and crazed. He looked around at all the people that had come to mourn and grieve with his family and just brushed past them nonchalantly, yelling and calling out for his sister without regard to or respect for the day's events.

"Vinia? Vinia?" Nate shouted, running up the creaky old stairs to their former childhood rooms. A couple of people called after him, trying to tell him that she was out back talking to her husband, but he didn't listen. The sound of doors slamming and furniture falling onto the floor echoed through the floorboards on the second floor of the 85 year old house.

"Vinia! I know you're here," his voice preceded him and floated down the stairs in front of him. Sister Tate, one of Momma's closest friends, tried to slow him down before he hurt himself or bumped into one of the guests. She grabbed one of his shoulders and tried to turn him around saying, "Nate, child, Ravinia is outside on the porch with Xavier. Is there something I . . ." Nate pushed Sister Tate aside and trudged past her in a fit of rage. Bumping into the edge of one of the coffee tables situated by the entrance to the kitchen, Nate briskly bounded through the kitchen, stepping down to the porch. In two long strides, he cleared the porch and made his way out the screen door and skipped down the stairs. He spotted Ravinia and Xavier talking by the birdbath and walked briskly over to them.

"Hey, Xavier--Vinia, I need to talk to you," Nate insisted, with a slow storm brewing beneath his voice. His eyes kept shifting back and forth between his sister and brother-in-law, and this made Ravinia nervous.

"Yeah, okay, Nate. What's up?" Ravinia responded, crossing her arms in front of her defensively. Nate anxiously looked at Xavier, who didn't seem to catch the subtle hint to give his sister and him some privacy. Ravinia looked at Xavier and motioned her okay for him to depart. Xavier acknowledged her and went about his way, walking along the trail of cars parked in the driveway and then disappeared around the front of the house.

"So, what's going on, Nate? You look like who did it and what for," Ravinia kidded in her dry sentiment. She still felt strongly about how Momma spoiled Nate so rotten that he could barely stand on his own two feet without her. She could see how helpless he looked without Momma, but knew he had to start being a man--his own man.

"Did you close Momma's account?" Nate questioned demandingly.

"Did I what? Close her account?" Ravinia repeated, playing dumb.

"You heard what I said," he responded accusatorily. "*Did* you close her account at the bank?" Nate restated, this time with a grunt.

"Uh, why do *you* want to know?" Ravinia asked, stressing the 'you' as if their mother's financial affairs were of no concern of his. She had a quizzical look on her face. He was up to something; she just couldn't put her finger on what it was.

"Ravinia, never mind *why* I want to know. Did you or didn't you?" Nate demanded from her, getting more and more enraged. He squared himself in front of her, grabbed her by the shoulder, and began to shake her.

Ravinia, being the older of the two, was playing the big sister card. Standing her ground, she firmly planted her feet in the grass and shook him off of her. She knew that he was getting ticked off. She also knew that he must have had the password or an ATM card. This bothered her because she had actually closed the account in order to help pay off some of Momma's bills and to offset the cost of the funeral.

"Nate, you were taking her money, weren't you?" Ravinia accused. She hated the fact that he was the favorite and that Momma had always overlooked his faults, even when they were detrimental to her *and* his well-being.

"Ravinia, for your information, Momma *gave* me a card so when I needed cash, I could get some. I wasn't *taking* her money. Why you always making me out to be a thug or something. I have a job," Nate said defensively, contesting her blatant accusations.

"Uh huh. Nate, you were tapping Momma for all she was worth, weren't you? And she loved you so much; she just let you do it. Well, somebody had to have some sense around here with all these bills she left. I paid off all the bills and used the rest for her funeral. How did you think she was going to be buried?

"I know you didn't just say you spent all her money. I know you didn't just say that," Nate continued, first looking at the ground and then around the yard in disbelief.

"I didn't stutter, did I?" Ravinia said, standing up to her younger, but much taller and stronger brother.

"I can't believe this. You and Xavier got all that money, living up in Highland Park, and you take the *last* of Momma's money. Why you always got to control things?" he said, pointing his finger down into Ravinia's face. "Momma was right about you. I would try and defend you to her, but now I know she was right," poked Nate, in an attempt to get Ravinia to break.

Ravinia looked at Nate and narrowed her fiery eyes. She wasn't having it today. "Listen, I am sick and tired of your sorry butt. Don't *think* you gonna come and start leaching off me and Xavier 'cause we ain't giving you any handouts. You need to start standing on your own two feet and be a man. Momma should have *never* let you back in the house."

Nate, so angered by his big sister's preaching, clinched his fists. Whatever he needed money so desperately for today would have to take a backseat, because there just wasn't any. He turned around so fast his wind hit Ravinia in the face. He walked down the same path Xavier did and stormed down the walkway until he got to his little blue Hyundai. He slammed the door and sped off, driving like a madman. His tires screeched as he peeled away from the curb.

Ravinia's crossed arms became chilled. She hadn't noticed how cold she was getting when she was talking to Nate. He had gotten her blood boiling and it masked her actual body temperature. Her head was pounding and she thought, *what else could go wrong?* The afternoon was almost over and the repast dinner had not yet been served.

Remembering the purpose of the day, she looked up in the sky as she climbed up the steps of the back porch. She could feel peeling paint underneath her fingers as she grasped the railing. It made her recall the summers she had spent painting and repainting the railings of the old, rickety porch. "Momma, did I do the right thing, this time?" she solicited the heavens. There was no answer. But deep inside, Ravinia received the confirmation she was seeking. She knew that she had.

Chapter 24.

MACARONI & CHEESE

"What are you doing here?" Ravinia sternly whispered under her breath, eyes glaring. Reverend Wright was making his way through the crowd, consoling the family at Momma's house. Ravinia felt his presence and was unnerved. She had not seen him since their last episode at the church, over 7 months ago and had not returned any of his calls. She was determined to make a clean break. She had decided she was going to start going to her mother's church when things calmed down. And here he was, smiling and acting all concerned. He was such a phony. Ravinia couldn't stand him. How could he step foot into her mother's holy house? The nerve of him!

"Ravinia, I haven't seen you in church lately and I was concerned," the mega pastor said in a sincere sounding voice. "I heard about your mother passing from one of the church mother's and figured you were having a difficult time coping with your tragic loss."

Motioning for him to move to a less conspicuous area of the house, Ravinia and the Reverend walked through the crowd of mourning family and friends to the back porch. Grabbing her mug of coffee off of the white, gold-speckled kitchen counter top, Ravinia reached the porch, turned and looked up at the solemn preacher and said in an exhausted voice, "Look. I haven't called you because I am tired of being used by you. My life has gone from bad to worse. You have taken the one thing I struggle with the most in my Christian walk and compounded it."

"Vinia, I really like you." The Reverend moved into Ravinia's space like he did every time they were alone. "I know we've done some things that were not right. I'll be the first to admit that. But, you've got to know that God forgives us when we do wrong."

"How can you stand here and say that? Yes, if there is something I do know, it is that my God is a forgiving and merciful God. But isn't there a change that we are supposed to make in our lives? There's got to be something that sets us apart and makes us different from unrepentant sinners and those who are just running around professing to be saved and not living as such? I mean, if we keep falling into the same temptations and do not overcome them by amending our ways, then are we really doing what God wants us to do? Even I know that being saved means more than merely going to church every Sunday and shouting around or dancing down the aisles. Aren't we supposed to at least try to do right the rest of the week? I've only been a Christian for what—a little over a year now, and I really wonder what I have done to make a difference in the way I live. There has got to be something more to this life than just living the same old way everyday."

"Yes, what you say is true. But when another's temptation is also your temptation, how do you counsel them when you struggle to overcome yourself? In all my years of being a minister, I've always struggled with that. I've prayed about it and asked God why I keep getting caught up in the same temptation. Honestly, I don't know the answer to that question," the Reverend expounded in desperation.

"Willie, you really have lost your way. You can't have me or any other woman that isn't rightfully yours. You must know that. What did you think, that I was going to divorce Xavier for you? You can't be serious," lowering her voice so her guests would not hear. Out of respect for her mother's house, Ravinia became aware that Katie Mae would never have approved of their interaction, and found it ironic that the Reverend and she were having this kind of conversation here of all places. Finding the strength she should have had in previous situations with him, Ravinia looked him squarely in the eye. Standing even shorter without the 3 inch heels she typically wore at church, she stood up to the towering preacher, took a deep, cleansing breath and said, "Look, it is over, Willie. I should have known when you first started looking at me cross-eyed on the very first day we met that something was wrong with you. Case and point, you need Jesus. You need to repent and start listening to what you preach about. You know, come to think of it, I don't think you ever preached about anything even close to infidelity in the year that I've been coming to First Baptist. Why is that?"

Unable to say anything, Reverend Wright just stood there, looking cut down with a silly smirk on his full face. He really didn't know what to say. It seemed like the women he pursued always ended up being wrong for him. Sapphire. Ravinia. But there was something about them that drew him. The ones who chased him down just didn't have it. Maybe it was the thrill of the chase, like in the case of Sapphire. Maybe it was the fact that he couldn't truly have Ravinia, so that way she kept him going. Whatever it was, it never served him well. Sadly, all this time, a good, noble woman, Mattie, was waiting for him to come running back to her. She was definitely guilty of chasing him down, but still, she was clearly worth slowing down for. He would have to settle down to consider Mattie's strengths later on. Being younger than both Sapphire and Ravinia, he was certain that his naïve soon-to-be preacher's wife didn't know about the rape. And if he had anything to do with it, she would never know, either.

Little did they know that Xavier had been listening to their conversation from inside the kitchen. Before they knew it, the porch door swung open and Xavier walked up on them, first glaring at the Reverend, then at his wife. His high forehead was beet red and his piercing sterling eyes began to redden as well from his boiling anger.

"I knew it! I knew something was going on between you two, but I just couldn't put my finger on it," Xavier said angrily shaking his head.

"Honey, I wanted to. . ." Ravinia tried to explain, thinking about the pictures she had downloaded off her phone of her husband and his imitation Barbie doll.

"Ravinia, I *knew* you were capable. I mean, all the signs were there. And mother warned me not to marry someone like you. I thought, I had given you more than enough to keep you busy." Xavier looked like he was putting all the pieces of their secret puzzle together right before their very eyes. "Huh, so this is why you always left the kids at your mother's when you went to church instead of taking them with you," Xavier pointed out, fitting the pieces together. That last comment stung Ravinia hard.

Reverend Wright started backing into the house, thinking that the troubled couple would be more interested in discussing the affair than dealing with his presence at the repast. He turned the knob on the screen door, when Xavier stepped in front of him.

Reverend *Wrong*, I'm not done with you," Xavier sternly said, looking up at the Reverend. He seemed proud for calling the pastor out of his name. It was obvious he had waited a long time to say that to his face. Xavier came up to the Reverend's shoulder, standing just about 5'11" with his shoes on. Ravinia noticed that Xavier was much better looking than the Reverend. She had never compared the two of them before, but standing together, she saw that what she had was a much more refined package.

"Well, this really isn't the time or the place," the Reverend replied in a deep, compromising voice.

"What? I know you didn't just try to patronize me. Look, I've known for some time that you've been making moves on my wife. You should really be ashamed of yourself, taking advantage of someone who really just came to you as a new member wanting a pastor to lead her. Instead, you saw another conquest. You saw, just another fine, but weak sistah to try to add to your collection. You knew that she was someone who could never be truly yours, but in all your assumed power, you still pulled at her. You didn't know her past. You didn't know her weakness. And from what I can tell, you didn't even try to know who she was. And if you did, or had any discernment, you didn't even act like you cared. How can you live with yourself?"

Ravinia was amazed that Xavier had paid so much attention to the commitment she made to God and her husband. She never thought she would hear anyone stand up for her like Xavier did. Apparently he really did understand that she was just trying to establish herself in a good church and to build on the vow she had made to God. Or maybe Xavier's sins were just as scarlet as hers and showing mercy would ease the pain on Ravinia when they finally talked about his infidelity.

In a firm voice, the Reverend restated his position, "Like I said, Mr. Hamilton, this is not the time or the place. Out of respect for your mother-in-law, perhaps we can take this up another time."

"See, Ravinia," Xavier said, now shifting his attention to his wife, "this ole joker ain't about nothing," sounding more ethnically Black. Xavier stepped out of the Reverend's way, slamming the screen door on his backside. As inappropriate as it seemed at the moment, Xavier's attempts at sounding ethnic *and* defending her against the Reverend, made her desire for her husband increase.

"I wonder how much of that money he is really using for the church." Xavier went on, "I wonder how many of his members really know how despicable he is." Xavier wanted to guarantee that Reverend Wright was off the premises. He followed behind him a few paces, weaving his way through the guests. When both men had reached the front porch, Xavier taunted him with lewd remarks down the porch stairs and all the way to his car. It was actually pretty strange to see Xavier going off on the Reverend, especially since he rarely interacted in such a manner with his fellow people of color. But Xavier kept following him down the block, jabbing the Reverend with statements about how much of a snake he was and that this was not the end of this situation. He even used the phrase, "nothing but a lying wonder," and "a sin and a shame," sounding almost like his mother-in-law, herself. Xavier was in rare form. It was just what the Reverend needed—a man who wasn't intimidated by his stature or his prominence to stand up and tell him the truth about himself.

For too long, Reverend Wright lived in the shadows of his most revered state. Only in his solitude, when the lights were off and the shades drawn, and he was by himself in bed at night did he allow his guilt to come over him and fully chastised him to the point where he realized the magnitude his sins. Even in his high esteem, he found himself buried in his sins; and yet, as he asked for forgiveness he felt like Judas—as if he could not be saved. As each morning broke, however, there was something necessary and familiar in his soul—the desire to do right.

Ravinia, unsure of how to react, was relieved that the affair was out in the open and that she had her husband's understanding to back her up in ending it. She was equally unsure of how this would affect her marriage, their children and her life.

Wiping her sweaty palms on her mother's apron, she went into the kitchen to pull out the sweet, yeast rolls from the oven. Their warm baked scent stirred the guests and a few meandered inquisitively into the kitchen. Ravinia shooed them away with a promise of just ten more minutes. She replaced the rolls in the oven with a beautiful baked macaroni and cheese that one of the church members had dropped off. The paprika was perfectly sprinkled atop the thin layer of melted cheddar cheese. It had been three hours since she had seen her mother lowered into the ground. She held on briefly to the counter to steady herself from the wave of emotion that made her feel light-headed. Recovering quickly, she reached into the cabinet for a basket to place the hot rolls in and set it on the counter. Ravinia then grabbed a cloth napkin to line the basket and placed them inside. She faintly heard her mother's voice speaking to her, again. *"It's over Ravinia, you did the right thing. The road may not be easy, but you will have to face whatever comes. After all, you made your bed, now you will have to lie in it. But if you trust in God, He will see you through."* Ravinia looked around, convinced that she would somehow be able to see her as well. But she wasn't there. Ravinia looked down at the basket of rolls in her hands and cried out loud. She missed her mother so much. The tears began to flow and she began to weaken again.

The screen door slammed and it was Xavier. He was fuming angrily and talking to himself. He saw Ravinia and was about to light into her, but when he saw her trembling and unsteady on her feet, he raced to catch her. He realized she couldn't bare any more pain, at least not today. Seeing his wife breaking down in her grief, he embraced her, holding her so tightly; Ravinia had to wiggle to find air to breathe. But she didn't push him away. He was close enough for Ravinia to smell the *Joop!* aftershave he had splashed on his face that morning before the funeral. Whispering, he tried to put his lips close to her right ear, moving her freshly coiffed hair, "Baby," he said gently. "We'll get through this. I haven't always been there for you either, but we'll get through this."

Burying her face deep into his neck, Ravinia cried bitterly. She felt so much compounded grief and pain; she didn't know what to do.

She released herself into his strong embrace and left the shame of the past year behind on the porch. Crying like a baby, Ravinia felt the comfort of her man surround her. She knew she had a good man, despite his own shortcomings and infidelity. Never had she in all the years they had been married heard Xavier sincerely speak faith into their relationship. Seeing their reflection in the window, she made a quiet discovery. Xavier's true strength had been hidden by a façade. He had spent years pretending to be what his peers wanted him to be, what the corporate image required him to be; whether it required playing the role of the sell-out, the racial token Black, or the laughing Uncle Tom. But now Ravinia saw through the layers he had created or borrowed and found something profoundly attractive about Xavier; something so sensual, she began to yearn for him. She realized that he was still hers and she smiled deeply through her tears. Setting the rolls on the stove next to them, Ravinia hugged her husband, encircling her lean arms around his neck. Despite the foundation that had been clearly shaken, she found a security in their marriage that still gave her a glimmer of hope. They *could* work things out. Stroking the fine curls that were tapered neatly around his neck, Ravinia knew that she would commit a lifetime to trying. Xavier pushed back from their embrace and looked at her and said, "Is that down home macaroni and cheese I smell?"

Ravinia laughed out loud for the first time since her mother's passing. Although Xavier's complexion was as light as snow and he acted at times as if he despised his own heritage, there was nothing he loved better than down-home macaroni and cheese, a mess of turnip greens topped with pickled beets and a splash of vinegar, and a big square of sweet cornbread on the side. Ravinia looked at her man, now peeking in the window of the oven, and knew that somehow everything would be okay.

Chapter 25.

LIBERATION

Sapphire went about her daily errands on Saturday morning as usual. She wasn't quite used to the freedom of not having to clean her house every week. The high-rise had a cleaning service that was part of the condominium's promotion. It was one of the perks they offered after sales plummeted due to the migration from high-rise commercial and residential buildings since 9-11. Migration to the city in general was at an all-time low, so Sapphire lucked out on a chance to live in the Gold Coast area for pennies on the dollar.

There were a few reasons why Sapphire was smiling that Saturday morning. Sapphire also enjoyed convenience and status. After losing Jake, she decided she wouldn't sell herself short anymore; living life to the fullest. So she didn't skimp on anything. When she needed her streaks redone, instead of calling her girlfriend Jade to bring over her handmade steam cap with varying size holes poked in it, she went to Yehia, an Egyptian stylist that everybody who was anybody went to in Chicago. She also stopped going to sleep with her shoulders stiff and her ankles swollen. Three times a week, she saw a Swedish masseuse and got a full-body, hot stone massage, seaweed wrap and facial. And once a month, she would go to Dr. Yu, a North Shore chiropractor, to get her joints realigned.

Jade, a hardworking housewife with a part-time job would make fun of her friend, calling her "bourgeoisie" and sidity. But Sapphire knew it was pure jealousy. Jade was consumed with the challenges of raising two growing boys, and wished that she could have the liberties that Sapphire experienced. She couldn't help but think that somehow she was not as worthy as Sapphire, because she obviously wasn't as fortunate.

With everything she had been through in her 42 years on this earth, surely she too deserved a little pampering every once in a while.

Jade's husband, Albert, was a simple man; the kind of man you could depend on. He didn't mind getting his hands dirty and breaking his back to make sure there was always food on his table and a deep-freezer full of meat. He was diligent about paying the bills on time and was not remiss in stopping at the store each night to pick up a gallon of milk and a loaf of bread for his growing boys. He was an engineer on the Union Pacific railroad and was very proud of his job. Working 15 years for them already, he was basically set for life as far as employment and pension were concerned. Jade knew when Al retired that they wouldn't have to worry about a thing. The railroad took care of its employees; Jade liked that kind of security.

Jade however, wanted more out of life. She enjoyed being a housewife and going to her part-time telemarketing job from noon to five, Monday through Friday. But deep down, Jade always envied the life of a single woman. At times, she would go shopping by herself or just drive around on a Saturday afternoon with no particular place to go. Occasionally, Jade would forget that she needed to be home with the boys so that Al could go out with his friends. She would always treat herself to something nice—a new blouse or lingerie to try to catch her inattentive husband's eye. She had to remind herself that she was a gentle flower. Being the only female in her home, it seemed that everyone else forgot. Her boys, she forgave for this oversight, but she wished that her husband would acknowledge her femininity.

Al performed all the husbandly duties that *he* saw fit to perform; and these more often than not *only* pleased him. He was an "old school" husband. When it came to intimacy: he saw, he took, he grunted a few grunts, and after a few boasts about how good it was, he fell fast asleep, snoring loudly. Five to ten minutes, at the most, was his average. Jade would just turn over in bed some nights trying not to cry. What was wrong with her? She had more than her share of *The Color Purple* moments of Al "doing his business" on top of her. She didn't want to complain, but she really wanted a lot more out of her husband intimately. She wanted to feel desired. Jade just couldn't bring herself to tell him that he just wasn't satisfying her. After all, Al didn't grow up understanding what it meant to please a woman. He was told to do like his father, and his father's father, to procreate a couple of times, and safely assume that all the other pleasure he experienced was a mutual experience for his wife.

Jade had grown up in the church, just like Al had, and unlike many of her teenaged friends, she kept herself virtuous until her wedding night, which turned out not to be what she expected. Al was practically "born and raised" in the church. The both of them were in Sunday school, youth group and choir together, and began to court in their senior year of high school. In fact, the only reason she began to go "steady" with him, was so she could go to prom with someone who wouldn't try to put the moves on her. Al was the "safe" kind. He never went too far with her, and at that time, that was just fine with Jade. He was always a gentleman with her, opening the door for her and saying "yes ma'am" and "no sir" to her parents.

Jade knew that she would one day marry Al because he was the "marrying kind." He was like a security blanket and Jade imagined that being married to Al would be pure bliss. He was her knight in a shiny new Cutlass, which he had bought with his summer job at the A & P food mart. He would fulfill her dreams and they would have a wonderful life together. Al would take care of her in their brick bungalow in Broadview, a western suburb of Chicago. They would have a couple of kids, a boy and a girl, and they would go to suburban schools, unlike she and her husband had. It was *her* American dream. People would look up to her and her 'married with children' status and desire to model their lives after her. Jade continued to dream like this until Al did ask her to marry him. Then reality hit.

It wasn't until he actually asked her did she start to believe in her mind that she was better than everyone else. Not only did Jade have a man that loved chasing after her, but she had accomplished something that was not as common in her mother's time: she had stayed a virgin until marriage. Some of her friends would tease her, calling her "Mrs. Jackson" or "Mrs. Albie," but Jade didn't care. She had what they wanted and she knew it. She wore the security of their relationship like a letter on the chest of the pristine, fuzzy-white sweater she always wore. It was as if her virginity was a status symbol. Jade used her "virtue" as a way to flaunt herself around, gaining clout every time she stood up to testify. She would represent the minority of young people who had never had sex by standing up boldly every Friday night in testimonial service proclaiming herself "untouched."

Many of Jade's peers felt like she was untouchable, and just plain unreal. The too-good-to-be-true Hollywood perfect life she invented for herself and her church-wide audience soon became a prisoner of her own design.

Chapter 26.

CRUISIN' FOR A BRUISIN'

"Jade, girl, what's wrong with you? You've barely touched your salad," asked a concerned Sapphire.

"I dunno, girl. I just don't know what's wrong with me," Jade responded in a low, despondent tone, prodding an orphaned snow pea across her clear glass salad plate, swirling it around in bleu cheese dressing.

"You want to talk about it? Is it your mom? How's she doing? I know she just had surgery and all."

"Yeah, she's all right, girl. You know she is as strong as a mule. Been seeing a chiropractor and taking herbs and stuff, chile. She should be back runnin' in a week or two."

"What?" Sapphire exclaimed. "Isn't she like 83 or something?"

"Yep," Jade acknowledged, pulling out a small tube of lotion. She squirted it out a little and spread it on her exposed mocha-colored arms. "She's 84."

"Wow. So what's the matter, Jade? You look so down. I know I need my hair done, but does it look that bad?" Jade, not able to resist, gave in to Sapphire's constant inquiries and cracked a smile at her lame joke.

"Okay well you can't tell Al though."

"Right. Like I talk to Al. When do I see Bighead anyway?" Sapphire laughed, trying to lighten the mood a bit. And without any warning, Jade started in, “Well, I don’t know if I am really happy with Al.”

“Uh, what you talking ‘bout Jade?” Sapphire mimicked, sounding like a young Gary Coleman. “What you mean you don’t know?”

“I just don’t know. I mean, I know I love him. He’s a good father and provider and all, but...”

“But what? What happened? Did he do something? Did *you* do something? Somebody had to have done something.” Sapphire anxiously jumped from question to question without breathing, waving her fork around. Jade responded, candidly, “Nuthin’. Just forget it.” Sapphire panned the expanse of the diner in search of her double cheeseburger and fries when she stopped suddenly and zoomed her focus directly back at Jade.

“Uh, huh. Nuthin’, my foot,” said Sapphire in a disbelieving tone. “I know, *something* had to happen and you need to tell me what that is. I mean y’all just came back from a *romantic* Caribbean cruise and all. I thought you had fun?” She put an emphasis on “fun” and winked at her girl, searching her face for a blush of confirmation. *Hmph. If Jade didn’t know what to do with Al, I sure do.* Sapphire relinquished the thought as soon as it entered her head, for the sake of their friendship and her ethics.

“Well, I did. You know how it is. The food was delicious, lots of tropical fruit and stuff. Our cabin was gorgeous and the beaches were fantastic,” Jade responded in a monotone voice, sounding less than convincing.

“So it wasn’t all that, huh?” Sapphire pointed out. She had a knack for reading between the lines. Continuing to inquire, Sapphire took a long sip of her Dr. Pepper and said again, trying to pump Jade for answers, “So what’s the problem? Was he looking at someone else?”

Jade, in defense of her devoted husband, blurted out, “No! He wasn’t looking at anyone else that I could tell. Nothing like that,” she said looking down at the floor.

"Okay, so now you've got me. Were *you* looking at someone else? Girl, if you were and didn't tell me . . ." Sapphire playfully changed her tone to become more stern when she talked, as she balled up her fist at Jade.

"No, no, no!" Jade sputtered out, rolling her onyx eyes. She was getting frustrated that she couldn't get her words out fast enough and that Sapphire was practically slapping more words into her mouth. She focused once again on getting her thoughts out completely, even though she had trouble expressing them. "Sapphire, would you please just let me finish before you start jumping to conclusions? That's just how rumors start. And you don't know who's listening to us."

"Girl, please. Stop dramatizing and get to it. Now, what is it?" Sapphire insisted, lowering her voice in an attempt to satiate her friend.

"Well, honestly, I think the thrill is gone," Jade said, giving a voice to the problem of her marriage. The words sounded worse after they were actually uttered and she wished that she could take them back. If there was something that Jade hated more than anything, it was admitting that anything was wrong in her life. No matter how bad, she would always portray her situation as if nothing was wrong. The rose-colored land of denial that she dwelled in most of the time would even convince her that her life was picture-perfect. But Sapphire, being a close friend for so many years, could always see through her façade. Jade liked and disliked this quality in her friend since college. Sapphire chuckled, "The thrill? Did you say 'thrill'?" rolling the "r" Latin style. Seeing that Jade was serious and actually admitting that something was wrong in her perfect marriage, Sapphire snapped her lips shut, hoping to gobble up her previous statement, but the words wouldn't pop back into her mouth. She decided on a hesitant, "Oh," determining it better to let Jade control the remaining conversation regarding Al. Taking a long, calculated sigh, the doctor ended with a genuinely concerned, "Really?" and waited for Jade to respond.

"Yeah. Well, you know we just celebrated our 25th wedding anniversary last month," Jade continued.

"Right, right. That was why you went on the cruise, right?" Sapphire pointed out.

"Yeah, like we've done every year for the past five years."

"So what happened this time?" Sapphire interjected trying not to look bored. It seemed like Jade was going to take all day to tell her story.

"Well, we do this every year. And every year, I get my hopes up that he's going to pull out all the stops and rock my world." Jade demonstrated what she meant by snapping her fingers back and forth three times. Jade still used euphemisms from the 80's and sometimes it was catchy and chic. Other times, it was just pathetic and simply played out.

"So, I guess he didn't, huh?" Sapphire empathized.

"Girl, the only thing rocking in our cabin was a chair with a broken leg." Both women erupted in sudden laughter, lifting the heaviness of their discussion.

"Girl you are such a nut!" Sapphire sighed, catching her breath and wiping a stressful tear from the corner of her eye.

"Yeah, it is kind of funny, but you know I feel bad. I mean, here I am, 43 years old, been married for over half of my life. Is it too much for me to ask for a little romantic interlude from time to time with my husband?"

"Naw girl, of course not." Sapphire added. "So, have you?"

"Have I what?"

"Asked him?"

"Yeah. A couple of times."

"So, what did he say?"

"Girl, he said leave the freaky stuff for when we have our anniversary and are out of the house away from the boys. And then when we get there, nothing. Nada. Zilch." Sapphire covered her mouth, trying not to laugh.

"Freaky stuff? Ha! Y'all be trippin'."

"Yeah, I know. Ain't it crazy?"

"I'm not even gonna ask. I don't want to know," Sapphire snickered putting her hand up as if to politely say 'Stop. That's just T.M.I. Too Much Information.'

"Well, it wouldn't be much to ask," Jade echoed bluntly.

Sapphire couldn't believe her ears. Here was little Miss Priss, fessin' up all her marital dysfunction without abandon. *It's was about time, though.* Sapphire thought quietly, knowing that there had to be much more going on behind that white picket fence of the Jackson household than had met her eye, and she knew it had to come out sooner or later. Jade certainly wasn't a Stepford wife, but she desperately wanted to keep up with the Joneses in her neighborhood.

"I see. Well girl, I don't know what to say." Sapphire said in a slightly serious voice, still surprised to learn that Jade desired some extra action from Mr. Jackson.

"So, girl, I am so messed up. I'm at the prime of my life. I still look good, right?" Jade slipped in, looking for affirmation from her friend. "Everything still works, you know. And we do get together from time to time, but I never feel fully satisfied."

"That's messed up girl. I do feel for you," Sapphire replied, secretly wishing she had *her* problem.

"Yeah," Jade agreed, sounding sad. Looking up she said, "So um, Miss Therapist Lady, what do I do?"

"Oh, so you think I can help you? Girl y'all crazy. And you know I can't counsel you. Ethics, girl, ethics."

"Yeah, ok. I see how it is. What if it were you?"

"Well, we both know that it wouldn't be me!"

"Yeah, that is true," Jade laughed loudly. "You ain't never lied about that."

"Well, think about it. If that is the worst of your troubles, you've got it made," Sapphire reasoned.

"No, not really. Just because we are okay in other areas doesn't mean that this is something I can live with. I mean, it has gotten *bad*. I don't like feeling unfulfilled. When I leave the house to go to work, all I think about is sex. And to me, that should be a part of marriage that is well taken care of." Jade's eyebrows rose for emphasis.

Almost choking on her Dr. Pepper, Sapphire tried to stop herself from coughing. Jade had said the "s" word. She *never* said that, especially not around Sapphire.

"You need to control that," Sapphire advised in a calm voice. She was a little taken aback by her friend's candidness. *This intimacy thing must really be bothering Jade*, Sapphire thought.

"I know. I can't help it, girl. I wouldn't even say anything if it weren't such a big issue. You know, it is entirely his fault. He won't even *try* to please me. I mean, he is so old school. And I know it's not because he is tired. When he gets home he'll play video games with the boys--some nights 'til ten o'clock."

Sapphire listened distractedly because her well-done burger had just arrived. All she could manage over her loud stomach growls was a "hmph."

"You know I see all these young boys half my age, trying to step to me. Sometimes they stare at me from across the way at work or on the street. I catch myself blushing, but the feeling that comes over me feels good. To know that a man—any man—still finds me attractive is an amazing feeling, at my age. And I need that kind of affirmation,

Sapphire. I just wish it was from my husband." Satisfied that she had pleaded her case, Jade took in a few more bites of food.

"Jade, watch yourself, now. In all seriousness, that's the last thing you want to start tampering with. Infidelity ain't no joke. And Al don't look like he plays when it comes to stuff like that. Besides, girl you got a good thing. You just got to build him up so he knows he is all that. You know, boost his lil' ego."

"I guess so, but you know I've never been with anyone except for Al."

"But, nothing," Sapphire interrupted. "Girl, you do that, you get him pumped up and feeling like a king, and that man will sweep you off your feet. I know Al can do that. Not many women can say that about their man in this day and age. But trust me, if you do what I said, it'll pay off. You'll be gettin' your groove back in no time."

"Hmmm. Well, I never thought of that. He is real sensitive when it comes to those kinds of things. That's why I've never mentioned anything before to him. But building him up—that might actually work. Girl, you are good. You know, just for that, lunch is on me today!"

"And if that doesn't work, then there's always Viagra and a lace body stocking." Sapphire added, winking her eye to signify that the next thing that would come out of her mouth was probably conversation reserved for grown folks. She stuffed a couple of fries in her mouth, to ensure she wouldn't go any further.

"Girl, pulleese!" They burst into laughter. "I don't want to give him cardiac arrest! And I'm sure I didn't say there was anything *wrong* with his equipment," Jade added with a gesture so Sapphire would get the hint. "Al would *never* take that mess. He would say it was just not natural. Can you imagine how he would go off?"

"Well, if it does turn out to be medical, explain to him as only a devoted wife knows how," Sapphire said in an almost patronizing voice, reminding Jade that she was a doctor. "Let him know your deepest thoughts, yearnings, your desires and wants. Perhaps he doesn't realize how desperate you want to be with him."

"Perhaps," said Jade, glancing down at her watch. Jade had the same Timex watch she had since high school. "Oh girl, I gotta go. The boys are at basketball practice and I need to pick them up."

"Ok. Well you better get a to-go box to take that chicken Caesar salad home to Al and those boys. You know that man would be upset if he found out you spent twelve dollars on a salad you didn't even eat."

"Yeah, you know you're right about that." Jade motioned for the waitress. "Miss, can I get this to go?" Sapphire thought, *I wish I had something I could take with me too and not this burned up burger, neither. Oh, well. It's probably better that I'm alone anyway.* Leaning over, Sapphire clutched her bloated abdomen, cringing in pain.

"Sapphire, girl, what's wrong?" Jade asked with a concerned look on her face. Sapphire, apparently used to the searing pain that came and went, tried to brush off Jade's apparent concern by saying, "It's just a lil' pain. It comes and goes." Sapphire tried to catch breaths between the pains to gauge their intensity.

"A little pain?!" Jade exclaimed. "That little pain had you doubled over."

"I'll be fine. I have a gyne appointment later today. We'll see what she says," Sapphire assured her concerned friend, in a low, shaking voice. She knew she couldn't fool Jade, but maybe she could pacify her a little.

"Your gyne? Girl what is wrong—I *don't* like the sound of that. It sounds serious. I should go with you," Jade insisted. She pulled out her cell phone. "I'll just call Al to pick up the boys. Let me call the school. Girl, you don't look so good."

"I'll be fine. No girl. See the pain is. . ." Sapphire braced herself for another wave and grimaced. "I'll be fine. Don't worry," she finished weakly, gritting her teeth. Sapphire was not convincing Jade. The therapist winced at each recurrence of the now throbbing pain in her abdomen.

"You are so stubborn, Sapphire! Lord knows you are one bull-headed child," Jade fussed noisily as Sapphire moaned quietly. The therapist tried to play it off, but ended up walking bent over like she was a 95-year-old woman, reaching for the wall for support. Managing to muster up a half-hearted smile in agreement, Sapphire uttered weakly, "I'll be fine—I'll call you." Sapphire carefully got up to leave, minding her facial expression.

"You sure you don't want me to come along?" Jade asked, wanting to help Sapphire out of the restaurant but stood by the way as not to offend her.

"Don't worry, everything will be fine," Sapphire assured her worried friend, tapping her hand gently. Jade said hesitantly, "It better be," as she whispered a little prayer under her breath. Her concern for her friend's situation overpowered her anger that Sapphire had not told her about this until now. "And you better call, too. Take care of yourself. Call me as soon as you know something."

"I will," Sapphire promised.

Chapter 27.

THIS TOO SHALL PASS

Reaching for the worn, plastic clipboard, Sapphire wrote her name on the sign-in sheet. She struggled whether to write down 'Dr. Sapphire Sykes' or just Dr. Sykes. Because of the sharp pains in her abdomen, she opted to keep it short and grab a seat as quickly as possible.

Hoping she would soon be called, Sapphire sat down and picked up a magazine from the collection on the table. Her fingers sorted through all the parenting and expectant mother options, and found a fashion magazine to her liking. Crossing her legs, she realized that there were several pregnant women waiting and she prayed they weren't waiting for Dr. Miller, too. Whatever it was, she wanted to get in, get seen and get out. For some reason, the pain seemed more intense today, more than she could ignore. Seeing the anxious expression upon the expectant moms' faces, Sapphire couldn't help but feel empty from her own maternal loss. She tried not to stare at their bulging bellies full of kicking life, but she couldn't help herself. She too had once known the joy of carrying a precious life inside. She also knew how it felt to lose that life, against her will.

Resentment began to surface and Sapphire's facial expression changed. She didn't mean to look obstinate, but there was no way for anyone else to decipher that. She disliked coming to the gynecologist, even for this once a year visit and the pure purgatory of the waiting room. But she had trusted Dr. Michelle Miller with her life once before and had developed a good patient-doctor relationship. Even so, she still did not like seeing the doctor, at any cost. Dr. Miller had been her obstetrician when she was pregnant and knew Sapphire's medical history even before coming to Chicago. Michelle was a kind soul. She was about

Sapphire's age and was one of the best female doctors on staff at Northwestern Hospital. Visiting her was convenient and Sapphire liked the fact that she could walk from the office to her condo in eight minutes flat. Although she loved to walk, it was just something about seeing the doctor that made her want to get home as soon as possible afterwards.

"Dr. Sykes?" the nurse called from the open door leading to the rear exam rooms and offices. Sapphire gathered her things quickly but rose up slowly. Walking carefully to the door, she looked back at her seat to make sure she had all of her belongings. She followed the nurse back to the examination room. "Step on the scale, please," the stout, little nurse instructed. Sapphire disliked getting on the scale but slipped off her shoes anyway. Placing her purse and coat down on the chair, she stepped up and the plate of the scale shifted loudly from her weight. Sapphire sighed, closing her eyes briefly as the nurse kept pushing the metal weight to the right. "One fifty eight," she proclaimed. "Okay, now. You can step down."

Wow, Sapphire whispered to herself in awe. *I must have lost twelve pounds. When did that happen??* Excited that she was lighter, the air of anxiety quickly came back over her and she couldn't help but wonder if this sudden weight loss somehow correlated to the pain she had been having for the last three months.

"Dr. Sykes? Dr. Sykes?" repeated the round nurse, jolting Sapphire out of her pondering.

"Oh, yes, I'm sorry," Sapphire said, still a little dazed. The pain reminded her of why she was there.

"Can you slip into this?" the nurse said in a less-than-friendly voice, flinging the flimsy, oversized, tissue-like smock on the exam table. It made a fluttering sound as it landed on the tissue protector sheet across the length of the table. "Take off everything, including your bra and panties. The doctor would like to do a full examination," she instructed. She then went over to the monitor on the desk and started typing in some stats. Sapphire waited and waited for her to leave, as she did not want to disrobe while the little round woman was still in the room. Sapphire didn't like to criticize, but the nurse's bedside manner left much to be desired. Not getting the hint, Sapphire sighed loudly, then coughed, and even rustled the paper protector, but the obstinate nurse kept making her updates in the computer, ignoring her perturbed patient.

Finally Sapphire, obviously frustrated and a little shocked, asked, "Can't you do that at your workstation? I need to get undressed before the doctor comes in here. I don't want to waste her time." She cringed from the added stress of having to instruct the nurse to leave her alone to disrobe.

The nurse finished typing the last bit of commentary, in an effort to further annoy Sapphire. Logging out of the session on the computer and casually lifting herself from the swivel stool, the nurse left the room and closed the door behind her. Sapphire, turned her back on the departing nurse, disregarding her backward glances, and began to unbutton her jacket. Feeling a bit rushed, she was still quite put off that the round, little nurse had been downright rude and had no regard for her patients. She lifted her mock turtleneck sweater over her head, catching the neckline on the clasp of her silver, hoop earrings. Unzipping her black, neatly pleated pants, she slipped them off, folded them on the crease and laid them on the back of the chair. She also took time to fold her sweater that she had just flung on the exam table and placed it on top of the pants. After dressing in the smock with her underwear still on, she remembered what the nurse had said, and peeled off her undergarments with the paper robe still intact. Wrapping the bra straps under the padded cups, she formed a collective ball of the two pieces and placed them between her sweater and pants to hide them from plain view.

Noticing the smock was hanging loosely, Sapphire remembered the tie and looked around the room. Scooping it up off the floor near the exam table, she tied it loosely around her waist. Dr. Miller would be coming in soon so Sapphire checked her presentation, content that she had left on her socks, even though nurse "Ratchett" had said to take off "everything." Getting holstered on those stirrups meant touching cold metal and she was not interested in being chilled to the bone. Sapphire, sure that her blood pressure had spiked after the episode, closed her eyes to relax until the doctor came in. Sapphire actually liked having a little "chill time" before seeing the doctor so that she could calm herself before being examined. There were still emotional layers that remained from the rape and the miscarriage that made her cringe when she was touched. But she would try to focus on good thoughts and regulate her breathing. She promised herself an ice cream treat afterwards or a walk down to Godiva for a little chocolate, to ease the anxiety.

The small, sterile pillow felt good. Sapphire began to close her eyes and in doing so, allowed herself a little nap. She welcomed any opportunity to find relief from the pain. Looking up drowsily at the ceiling, she lowered her glance to the pictures on the wall. There were lovely Monets and Renoirs, full of vibrant colors and flowers. They were a soothing complement to the sterile whiteness of the walls and stainless steel instruments used in the small space. The waiting time seemed much longer with her clothing off. Only six minutes had passed and she started to feel restless and a bit chilled from her partial nudity. The pain was still there, but had seemed to dull a little.

The sound of the doorknob turning startled Sapphire out of her twilight sleep. Dr. Michelle Miller walked in with a pleasant smile on her face. She looked at Sapphire and said, "How have you been? How's the practice doing?" making small talk to break the ice. Dr. Miller was a Caucasian woman about 40 years old with mousy, brown hair. Standing at five-foot-ten, the doctor's thin athletic build made Sapphire self-conscious about her own weight. Her smiling brown eyes lit up the room. She was well aware that Sapphire greatly disliked coming to her office, so she knew there had to be a reason other than a Pap smear for her visit.

"I've been pretty good. Same ole, same ole. How 'bout yourself? Oh wait, that nurse who was just in here, was not very pleasant," Sapphire said honestly, strangely void of pain. She still had a sour taste in her mouth about the intake nurse's demeanor.

"Tammy?" Dr. Miller inquired. "Yeah, I don't know. I think it's a cultural thing for her. She isn't very warm or pleasant to *anyone*. She is a skilled nurse though, one of the best in our practice. Did she say something inappropriate? If you'd like, I can talk to her."

"Yes, well, never mind," Sapphire ended abruptly as she started to feel another pain, sharp and precise, cutting through her. This pain wasn't like gas, which felt almost superficial, but a deep searing sensation that made her hold her breath and rub her rounded abdomen to try to make the pain go away. Before she knew it, she was rubbing her belly, with a slight grimace on her face.

"How long have you been having those, Sapphire?" Dr. Miller asked as she stretched the opaque-canary yellow examination glove over her slender fingers. Her smile was erased from her semi-freckled face and replaced by a couple of worrisome frowns and a fire-red, matte line that was firmly pressed lips.

"About six months, I guess. It comes and goes. And the intensity is never the same." Sapphire admitted.

"Is there any activity that seems to aggravate it, you know like sexual intercourse?" the doctor asked, motioning for her to lie back and put her feet in the stirrups. Sapphire didn't respond. As Dr. Miller prepared her table for a Pap smear and examination, Sapphire's lower body began to turn numb at the cold sound of the medical equipment clanking together. As the doctor helped Sapphire maneuver herself in to the appropriate position, she gently touched her leg. "Scoot down, Sapphire," the kind doctor coaxed, lightly guiding Sapphire's movements.

"That's it. Good. Right there. Now, relax and take a deep breath." Nothing the doctor could say could make her relax. She was tingling nervously all over, but she tried. Taking in a deep, cleansing breath, she released the air just as the doctor inserted the cold speculum inside of her. Sapphire always felt numb when she was touched there. The feeling would only last a few seconds. Then there was excruciating pain; a strong searing pain. Somehow, this pain was intensified by the instrument's insertion. Sapphire started to cry. *What is wrong with me?* She questioned in her head, not realizing the examination was over.

"Okay, Sapphire, that's it. You did well," Dr. Miller said in a bland voice. Sapphire heard what the doctor said and closed her legs. It was what she wasn't saying that troubled her.

"I am setting you up for some scans and blood work. I have an idea of what it might be, but I want to make sure. You'll need to get these done as soon as possible."

"Michelle, be honest with me," Sapphire requested, lifting her torso up off the pillow into a sitting position on the table.

"Yes?" the doctor questioned.

"What do you think is wrong? I don't like the tone of your voice and I want to know what your impression is."

"Sapphire, you know we don't like to talk about a possible diagnosis unless we have a good indication of what it may be. Honestly, even after the scans, we are going to have to go in and remove those fibroids. There is a possibility that it is more serious than that. We just don't know yet." *Serious—what could be that serious. Oh God, please,"* Sapphire prayed. Then she began jumping to conclusions.

"Cancer? Are you saying I might have cancer?" Dumbfounded, she lost the feeling again in her lower extremities and just stared blankly at her doctor then at the vibrant Monet on the wall.

"I didn't want to suggest that as it is too early to tell, but there is a possibility." Sapphire just kept looking at the wall, hoping for a word or phrase that would snap her out of her daze, but none came. Dr. Miller continued, gently touching her friend's knee to bring her focus back to her. "It could just be the fibroids," Dr. Miller hesitated, noticing Sapphire's eyes begin to water. "Sapphire, I know how you hate to see doctors, but if the scans come back with something, I want you to see a specialist at the University of Chicago. He is a personal friend of mine."

Sapphire couldn't believe what she was hearing. Certainly she wasn't prepared for the possibility of cancer. With everything that she had already endured in life, this was the clincher. Why her? Just the thought made the pain deepen and her swollen belly ache sorely. Taking the card from Dr. Miller's grasp, she looked at it timidly.

"I wish there was more we could do at this point, Sapphire," the doctor consoled, putting her warm hand on top of Sapphire's hand.

"Yeah," Sapphire said, still oblivious to reality. The warmness of the doctor's hand was too much for her to accept at this point without crying. She started to rustle around, to signal that she wanted to get dressed.

"If you want to talk, I'll be in my office, or if you want to call me, feel free. I'll try to answer all your questions, but you need to make sure you get some rest," Dr. Miller advised.

"Okay," Sapphire said insipidly. None of this conversation was sinking into her long-term memory. Sapphire blindly waved at the doctor, as she left the room, not even bothering to move her facial muscles into a half-smile. She numbly got dressed as she felt a rush of emotion wash over her. She dressed quickly and left the office. Today was a Godiva, Coach and 31 Flavors day all mixed into one. Looking at her watch, she realized she had only 22 minutes before the Michigan Avenue Coach store closed. Sapphire only bought expensive things when she was either rewarding herself for being extremely good, like going into business for herself, or really upset about something and needed a distraction.

After stopping at Godiva for a chocolaty treat, she walked briskly back home where she could cozy up to a new book and some tea. Throwing her red and white coach shopping bag on the couch, she dropped her purse on the floor. The twice-folded blue lab paper fell out and Sapphire gingerly reached down to pick it up. Feeling the pain teeter back and forth within her, it was as if it was trying to decide if it wanted to cripple her or just annoy her to the point where her rocky road ice cream tasted bitter. She reached down and grabbed the paper, only to find the intensity of the pain almost knock her to the floor. Forgetting what it was for, she opened it only to remember it was a lab referral to get the CAT scan and ultrasounds her doctor had ordered. Feeling herself wince at the idea of having to endure the tests, she knew that whatever was causing her pain was more than just fibroids and she'd have to do whatever it took to find out the underlying cause.

Thinking back to the first time she felt like something was wrong; Sapphire realized it had been almost six months since the first twinge. She was sitting down eating dinner in her living room after an exhausting day at the office. As she began to relax, she felt a sharp pain that she likened to a butcher's knife grinding through her belly button, landing deep into her uterus. The pain was so quick and concentrated she almost lost her breath. Lying down, she attempted to ease the throbbing; hoping that if she laid on one side or the other, it would subside or go away. Reaching for the bottle of Tylenol that was conveniently resting on her glass end table, Sapphire took a few of the white capsules to take the edge off the excruciating pain. Then she reviewed the events of the day. Not once did she think what she was facing could be that serious. Sapphire was well aware that she had a few fibroids from when she was pregnant and thought maybe one of them was acting up. Never did she think it could be cancer.

Chapter 28.

THE SILENT KILLER

Rainy. Drizzly. Cool. Barely 20 degrees, it was seasonably cold for Chicago in mid-January. Four days of pouring rain and the clouds seemed to droop so low over the Sears Tower that it seemed a mere seventy stories high. Canceling all of her appointments that Tuesday, Sapphire decided she couldn't put off getting the tests that Dr. Miller ordered any longer. Taking a cab to the hospital, she walked into the women's hospital corridor and looked around at the place. The atmosphere, warm and friendly, was a paradox in itself. In all the revamping to make the look and feel more like a sanctuary than a medical facility, Sapphire still had chills whenever she walked into a hospital or doctor's office. Even though the rape was long in her past, the after affects of having to get a D & C pounded her head, making her heart palpitate unnecessarily. She decided it was best to get in and get out, although she could see that there were probably a number of people there who might be in the same predicament as she.

Life had taken a taxing toll on Sapphire the past few days after seeing Dr. Miller. It was like she could barely scrape up any energy to want to do anything worthwhile. Staying in her powder blue sweats all weekend, she almost ran out of food to eat. That didn't seem to matter as much to Sapphire who didn't have an appetite in the first place. Worry made her belly full and the pains that she felt were riddled by anxiety. Ignoring all of Jade's calls, she knew by Tuesday that she had better do something or Mrs. Jackson would be sending out a search party for her.

Sapphire watched the expression on the technician's face as if it would relay a diagnosis. This tech was good. She smiled often, reassuring Sapphire that everything was moving along smoothly. Sapphire knew better, though. She looked at the monitor that was cleverly turned away from full view to see if she could see anything. Every time she looked towards the screen, the technician would move the scanner to the opposite side of Sapphire's abdomen. Sapphire picked up on it and got frustrated. There was nothing she could do until the doctor received the results from the Radiology department. Nonetheless, Sapphire was curious. She wanted to know what was wrong with her now. After ten minutes of feeling the warm clear gel gloss over her lower belly, she just pushed the technician aside and got up off the table. "I know what you are doing," Sapphire accused, and started wiping herself off with the paper blanket that was provided.

"I can't say anything about the ultrasound. I am not a doctor," the technician responded almost robotically with the only authority she had.

"I know, but it is just really frustrating waiting to find out what is wrong with me. You see something. I can tell by the way you keep going back and forth in that one area and you hit those buttons over there to get a close up. I know that you're trying to play it off and hide what's really going on with me. Honestly, I am not blaming you. I'd probably do the same thing with my patient. It's just that I am just having a really hard time dealing with all of this right now," Sapphire said, trying to hold back tears heavy with anger, uncertainty and fear.

"I'm sorry. Really, I am. I see so many patients and it is never easy to look them in the eye, knowing that they want more than a 'you can get dressed now, have a good day' from me. You don't know how many times I wish I could make this better for you and any other cancer patient who comes in here."

"That's okay. You don't have to apologize," Sapphire answered, remorsefully. She then realized what the ultrasound technician had just said and she knew that she had cancer for sure. How did the technician know she had cancer? Sapphire didn't know, and her doctor although she suspected it could be, didn't know, either. Feeling the muscles in her face tense up, she tried to relax them, but nothing would ease her numbed facial expression.

Blindly, Sapphire slipped on her skirt, grabbed her purse and wintry wears and walked out of the door with the ultrasound technician still standing over the table with the gel-coated scanner in her gloved hand. She walked out of the room and down the hall to the exit. Her life seemed out of control. Sapphire knew that whatever she did, she needed to stay strong. But that was the furthest thing from her mind at that time. Feeling the below zero lakefront air hit her face when she walked out of the North door of the Women's Pavilion, she reached in her purse and grabbed her cell phone. Without even thinking, she pressed '2' on her speed dial. Hearing an answer, she blurted into the phone, "Jade—I need to see you, girl."

Before she could finish her voice message, the second line beeped. It was Dr. Miller's office calling.

"Hello?"

"Dr. Sykes, this is Dr. Miller's nurse."

"Okay," Sapphire whispered coolly, inhaling the crisp lake air.

"Dr. Miller would like to see you today. Can you come in at 7:45 p.m.?" Dr. Miller customarily saw patients until 8 p.m. on Tuesday nights.

"Sure," Sapphire responded although she wasn't "sure" about anything anymore. She clicked off the line and turned her phone off.

Sapphire knew that when Dr. Miller's nurse called her personally on her cell phone, that her situation had to be serious. It was only a matter of time before she would know what was going on with her. She decided to push the worry out of her mind. There was no use in thinking about something that had not been discovered. But, as much as she tried to shove the thoughts outside of her head, one stubborn thought kept reminding her of how vulnerable she was. The deepest, darkest crevice of her past kept creeping up on her when she would try to drown her concerns. All she could do was wait for the evening to come when she would see Dr. Miller; then she would have some idea of what she was dealing with.

Time seemed to stand still. It took almost seven painstaking hours for the dreaded appointment time to arrive, and Sapphire could barely stand it. Every little thing distracted her; she didn't know whether she was coming or going. Allowing herself to get into a rut, she paced back and forth when she got to the doctor's office. The impatient therapist couldn't sit down for long and be party to the waiting. Her situation was serious, if the tone of the nurse's voice was any indication. Sapphire decided she wanted the news quick and straight. Her mind jumped around and flipped through a hundred slides before the nurse called for her to come back. This time, it was just a matter a minutes before she was called. Sapphire was escorted back into Dr. Miller's office and found her typing some notes into her laptop.

"Have a seat, Sapphire," the doctor said, sighing after barely getting the words out. Sapphire refused to speak. She pulled out the chair and sat down. Her body grew numb and light as a feather. She didn't like the feeling she was getting from Dr. Miller.

"Well, I am gonna be straight with you. I saw the report from the radiologist regarding the ultrasound and CAT scan. There is a collective mass attached to your uterine wall about the size of a golf ball. It appears to be a tumor, but we would have to do laparoscopic surgery to be sure. You also have several large fibroids, and those may be causing the pain." Still not saying a word, Sapphire faded in and out of the report from her physician. She heard about every other word that was said. Dr. Miller continued, "So, Sapphire, I've asked Dr. Cankar to perform the procedure if you consent to have it done."

Realizing the doctor had finally asked a question that she needed to answer, she responded, "Yes, that will be fine." Sapphire nodded and took out her Blackberry. "Can we schedule the procedure now? I'd like to get this over with."

"Sure. I already took a look at the surgery schedule for Friday. How is seven-thirty a.m. for you?" Sapphire nodded submissively. "I'll go ahead and schedule you at that time so we can hold that date/time slot. Remember, this is just exploratory; to take a biopsy to see what we are dealing with. Unless something major happens, I should be able to be there with you for the procedure."

"I understand. Seven-thirty is fine," she said, logging the information into her cell phone. Sapphire hadn't felt any pain that morning, just numbness. She wasn't easily influenced by the lack of pain. She knew that it was temporary and would be back in full force.

"Dr. Cankar is an excellent surgeon," Dr. Miller assured.

"I'm sure he is. I know you all will do what is best, Michelle." Sapphire looked directly into the doctor's eyes, affirming her belief in her physician.

"If you need anything, Sapphire, you have my cell. You call me. All right?"

"Ok, I appreciate that, Michelle. I really do. But you know, I feel like this is the last straw. I know whatever it is, benign or malignant; I have got to fight it. I am so tired all the time. I have no inspiration at all and my strength is constantly being sapped. I need to take some vitamins or something. But honestly—I-I just want my life back."

"The vitamins will definitely help. You probably are riding high on emotions also and that can be draining. Try and get some rest over the next two days, and if you can, try not to think the worst. Whatever the outcome, you are one of the strongest women I know. You've been through some difficult things, and yet you always pull through, and you bring yourself out. You fight and you fight hard. It's okay to lean on someone else now. Are you still seeing patients?"

"No, not really. I haven't officially taken a leave yet, but I'll call and let them know I'll be out for a while," Sapphire sighed, blowing out a stressful breath. "Thanks, Michelle. I, uh, well, you know. I don't want to even speak it."

"We will get through this. If any woman can, it is you, Sapphire," Dr. Miller reassured, trying to regain Sapphire's eye contact.

Sapphire left the doctor's office feeling as if she had lost her best friend. Although she didn't know exactly why, it was like the uncertainty didn't bother her as much as knowing she would be going under the knife in less than three days. Feeling weary and drained, she took a taxi to

State Street. She got out and walked around, breathing in the cold dampness of the rain. It felt more like London than Chicago. Enjoying the cold drops splashing on her face and head, she soaked in the wet cleansing rain of the day. In all their grayness, it was amazing how much beauty lie in the silver-gray of dark drooping clouds. Pregnant with water, they birthed a purity needed to regenerate the earth, even in dormancy. But today of all days, rain symbolized more than just the beginning of dark clouds.

Realizing she had spent too much time worrying about what she could not change; Sapphire felt her spirit lift when she left the worries of the world behind. She whispered into the atmosphere a gracious, "Thank you" looking towards the heavens, watching the magnificent handiwork displayed in the electric fingers that stretched across the blackened sky. *Life was worth living,* she re-emphasized in her mind. Thinking back, she remembered her mother singing a song in church. Sapphire's mother had a strong alto voice that made those listening tremble when she sang. She couldn't remember all the words to the old spiritual, but she knew that it had something in it about not complaining. Closing her eyes, she squinted hard trying to remember the precious words her mother would say to Sapphire, or to no one in particular: "All of my good days, outweigh my bad days, so I won't complain."

Such a simple truth. Profound in the element of life's revelation lived the fact that for every bad day, there has to be at least one good day that makes it all worthwhile. Thinking of how her mother must have had her own set of daily woes, Sapphire knew that she must continue to hold fast to the very promises that God had given her when she was a little girl looking for her mother to hold her in the middle of the night.

Chapter 29.

MOVING ON

Gray clouds passed over the Midwestern sky as the sun begged to peek through, revealing white strips of cirrus. It was just a few days since the funeral and Ravinia went to face the loneliness that lingered in her childhood home. Still numb, she parked her car on Dempster Street, not wanting to attach herself too closely to the familiarity of the neighborhood. Walking a block down to the house, she paused briefly to look down to the street at the porch of the gray and white frame house. "Momma, *loved* that house," she said aloud to the eavesdropping clouds. Thinking back to the days that embraced her innocence, growing up in a prospering Evanston, she knew that only she could reclaim her life, whether it was here or with her husband. Trying still to bravely hold back tears that were long overdue, she finally broke down, sobbing loudly. Xavier wasn't here to console her this time and these were unmistakably tears of grief, not remorse for her affair with the Reverend.

Large pools of salt water began to fill her tear ducts and started to flow from her almond shaped eyes. It felt good to cry out loud. Wiping the droplets to no avail, she continued to walk down the sidewalk to the house. Feeling her cheeks flush, she became aware that her mother's neighbors were watching her, and rushed quickly to get inside. More than anything she did not like being watched, especially in a moment that was supposed to be all her own. Although she could not feel her feet touch the pavement, she could hear the clicking of her heels and the scrape of her boot along the path as she tried to pick up her feet. The last thing she wanted was sympathy *and* company. *Please God, don't let any one see me and decide I need help sorting things out. I really rather be alone today. No Ms. Johnson, no Mrs. Smith, and no, not even little Ms. Poole. Bless her heart. I know she means well. Please Lord, just me this time?* She pleaded selfishly as she prayed.

Making it to the stairs, without interference, she was convinced that the angels were standing guard. The feeling that someone was watching her suddenly ceased and calmness enveloped her. Ravinia muttered a sigh of relief and slipped a muted, "Thank you Jesus," out into the atmosphere, hoping one of the angels would take it right up to Him. Katie Mae had kept a very tidy house on the inside and out. Her shrubs and lawn were always neatly manicured and the stair railing received every spring a fresh coat of light gray, glossy paint. It was due time for a touch up. Even the welcome mat was shaken and brushed every Saturday morning, just in case visitors might come over. The mat intensely needed grooming. Old, dried up autumn leaves were stuck in its casing. Wedged in the creases of the sidewalk, new weeds had begun to pop through the cracks in the walkway. These all served as evidence that Katie Mae was definitely gone.

Opening the screen door, Ravinia went back in time to the day Mr. and Mrs. Weiss brought her and her mother to the house. Katie Mae was so embarrassed that her employers had bought her a brand new house in the suburbs, free and clear, that she refused to get out of their car. Momma was a bit stubborn. She believed in making her own way the best way she could. She didn't accept any handouts and she certainly wasn't going to let some white folks put her in a house without paying a mortgage or a little something for it. Certainly, she expected she would have to work more hours and Katie Mae would not be able to be away from her children that long. In her finite thinking, she could not see the reason for such an extravagant gift and as such, she blocked out any notion that this beautiful home was truly her very own. No matter how nice they were, Momma always took the Weiss' gratitude with a grain of salt. Ravinia, however, in her child-like trust, was so excited that she bounded out of the Cadillac and started running down the walkway back to the backyard, like it was already her house. Her childish abandon briefly embarrassed Katie Mae until she remembered that Ravinia was a child; a beautiful, brown child that needed to be nurtured and loved. She needed to learn how to play without worrying about broken glass and hypodermic needles lying around on the play yard. She needed grass and trees, not concrete and metal bars. Katie Mae had a good mind to run after Ravinia, but she knew that her argument would be much less effective if she budged even a little, so she stayed in the back seat of the car with her thick arms crossed.

Little Ravinia emerged from the rear of the house, ran back to the car, leaned into the rear passenger window, pleading with her mother in her little girl way to accept the generosity of the Weiss'. Katie Mae, for the first time, saw a vibrant life in Ravinia's eyes along with an opportunity to give to her baby girl the life she had always willed. No more inner city living. No more ghettos. No more hustling. No more ducking and dodging bullets! Seven eighty-one Dodge became their new home.

That was 1969. Now, Ravinia walked inside of the house she grew up in and inhaled all the memories she could in one breath. She knew it was time to sort through Momma's things—keeping some memories and giving away others. Since Momma had only a few things written in her will -- something she had Ravinia type up the first time she went into diabetic crisis -- Ravinia and Nate decided it best that Nate keep the house.

Ravinia sat down on the couch and heard its plastic cover hiss trapped air. She got right up and lifted the cover off the olive-green couch, and then off of the two maize-colored Queen Anne chairs. She thought to herself, *I know Momma probably never enjoyed the comfort of actually sitting on her own couch without plastic.* Ravinia commenced to remove all the covers off the furniture, letting them finally breathe again. And when all the plastic covers and runners were off, Ravinia sat down on the firm French provincial couch feeling like a queen. *It's a shame that Momma had all this beautiful furniture and never truly enjoyed it*, she muttered in her head. Ravinia didn't believe in having untouchable rooms or furniture. In her mind, it didn't make sense to have things she couldn't enjoy.

Ravinia really didn't feel much like sorting through her mother's things today. But she did want to do something other than just sit around. She scanned the room and saw the hi-fi console. Lying on the console were a couple of orange and lime floral-patterned photo albums obviously purchased in the late 60's or early 70's.

Someone must have been looking at them during the repast because Katie Mae would never have left anything out of place. Ravinia grabbed the albums and brought them over to the couch. Turning the pages, she saw pictures of herself as a little girl and Nate as a baby. Ravinia smiled because she remembered being glad the day Nate was born. As she kept turning the pages, she came across a couple of pictures of herself and her father. She was standing in front of a corner candy store not too far from the projects. Her father had just bought her a Chick-O-Stick. She grinned from ear to ear like it was Christmas Day. Ravinia wondered who had taken the photo, but not as much as she wondered where her father was. Her dad looked so handsome back then. He was holding Nate in his big strong arms. Ravinia was the spitting image of her father with dreamy, burnt orange colored eyes set in his smooth, mocha colored skin. His keen nose and full lips complimented his shiny, tightly curled black hair. Nate took after their mother's side of the family with his lighter skin, hazel eyes and wavy hair. That picture was the last one they would ever take together.

Ravinia took the well-preserved photo out of its square cellophane sleeve. 'August 1966' was written on the side. She tried to remember back to that day but she couldn't. Her head was still cluttered with all the post-funeral things she had to do. Laying the single photo down on the cocktail table, she continued looking through the album. The cellophane casing had become dry, cracked and yellowed with age.

Just then, she heard the back screen door open in the kitchen. She leaned over to see who was coming through it. She figured it was Nate since he was the only other person who had a key besides her. She looked up briefly to acknowledge his presence and then quickly back to the album she was viewing. Wiping a stray tear from her face, she looked up at him and breathed out a heavy, "Hey." Nate returned the greeting in a southern drawl and replied, "Hey yourself." He didn't seem to be in a particularly good mood, especially since Ravinia was there. It seemed like every time he would come over, she would be there, too. All he wanted was to get their mother's stuff out that Ravinia was taking so that he could start moving his things up from the basement.

"I just stopped by to gather a few things of Momma's that I figured you probably didn't want," Ravinia said looking up at her baby brother. She remembered how fat he used to be when they were just kids. Nate had grown out of his baby fat into a lean, medium-build man.

Since he had gotten out of being a gangster, his image had softened a bit and he was beginning to look like her brother again.

"That's fine," he responded, looking down at his feet then everywhere else but in Ravinia's direction. "I'm gonna go in the basement and start bringing some of my stuff up here."

"Okay, well, I'll let myself out when I go," Ravinia said matter-of-factly. Things were still awkward between them since the funeral. Nate went downstairs and Ravinia settled back into her place on the couch. It felt much more comfortable without the sticky plastic covers that had covered them for almost 40 years. As she settled herself into the back of the couch, she heard what sounded like paper rustling behind the cushion. Reaching down, she pulled out a folded piece of lined notebook paper. The left edges were frayed from being torn out of the spiral book. Looking around, she wondered what the paper was. Carefully opening the paper, she saw that it was dated just two days before Momma's death, a week before her 73rd birthday. A cold chill ran down her spine as she began to read the contents of the letter. It read:

Dearest Momma,

I want to thank you for being an amazing woman. You've managed more in a day than many folks have done in an entire lifetime. You wore many hats in our household. You were a chef, psychologist, physician, teacher, pastor, housekeeper, personal shopper, chauffeur, and more. Not one complaint.

As a teenager, you gave me direction. I can remember times when I felt confused, lonely and discouraged about life, and you encouraged me to always stay strong. You told me to keep my faith in God that He would never leave me, and for this I thank you.

Thank you for giving me the gift of honor both as a child and now as a man. You and I went through some very rough times when I was a teenager out on the streets. While I was too busy hating myself, you were finding ways to show me how much you loved me. I appreciate you. Without you, I could not have made it this far. I hope that I am worthy of your love.

Thank you, Mom, for your patience and allowing me to make my own mistakes. You truly are a Godsend and I wonder where I would be if it had not been for you. You touched my soul and I am so blessed that you are not only a brilliant mother, but an awesome friend as well. I know you have the weight of the world on your shoulders when it comes to me. But Mom, because of you, I SURVIVED.

In my years, I've seen people come and go, young and old from all walks of life. But you never left my side. I've hurt you, disappointed you, and shamed you. Momma, I've never been good at apologizing but please forgive me. Thank you for doing the very best anyone could ever do.

There were times, Mom, that I did not really appreciate your spirituality, just how important God was to you. As a teenager, I found church boring, meaningless, and irrelevant. Thank you for not condemning me when I strayed from the church. Thank you, Mom, for never failing to pray for me. I believe that it was your prayers and the prayers of others that softened my heart. I have come to believe from personal experience that the persistent prayers of a loving mother are one of the most powerful forces in the universe. Thank you for being such a beautiful example of what a mother should be. Thank you for admitting your faults and in turn teaching me to do the same. Thank you for the freedom to be who God called me to be and to go where He's called me to go. Thank you for not letting ME settle for anything less than God's best.

Mom, I also thank God for your precious hands—the same tender hands that rubbed my back, stroked my face, dried my tears, disciplined, and held me. I love you, Momma!

Your legacy, Nate

Ravinia didn't know what to do. The letter Nate wrote was such a beautiful expression of what her younger brother just couldn't say. No wonder her mother spent so much of her energy nurturing Nate. She knew that the world was cruel, especially for Black men. She knew that her mother could never let the clutches of destruction get a hold of him completely and snatch her little boy away from her. He was her only man-child, and to Momma, he needed to be able to take care of himself like she took care of him. Momma knew that Ravinia would be okay. After all, she was just like her. But Momma did not want Nate to turn out like their father Grady Brown. And she would spend every day until her last, praying and praying Nate's soul from the gates of a burning Hell. With all that Nate went through, Momma saw right through his wrongs. To Ravinia, her mother was looking at Nate through the eyes of Jesus. No matter how many times he stole from her, lied to her, turned his back on her, Katie Mae still had faith and loved him, welcoming her "prodigal son" back into her home. Folks thought she was crazy; that she had lost her mind. But to Momma, Nate was not a lost cause. She used to tell Ravinia, "Lord willing, as long as I have breath in my lungs, I'm gonna pray my Nate home, back where he belongs." And she did.

What Ravinia had just read made her realize how selfish she was in being jealous of the love her mother had for her little brother. Her heart was softened like sweet creamed butter and she felt horrible at how she had perceived her mother's undying love for her brother. It probably took all Nate had to write that letter to Momma. Realizing that this must have been meant for her mother to receive while she was still alive, Ravinia wondered what Nate must have been going through. This was his way of thanking her, but she never got a chance to even see it.

Tucking the letter in her jacket pocket, she walked over to the door that led to the basement. Ravinia stepped down the stairs and met Nate coming up with a box of old picture frames. "What are you doing?" Nate asked with a grumpy disposition written across his face. He was seemingly upset that Ravinia was walking down the stairs of what once was their childhood home. He thought she was checking up on him like she used to do when they were kids. "I thought you might want all these pictures and stuff. Momma kept all this stuff down here and never did anything with it." Then he noticed Ravinia had been crying and impatiently asked gruffly, "What's wrong with you, now?"

Ravinia just looked at Nate and the scar on his right cheekbone. She remembered someone had slashed him with a broken bottle when he carjacked them. That was the night they were at Evanston Hospital and Nate had to have seven stitches. Tears started streaming down Ravinia's face as she pulled out the letter from her pocket. Nate, looking puzzled, put down the box of frames on the step between them. He took the letter from her and unfolded it. After taking one look, he folded it up and his expression changed from puzzled to perturbed. His eyes started to get red and Ravinia knew he was upset. "Yeah, and?" he asked picking up the box. Stuffing the letter between two metal gold-tone frames, he looked at Ravinia like she was crazy and said, "What?"

"Momma didn't get to see this did she?" Ravinia asked, hoping Nate wouldn't shut her out.

"No," the younger sibling said blankly, trying to hold back the tears. His nose was starting to redden at the tip as his cheeks blushed with emotion. After being in a gang for so long, Nate rarely cried and when he did, no one ever saw him. Ravinia sat down on the step in front of him. Reaching up, she touched his face, just like Momma used to do. Nate tried and tried not to give in, but the hurt that was tearing him up inside wouldn't let him be. His high yellow face started getting splotchy as Ravinia could see one little teardrop trying to pull itself through. Ravinia didn't relent. She wanted him to break his tough shell and cry like a big baby. She kept stroking his face until the one little tear fell with such force that it bounced off of Ravinia's nutmeg-brown hand. Nate started to weep, making loud, guttural yelping sounds with his throat. He had held in his mourning until now when all the sorrow from the past two months came flooding out of him.

Ravinia reached out to her little brother and tried to hug him. Nate was crying full force at this point and almost collapsed on Ravinia. Helping him sit next to her on the step, she held his head on her chest like she had held her own son, Justin, as a little boy. Ravinia knew she was the stronger of the two and that she was the one who would fight the battles when they were kids. And even though Nate had always been her pupil when they played school, Ravinia was learning something now about life that she couldn't have found out on her own: Just because something doesn't seem fair, doesn't mean it isn't right. In all her mother's attempts to raise her children to be independent, her mother was the only one who could love Ravinia so much that she had to push her away in order to draw her back in.

Chapter 30.

EMPTY

"You're going to shave me *where*?" Sapphire exclaimed. Glaring at the male nurse with the blue puffy cap, Sapphire rolled her eyes at the request that had just been made of her. "And you have to shave the whole thing? Why? What is the purpose of that? The surgery that Dr. Cankar described isn't anywhere near there. It's a laparoscopic procedure, not a C-section!" Sapphire insisted on the verge of tears.

"I understand that, Dr. Sykes, but this is a precautionary measure. It is required that we shave the area in order for it to be properly cleansed prior to the incision to reduce the risk of infection."

"Uh huh, okay. I know all of that, but it seems a little extreme, don't you think?" said Sapphire, relenting weakly even as she felt her blood pressure creep higher.

"So are you refusing to have the procedure done?" the male nurse questioned, getting a bit frustrated at Sapphire's resistance.

"No, and I'm not trying to give you a hard time either," softening her tone. Sapphire sounded exhausted and it wasn't even seven a.m., yet. The back and forth conversation was making her tired and she needed her strength for the surgery and recovery. Giving in, she closed her eyes as she heard the razor grate quickly over her. Biting her bottom lip, she knew that this would be the beginning of many unexpected events to come.

"All done," the male nurse said, touching Sapphire's right hand in an attempt to comfort her. Sapphire nodded and muttered a low, "Thank you," even though she hardly felt any gratitude for what he had just done. But protocol was protocol. Who was she to oppose standard operational procedures or the hospital's JACHO standards? Besides, she was not willing to fight all the blessed morning about such a little thing. Starting to feel jittery because the pre-op room was inhumanly cold, Sapphire pulled up the covers. A large band of butterflies seemed to collect in her stomach and she was feeling extremely anxious about going through with the procedure.

Another nurse, this time female, came to insert the IV into her arm. This would be the same IV that the anesthesia would be put in. The pain was minimal considering that she would be facing surgery in less than a half hour. Waiting for the fluid to circulate through her body to ensure that she was fully hydrated for the procedure, Sapphire thought about her mother. She would be worried about Sapphire until she got out of surgery if she had been here. She wanted her mother to be with her, but Sapphire did not tell her about the procedure until the night before. Thinking it would be too hard on her to deal with her mother's emotions, let alone her own, Sapphire opted to tell her without any notice. Envisioning the images of her mother from her childhood with the ones she had recently taken and sent to her via email, Sapphire began drifting into semi-consciousness.

Before long, Dr. Cankar came in to see her and explain to her the procedure. It was to be a simple exploration. If, in the event a tumor were found, he would remove it. Sapphire signed the release that stated his course of action, and laid back on the gurney. Dr. Miller was also there and grabbed her hand squeezing it tightly to reassure her that Dr. Cankar was the best man to perform the procedure and that they would talk in a few hours. As Sapphire was wheeled into the operating room, she noticed how bright the lights were around her. Everything looked so white and smelled so sterile. Looking around, Sapphire was flat on her back. The arch in her back refused to relent and ease into the firm mattress. The pillow had been removed from behind her head and the anesthesiologist had arrived. Dr. Miller was there to observe and watch Sapphire from behind her mask. A team of nurses and doctors had now gathered in the room and Sapphire started feeling drowsy. Her eyes grew heavy and, as if on cue, Dr. Cankar instructed her to count backwards from ten.

ꕥꕥꕥꕥꕥꕥ

Oh God. What happened to me? This doesn't feel right, Sapphire thought loudly. The raw, searing pain in her abdomen awoke her. It was like she had been sliced open and now she was awake to feel it. The last thing she remembered was saying the number seven as she counted down from ten. Barely conscious, Sapphire was aware that she was in the recovery room. It was apparent that she had survived the procedure and was beginning to wake up. Hearing what sounded like the nurses talking around her, they carried on as though she wasn't even there. The conversation was casual; discussion about last night's dinner and what choices they had for lunch. As she started to move back into consciousness, Sapphire had no desire to be fully awake. The pain was so alive and fresh that she wondered if the anesthesia was wearing off too quickly. Barely able to move and afraid of something falling out onto the floor, she lifted her head slightly to look around the room. "Ouch," Sapphire moaned, not realizing that just lifting her head off the pillow would cause so much pain. Her vision was clear but her mind was still fuzzy and that distorted the images she saw around her. There was a lot more color in this place than in the operating room and Sapphire felt more and more alive with each passing minute. As the nurses kept ignoring her waking signs, Sapphire realized that it was time to make her presence known. Lifting her arm that was attached to an assortment of tubes pumping her with fluids and other sustenance, Sapphire tried to make an audible sound. However, the oxygen mask that was over her mouth and nose made it hard for anyone to hear her, especially since she wasn't talking very loudly. Her throat was sore and ached terribly from where the breathing tube that had been inserted. As she waved her arm unsteadily, the male nurse that had shaved her earlier came over to her.

"Dr. Sykes, welcome back. You're going to feel a bit groggy, but that's normal. Are you in a lot of pain?" Sapphire tried unsuccessfully to glare at him for asking such an asinine question. *I just had surgery, you moron. Of course I am in pain.* She hoped that her telepathic message reached him although she was sure he was brain dead by the last apathetic comment he made. Sapphire tried to nod to signify that the intensity of the pain was more than she wanted to deal with.

"You can take the mask off if you feel like you are okay to breathe and are not short of breath." Sapphire was too tired to pull the mask off. All she wanted to do was rewind and go back in time before the surgery, when the pain was periodic; before she had been shaven to a pubescent baldness; before she had to inwardly digest the words 'cancer' and 'tumor'. If she could just have something to knock her out so that she wouldn't feel anything for a day or two, she thought she'd be able to cope with it. Realizing that she probably needed to verbally communicate that little bit of thought to the attending nurse, she feebly lifted her hand to her face and pulled down the mask. In a scuffled voice she made her request known, "I am in so much pain. I need something *now*."

"Yes, I know. It is going to be a little edgy, but you'll get used to it." Sapphire strained to look at the flippant male nurse. She wondered if he had ever had any type of surgery and resisted wishing a procedure on him.

"I am only going to say this one more time. Put the order in *now*! I can't deal with it and I refuse to deal with it now. If you can't do it, give me the phone and I'll order it myself." Sapphire's ire rose above her physical fatigue, her grogginess and her patience. She would not rest until she had a new nurse and a few liters of IV drugs laced with Demerol or Morphine.

"Let me get the doctor," the young nurse replied, scurrying away in his post-op scrubs. His covered feet barely touched the floor when he almost ran out of the recovery room. Looking around, Sapphire saw a couple of other people still unconscious lying around her. She hadn't noticed them before. It was odd to see other people right after surgery. Some of them looked inflated, lips puffy and cracked. Others looked like they had the life sucked right out of them, deflated and shriveled up. Either way, they were all knocked out. Sapphire wondered if they would all wake up, whether in comas or in a drug-induced sleep.

Dr. Cankar bolted through the door of the recovery room. He looked like he had just awakened, too and was walking straight to Sapphire's bed.

"You woke earlier than we expected."

"Really?" Sapphire wondered what that meant. Perhaps she wasn't given enough anesthesia, which could explain why she felt like she could remember bits and pieces of the procedure.

"Well, I understand you are asking for pain medication."

"Yes. When can I have it?"

"Well, soon. I wanted to talk to you about the surgery first." Sapphire knew something was not right. The events were not shaping up as she thought they should. All she wanted was some Demerol -- that was it. But now the doctor wanted to "talk." This was not a good sign.

"Okay," Sapphire replied as she still lay at an uncomfortable angle to fully see the doctor. The pain was too intense to fully concentrate, but Sapphire tried to focus as the affects of the anesthesia wore off.

"Well, there is no easy way to say this, but we found a large malignant growth in your uterus and several smaller tumors or cysts in your right ovary. We did a pathology screen of the cells of both tumors to find that they were indeed cancer, which I am sure you expected. As the surgery progressed, we found that some of the cells in the larger tumor leaked in the uterus, and to prevent further damage, the surgery team determined it was best to perform a radical hysterectomy." Sapphire could not believe what she was hearing. First of all, she had cancer. Second, she had two different types of cancer in two different places. Thirdly, she didn't have any more reproductive organs. The last one made her go from flabbergasted to down right outraged. When did the "exploratory" surgery go from being simple to removing everything that produced estrogen within her? She wanted answers. She attempted to sit upright and was blinded by a triple threat: rage, pain and truth. She passed out from shock as codes blared and IV's were ordered, rushing to sedate the good therapist.

Sapphire awoke again, this time uncertain of how much time had passed. She could not feel her lower extremities but had a clear view of

Dr. Cankar. He approached her bed gingerly, announcing that she had been sedated and that twenty-four hours had passed, and that they should continue their discussion. Dr. Cankar tried to continue his dissertation of the results of the surgery when Sapphire focused again on her reality. A hysterectomy—no. A TOTAL hysterectomy! With all the medical, technological and engineering advances, leaving her with no options was unacceptable and simply unheard of in this day and age. The therapist was not ready to comprehend the necessity of this. Sapphire knew it was not a dream, although her hope willed it to be. The procedure Dr. Cankar spoke so callously about was a harsh but true reality; one she could not reverse or change.

Seeing that Sapphire was again getting infuriated, Dr. Cankar motioned for the nurses to bring the pain medication and sedative for her. She shook her head violently to protest. She wanted to deal with this right now. As Sapphire began to grit her teeth in anger, trying to breathe, cough and tell the doctor that he did not have a right to remove her uterus; she barely noticed Dr. Miller had slipped into the room. Sapphire zeroed in on her, searching her doctor's face for an answer. In a raspy, strained voice, she asked, "Michelle, tell me. Tell me you didn't do this to me." Dr. Miller eyes spoke the truth Sapphire couldn't bear to hear. Dr. Miller tried to open her mouth to explain the necessity of the outcome of the procedure, but as a woman, she couldn't even bare her lips to utter the justification her male colleague had maintained during the surgery.

Through the night, Sapphire would awaken, sweating feverishly, going in and out of delirious dreams that turned into hallucinations then back to dreams again. To Sapphire it was like being in the Wiz, in a fantasy world that overlapped with her reality. She didn't like this feeling--completely detached from the pain in her body but totally attached to the drugs plaguing her subconscious mind.

At one point in the fight between streams of consciousness, Sapphire was awake long enough to envision her mother. This must have been what her mother felt when she was given antidepressants and other stimulants to alter her state of mind when she wasn't at all insane. The turmoil of trying to chase her sanity through the hurdles of unnecessary medications must have drained her. No doubt, her spirit must have been broken, time and time again.

Imagining what her mother must have gone through made Sapphire pull through the depression that was starting to overtake her so quickly after the surgery. It would take God and time to heal her from the emptiness she felt. And even then, she needed more than a cliché of "everything is going to be all right." She needed intercession. She needed a faith that she hadn't grabbed hold of since her last tragic circumstance. Even though she knew that God would not fail her, she kept thinking, *but this is really big Lord*. So she began in the only way she knew how; in a soft, simple meditation. *Jesus. Jesus. Jesus.* Over and over again, she repeated His name, until she lapsed once again into unconsciousness.

Sapphire awakened to an unusually bright sky. Someone had taken it upon them self to open her blinds. She sat up cautiously. Looking around, questioning the purpose of her existence, she looked out at the view. As far as she could see were the sky and the lake, one cerulean and the other almost teal. They were different and yet reflected off of each other. Sapphire just stared blankly wanting to cry but unable to find a tear to moisten the sclera of her eyes. She wanted her reflection to bounce off of her ability to rise above this situation and move on with her life. The point was nobody could tell her anything she wanted to know. And that made Sapphire question every principle she knew was right. It was now a matter of life and death and even the most reasonable explanation of why this happened to her failed when she put her life next to it. And for once in her life, Sapphire wondered if her life had actually been spared or if living would be worse than dying. Sapphire couldn't face the person in the mirror. Not now.

Chapter 31.

MORE BLESSED TO GIVE

Ravinia knew this hospital all too well. She had given birth to the twins here and remembered the wallpaper in the birthing room. It was pink and blue pastel with little knitted stockings stamped on the print. Feeling her face smile, she remembered why she had come back to this place. Reaching the information desk, she asked for Sapphire Sykes' room. The white-haired woman manning the desk asked was she a family member or a friend. Ravinia replied in non-response fashion, "Yes," but the lady gave her an admission card anyway.

"She's on three South, Women's Health," the elderly volunteer advised. Just take the elevator to your left up to three and make a right. Stop at the front desk to make sure she can have visitors."

"Thank you, ma'am," Ravinia kindly replied. The clear cellophane wrapping barely covered the ivy leaves of the plant arrangement she had brought for her therapist. Hesitant that Sapphire would not receive her for fear of breaking patient-doctor confidentiality, Ravinia bit her bottom lip nervously. When she found out what had happened to Sapphire, her heart went out for her. She had to do something to redeem herself after walking out of their last session and never returning. There was a deep yearning that made her want to go to see her, and until she did, that pervasive sensation would not go away. As she got to the elevator, the doors opened and she saw a very tall man.

Why is he everywhere I go? Ravinia asked herself. Reverend Wright was exiting the elevator that Ravinia was about to enter. He looked different though, than the last time she saw him. His countenance was glowing and he seemed very peaceful.

"Sistah Hamilton. What a pleasant surprise!" the Reverend greeted her wholeheartedly, slightly chuckling. You would have never thought the last time Ravinia saw him her husband was chasing him down the street. His eyes still had that intricate pattern of greens and ambers that floated in symmetry. "Sistah Ravinia, it's so nice to see you again," a deep female voice dropped amiably. Faintly recognizing the voice, Ravinia turned to see Mattie Reynolds standing calmly behind her. She was holding a medium-sized basket of flowers and several stringed balloons, smiling coolly at Ravinia next to the Reverend. Ravinia was speechless. She felt her lower extremities go numb and her mouth begin to feel dry. Never in a million years had she expected to see either one of them at the hospital. She braced herself in case there might be a confrontation. Ravinia wasn't sure what the Reverend had told Mattie about them. She recalled that at one point Mattie had been suspicious of her and the Reverend's counseling sessions.

"Sistah Hamilton, are you alright?" the Reverend asked in a concerned voice. Apparently, Ravinia was so stunned she hadn't said a word. Yet, Ravinia didn't even blink. Scenes from her escapades with the Reverend flashed vividly before her blazing eyes. She could feel the heat burn in them as she watched the sinful acts they committed in the church itself. Feeling so ashamed to be facing a woman who truly seemed to care for the Reverend, Ravinia started feeling flush. Guilty thoughts began to inundate her mind as she wondered if Mattie ever forgave the Reverend for what he did with her. Certainly, Ravinia did not want to be the reason a young, eligible bachelorette like Mattie would be cheated out of a chance to have the Reverend for life and for love.

"Uh, oh, yes. I'm sorry," she stammered after a moment, blinking the stray memories away. Just then, the light tan leather straps of her Louis Vuitton bag started to slide down the length of her slender arms from the bend in her elbow. She panicked as she thought the sliding bag would cause her to drop the ivy plant and the book she had gotten for Sapphire.

"Help her, baby," said Mattie as she motioned to the Reverend, quickly popping a wad of what smelled like Double-mint gum. She had a slight grin on her face as she watched Ravinia struggle. Realizing she was delighting in her rival's difficulty to manage her parcels, Mattie changed the expression on her face to be one of concern. It wasn't necessary to monitor Ravinia's behavior because it was obvious who was with whom. But Ravinia had caught a glimpse of Mattie's face before it had changed and she understood within her spirit that Mattie knew that she had been the competition.

The Reverend's face turned a mild shade of rose when Mattie uttered the word "baby." His reaction seemed to please Mattie so she joined in the effort and stretched out her hand to help Ravinia juggle her things. Ravinia looked up at the way Mattie referred to the preacher. Then she noticed the younger lady's left hand and saw a stunning almost two carat emerald cut engagement ring on her ring finger.

"Oh!" Ravinia gasped. "What a gorgeous ring, Mattie," she added in amazement, rising up from almost dropping the plant again. Mattie blushed deeply. Her low southern voice was characteristically sultry and suited her dainty demeanor. Mattie was from Georgia and her demeanor was certainly befitting of a Georgia peach—sweet and gushing. The fine downy hairs that traced her jaw line revealed that she was naturally hairy; a trait some men found attractive about her. Combed back off her almost peachy-bronze complexion, Mattie's silky-fine, waist-length hair was always pinned up in a chignon or French roll. Mattie characteristically did the "Creole stroll" when she walked down the aisle at church. Today however, she strutted proudly, hips swaying in her peplum suit. Her figure was so tight it was reminiscent of the character *"Sandra"* on that popular, Black 80's sitcom, *227*. She worked her hips so fine, she could make a Septuagint stand up and holler. Mattie was an honest to goodness southern belle--hat wearing and all. The only thing she didn't have was a parasol, but of course, this was Chicago, not Georgia. For the life of her, Ravinia could never figure out why the Reverend passed Mattie over for her. They were a perfect match. And how could he possibly cheat on *her*? But it didn't seem to matter now.

"Willie just proposed last Sunday in service. He was so bold, I couldn't even move. I just sat in my seat looking up at him 'til somebody nudged me to go up there and get the ring." Mattie nudged in closer to the tall Reverend's side, marking her territory securely. And as if on cue, the Reverend pulled little Mattie into a warm embrace making Ravinia aware that she was alone.

"That's so wonderful. I am really happy for the both of you," Ravinia said truthfully. She felt like a yoke had just lifted off her shoulders. They looked so happy, though she could tell that the Reverend had a slight look of concern in his eyes, as if he was hoping Ravinia wouldn't go delving into their past affairs and mess things up for him. What he didn't know was that Ravinia was more over him than he would ever know. She was glad someone was finally making an honest man out of him.

"Well, we need to get going. Oh yes. Ravinia, do you remember little Shirley Mays, the youth choir director?" Mattie asked Ravinia.

"Yes," Ravinia nodded in implicit acknowledgement.

"She was in a car accident and broke her leg. I just went to get these flowers and balloons for her. Can you believe no one had even sent her a card yet and the accident was on Tuesday?"

"That's a crying shame. Well, I'm sure she'll love this," Ravinia smiled. She felt so good on the inside. Finally, there was some closure on that chapter of her life.

"I need to get going myself. I am here visiting a friend."

"Well, we hope to see you at church, soon. The wedding is going to be in June," the future Mrs. Wright's voice trailed off as the couple waved.

"All right," Ravinia waved back to the exiting couple. She had noticed that Willie had not said much the whole time, but it was just as well. It was probably best that way. Ravinia knew that Mattie only invited her to church as an open invitation and not a personal one. She knew that she would probably never step foot back into First Baptist again.

Pressing the Up arrow to call the elevator, she waited patiently for the car to arrive. Getting in, she pressed "3" and stepped towards the back, allowing the other passengers to step inside. Reading the digital panel, she saw it said, "7:44 p.m." and "Visiting Hours are from 10 a.m. to 8 p.m." She thought, *I hope I have enough time to get up there.*

The doors opened as the chimes signified the arrival to her floor. Ravinia exited the elevator and headed toward the nurse's station. Asking for Sapphire Sykes, she was told to be quiet and keep her visit brief.

Sapphire's door was slightly ajar. Ravinia tiptoed into the private room and looked at her former doctor. Her eyes were shut tight and her face was a little puffy. Her lips were rosy lavender and were chapped. Her swollen fingers also told the story of what had happened to her. Ravinia placed the ivy plant she had brought onto the window ledge. She looked out at a northern sky and saw traces of Lake Michigan. It hurt to see Sapphire like this, all vulnerable and exposed. Hearing a slight moaning sound from Sapphire, Ravinia turned to see her therapist's face grimace.

"Who's here," a painful, scratchy voice uttered. Ravinia wondered if she should say anything. Sapphire hadn't even opened her eyes yet. She was reaching for the control buttons to lift her bed to a position where she wouldn't have to move much to see her company. Finding the Up button, she pressed piecemeal, making "ouch" sounds on the way to a more upright position. Her loud breathy sighs were more than Ravinia could take.

"I know what you're gonna say, Dr. Sykes, but I had to come see you," Ravinia explained.

"Ravinia, is that you. How did you get. . ." Sapphire began to ask with a strained look on her face.

"How is not important," Ravinia interrupted. What *is* important is that I am here and I want to help in anyway that I can," Ravinia said, reaching her hand out to Sapphire for support as she tried to adjust herself without moving her abdomen.

"Can you hand me that pillow?" Sapphire pointed to the chair. "I need to cough," she said candidly. Ravinia quickly walked over to the hospital's rendition of a Lazy Boy recliner and brought the pillow to Sapphire.

"Hold it firmly on your belly," Ravinia offered, remembering the C-Section she had with the twins.

"I know how to do it," Sapphire said coldly, finding it difficult to talk and resist the tickling in the back of her throat.

"Of course you do," said Ravinia, feeling a bit cut down. Looking around, she knew it would be difficult trying to get through to Sapphire. They weren't very close and certainly the currencies were imbalanced in what Sapphire knew about Ravinia versus what Ravinia knew about Sapphire. But she didn't let that stop her. Something kept compelling her to persist.

"Do you want some water?" Ravinia asked cheerfully, looking at the pink pitcher prepared for Sapphire on the ledge.

"Yes" Sapphire responded slowly as she watched Ravinia pour the water into her cup, eyeing her perfectly coiffed hair and the way her pink Guess tee shirt was neatly tucked into her jeans. Looking at Ravinia made Sapphire ache. *Why is she here?* Sapphire asked herself, over and over again. Sapphire barely wanted to see anyone she knew, let along a former patient of hers. She inattentively smiled back at Ravinia when she handed her the water and said a gracious "thank you," but she felt like she was being pitied.

"So, how are things at home, Ravinia?" Sapphire asked. She tried to think about something other than herself since she wasn't in a very good mood after having found out yesterday that the doctor had removed both her ovaries without saving either one of them. Devising several legal plans to sue, she knew that she needed to remain positive if she was going to overcome this.

"Actually, pretty good. But I don't want to focus on that right now. How are *you* doing, Sapphire?" Ravinia asked, looking as if she didn't have a care in the world and also redirecting the attention and conversation off of her and back onto Sapphire. She took the liberty of calling the doctor by her first name, not even knowing if it would be acceptable. Risking more than just her relationship with her former therapist, she also wondered if her decision to visit Sapphire was a help or a hindrance.

"Oh?" Sapphire questioned, as she sipped the ice water. She was quite warm and still a little feverish. Her face shone from the sweat that had formed from the post-operative fever. The doctors had given her antibiotics in case she developed an infection. There was a small section of the cancer that had metastasized in Sapphire's abdominal wall. The doctor told her that she would have to get chemotherapy to kill off the remaining cancer that could not be removed from surgery without damaging her intestines. Not knowing what she would have to face, her thoughts flicked from scene to scene. She wasn't much company for Ravinia and didn't bother to apologize for it because she had not asked Ravinia to come see her. She also didn't care much that her hair was all over her head and getting thick at the roots. She didn't care that she was dressed in a soiled gown and needed a sponge bath. She just didn't care.

"So, Dr. Sykes or can I call you Sapphire?" Ravinia asked, setting the water pitcher down on her tray table.

"Might as well just call me, Sapphire. You know this ruins our client-patient relationship. Ethically, I can't see you anymore," Sapphire said in a perturbed tone as she tried to maneuver her aching body upwards in the hospital bed.

"Yes, I didn't really think about that, you know, but I'm all right with that. I really wanted to do this—come and see you and all," Ravinia replied honestly looking at Sapphire grimace and almost curse under her breath. Sapphire didn't know whether to be offended at Ravinia's response or take it as a compliment.

"Well, you should have. We were really starting to get somewhere with your situation. Why did you come here in the first place? I don't understand."

Sapphire was getting suddenly more and more frustrated at her guest. Ravinia hesitated for a minute and bit down on her bottom lip to fight back her impulsive response to leave.

"I really don't know myself. I felt an urgency to come and see you after I heard about your situation at church. Sister Jade Jackson asked the church to pray for you. You know her right? Anyway, it was as if I needed to fulfill something in my life, and that something was to put my concerns aside and do something good for someone else," Ravinia said, pacing the floor as she talked.

"Uh huh," retorted Sapphire, glaring at Ravinia in disbelief. "Whatever." It seemed as if Ravinia's need to feel good about herself was coming at the expense of the doctor. And that did not sit well with Sapphire since Ravinia was the messed up one. She was the one that needed psychotherapy, not her. Sapphire just couldn't see the good in Ravinia's intentions.

Ravinia could barely believe what she was witnessing. Usually, Dr. Sykes was upbeat, chipper, and happy to see her. Now she was downright rude, nonchalant, and seemingly angry at something more than just Ravinia coming to see her uninvited and unannounced. Ravinia didn't want to take offense to her former therapist's attitude, but it did hurt her feelings a little.

"Well, I am sorry if I intruded. That wasn't my intention," a meek Ravinia commented. "I'll be praying for a speedy recovery."

"Thanks for coming. Be sure to close the door on your way out," Sapphire expressed loudly as Ravinia picked up her purse from the chair. Sapphire was feeling worse than any day of her life--including the rape--and she didn't care who knew it. When the door slammed from its weight, she felt like she had been slapped in the face. *That Jade,* Sapphire thought but quickly erased the ill-willed thought. Knowing she shouldn't have been so harsh with Ravinia, she felt remorse. If she could have mustered up some tears, she would have cried. But she did feel a slight stinging in her tear ducts.

As she tried to wipe the tear in half formation, she realized that her IV didn't feel right. Looking down on her left arm, it was swelling up and she started feeling a great amount of pressure where the needle had been inserted. She reached over to the call button on her bed and paged the nurse's station. Instead of someone coming right away, they took their time. It was nearly fifteen minutes before someone came and turned the call light off. Sapphire was livid at that point. Apparently the IV had come out of place and the fluid was leaking outside of her vein. It had been three days since she had gotten the IV, and apparently the vein wanted out of the whole deal. This time she couldn't repress her emotions. Sapphire was so angry she found the strength to make tears and forced them out of her. Slowly, she let each tear flow, hot and wet down the apples of her cheeks. The Philippino nurse noticed her tears. Her badge said, "Ligaya," and she seemed unconcerned until she saw that Sapphire was crying.

"It's going to be okay, honey. You'll get through this," nurse Ligaya consoled.

"That's easy for you to say. You didn't just have a hysterectomy."

"No, I didn't. But that doesn't mean your life is over."

"Really? How would *you* know anything about my life?" Sapphire screamed at the nurse. The sound of her own elevated voice startled her. It was an odd occasion when Dr. Sykes raised her voice at anyone. "You don't know anything about me."

"I know that life is worth living. I know that if you believe, all things are possible. I know that you could be dead instead of alive, and you are alive."

"Great. I am alive. Now what? Cancer is hopeless," Sapphire said, spitting out the words she had been thinking but felt she should not utter. Looking out the window, she winced as the nurse rubbed her sore inflated arm.

"It is not hopeless. I survived cancer because I fought it. I prayed to God that He would let me live because I wanted life. You can never give up. If you do, then you've proven that you are not worthy to live and that makes you lower than any living thing, including a cockroach."

Sapphire sat there listening to this nurse go on and on about life and living and now cockroaches. The woman's words danced around Sapphire's aching head like lightening bugs flittering around a porch light on a hot summer's night. Eventually, they would sink in, but for now, they just danced a dance out of sync with Sapphire's understanding. All that talking and listening made her tired. Deciding it would be better to sleep her worries away than try to face them awake, she asked the gentle-faced nurse for some pain medication and sleeping pills so that she could rest. The nurse put in the order over the phone to the pharmacy and stayed with Sapphire until it was transported to her floor for dispensing.

Helping her get as comfortable as a woman who had just had a radical hysterectomy could, Ligaya stayed close by sympathizing with Sapphire. She could feel the pain that Sapphire felt and the anger and emptiness that filled her soul. The rage of injustice brewed within Sapphire as she held the feelings inside of the emptiness that remained. She wondered how long it would take to heal from the scars that the previous days had brought. In all her experience with cancer patients, the compassionate nurse knew that if Sapphire truly wanted to survive, she would have to do it on her own. Most of all, she saw something in Sapphire that she had once seen in herself. It was apparent that Sapphire wanted to live. It was her words that fought back and resisted everything in her presence. Her will to survive was greater than the journey she had traveled. But even more than that, Sapphire had to realize that God had not brought her this far just to leave her.

Chapter 32.

IF AT FIRST

After the way Sapphire treated her, Ravinia should have been discouraged; but she would not allow her 'calling' to be squelched by her current face of dismay. She could not relate to the ordeals of having cancer or a hysterectomy, but she knew that she could do something to help, even if it was to just sit with or hand her former therapist a cold glass of water. This was a lot for Sapphire to face on her own. Perhaps her rudeness to Ravinia was justified. Deciding instead of giving into Sapphire's antics, Ravinia determined that she would persevere in her personal ministry. It would take a lot more than Sapphire telling her to let the door hit her where God created the great divide to make her stop caring about visiting the sick and shut in. In fact, Ravinia decided she wouldn't let a day go by without seeing Sapphire again.

At the hospital, Ravinia ended up parking near the front entrance. As she walked through the reception area of the large hospital, she heard a piano playing. It was odd to hear music within hospital walls, so Ravinia was drawn through the concourse to the atrium. When she entered the arched door of the elegant open room, she noticed a man playing a grand piano right in the middle of the floor. The acoustics of the hollowed room were perfect and the melodious notes bounced off the walls as if it were a grand ballroom. Ravinia stopped at the café for a French vanilla cappuccino latte and leaned on the exposed brick wall across from the piano, holding her hot drink as she soaked in the music. Scanning the room, Ravinia noticed that there was a mixed audience of hospital employees, visitors and patients lined around on the second story balcony overlooking the atrium. Spotting Sapphire, Ravinia decided to go up to the second floor and casually talk to her. When she arrived, Sapphire looked at her and smiled sheepishly.

"I'm surprised to see you here today," Sapphire said, looking up at Ravinia from her wheelchair. "That smells really good."

"You want me to get you one?" Ravinia asked.

"Nah. I probably shouldn't have any. I'm already getting hot flashes or whatever this is and that caffeine will probably mess me up," she laughed gently, fanning herself briskly.

"Right," agreed Ravinia. She briefly wondered what it felt like to not have her ovaries and uterus anymore, but quickly dismissed that thought from her head.

"What is this?" Sapphire asked Ravinia. She looked up at Ravinia gazing longingly down at the pianist. It was as if she wanted to join in with him, but knew that she shouldn't.

"Chopin. Isn't it just exquisite?"

"Didn't you tell me that you play an instrument?" Sapphire inquired of Ravinia tracing her memory. "What was it, a cello or something?"

"Close. I played violin in high school."

"Were you any good?"

"Pretty good. I was first chair and I ended up taking music theory as a minor in college."

"Really. Wow. I always wanted to play something, but my father wouldn't let me. He said it was a waste of time."

"Well one thing it is *not* is a waste of time. I haven't played seriously in years, though. But you know, it is something that really has helped me through some tough times."

"I bet. I love orchestra music. It is so soothing, and healing, too," commented Sapphire over her shoulder as she started to wheel herself back to her room. Ravinia, realizing Sapphire shouldn't be using her abdominal muscles yet, grabbed the handles and pushed Sapphire toward her room.

"Yes, it is." Sapphire noticed how lost Ravinia seemed to be in the rapture of the music being rendered, and it made her think.

"You know, you should really think about signing up with the Arts Department at the hospital. They have a volunteer program where musicians come in and play for the patients. It is sort of like music therapy."

"I never thought about that," Ravinia said, walking next to Sapphire in her wheelchair. She opened the door to Sapphire's room to find the nurse turning down her bed.

"Oh, I think that would be awesome for you."

"I definitely have to check that out. Thanks."

"Not a problem," Sapphire said as she carefully lifted herself out of the wheel chair. The hardest part was standing up and moving those muscles that had been expanded in the surgery. She was still extremely sore, but was trying to get used to maneuvering through the pain.

"So Ravinia, tell me about what's been going on?" Sapphire asked, trying to divert her attention while she eased herself back into bed.

Getting up to assist, Ravinia said, "You sound like you are about to start a session."

"I do, don't I? Guess I can't do that anymore, huh," Sapphire chuckled.

"Yup. But we can still talk can't we?" Sapphire nodded, permitting Ravinia to continue.

"Everything is kind of touch and go between Xavier and me. After my mother's death, we were going to work on finding out what we were going to do about our marriage. I think we both just avoided the situation for a while and that didn't help. Xavier just kept staying away from the house. Finally, I called him one day at work and, well, we ended up deciding that we would try and work things out."

"Are you sure that is the best decision? He did cheat on you, right?"

"Yeah, we both did. You know that. I think that we left out some important things in our lives when we started to drift. I am not even sure if we married for love, or even for the right reasons. But something happened when we were apart from each other. I think we both wanted wholeness."

"Uh-huh. And did you find that?" Sapphire questioned, catching herself going back into psychoanalytical mode again.

"I think so. I think it is something that we both have to invest in. I can't make our marriage work all by myself. He has to want to be committed to it just as much as I am. And you know, I think I am falling in love with him," Ravinia confessed as a blush formed over her cheeks. Ravinia could feel the excitement of knowing that her man would be there at home waiting for her.

"Ah, sounds like you are well on your way. I was concerned when you didn't come back. I didn't know what happened to you."

"Yeah. I am sorry about that. I think that I had to find out for myself what I needed most in life. And it wasn't my kids or Xavier. I needed to know that I could be forgiven. That in all the wrongs in my life, there was something that made sense. Something that was good and right."

"Hmmm. Now that's interesting." Sapphire's voice dropped. "So it sounds like you aren't still seeing 'the Reverend.' When Sapphire said 'the Reverend,' Ravinia looked up. She thought about the encounter she had just yesterday and started to speak.

"Yes. I ended it with him."

"Good," Sapphire snapped quickly. Thinking about her next sentence, she hesitated before speaking. What she was about to reveal could cost her everything, but at that point, she was beginning to see Ravinia as a friend, not a former patient.

"As your doctor, I could not tell you this. And I probably could still get in a lot of trouble revealing this to you. But. . ."

Ravinia looked strangely at Dr. Sykes. Sapphire's face was drawn and serious. Her eyes grew distant and cold.

"What is it? It's ok. You can tell me," reassured Ravinia, trying to instill confidence that she would not turn Sapphire into the review board for whatever it was she was about to say.

"I can't. It's—it's—it's just too bad." Sapphire dropped her head and then looked away. She struggled intensely with what was heavy in her heart. Ravinia didn't want to push, but she could tell it was something she needed to know. Then a sickening thought came over her. Ravinia tried to cancel it, but it was just too real to retract. *Was my doctor sleeping with him too?* Just then, Sapphire opened her mouth to say something, but the words didn't come out.

Dryly she finally cleared her throat and blurted out, "William Wright raped me." The doctor felt relieved that she got those four little words out but uncertain if she had made the right decision in telling her former patient, especially this one. Hoping some finality to Ravinia's decision not to see him again would be solidified by her revelation, Sapphire looked away trying to see what the window cleaners were doing.

The silence between them was deadening. Ravinia was in pure shock. She couldn't say a word. All this time, she had been talking to this woman about her infidelity and she had experienced a violent crime at the same man's hands. The gamut of possibilities flooded Ravinia's head and she couldn't sort out her thoughts. Realizing that she had to move on through this, for the sake of Sapphire's condition, she quickly came back to her senses. Kneeling down in front of Sapphire so she could be on the same level with her as she sat on the side of her bed, she quietly said in the most concerned voice, "Oh, I am so sorry, Sapphire. I had no idea." Sapphire tried to smile, but the muscles in her face wouldn't lie.

"You couldn't have. It happened a long time ago, in Boston." *Boston?* Ravinia thought to herself. *When was the Reverend in Boston?*

"We were in college and were dating. He raped me and I've never been able to fully recover from it."

"How could you?" Ravinia lingered. Sapphire jumped in and said, "I mean, listening to you talk about how you two were together just ripped me apart. What he did to me messed me up. But I overcame it."

"I don't even know what to say, Sapphire," Ravinia said in sounding despondent.

"Don't say anything. I see something in you, Ravinia, that I know will get you through this rough time in your marriage. Whatever the outcome, you are a survivor."

"Reverend Willie Wright," Ravinia repeated in disbelief, shaking her head in disgust. All the respect she had gained for him by seeing him for a short time with Mattie was just flushed down the drain in a matter of minutes.

You know, that's all I am going to say about that. I made up in my mind, I want to live," Sapphire confidently said, changing the subject. The therapist continued on. "Jade was talking about you just last night on the phone. She said she really thought you were sincere. How you joined her church and have really been making a difference in your life."

"Yeah. I guess I had to lose some pretty important things in my life to realize that I needed to find out the truth about myself," Ravinia admitted. "I'm still searching for that truth. I mean, I know it's out there. And, I'm not talking about X-files," Sapphire smiled briefly. It was apparent she was getting tired.

"I believe in God and His power in my life. But, you know, being in this situation just really makes me question my purpose in life. At one time I used to be so sure of myself. But these days, I don't feel like I know much about anything--least of all, what I'm doing on this earth."

"Sapphire, one day that will ring clear. You'll be able to fully understand your purpose."

"I hope so. I just feel so raw and bitter right now. I mean, what else do I have to go through in my life?" the former therapist admitted, gritting her teeth.

Ravinia's life and situation paled to Sapphire's. It was hard to know what to say, if anything at all. She couldn't fathom being raped, and then living through it to find out that she would never be able to have children due to cancer. Ravinia didn't know what else Sapphire had not revealed, but that was enough to make her count her blessings and pray for Sapphire to find comfort in the midst of her situation. Ravinia opened her mouth to say something, but snapped it closed. Then, forcing the words, she blurted out, "You, too, Sapphire. You will survive. You've got to. I didn't tell you this because I was so guarded with you before, but something brought me to the hospital to see you. When I heard what happened, my heart ached for you. I felt, in some strange, inexplicable way, that my good friend was in pain. And the truth is, I missed you. I know that we weren't really friends, but I felt that we were. And if we are somehow connected and I am a survivor, then you must be, too. And one more thing you must know. I am honored that you have trusted me with your confidences. I will always guard them with the same level of trust and respect as if we still had a patient-doctor relationship."

When Ravinia finished her soliloquy, Sapphire sat quietly with tears in her eyes. She whispered a weak, "Thank you," before clearing the lump in her throat with a cough. "It's funny. I had that exact same feeling." Letting out a heavy sigh, Sapphire rested her head back on the pillow. "Wow, I guess all this female bonding has tuckered me out," she said, chuckling low and satisfying. "I'm really glad you stopped by, Ravinia. I'll be getting out in a day or so. As soon as all my bodily functions start again, we should do lunch when I get out," she winked.

"Sounds like a plan," Ravinia said, slightly taken aback by the doctor's candor. Closing the door behind her, Ravinia felt better about the day's events. Not only had she overcome the previous day's rejection, she had been a friend to someone. Life was beginning to turn around. If only she could stop thinking about Reverend Wright.

Chapter 33.

REMINISCING

To be a good Christian, Momma, rest her dear soul, sure was color-struck. Whenever she got wind of me courting some young dude from school, she would peek out the window to take a good, long look at him, giving him the stern eye, should he look her way. And if he didn't meet her color specifications, she'd say I couldn't make time with him. I felt bad for all the dark skinned boys who were fond of me, because Momma would never let them set foot in our house--not talking about going out with *me*. She would always say, "Ravinia, you got to think about how your kids will turn out. You're dark enough. You need a real light skinned boy, like Nate, to pull your complexion out and ease the tension in your hair." I loved the tension in my hair. All in all, its coil and spring spoke to my spunky personality. Yet, there came a time when I wanted my nappy edges to be hot combed. I would heat up the comb on the stove and tap it on a clean washcloth. If it didn't make the cloth yellow and still smoked, it was probably just right to zip through the new growth on my temples. I tried hard not to burn myself, lest I would have to rub cocoa butter on it so as not to leave a mark.

I never understood why Momma could feel so strongly about complexion. It didn't much matter to me. I liked boys. Period. No matter what their color, I liked them. I even liked some boys who weren't Black, and that was awkward at times, but adventurous. I wanted to see if they would go out with me, but they never asked. It was unthinkable back then; but in Evanston, a suburb just north of Chicago along Lake Michigan, it seemed that interracial couples were more common there than in other areas in and around Chicago.

We lived a convenient, direct path across from Evanston High School. Unfortunately, Nate and I could never get away with anything because Momma could just pop over at any time. There were days when she would get off early from the Weiss's and "drop in" on us. We never knew if we would just see her walking the hallway, or find her checking on us with one of our teachers to see if we were up to something. And if we were, she'd be on our behinds like white on rice. And Momma didn't particularly care where we were or who was watching. She would set us out right in front of the street, in front of our friends, teachers or whole class. Nate hated it because he was always up to something and she would call him out, embarrassing him in front of all his wannabe thug friends. Call it intuition, mother wit, or that extra somethin'-somethin' God put in her spirit, but Momma seemed to run right into us acting up. After a while, we caught on and started looking over our shoulders just about all the time. It was at the time that I would be at my locker or in a secluded place near the auditorium lip-locked with an anxious little boy who wanted just ten minutes to prove he was a man that she would show up. It was as if she knew exactly where I would be and when. Boys were scared of my Momma, and it took having girls of my own, to understand why my mother did what she did.

She loved us and wanted the best for us. She worked hard as a single mother, with barely more to offer us than her ex-husband's last name. She had to work for someone else's family, keeping them fed and their home clean, in order to provide us with a decent household. That made her more than just a mother. Her sacrifices were not always her heart's desire. She had always wanted to go back to school and become a nurse or something. But, in her day, going to college was a gift, or something otherwise reserved for 'well-to-do' Blacks. Coming from the deep South, a lot of talented kids got passed up. Some of them got lucky, though, if a rich benefactor would sponsor them--taking them under their wing, mentoring them through the world of knowledge. I never knew my Momma wanted to go to school until I became an adult. I knew it all too clearly the day I graduated from college was the happiest day of her life. It wasn't easy, though. College was one of the hardest things I ever had to do.

All through college, Momma would call leaving messages on my dorm room answering machine telling me, "I hope you getting your studies, Vinia. I ain't got you in school to be messing around, whoring. You need to come to church so you can get some prayer to keep you going. And you bet' not get pregnant. That's all I need is a bunch of grandbabies running 'round. I just got Nate out the house. You hear me, gurl. You hear me?" Click. On the days when I was actually in my room to answer, I would always say, "Yes, ma'am, Momma," only half-listening to her ranting and raving. But in my heart of hearts, I heard her. It was her voice that I would hear when I would be pushing some nasty dude I barely knew up off of me, on the verge of a one night stand, trying to maintain some dignity for myself. It was her shrill little voice I heard when I was given a joint to smoke. I would always end up turning it away because the constant warning in Momma's voice always drowned out all the other voices I could devise in my confused little head. When I couldn't make decent decisions on my own, her voice seemed to always come through, loud and clear.

I made her proud, even though she never said it. It wasn't until after her death did people come up to me and tell me how much she talked about me and how proud she was of Xavier and me. She wanted so much for me; perhaps she thought that if I knew how pleased she was that somehow, things wouldn't turn out right. One thing was certain: she didn't want me to mess up my life. I didn't always understand her ways or appreciate why it was so important to her that I be a success. What I needed from her was acceptance, love, and understanding. What she wanted to give me, though, was the removal of the curse—the cycle of destruction that was so prominent in African American families. She kept standing in the gap and that gap represented what I ran so desperately from when her voice would chase me from every appearance of evil. Momma wanted to have the fruit of her womb go to college, finish and make something of themselves. She didn't want us to be another mere statistic. She didn't want to look up on the news and hear about us doing something that would cause her shame. Our mother raised us better than that and wanted us to honor her and her teachings.

If ever Momma were called to pick us up from school, she would be there within minutes with a stressed, stern look on her long face, like we weren't supposed to get sick. We knew if she had to get up from watching "The Price is Right" with Bob Barker, our behinds were toast. I miss Momma. Nothing in the world can change that. I know she is in a better place, but I still miss her presence.

Nate and I had finally finished getting all of Momma's things moved out. He had brought his things upstairs and the house was starting to look more like Nate's house than our family home. I held on to the precious memories. I quickly thanked Momma for swallowing her pride and allowing herself to be taken care of. Eventually, I think she realized it was the best thing for her. I wondered for a moment how she could have lived for so long without a companion. Not once after our father left us did she date or make her acquaintance with another man; it didn't even seem to concern her. I think that is how she justified being so hard on me and my need to define myself through men. Keeping herself busy with church activities, knitting, and watching her grandchildren, Momma had no time to feel the need for a male companion. It was not as if they didn't try. Katie Mae could still turn heads; but she was determined not to go back to a life of misery caused by someone she loved.

She would say, in her Creole-sounding way, "The Lord, He keeps me. His spirit comforts me, ev'ryday. He is my ev'rything, chile. Ev'rything." It seemed to me an awesome thing to be satisfied with reading the Bible, praying and fasting. I could not relate to the level of spiritual satiation my mother had. Just couldn't ignore my needs and desires as a woman. But she did. And she knew true contentment.

Chapter 34.

THE THRILL IS GONE

Jade had thought about what Sapphire had told her nearly a month ago at lunch. She had been so busy tending to Sapphire's affairs while she was in the hospital that she had forgotten about her own life. Things had not changed between her and Al and she realized that she needed to talk to him, just as Sapphire suggested. She decided to make him a romantic dinner with candles and send the boys to her mother's for the weekend. Stopping at Victoria's Secret on her way back from the grocery store, she found some lingerie that she was sure Al wouldn't be able to ignore. She rushed home to get back to the pot roast she was stewing in the crock pot and decided to greet him in her new lingerie.

Drawing a warm bubble bath, she laid back in the tub thinking about how she would seduce her husband. The thoughts of him swept over her and she quickly finished so she could get dressed. Stepping out of the tub, she toweled off and put on some baby oil to keep her skin moist and touchable. She hoped he was in a good mood because she wanted tonight to be the night he rocked her world for more than fifteen minutes. Tying the sash of the light pink satin robe around her waist, she rushed downstairs to fix the salad. Al was a simple man, so she knew she didn't have to put on much makeup or anything. She thought it best for him to start eating his meal before bringing up the needed discussion. If he did have a bad day at work, the food would comfort him and she would soon follow.

Lighting the vanilla scented candles she looked at her watch. It was seven o'clock and she knew he would be pulling into the driveway soon. The neighbor's dog always barked when he pulled into the driveway, so she would have a three-minute warning before Al actually got in the door. She stepped into the bathroom to take a once over to make sure everything was in order, then went to the living room and sat on their sectional. Jade grabbed the remote to the stereo to put on some mood music. Jonathan Butler. That South African brother sure could play the guitar. Trying to play like she was reading a magazine, she realized the time was passing and Al had not come home yet. She went to the bay window of her living room and peeked out into the street to see if his car was coming. There was no sign of him. Jade started to worry. She went to the kitchen and grabbed the cordless phone off of the counter. Starting to dial the number of his cell phone, she heard the dog bark. Relieved that he was finally home, she ended the call and went to the sink to wash her hands. Al came through the door, looking for the boys. He called out to them with his masculine voice echoing through the house. "Jade, where are the boys?" he bellowed, with a bag full of video games and snacks from the local video store.

"Uh, baby, I sent them to my Mom's for the weekend. I hope you don't mind," she said, walking into the hallway near the side door leading to the garage. She hoped he would look up from untying his shoes to notice she was wearing a new peignoir.

"Well, I wish I had known your plans before I stopped at the video store and got all these games for them. What is on your mind anyway? And why are you dressed like that?" he asked, apparently unmoved by her appearance. Jade realized he was not getting the hint and decided to get straight to the point and bring up exactly what was on her mind. She hoped it would, in turn, bring him back to one of his roles as her husband. She walked over to him and looked him in the eyes. Placing her recently manicured fingers around the back of his neck, Jade tried to pull him in for a kiss. Sorting through the mail on the counter, he pushed her away and said, "Woman, what is wrong with you? I am just getting home from a long day at work and I am tired and hungry. I just took off my jacket and stinky shoes," he said roughly as he walked toward the comforting scent of russet potatoes, carrots and juicy pot roast simmering in the crock-pot.

Jade looked at the series of rolls on the back of Al's neck and tears filled her eyes. She crossed her arms in a defeated gesture, time, money and now emotions wasted. Running upstairs, she took off the pink, lacy peignoir and stuffed it in her dresser drawer. She put on a pair of black jeans and an old T-shirt and ran back down to the main floor. Opening the closet door, she pulled out her black leather boots and her leather jacket and grabbed her purse and keys off the hall table. Without even saying goodbye, she stormed out the front door heading for the garage. She was so upset that she could barely feel her feet hit the pavement.

In a matter of minutes she was driving towards the toll way, trying to decide if she was going to head north to Milwaukee or straight south on Interstate 294. She had to get away. She was hungry *and* angry and that combination scared her. She didn't know what to do. After making a pot roast dinner, she didn't want to get fast food. She needed to sort things out. She kept driving until her stomach growls were louder than the radio. Spotting a little café, she pulled into its lot and parked. She figured she could get some soup and a quaint dinner. Jade kept thinking to herself, *what is wrong with me? Why can't I get him to be with me to meet my needs and not just himself? What did I do to deserve this? Is this what it is supposed to be like?*

She waited to be seated at a booth in the corner of the little restaurant. Looking at the patrons, she noticed there weren't many people there on a Friday night. Adding to her misery, she followed the waitress to her table, feeling sorry for herself. She questioned her rationale for walking out and not telling Al where she was going. Her cell phone had been ringing nonstop for the last ten minutes, as Jade ignored Al's calls.

Scooting close to the window so she could look out and think, she noticed a man coming into the café. He was about six-foot-one, medium build wearing a red and black Bulls tee shirt, blue jeans and a black leather jacket. The tip of his nose was slightly red and his skin deeply tanned from the sun. His smile was genuine and it was obvious he frequented the place. His straight, thinning jet-black hair and laughing brown eyes only added to his friendly demeanor. He had an Italian lilt to his voice, and when the waitress called him 'Gino', it was safe to assume that he was. Jade returned her gaze out the window, and sighed. She didn't know what to order, and with Mr. Congeniality walking through the door, it may take even longer to get her Coke.

Gino waved to the waitresses and they smiled back, making small talk. Looking around the restaurant, he spotted Jade, with her hand under her chin, pensive but approachable. Jade was so wrapped up in her world that she hadn't noticed the stranger's verbal acknowledgement of her. He sat at the counter and ordered a soda, still looking back at the beautiful African-American woman seated by her self. Jade realized that she was the only woman of color in the place and it made her a little nervous at first. She had been driving in such a frenzy she didn't realize she was in Norridge, a near Northwest suburb of Chicago. It didn't much matter to her. She just wanted prompt service and a good hot bowl of clam chowder, if they had it.

The 40-something Italian guy got up the nerve to walk over to Jade's table. Jade didn't even notice until she saw his reflection in the window. She turned and looked up at him with eyes full of curiosity, sadness and a slight tinge of angered disappointment. Wondering what he wanted, she thought that perhaps he needed some change for the phone. Clutching her purse, she said, "May I help you?" Gino smiled and looked at her with warm eyes, "I certainly hope so. Do you mind if I sit with you?"

Slightly startled at his forward approach, Jade asked, "Why? Why do you want to sit here? There are plenty of empty tables in this place. Why do you want to sit with me?" The man looked at her and smiled proudly at her pointed questions. It didn't seem to faze him that she was a woman of color.

"Well, you looked like you were alone and needed someone to talk to," the perceptive gentlemen responded, still looking admiringly at Jade. She sensed his genuine interest in her and her despondency; Jade nodded her head and motioned to the empty side of the booth.

"Sure, go ahead and sit down," she invited, hoping the smiling man was not a convicted felon.

"Boy you must have had a really bad day or something. I haven't seen a face that long since Diana Ross did the Wiz," he joked. Jade questioned his audacious poke at Diana Ross, hesitated a moment, then laughed. It was actually quite funny.

"My name is Gino, Gino Valentino. What's yours?" He slurred his "s" in characteristic South Side Chicago flair.

"Jade," she said, cautiously looking up at him. She was reserved with this stranger as she was with most people she didn't know, making it difficult for them to penetrate her demeanor; just in case they were not on the up and up. "Jade is sufficient," she added to end his further inquiry.

"All right then, Jade-is-sufficient," he mimicked, smiling at her. "So what's bothering you? A pretty lady like yourself shouldn't have any worries." There was that classic smile again. He was certainly charming, but Jade was too distraught to reveal her personal issues to him. Gino signaled to the waitress for a couple of menus and suggested she try the clam chowder. Jade looked at him in amazement. There was something about this guy that struck her. She was hoping the restaurant had clam chowder. When the waitress came, she spoke up and said, "Let me start with your biggest bowl of clam chowder." She smiled and laughed heartily throughout the meal with the kind Italian man, and thanked him genuinely when they departed for distracting her from her own thoughts for a while.

Jade drove back towards home, thinking about her encounter at the restaurant. She really had a good time in the company of Mr. Valentino. He had really listened to what she had to say and had a great sense of humor. Making her forget her worries for the moment, she found his carefree personality appealing. Having many preconceived notions about people of other cultures and ethnicities, Jade wondered what it would have been like to be married to someone like Gino. She wondered if the passion she sought would be fulfilled or if things would be the same. Her mother always told her that the grass always seemed greener on the other side; but what her mother didn't tell her was that often times it actually *was* greener.

Gino was raised privileged but made it his business to overlook things that just didn't matter. He woke up every morning and thanked God for his life. He started each day on a positive note, saying that he was going to make this the best day of his life. Seeking out opportunities to share his pleasant outlook on life with someone else, he made it a point to talk to people who were different than himself and saw the good in them, regardless of their skin color, economic status or background. He gave Jade his phone number because he saw something in her that was extremely wholesome and attractive. She looked like a good woman and that was hard to find, even for Gino.

Jade didn't know what to do. She knew that Al would be waiting for her at home and she didn't want to face him yet. Having such a good time with another man made her feel guilty, although all they did was share a table, some pleasant conversation and a curiosity about the other's background. The fact that Jade found him attractive made her feel like she cheated on Al. She hated feeling that way, especially since she hadn't done anything wrong. Al had a way of making it seem like she was at fault for feeling the way she did. She just wanted more out of Al as a man, as her husband and lifetime lover. Not knowing which way to turn, she pulled over to the side of the street on Dearborn, just minutes from Sapphire's place. She dialed her number, hoping she was not yet asleep. It was hard to gauge when to call Sapphire since she was still getting chemotherapy. Depending on how she was coping, she could be sleeping days or nights or both. The phone answered and Sapphire's weak voice came over, barely above a whisper, "Hello?"

"Oh, girl, did I wake you? How are you feeling?" Jade asked apologetically. Sapphire sounded like she had a Brillo pad stuck in her throat. The chemo made her throw up all the time so her throat ached constantly.

"Naw, girl. I was just sitting here reading and writing in my journal. I guess I was really messed up the last time I wrote in here," she said, slightly slurring her words. "What's up?"

"Well, I tried what you suggested with Al."

"Yeah, okay," Sapphire said blandly, not really interested in wanting to expend energy thinking about someone else's intimate affairs. "Well, good. Did it work out?" the weak doctor inquired politely. She felt like her insides would explode at any minute, but didn't let on that she was feeling miserable.

"Not exactly. He didn't go for it. I made a nice dinner with candles. Bought some new lingerie from Vickie's and nothing. He complained about me getting too close to him." Her voice cracked as she tried to speak. "I can't even remember what he said but it made me so angry I walked out and went for a drive," Jade admitted to her sick friend.

"A drive?" Sapphire questioned.

"Yes."

"So where, pray tell did you end up, Ms. Jade?"

"I think it was Norridge."

"Norridge? Um, excuse my ignorance, but there aren't too many of "us" driving around Norridge, especially at night. What possessed you to go all the way out to Norridge?" Jade knew what Sapphire meant by the racial inference, and admitted that she was concerned herself at first, but was too distraught to care about a racial incident occurring in the near Northwestern suburbs.

"Well, I dunno. I was just driving and hungry cuz I left before we ate, you know. I pulled off the expressway and kept driving until I saw a little café where I could get some soup."

"Uh huh, keep going," Sapphire nudged.

"Yeah, well, that's what I'm calling about. Al got me so upset. He never wants to do anything out of the ordinary," Jade whined to her friend.

"I know. I mean, I can imagine," Sapphire quickly corrected.

"Anyway, I was so upset that all I wanted was to have a nice bowl of clam chowder and calm down. You know it's so unlike me to just go out on a Friday night by myself."

"Yeah, I know," thinking back to all the times she wanted Jade to go out with her and she refused because she was working on a jigsaw puzzle or knitting an afghan for her mother-in-law.

"I met a man, Sapphire," Jade blurted out anxiously. Her cell phone had some static in it because she was parked by the traffic signals.

"Did you say you met a man?" Sapphire repeated.

"Yes. Yes, I did."

"Okay? And?"

"Well, his name is Gino Valentino and . . ."

"Gino, what? Girl, that sounds like an Italian name. Is he Black?"

"No, he is Italian," Jade said positively.

"Hmm," Sapphire sighed, adjusting her slender self in her easy chair. She was barely 107 pounds now, and the bones supporting her frame ached when she was sitting in one place too long.

"Girl just let me know when you get too tired. I'll just call you tomorrow."

"Where are you and where is this Gino guy?"

"I'm actually just a couple of blocks from your condo. I don't know where Gino is. I left him at the café."

"Why don't you come over and bring some Häagen-Dazs with you. There's a White Hen just down the street from you." Sapphire requested, grinning slyly across the phone.

"Oh, you sure? I don't want to keep you up or nothing," asked Jade concerned about Sapphire's well being.

"Just bring the ice cream and some whipped cream. Oh yeah, grab some Planter's Honey-Roasted peanuts, too. I got a craving for something sweet and crunchy."

"All right. I'll be there in a few."

"Cool, thanks."

Parking on the street, Jade walked over to the White Hen Pantry and grabbed the honey vanilla ice cream from the freezer case and a pint of Ben & Jerry's Butter Pecan for herself. Remembering the whipped cream and nuts, she paid for her purchase and ran across the street to Sapphire's condo. Since she had been visiting Sapphire several times a week for the last four months, the doorman knew her and let her up to the 39th floor. Jade wondered how Sapphire could live in this big place all by herself, being so sick, and all. But Sapphire loved it. She enjoyed looking over the vastness of a periwinkle Lake Michigan during the day and at the brightly lit, picturesque skyline at night. Chicago nights were the best. Seeing the stars above, Navy pier to her left, and the sparkling impression of corporate lights against the midnight sky, the city life enraptured her. The blur of streaming red and white against the ribbon of Lake Shore drive was better to her than Paris at any time of year. That is how Jade found her, lights out, starring out at the panoramic view of night sky. Sapphire loved this town and through sickness and health she wanted never to leave.

Chapter 35.

RESURRECTION

For the life of him, Al couldn't figure out what had gotten into Jade. It seemed like she was going through a mid-life crisis or something. He wasn't sure if she was going through the change because he just didn't pay that much attention to her cycles. Never being one much interested in anything but what would give him satisfaction, he didn't even give it a second thought that his wife may be starving for affection.

Jade hadn't talked to Al all weekend, and that concerned him. Jade was a talker. She wanted to know every detail about everything that went on with him, and she also told her husband every detail that went on with her. It was like she was certain she would miss some imperative detail if she didn't know what was going on at any given moment. The way she was acting just didn't add up to Al. He didn't understand that besides the basic needs he provided for her, a roof over her head, food on her table, clothes on her back, and money in her pocketbook, a woman needed much more. She needed her sensuality to be fed as well as her body.

As a woman who knew nothing of another man's touch, Jade needed Al's attention more than ever. After all, she waited for him. She waited years and denied herself the pleasures of the flesh, to be his wife. Certainly, that deserved bringing the chapters of the Song of Solomon alive in their bedroom. But Al couldn't see beyond himself to see Jade, his Nubian queen.

Going back to work early on the Monday after falling out with Jade, Al sought out advice from a few fellas at the yard. It was before his morning run and he knew he could ask them what he should do to make things better between himself and Jade. He went to grab a cup of coffee from the Dunkin' Donuts when he saw the brakeman, Gino, talking to a couple of conductors.

"Hey, Gino, my man. What's shakin'?" Al asked, hoping he could bring up Jade and get a second opinion. Gino always seemed to have the right answer for everything.

"Al, my friend. How are you? Ready for another day?" Gino nudged him in the arm with a big grin on his face. He always had a good attitude about most things. Today though, he was very enthusiastic about something and Al decided he would wait until Gino finished his conversation with the guys to ask for advice.

"So, as I was telling the fellas, Al, I met this gorgeous African-American woman at this café by my house last Friday night. She had the deepest, darkest brown eyes you ever want to see. Al, you would have forgotten you were married, she was so fine," Gino added.

"I doubt that. Nothing can make me forget that." Al said sarcastically, thinking about leaving Jade with her back turned to him in bed that morning.

"Well, I tell you's! She was a beauty. They don't make 'em like that no more. And she was very sweet, too."

"So, you give her the digits, Gino, huh?" one of the conductors inquired, slightly grinning.

"Of course. But only with good intentions. She was the kind you would wait for-- if you know what I mean." The guys laughed, wondering what kind of woman Gino had met that would make him do such a thing.

"Al, you know what I'm talking about. How long you and your lady been married? Twenty years or something like that? See, I want that. A good woman I can come home to."

"Yeah, it's cool, man, when they acting right."

"I understand. But you know, you gotta give something to get something. When's the last time you brought her flowers and candy? Or taken her out and made her feel like she is the only woman on earth?'

Al thought long and hard. He honestly couldn't think of the last time he really was attentive to Jade. There was the cruise, but he really didn't remember them doing anything together except eating.

"So, what's this looker's name?" another conductor asked, sipping his coffee.

"Jade. Just like the rock. Oh man, was she solid," Gino said with a twinkle in his eye, seemingly reminiscing back to the night he met her.

"Did you say Jade?" Al repeated, as the name penetrated his heart. For a second, he felt his life flash in front of him and he panicked at the thought that his Jade was the woman Gino was talking so candidly about. His mind flipped through suspicious random thoughts like a slide show. Al hoped it wasn't her.

"Yeah, isn't that a beautiful name?" Gino said, looking at Al.

"Uh huh," Al said, still wondering about Jade's whereabouts on that past Friday night. When he came from the kitchen to ask her if they had any hot sauce, she was gone. Al was getting concerned and wanted to know more about the woman Gino met.

"So when did you say you met this woman, Gino?" Al questioned cautiously. He didn't want to let on that his own wife bore the same name but he wanted to make sure it wasn't his wife.

"Friday night, weren't you listening to me? Man, I'd give anything to be with her. She definitely had it all. Only thing, she was upset about her husband not paying any attention to her, you know. I told her that she deserved better than that. Someone who would be attentive to her needs and wants, you know. Women need to know that they still got it. Makes 'em feel special. They need to know you appreciate them," Gino added with a smile on his face.

"Right, right," Al said quickly, still contemplating his wife's possible actions. It could have been her. Al thought back to the conversation they had before she left. He had been so inconsiderate. There she was in lingerie he had not seen before, laying there waiting for him to come home. The house smelled like warm vanilla from all the candles lit in the dining room. She had his favorite dinner hot and ready for them to sit down and eat and he didn't even say, "How was your day, honey?" Al knew that he was wrong and he hoped that he could somehow redeem himself.

"So Gino, let's say you had an opportunity to go out again with this, Jade lady. What would you do to express how you feel to her? Would you take her to dinner or buy her a gift? What would you do to make her yours?" Al tried hard not show any emotion as he questioned Gino.

"Well, you know, I would invite her to a nice home cooked meal, one I prepared. I'd send her some flowers with my invitation to a date. Women like Jade love flowers. I could tell she probably never got any from her husband. And then I would see where the evening would take us. We may take a walk afterwards, holding hands, looking at the stars. Or we could go for an ice cream. It depends on the lady, and that Jade, she was a lady. Very classy."

Al was relieved that Gino spoke so highly of this "Jade" in case it was his wife. He started thinking of ways to win back his wife and bring back a little excitement to their marriage. He decided he didn't want to wait too long, because not communicating with Jade was too much for him to handle. Deciding to take it slow, Al thought about stopping at the grocery store after work and picking up some whipped cream and fresh strawberries. Then he thought about dinner. He wasn't a very good cook, and there would be no way for him to prepare dinner with Jade getting home first. He decided he would call her and tell her not to prepare dinner and that he would bring something home. Hoping she would not resist the idea, he decided to call Red Lobster and order her favorite. Since it was a weeknight, he was uncertain what to do with the boys, but he would figure it out when he got home. Al's plans were going well, in his head. If he could just make them happen, they'd be back on speaking terms by tonight.

Al pondered what went so wrong. It wasn't that he didn't love Jade. Lord knows, the sun rose and set upon her and the joy she brought to him made him grateful he was alive. He remembered the first time he saw her. She was a straight-laced, graceful girl. Her rich, dark cocoa skin always glistened against the church's bright lights. Jade's smoldering eyes were slightly slanted and lined with tightly curled black lashes that made her look like a Nubian princess. Her clothes always fit her perfectly, not too tight, not too loose. You could see her 34-26-36 figure through her modest clothing and her big calves were the perfect complement to her knee length dresses. Al knew she was going to be his wife the first time he saw her in his uncle's near North Pentecostal church. He also knew she wouldn't make it easy, and that was just fine with him. Mr. Jackson knew the value of waiting for a good thing.

Al had always been the type of husband who had to muster up affection for his wife. A peck on the cheek in front of the kids was his best effort at public displays of affection. He knew that this was not going to cut it anymore. Five minutes of pleasure was not nearly enough for all the woman that his Jade was, and Al knew it. Al was becoming increasingly aware that Jade's needs were greater than his own. Uncertain if he could fully meet her desires, he decided to make a call to someone else. A woman who would perhaps know what Jade was yearning for.

"Mom, its Al," the desperate husband admitted on the phone.

"Hi baby. How you doing? Is everything all right? You don't usually call unless something's wrong," she said in a voice that made Al cringe, wishing he hadn't called in the first place. If his father were still alive, he would have talked to him. He didn't quite know how he was going to even ask his mother such a delicate question 'like what can I do to please Jade intimately,' but decided, for the sake of his marriage, he better think of something quick.

"Yes, everything's just fine. Well, mostly," he stammered. "Momma, I'm just gon' come right out and ask you a question that makes me a little shame, but I got to figure something out."

"What is it baby? You know you can talk to me about anything," she encouraged him.

Al hated when she said that. There were certain things he just was not going to talk to his mother about, no matter what she said. But he forged ahead, nonetheless.

"Well, it's me and Jade. Things just ain't too good in the sexual department and I was wonderin' if you had any suggestions." There. He said it. It hadn't sounded too bad, either, although he had almost choked on the word 'sexual.' It got all tangled and tied up as it tried to escape his mouth.

"Ain't nothin' to be shame 'bout askin' me this and all, but you know, I ain't dead yet."

"Yes ma'am," Al replied obediently.

"Albie, you gots to ask her what she want from you. Spend some time getting to know the things she want you to do with her. The key is giving her time to be a woman with you, not you just being the man all the time. You may think having relations once a month is more than adequate, but a woman like Jade is in her prime. Nurture her like the earth and heavens caress a flower in the springtime. Rain, fertile ground and sunshine. All those different things go into bringing a flower to life. It's one thing to plant a seed. It's another to grow a flower into bloom. But when it comes forth, it's a beautiful thing ain't it, boy?"

"Yes ma'am, it is," Al answered respectfully. He hadn't given their relationship that much thought and realized his mother was a wise soul. He loved her dearly and saw so much of her feistiness in Jade. He really needed to talk to her more often.

"Now, you get off this phone and gon' and make Jade a happy woman." Al thought about the last time he made love to Jade. After three minutes of trying to remember, he felt embarrassed. He recalled that Jade was barely touched by the activity, and had started laughing, deciding not to spare her husband's feelings. Al knew that something was wrong, because she never had reacted that way before.

"Al, boy you still there?" the tender voice on the other line asked.

Al, quickly jolted out of his delinquent daydream, cleared his throat and said, "Uh, yes ma'am. Thank you, Momma. I got to go."

"All right baby. Why don't you bring the boys over here so y'all can have the house to yourselves tonight?"

"Okay. Thanks, Ma. I'll stop by before five," Al said, smiling. He knew exactly what to do. It was going to take some work, but he was willing to change his old stubborn, chauvinistic ways if Jade was willing to find some value left in her old man.

Chapter 36.

THE FACE-OFF

All of the useless men in my past would come to me from time to time, visiting me in my dreams. I never remembered all of their names, but there was always a scene that replayed like clockwork when my memory of them was released from my mind's eye. At times, it was profoundly overwhelming. If I kept thinking about them and the various things we had engaged in, I would end up consumed with remnants of the love we shared and the selfish memories they left behind. I grew sick every time I thought of the many narrow escapes I made, walking the streets of Chicago alone, looking for the answers that I could never find in the forbidden arms of these nameless, sometimes even faceless man. I thank God I am still alive today. Lord knows, some of the choices I made seeking love could easily have cost me my health, my sanity, my life.

Never did I think through my escapades as I recklessly lived in the moment. *Carpe diem*, yes, I seized the day, the night and everything in between. I did what I thought I wanted to do, but in retrospect, it really wasn't what I wanted. They say women want romance, love, and intimacy. Men, in my experience just want. And they want so that they can get and get some more. Then they get bored. It's right about the time when they get bored that women think it's their responsibility to keep them entertained. In this period of time some of the most insane choices are made. Women fall into desperation when they feel that love—or whatever they found in the arms and loins of these men—has been threatened. Some go on death-defying crash diets, have liposuction or other cosmetic surgeries performed, trying to reinvent themselves for a man that can't keep focused long enough to comprehend that he has a good thing in her. Losing weight does not help the wayward man regain his focus.

Other women use the tactic of going on expensive spending sprees, buying new clothes, new furniture, new anything, including satisfying *his* every whim in trinkets for him, hoping that the "new" will attract and some how keep their man interested. Buying his affection becomes superfluous when it is, in fact, her unattractive attitude that drove him away. And other women just act crazy, talking out the side of their necks—threatening to leave or kill themselves. The saddest of these women are the ones whose mothers, aunts and sisters could not convince them that no man is worth killing herself over. But, most vengeful is the scorned woman who will destroy herself and the man that has done her wrong. The destruction in the path of an angry Black woman makes a Florida hurricane and a California mudslide pale in comparison.

Fortunately, I got out before things got that bad with Markus. I vowed that I would never go down that road again with the likes of a man. I'd leave first before I would even think of destroying myself. In all this contemplation, I still didn't know what to expect with Xavier. I knew it would be awkward at first trying to work things out. Part of me was looking forward to it, and the other part simply fought back. He frightened me—his power, his control, his ability to severely alter the life he represented for me. Without Momma, I was unsure of how I would face him. Knowing that he was just as guilty as me gave me some leverage. I figured that we would meet on equal ground. I hoped he would be compassionate and not vindictive. I hoped he would not pit our children between us and make us choose. I could not bear losing another child to divorce. It tore me up inside that I had allowed myself to go down the adultery road again. I knew I could overcome (with a little divine intervention) this demon inside of me, but I needed his strength as my husband, my covering, to hold me and be "the everything" I needed.

Of course, I needed to stand on my own two feet, but he had to be the man who had my back. He had to make himself available for me to communicate and to love. I needed from him the love and passion that keeps two hearts panting for each other eternally. I prayed that this wouldn't be too much to ask. In a way that I had not done in a very long time, I got down on my knees before God. It was 4 a.m. and I knew that Xavier would be coming home soon. I began to cry because I didn't know what to say, but my heart was so full of passion for my husband. For the first time ever, I felt a love deep inside of me for him. I found myself praying as the tears flowed, asking God to restore our marriage and bring forth a love unlike any that we had ever experienced.

I prayed that we would renew our vows and that the wounds we had created in each other's hearts would be made whole. I prayed that we would remember what our marriage symbolized and the sacredness in the words we said before we promised, "I do." I prayed that we would cherish each other and learn to understand what it took to make this thing work. Up from my belly like a wellspring, my spirit began to rejoice. I had never thought in all my years of being "churched" to give my marriage to God. I trusted too long in my finite ability to resolve matters. My bull-headed attitude constantly got me into trouble and this time I needed more than just an opinion to get me through. I knew that I felt good about what was to come. It would take more than thirty minutes on my knees to bring us back to a place where we could live harmoniously and find love again. But it certainly was a lot better than fussing and fighting.

I had to change myself, to be receptive to Xavier. And that also meant changing churches. Going back to my roots brought me right into the life of someone who would intercede for me. When I started going back to my mother's church, I barely knew anyone my age. But then I met Jade Jackson and her husband Al. Jade and I spent many nights talking and praying together. It wasn't until she shared with me about her friend Sapphire, that I found the link I needed to push beyond my troubling situation. It was just what I needed to stop feeling sorry for myself and to start praying for someone else who was worse off than me. Dr. Sykes never knew how much she helped me by pushing me away from her room that day. I needed to keep coming back and have faith that God would take me where I needed to go, for His purpose. Not giving up on her gave me the strength to know that I shouldn't throw in the proverbial towel and give up on Xavier.

I didn't know how he would accept me after all we had gone through over the past year, but I was willing to give it all I had. After all he was worth it, and not just for the money, either. He really was worth it. It was my turn to prove my worth to him.

ନ୍ଦ୍ରନ୍ଦ୍ରନ୍ଦ୍ର

Ravinia knew that Xavier was still having a reckless affair and in spite of her being caught, she was still worried that he hadn't broken things off with the girl. She had to confront him with the evidence she had, hoping he would make the first move, either to end the marriage or to try and work things out. She feared the day they would have to admit their wrongs before each other. It seemed so right when she was in the arms of the one she thought could bring her closer to the truth she sought. Sadly, he fell into the group of all lovers past, leaving her with desires unfulfilled and scars etched across her heart. This last affair sparked by the Reverend's misleading advances was the worst of them all.

Ravinia couldn't stand it anymore. Since the day she prayed, she could count on one hand how many times she had seen her husband. Xavier constantly had events, clients and things he needed to do after work, and oftentimes he would spend nights at hotels, because he claimed it was "just too late to come home." Ravinia was tired of making excuses and decided to call Xavier at work and just let him have it.

"Xavier Hamilton, please," she crisply requested of the Omicron Consulting switchboard operator.

"One moment," the deep, British male voice said on the other line. The phone line rang three times and was answered.

"Xavier Hamilton speaking." The distinct voice thundered forcefully. Xavier's medium-pitched, distinguished voice still made Ravinia quiver after all these years of listening to him snore and talk to himself in the mirror about how fine he was. She knew he was full of himself but that didn't matter much now.

"Honey, it's me," Ravinia softly answered. She intentionally lowered her pitch and evened out the tone of her voice in order to appeal to Xavier's sensibilities. Her mind quickly changed about telling him off.

"Hey, Vinia. What's wrong? Is it the baby?" Xavier questioned, slightly startled to hear Ravinia on the other line of his office phone. Ravinia knew he would jump to conclusions first.

"No, everyone is fine. Uh. . ." she stammered, trying to think of something quick and witty to say to keep his attention. Perhaps honey was better than vinegar. She had to figure out a way to get him away.

"Well, what's going on?" Xavier questioned, raising the tone in his voice to almost serious. He was tired of the games Ravinia played and continued scribbling on his note pad about the plans he was making for the weekend with Heather, his intern. Xavier knew that he had Ravinia in the palm of his hand. He had found out about her and the good Reverend and yet she had not found out about him and his mistress, or so he thought. Believing that he could have his cake and eat it too, he frolicked in his wanton desire night after night. He couldn't get enough of his blonde pawn, but wondered why Ravinia was calling him so early.

"I was on my way to meet you for lunch. Did you have any plans?" Ravinia asked as she grabbed her keys and distressed taupe leather jacket off the couch. Slipping on the sleeves of the supple, lambskin, she zipped up the princess-seamed jacket that barely reached her hips. Sizing herself up in the mirrors aligned in the foyer, she turned and took a quick look at her backside. *Not bad*, she thought. After Momma's death, she had noticed that she had lost a few pounds and had started working out again. Her jeans fit nicely and her matching cream three-inch pointed toe boots accented her cinnamon complexion perfectly.

"Uh, well. Actually, I didn't have plans," Xavier admitted honestly. He came off as if pleasantly surprised, although Ravinia could see through the deceptive truth of his response.

"Good. I'll pick you up in about 15 minutes. I don't need an ID or anything do I? They'll still let me through the gate, won't they?" Ravinia asked. Omicron was located in the northernmost point of Glenview on an enormous landscaped campus. Ravinia had once loved working there. It was always so peaceful in the summer with the lazy swans and restless trees; it was like having an office building on a resort. Most every amenity possible was made available for the employees—hair salon, spa, dry cleaners, café, concierge, automotive service, and more. If it was requested and possible, Omicron had it.

"Okay. I'll see you at the guest entrance at 11:45," Xavier said, trying to sound confident. He didn't know what Ravinia was up to, but it couldn't be good. They hadn't had an opportunity to talk things through since her mother's funeral and Xavier had hoped she'd forgotten about the whole incident. Although he meant what he said about working things out and all, he wasn't ready to end his tryst. His pretty intern showed a lot of promise and did everything he wanted her to do and more. A recent Duke graduate, she was smart and bubbly. Ambition was her middle name and there was nothing that was going to stop her from working her way up the corporate ladder. Xavier just happened to be one of those rungs and he didn't care that her affections were shallow. His middle-aged ego was being stroked and he welcomed the mid-life crisis he was having at 45.

He had the wife, kids, a great home and a secure job at a very prestigious consulting firm. What more could someone like Xavier with so much financial power want? "More" was his answer. The things Xavier had were appreciated, but they were never enough. He always wanted more: bigger, better, younger, prettier, hotter, and faster. Xavier was insatiable, and that was his weakness. In all his greatness, his weaknesses lie in his rapacious hunger to satisfy that drive to impress the Joneses, however, in the beginning, Ravinia kept him intrigued. He could not figure her out; she was a mystery to him. He wasn't very discreet about his office affair, so if she knew—and in all likelihood she did—why hadn't she said anything? He hadn't really thought about it until now. Xavier started to worry. Was Ravinia going to ask for a divorce? He wasn't ready for that. Being a partner had its advantages, but being married with children with a pristine background as a partner was even better. Being only one of twelve current partners in the entire firm, he realized that he needed to ensure that he was always portrayed in an appropriate light.

Sitting down at his walnut desk, Xavier looked around the perimeter of his corner office. There were pictures of him and Ravinia at a couple of company functions when she was still working at Omicron. She looked so beautiful with her straightened shoulder length dusty brown hair framing her oval face. Radiant, she barely showed her age. The richness of her brownness juxtaposed to Xavier's café au lait complexion reminded him of what she represented for him: a symbol of the Blackness that he still needed desperately to hold on to. Even in her small stature, she was a strong, woman; confident and an amazing force to be reckoned with. He decidedly looked forward to the unplanned lunch date with his wife, but grew concerned as to what she possibly was devising behind his back.

Xavier remembered the first day he saw his wife. He was in awe of how her presence filled the room. All eyes were on this profoundly attractive, five foot seven inch Nubian queen. No one questioned her authority, in those days. It was as if she ran the company and everyone else just followed suit. She was only a senior manager, and yet, she wielded the weight of a managing partner as people stepped out of her way when she walked into a room. Xavier had taken that former corporate strength Ravinia possessed for granted all these years. She had found a way to make it work to build the life they had together. Just because she no longer worked didn't mean she wasn't capable of that same power and capacity to move mountains. That was the woman he had chased down, wanting to know what made her sing and what made her smile. He lived for the days of their courtship, devising ways to distract her in board meetings, trying to make her forever his.

Walking out to the revolving door of the guest entrance, Xavier saw Ravinia in her silver Mercedes. He slightly waved at her and surprisingly smiled, as his thoughts carried him back to the day he first handed her the keys to the Benz. It was her 40th birthday and life was just beginning to make sense. Nearing the car, he almost skipped. Ravinia took off her sunglasses and leaned over to move her purse from the passenger seat. Opening the door, Xavier got in, laying his suit jacket on the back seat. He leaned over to his wife and gave Ravinia a gratuitous kiss on her full lips, palming the smooth roundness of her cheek in his right hand. This felt so good. Ravinia cupped Xavier's cleanly shaven face in her hands and kissed him completely, closing her eyes to fulfill the emotional exchange. Xavier always smelled so delicious and looked so dignified with his suit on. Omicron's dress code was business casual, but Xavier met with clients on a regular basis, so he customarily wore a suit.

Still parked in the guest entrance, Ravinia realized that they were on public display and opted to end the embrace in order to drive on to their lunch destination.

"So, what did you have in mind, cutie," Xavier said, playing with the tuning presets, trying to find a suitable station to keep the mood. Ravinia realized that Xavier's mood was playful and he was "feeling her." He also knew that eventually they would have to talk. It had been so long since she had her husband in a mood where all he could think about was her, and she knew better than to blow it. Xavier's mind moved quickly as desire for his wife began to knock on the door of his mind.

"I don't have any client meetings this afternoon, baby. You want to skip lunch and maybe just relax somewhere and, you know. . ." Xavier had that look in his eye and Ravinia knew that look all too well. He was ready for her and it was just a matter of time before he would completely forget about the purpose of her visit. Ravinia spotted a Shell station and pulled into it. She parked the car on the side, careful to avoid any oil spills, and looked squarely at Xavier.

"Xavier, we need to talk," Ravinia said looking desperately into Xavier's gray eyes. She was putting it all on the line and knew that this could be the end of them.

"Yeah, I know baby. We were supposed to talk a long time ago," Xavier said, starting to cool off. "I don't even know where to begin," he continued honestly, looking out the window.

"Well," Ravinia said boldly, "I don't either. But if we don't get this out, we are never going to know what is really going on with us."

"You're right, baby. You're right."

"So, honey, I know that we've both been wrong. We've both done unforgivable things to each other." Xavier looked at Ravinia with slightly pouting lips and doleful eyes. He felt badly that she was the one admitting his shame.

"Ravinia, we need to stop this. I need you. I want my wife back. We cannot keep living a lie. I know I did you wrong. And you know what you did. I just can't keep fooling my old self into thinking I need someone else to make me a younger man."

A younger man? Ravinia could not believe her ears. Her husband *was* having a midlife crisis. Almost ashamed of herself, Ravinia looked at Xavier. He barely showed signs of aging except the graying in his temples and sideburns. Even if Xavier was feeling like he had to prove that he still had it, that didn't excuse what he did and with whom. But Ravinia was going to table that conversation today.

"Well, honey, you *aren't* getting any younger. That's fer sher," Ravinia said valley girl style, making sure she regionally accented her words to depict the California blonde that had captured his attention. Xavier squirmed appropriately. He knew what she was doing.

Xavier turned and looked at his wife, then turned to pull down the visor and flip open the mirror. Examining the sides of his face, he spotted the graying areas and flipped up the mirror again. Ravinia felt sorry for her husband in all his vanity. Caressing his face with her right hand feeling stubble forming, she said, "Baby, you still got it."

Xavier looked at his wife and from his view; she just didn't seem a day older than when they got married. Ravinia was looking longingly into her husband's eyes and he knew that this was the feeling he had been trying to fill. He felt like he wanted to be with his wife, in the sanctity of their marriage. For the first time in years he wanted Ravinia just like he did when they were dating and she wouldn't let him have it.

"Xavier, I just need to know one thing," Ravinia implored looking deeply into his sterling eyes. That precursor scared the Omicron partner. She had a look painted on her face that made him regret he picked up the phone to speak with her just a few short moments before. Xavier thought it best to just to look at her intently and not say anything. Taking a deep sigh, Ravinia prayed for strength to ask the million-dollar question that would decide the fate of her marriage. "Are you still committed to this relationship?"

Xavier hesitated. The question was loaded. He knew the right answer, the one that was in his heart. But he had also strayed away from the one good thing that made him honest before God. He knew he couldn't wait too long to answer because the silence would answer for him.

"I am committed to recommit myself to you--mind, body and soul, if you, Ravinia Lynnette Hamilton recommit your mind, body and soul back to me."

Ravinia looked at Xavier. He had almost taken too long to answer, but his answer was what she wanted to hear. She looked at her man and quietly said the words she never thought she would say again, "I do."

Xavier smiled and said to Ravinia, "Baby, let's go home." Picking up his Blackberry from its sleeve, he sent an email to his secretary that he would not be back for the rest of the day, something about keeping a very important appointment with his wife. Ravinia put her foot on the pedal and sped off going east on Lake Cook Road. The wind felt good combing through her dark, silky, feathered hair. She knew that she had fought to get back what the enemy had stolen from her. It felt good to get back what was rightfully hers.

Chapter 37.

WILL TO SURVIVE

Journal Entry #17

February 20, 2005

The days grew long as the night sweats drenched my sheets. I felt so restless and worn out, I wanted to just lay out and let life sweep over me. I'm so tired of seeing the same ole people everyday, people who smile in your face and stab you in the back. People who say they have your back (you know, the one they just stabbed) and in the end, they're self-serving. A lot of people came to visit the first couple of days, even weeks after my surgery, but now it seems they have forgotten about me. Even my Christian friends appear to have grown weary in their well doing. Over and over again, I tried to smile and go through the motions, but I knew they knew too much about my past, my life, and me. I needed to get out of this place that cradled so many memories; this place that left me wallowing in space only to feel the remains of pain and sorrow.

I hated moving, but I knew it was time to go. I wanted stability in my life, and at the same time, I didn't know where that would come from. Night after night, I prayed and poured out my soul before God, questioning my purpose, my existence, the very essence of my being. I searched the scriptures for answers and found many comforting words, but I needed to know within myself, that in all I had lost, that I still had worth. What could I, of all people, offer a man? It was so ironic that at the hands of men, I had lost so many precious things, yet it remained the one thing I truly needed to survive. Looking into the cold, dark eyes of a man who took away my choice to bring forth another life, I realized that he would never know the extent of what he had done to me. In his blatant medical disregard for my womb, he removed the substance that flowed through my veins. He left me barren and empty, and only time would heal the scars left by the cancer that ravaged my femininity. I trusted him with my life, and yes, that *was* saved. But my choice to preserve my legacy--the part of me that had survived generational curses that severed soul ties with the men of my past had been mutilated. I had lost my precious alabaster box, not just to a silent killer, but to the one who took an oath to "first, do no harm." What could I offer? What could I give?

Forgiveness. I tried and failed miserably at times. I grieved deeply at the loss of my life-giving organs. I had given so much of myself to men in an honest attempt to receive love and acceptance that, at times, I truly forgot who I was. I didn't choose them; they sought me out through birth, through life, through death. I knew that I had more love to give than the average woman because it hurt so much when they looked the other way. I wanted to please them, build them up into strong men, but they couldn't even handle the pressure of knowing that they were adored. It was more than I could bear, giving of myself in emotional exchanges that only a fool would waste their time on. These ways of compassion I paid dearly for, but I never toughened from the disappointment. I knew that someday, I would feel true love and it would be reciprocated. That hope--some would call it insanity would be my reason to love again and wait patiently for it. Even when my hair started falling out and my skin turned ashy, sallow and dull, I knew there would be someone out there who would call me beautiful; someone who could see into my soul and find the rare, intrinsic beauty that only my heart could design.

Sometimes the things we encounter in life seem insurmountable, as if our very existence would fade if we were to continue to endure the searing pain perpetuated by ignorance. Sometimes we emerge from our own struggle scathed and broken, thinking, if not for God keeping us alive, we would surely die. But knowing that there is nothing that we cannot endure, we press forward, realizing that in our weakness, we are strong because we are more than overcomers. We overcome through our trials and tribulations this life has thrown us. The words we speak in faith and the power that comes forth when we voice out our beliefs transcends even our worth and ourselves. Standing strong on those unwavering truths, we face those things that so easily beset us. These things take us back to our infancy and singe us to the quick, but yet we thrive in our living.

Life is much too short to sit around and feel sorry for ourselves. Even in the midst of all the chemotherapy, there were times I just wanted to give up, but didn't. I persevered beyond any measure I thought was possible. And although I often was left to myself and didn't have anyone or anything to depend on, I knew that the best woman would win in the end, surviving life's challenges. And in bouts of *loneliness* that were so profound that the word itself no longer held its own definition, I found signs of my breaking vulnerability every time I looked in the mirror. I actually had to challenge myself to stand before the vision of destruction that the incurable disease had caused and speak life to myself. I would speak to every cell and membrane, living or dead, in my body, and command life to flow through and to it, by the undeniable power of God. And with the prayers of many, I found strength in the faith that they would stand in the gap for me. Having fallen victim to a chronic illness like cancer, I came to know who my true friends are. Those that came to see about me, called and sent cards truly understood the impact of a friend bearing the gift of their own sacred presence. I made a point to tell them that it made all the difference in the world to know that they cared.

Jade would pray for me. She stood by me, cooking meals for me. She even stayed and fed me when I was too weak to feed myself. When the poison of the chemo surged through my veins and made everything good feel bad, she was there to clean me up when I was too sick to know up from down. It was comforting to know that she diligently kept me in her prayers and that she had put me on the prayer list at her church. Never before in my life had I felt so strongly the power and the humanity of my own soul, as I did during the treatments. I had never felt so close to God as when I was recovering from the surgery. Truly there were times when I would feel my strength being renewed, as if the wings of angels were encamped around my bed, and their hands were underneath my body raising me up to survive the worst of it.

Journal Entry # 19

April 14, 2005

It's incredible how folks who have never endured anything even remotely close to your situation, or suffering, or a near death experience, pretend to be able to relate to your situation. Either they know of someone who has gone through it or read about it, but not actually experienced the depth of your pain well enough to just silently care. It may not necessarily be true that you actually have to walk in someone else's shoes in order to understand what they are going through. Of course, they can empathize, comprehend and acknowledge your ordeal, but they honestly cannot know what it is like to be trapped in a pain so severe that the only thing you can do is hallucinate to rid your body of the excruciating thoughts that are larger and louder than life itself.

These thoughts penetrate to the core of the soul, revealing a direct-connect to God. It is true that some folks actually do get closer to God because there is nothing else for them to do but pray when going through a traumatic or life and death experience. All I know is that it was seven months of grueling pain and suffering. The surgery pales in comparison to the chemotherapy, which at times I was certain would end me. The weight loss was horrific--watching my muscle and fat waste away and the remaining skin hang loose from my bones. Everyday, I feel the gag reflex that never relaxes because the poison they put inside of me to kill off the remaining cancer made me so nauseous I had to vomit constantly. Most times I am unable to talk because the acid resulting from the vomit has eaten away at the membranes protecting my throat.

I was forced to internalize my feelings. At times, this was more than I thought I could bear. After going through all that, losing my hair was simply heartbreaking. It wasn't like I didn't know what to expect. I'm a doctor. I know the side effects of chemo and radiation. Yet, when it happened to me, I was not prepared for it. My self-esteem fell away to the floor with each strand of hair, and locks of ego clumped worry in my comb and brush. I was humbled.

I have decided, as Ravinia declared, that I am a survivor. The Bible says, I am "more than a conqueror." One thing I do know is that God was there with me all along the way. He had to be watching over me during the rape and yet, that is still a mystery to me. How could He let one of His own do that to me? One who still questioned my faith. Man is truly weak, but God is strong. I know that there is a God. I know He helps me survive each day with strength. I just want to know that God truly knows me.

Today, I tried on the wig that Ravinia brought me. I look like Whitney Houston in *The Preacher's Wife*, but I am still alive. I put on some mascara today and a little lip-gloss to brighten my face. I am coming out of this thing. With God as my strength, I know He is my help and I look to Him to bring me through. My mother called yesterday and said she was coming to see me. I hate for her to see me this way, but I know that I have got to start facing my fears head on. And Lord knows I need a good meal.

ꕥꕥꕥ

Journal Entry # 24

May 29, 2005

If someone had of told me I'd be running along shoreline of Lake Michigan just eight months after my surgery, I would have told them they were terribly mistaken, because I didn't even run before the procedure. Life has taught me to pay attention to things that should be most important to me—God, family, friends—you know, the things we take for granted the most. I used to think that I could do anything, that I was superwoman. Because I had overcome so many things that most people who knew me didn't even have knowledge about, I wore this outlandish facade that perpetrated complete wholeness when, in fact, my life was anything but whole or wholesome.

It's funny how things come full circle. Jade called me the other day apologizing for being so distant and not calling or stopping by like she used to. She was all excited that her and Al were taking another cruise around Christmas and that, since that night in Norridge with Gino, they had been acting like newlyweds. Jade said it was like he was a new man. I knew that bigheaded man would come around one day. Men sometimes need to be reminded of the good thing that they have right under their noses. The problem is that sometimes their noses are stuck up so high, they don't want to look down at what they left there. But apparently, Al came to his senses and is now making Jade a very happy woman. So happy, in fact, that she quit her telemarketing job to be a full time wife. Again. I am really happy for her. She's my best friend and has bailed me out so many times. I am glad we are still friends. Al is really good for her, too, and I am delighted he is reinventing himself. A couple of times, Al came home on his lunch break to surprise her and needless to say, he went back to work with a big smile on his face. Sometimes it is the little things that make the biggest difference in a woman's life, like reassuring her that she is still the only one who can turn your eye. One day maybe I'll find that kind of man again. But I can't worry about that now. I've got to get myself back, and that takes all I've got.

Ravinia called yesterday wanting to know about the idea Jade had about starting a boutique. Jade had mentioned the idea before Bible study to a couple of members of the church and wanted to know if anyone knew of a good bank to get a small business loan. I haven't told Jade or Ravinia yet, but I really want to help with the boutique. It is something I could do while recovering to get myself out of the house and back to leading a somewhat normal life without the stress of managing a practice. Although I love what I do, I need for my life to have purpose and meaning. Giving back to help Jade set up a place where the proceeds will go to cancer research and help for abused women is exactly the type of job I want to have. There has got to be a cure out there for cancer, and someone has to find it. Ravinia said she hoped she could talk her husband into financing the startup, though it would be a win-win for all parties involved. Jade would have her money free and clear and Xavier would have a mega tax break next year. If he timed things right, he would get it right under the wire for this year.

The weather's getting much cooler and you can tell it's almost Christmas again. Thanksgiving was last week and Mom came up to visit. It was just us this time, and that was fine with me. I was concerned that she wasn't with her other family during the holiday, but she assured me this would be okay. Finally, some selfish time with my mother. Don't get me wrong. I love Raquel and all, but you know, after over thirty years without her, I wanted to spend at least one holiday with my mother. And it felt good just to be with her. She made a small turkey with dressing, green beans with the tiny red potatoes, macaroni and cheese, and a sweet potato pie that was so delicious, I felt like I was a little girl again in California. I had missed her cooking so much that after about the third day of her visit, I started rationing my portions. I wanted plenty of leftovers for when she returned to Arkansas. I wanted something to savor. But no matter how I tried to skimp, she wouldn't let me. She convinced me that there would be plenty of leftovers.

When my mother went back to Little Rock, I missed her so much, I went into the kitchen to get some peach cobbler. Before she came to visit, I had been trying to cut down on sweets because the sugar seemed to make the hot flashes worse, but compared to my mother's down-home cooking, I didn't mind sweating through it. To my surprise, the refrigerator was full of new Tupperware containers with all my favorite dishes in them. Chicken and dumplings, lasagna, black-eyed peas. I craved them all. And what couldn't fit in the refrigerator was put in the freezer. I had food to last until the New Year. I could have cried, there was so much food.

The days are getting better. I am feeling stronger and stronger. I can almost walk to my doctor's office now without having to catch a cab part of the way. I am truly blessed to have my life come back into focus. For a while, I didn't think I had anything to live for. But I realize now that life is worth living if you have purpose. Without that, nothing makes sense. I finally see that. I used to get down on myself for all the tragedies I had to face through the years. But there are so many people who face far worse than what I've lived through, and they are grateful to witness another day. For once, in a long time, I am actually looking forward to tomorrow when I get my first scan since the surgery. No matter what happens; I am going to be okay. Things are turning around. Finally.

Chapter 38.

MAGDALENE'S

Ravinia was rushing in traffic that bright Saturday morning in December. Driving down I-94 towards the Loop, she realized that she had forgotten a bag of vintage designer clothes and shoes in the garage. Hitting the steering wheel out of frustration, Ravinia glanced out of her passenger side window to see someone staring at her from the SUV next to her. She had promised Jade she would bring them with her so they could get the clothes priced and hung before the big sale. It was the grand opening of Jade's new store; ***Magdalene's*** and she wanted everything to be perfect.

It would only take her a few minutes to get to the near north boutique. ***Magdalene's*** symbolized the freedom of a new day, and through its birth came the realization that the power to overcome and survive lived within the sacrifices made to open the little store's doors. Pulling up to the back of the boutique, Ravinia jumped out of her car slamming the door behind her. Switching back and forth, Ravinia walked to the back of her car to get the items she did remember to bring from out of the trunk. Reaching over, she grabbed a bag of rolls in one hand and a case of punch with the other. Sapphire came to the door to see whose screeching tires had landed in the back alley of their establishment. It had been 11 months since the surgery and the formerly vibrant therapist looked gaunt. Her deep-set, doe-like eyes in their bluest hue were almost purple as the dark circles lined around them intensified her vulnerability. It was obvious she had been through the ringer, but with each calculated step, her fight preceded her setbacks.

"Ravinia, it's about time. We were wondering if you were going to show," Sapphire's scratchy voice smiled as she gave her friend the once over.

"I know, I know. I am always late. But, I am here," Ravinia beamed. She still thrived on the principal that fashionably late was chic.

"You look gorgeous as ever," curving her full lips while eyeing Ravinia's six-hundred-dollar purse.

"Uh-huh. Sapphire, you are looking good." Ravinia tried to avert Sapphire's attention back onto herself. "I like that hat you're wearing." Sapphire was still growing her hair back, and even though she wore a wig, she always wore a hat as well. Trying to remain positive, she focused on Sapphire's strength and not her weakness.

"Yeah. I am starting to actually feel like myself again. I've put on a few pounds and things are staying down pretty good now."

"Well, thank the Lord," Ravinia shouted as she reached out to hug her former therapist. Sapphire had decided to give up the practice and go in with Jade's idea of opening up an upscale designer boutique and resale shop. This way she could contribute her time when she felt up to it and also provide a service to the community. A portion of the earnings would go to the North Side of Chicago Battered Women's Society and towards the Northwestern Hospital's Cancer Research Institute. It was Ravinia's idea, though, to combine the boutique concept with a designer resale shop especially since Ravinia could begin to fill the store from her recycled closet, until steady donations started coming in. Sapphire wanted the rest of her life to have purpose, and if she were going to work, then it would have to be fulfilling. She had learned from Ravinia that by helping out someone else, she could help herself.

"You're gonna come out of this—you know that right? I believe it, girl. You are so strong and your faith is so big! You are one powerful woman. You hear me, Ms. Sapphire Sykes?"

"Yeah, I have to tell you. It was hard though, Ravinia. Some days I thought I was gon' die. And some other days, I felt so bad I thought I wanted to die. It just was not my time, though. Apparently, there must be something left on this earth that God wants me to do. I don't know what it is exactly, but it's waiting just for me. Well, come on in. Set your stuff over there and get to sorting. We are expecting a huge crowd today. Jade's up in the front waiting on you."

"This is such a beautiful thing. I am so proud you all asked me to help with this place. This is going to be such a blessing for so many deserving women around the city."

"Yes, it is. Without your support, Ravinia, we couldn't have done this without taking out a loan. Let Xavier know that we really appreciate him paying to fix up this old place."

"Girl, its just money. I'm just glad we were able to help. You know he throws around so much money on worthless stuff and events. It's about time we invested in helping people out of desperate situations like domestic abuse, rape and teenage pregnancy."

"Yeah and *Magdalene's* is also going to sponsor a 5K walk for ovarian cancer research for next year's 4th of July weekend. Jade just got the paperwork about that. I am really excited about that. You know, I spent a lot of time up in my high-rise condo on Lake Shore Drive and in my corner office overlooking Lake Michigan counseling people *only* if they could afford to see me. Do you know how many years I wasted, thinking that I was really helping somebody?"

Ravinia looked at Sapphire in disbelief. Truly she helped many people with their problems. She was saddened that Sapphire seemed to think her efforts were in vain.

"Sometimes I wonder why I was stricken with cancer so early in my life. Why did God allow me to go through yet another demoralizing life event before I reached 45 years old? And then, one night when it was just God, and I alone in my bedroom, He spoke to me. In an audible voice, He said,

> *"Sapphire, I chose you because you will go. In all your struggles, you have always searched for the truth. And to overcome is to conquer. You are a warrior, mighty and powerful. I wanted you to feel what my people felt when they were persecuted for my sake. I wanted you to empathize with the pain and suffering of those with chronic illness who are left by the wayside in nursing homes and hospital beds. I wanted you to witness these horrible things so you would know that I*

am a rewarder of those that diligently seek me. You sought me, but didn't find me until you were on your back prostrate, stricken with what should have been fatal. It wasn't until you could not do for yourself anymore that you found me."

"Whoa. What a powerful message!" Ravinia marveled, awe-stricken from the revelation she had heard. The sheer strength in Sapphire's voice humbled her to a point where she felt there was a great divine power speaking through her former therapist.

"So now, I know for myself. There is a God. Without a shadow of a doubt. One who abounds in love. And I've come to terms with the fact that if He never heals me, I know that He is able and that He can. And in that confidence is my healing. You know the amazing thing about this whole journey these past few months?" Sapphire said with her countenance glowing.

"What?" responded Ravinia circumspectly; hanging onto the doctor's every word.

"You know, God isn't all concerned about the religions we wear, all the intricacies of fighting over who is going to sing the sermonic solo for next Sunday. God is concerned with love—an amazing, profoundly, peaceful love that surpasses anything we could ever experience on earth. People don't love each other like God wants them to, Ravinia."

"You're right about that, Sapphire," Ravinia added knowingly.

"If we just took time to love, there would be less hate, less murder, less sin in the world. It is so simple, yet people try to complicate God's message. It is really all about love," Sapphire finished with a big sigh. It seemed to take the wind out of her to talk that long and intently about something she felt so strongly about.

"That is so beautiful, girl. You are so on point, because love forgives, and that is what is mending my marriage back together," Ravinia said, wiping a stray tear from the corner of her eye.

"Okay. So, do I have to be the one to cut the ribbon when the Mayor gets here?" Jade trumpeted as she walked into the storeroom where Sapphire and Ravinia had been talking and crying.

"Thank God Starbucks donated all that coffee. All those folks are waiting outside in the cold for us to open," Jade fussed with a grin on her face. Wiping her eyes, Sapphire said, "Girl, I wouldn't miss this day for all the Häagen-Dazs in the world." She wrapped her bone-thin arm around the lower half of Jade's thicker waist.

"Me either, girl. Me either," chimed in Ravinia, smiling at the other two proprietors.

"Then let's do this," proclaimed Jade, as she pulled Ravinia in, wrapping her arm around her. Squeezing her friends tightly, with Ravinia on the left and Sapphire on the right, Jade shouted, "*Magdalene's* is now open for business!"

Chapter 39.

LULLABY

Looking at her daughter, Randella, who was rocking her baby doll to sleep, Ravinia reminisced back to the days when her mother used to hold her in her arms. In child-like innocence, Randella sang:

Rock a bye baby in the treetop
When the wind blows the cradle will rock
When the bough breaks the cradle will fall
And down will come baby, cradle and all ...

Ravinia closed her eyes, lulled into cavernous thoughts that churned around the charming, yet dissonant lullaby. Seeing herself perched up high in a tree, Ravinia daydreamed that she was lying in a fetal position, wrapped tightly amongst her fears. As she stretched out on the shaking limb, she could not see that there was a large crack near the trunk. Feeling the branch tremble, she realized that the tree represented her life and the branch that was broken symbolized every vow she had ever failed. Blinking a couple of times to clear her mind, Ravinia swallowed the wondering truth that she had to face every day for the rest of her marriage. The reality of life was going to be bittersweet; and she had to take the bitter parts with the sweet in order to survive and then, thrive in her own.

Not more than a few seconds after the lyrics had left Randella's little mouth, Ravinia knew that her daughter's precocious curiosity would not allow her to finish the song without having to explain the third stanza. Randella looked up at her mother with big mahogany eyes and asked in a tiny, inquiring voice, "Momma, what does the baby do when the bough breaks?"

Ravinia responded cautiously, regretting this part of motherhood. It was the Q and A sessions that seemed to unnerve her the most. Trying to remain reasonably calm, in a still voice she said, "Well, the baby falls," thinking about her own most recent experience that practically knocked her flat on the floor.

"I don't like that song anymore," said Randella, shaking her pretty, little head full of plastic barrettes back and forth. The soft curls of her reddish-golden hair blended with the bronze undertones of her caramel-colored skin. "The baby got hurt," her soft voice pouted, as she held her American girl doll, Addie, close to her heart, lest she too fall like the baby in the song.

Ravinia looked at her daughter and stroked the fine baby hair that traced her daughter's hairline. Smoothing Randella's ash blonde edges, Ravinia wondered about what her adopted daughter's parents must have looked like. She then thought about her marriage and how she and Xavier had survived, though the vows they had made had been broken. In mother-like wisdom, Ravinia kissed her daughter's forehead, where one of the plastic barrettes had left a jagged white scratch and said, "Sometimes things happen and we fall. Whether someone pushed us, we were put up too high and allowed to fall, or we just fell down on our own accord. But every time we fall, Della, we must get up. There may be some broken bones, some hurt feelings and bruises we must bear. But we must get up baby. We must get up."

Ravinia knew Randella would not fully understand the magnitude of the revelation that had just dropped off of her own lips. But the message was not for her daughter, but for her.

Vows are not meant to be broken, but people are meant to be forgiven . . .

And now abide faith, hope and love, these three; but the greatest of these is love.

I Corinthians 13:13 NKJV

Reading Group Guide

WHEN THE VOW BREAKS

1. During the scene at the church, Ravinia had several opportunities to get away from the Reverend before any mischief occurred. Why didn't she? What made her stay? If you were in a similar situation, what would you do?
2. What explanation can you provide as to what were causing Sapphire's illnesses as a child? Did she need psychological treatment or just deliverance through prayer?
3. Do you feel that Sapphire was raped? Or was it her fault because she was already dating the Reverend? Could she have prevented the situation from happening?
4. Who made the greatest change in their life—Ravinia or Sapphire? Why?
5. Discuss at least two (2) instances of two (2) different characters that endured domestic violence in this novel.
6. Who was the tempter?
7. What did Ravinia want from her mother? Did she ever get it?
8. Symbolism plays a big part in conceptualizing the characters in this book. What types of symbolism can be found in the names of some of the characters and their roles in the story?
9. Why do you think Ravinia kept hearing her mother's voice after she was deceased?
10. Is Jade justified in not being complacent in her desire to have more excitement in her marriage? Or should she be happy with what she has and not complain?
11. Will the Reverend amend his sinful ways? Will being married to Mattie change his philandering?
12. Describe the various ways in which vows were represented and subsequently broken in "When the Vow Breaks" and why.
13. With all the infidelity and law-breaking present in today's society, are vows a thing of the past?
14. Describe the spiritual strength of Jade, Sapphire and Ravinia. How do they differ and how are they the same?
15. Do you think Xavier is sincere about reconciliation with his wife?
16. Why do you think Ravinia had such a difficult time with Xavier's extramarital affair with a woman of a different race as opposed to the many affairs her first husband had?
17. After reading the journal entries that Sapphire wrote, who was she angry at the most? Do you think she resolved that anger? How?

Reading Group Guide

18. Do you think Sapphire gave up her practice for friendship or did she give it up because it was too much responsibility while she was trying to heal? What do you think?

19. Ravinia found that the power of prayer brought her through a challenging ordeal in her life. Have you ever found prayer to be a solution to a situation you are facing? Can prayer change a life?

20. In this day and age, there is so much corruption in the legal system, government and the church. What can you do to make a difference?

21. The last line of the book talks about how vows are not meant to be broken but people are meant to be forgiven. What does that statement mean to you? Do you agree with that?

RESOURCES

Professional Prodigy, Inc. takes no responsibility for, and exercises no control over, the organizations' views.

National Domestic Violence Organizations

Family Violence Prevention Fund
383 Rhode Island Street
Suite 304
San Francisco, CA 94103-5133
Phone: (415) 252-8900 Fax: (415) 252-8991

National Coalition Against Domestic Violence Policy Office
1532 16th St. N.W.
Washington, DC 20036
Phone: (202) 745-1211 Fax: (202) 745-0088

National Coalition Against Domestic Violence
P.O. Box 18749
Denver, CO 80218
Phone: (303) 839-1852 Fax: (303) 831-9251

National Resource Center on DV
Pennsylvania Coalition Against Domestic Violence
6400 Flank Drive
Suite 1300
Harrisburg, PA 17112
Phone: 1(800) 537-2238 FAX: (717) 671-8149

National Health Resource Center on Domestic Violence
Family Violence Prevention Fund
383 Rhode Island St.
Suite 304
San Francisco, CA 94103-5133
Phone: 1(800) 313-1310 Fax: (415) 252-8991

Battered Women's Justice Project
Criminal Justice Center and Administrative Office
Minnesota Program Development, Inc.
4032 Chicago Avenue South
Minneapolis, MN 55407
TOLL-FREE: 1(800) 903-011 Ext: 1
Phone: (612) 824-8768 Fax: (612) 824-8965

RESOURCES

Battered Women's Justice Project
c/o PCADV - Legal Office
524 McKnight Street, Reading, PA 19601
Phone: 1(800) 903-0111 Fax: (610) 373-6403

Battered Women's Justice Project
National Clearinghouse for the Defense of Battered Women
125 South 9th Street
Suite 302
Philadelphia, PA 19107
TOLL-FREE: 1(800) 903-0111 ext. 3
Phone: (215) 351-0010 Fax: (215) 351-0779

National Clearinghouse on Marital and Date Rape
2325 Oak Street
Berkeley, CA 94708
Phone: (510) 524-1582

Center for the Prevention of Sexual and Domestic Violence
936 North 34th Street
Suite 200
Seattle, WA 98103
Phone: (206) 634-1903 Fax (206) 634-0115
E-mail: cpsdv@cpsdv.org

National Network to End Domestic Violence, Inc.
666 Pennsylvania Ave. SE
Suite 303
Washington, DC 20003
Phone: (202) 543-5566 Fax: (202) 543-5626

Chicago Domestic Violence Organizations

Southwest Women Working Together
Provides direct services and advocacy to help women, children and families to lead empowered, self-sufficient, and violence-free lives
6845 S. Western Ave.
Chicago, IL 60636
Phone: (773) 737-2500 Fax: (773)737-1925
E-mail: info@swwt.org
Website: www.swwt.org

RESOURCES

A Friend's Place
A free walk-in counseling center for women and children in Chicago, IL.
24 hour crisis referral Hotline, court advocacy, and community education
A Friends Place
P. O. Box 5185
Evanston, IL 60204
Phone: (773) 274-5232 or 1(800)603-HELP

Sexual Assault Hotlines

National Sexual Violence Resource Center
24-hour access to information, resources, and research regarding sexual assault
Phone: 1(877) 739-3895 (toll free)

Rape, Abuse & Incest National Network RAINN)
635-B Pennsylvania Avenue, SE
Washington, DC 20003
Phone: 1(800) 656-HOPE *(Note: This number will connect you to your local rape crisis center.)*

Cancer Survivors Organizations

Sisters Network
Founded in 1994, Sisters Network® Inc. (SNI) is the first national African American breast cancer survivorship organization.
http://www.sistersnetworkinc.org
8787 Woodway Drive, Suite 4206
Houston, TX 77063
Phone: (713) 781-0255 Fax: (713) 780-8998
infonet@sistersnetworkinc.org

Nueva Vida
Spanish resources
http://www.nueva-vida.org
2000 P Street NW, Suite 740
Washington, DC 20036
Phone: (202) 223-9100 Fax: (202) 223-9600

Native American Cancer Research
Information about the Native American Cancer Survivor's Support.
Network, educational resources and information about clinical trials.
http://natamcancer.org/

RESOURCES

Survivors Network
3022 South Nova Road
Pine, CO 80470-7830
TOLL FREE: 1(800) 537-8295
Phone: (303) 838-9359 Fax: (303) 838-7629
natamcan2@aol.com

SHARE
SHARE is a not-for-profit organization that offers survivor-led support to women with breast or ovarian cancer, their families and friends.
http://www.sharecancersupport.org
1501 Broadway
Suite 704A
New York, NY 10036
Phone: (866) 891-2392 (212) 869-3431

Facing Our Risk of Cancer Empowered (FORCE)
http://www.facingourrisk.org
Toll-free: 866-824-RISK (7475)
16057 Tampa Palms Blvd. W
PMB #373
Tampa, FL 33647
Phone: (954) 255-8732

Gynecologic Cancer Foundation
http://www.wcn.org
230 W. Monroe
Suite 2528
Chicago, IL 60606
Phone:(312)578-1439 Fax (312)578-9769
info@thegcf.org

Ovarian Cancer National Alliance
http://www.ovariancancer.org
910 17th Street, N.W.
Suite 413
Washington, DC 20006
Phone: (202) 331-1332 Fax: (202) 331-2292

RESOURCES

The Wellness Community
International non-profit organization dedicated to providing support, education and hope for all people affected by cancer – at no cost.
http://www.thewellnesscommunity.org
919 18th Street, NW
Suite 54
Washington, DC 20006
Phone: 1(888) 793-WELL (9355) (202) 659-9301
help@thewellnesscommunity.org

PROFESSIONAL PRODIGY, INC.

Changing the Course of Your Future One Path at a Time

Professional Prodigy Inc. The goal of the organization is to bring women together to create a forum for women to empower and educate themselves while inspiring other women. Although the focus is on minority women, all women are welcomed and encouraged to participate in activities and use the organization's resources. The organization seeks to create opportunities for women to network with other women and pool resources of women's organizations and businesses of interest to women. We have a special focus on leadership development for girls and teens. We feel the importance for women leaders to invest in the next generation of women leaders is significant. After all if we don't do it...then who will?

Our workshops are designed for the empowerment of all women of all ages and business levels. They are to educate, entertain and guide women on their journeys to personal and professional achievement.

Our Vision:

To create forums that will educate and empower all women.

Our Mission:

To offer training in education for both career opportunities and entrepreneurship which will:

- Provide the essential skills and relevant knowledge which individuals need to achieve success,
- Foster and promote personal and professional development leading to entrepreneurship, and
- Prepare individuals for success in business and professional environments.

Our Goals:

To promote awareness on the positive contribution of women of all ages and business levels.

For seminars and workshops, please contact:
Website: www.professionalprodigy.com
Ph: 708.449.8058, fax: 708.449.0001
Email: www.professionalprodigy@sbc.global.net

Ready or Not . . . Get Set Go

(An Entrepreneur's Guide to Starting and Maintaining a Successful Business)

By Sheila Taylor-Downer

ISBN: 0-9702909-0-X

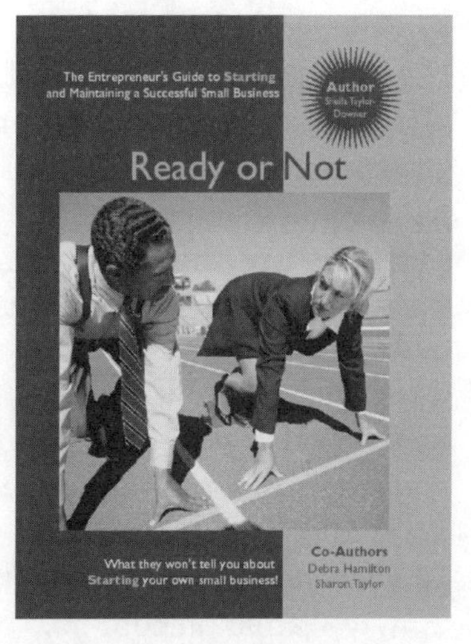

Midwest Book Review says: Ready Or Not...Get Set Go is the ideal "how to" book for anyone aspiring to become their own boss through launching their own business enterprise. Debra Hamilton and Sharon Taylor effectively collaborate with Sheila to offer the reader an informative and practical guide and reference to starting and operating a successful business as they survey such essential issues as the legal structure for a self-owned business; "law & taxes"; do-it-yourself evaluation for personal qualities necessary for running a business; the start-up costs of a small business; creation of an effective and goal oriented business plan; marketing; and much, much more. If you are contemplating having a business of your own, begin with a careful reading of Ready Or Not...Get Set Go -- it will be the best investment of your time and money that you could make in deciding whether or not to go out on your own in today's highly competitive marketplace.

Order information:
$13.95
Website: www.professionalprodigy.com
www.amazon.com
P. O. Box 641, Hillside, IL 60161
Ph: 708.449.8058, fax: 708.449.0001

Women In Power
(A Narrative of Triumphs and Defeats)

By Sheila Taylor-Downer

ISBN: 0-9702909-1-8

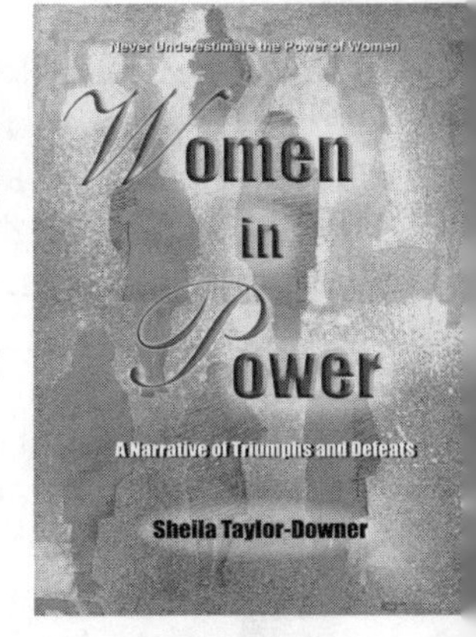

Chicago Defender says: This extraordinary work explores powerful, insightful, invigorating short stories about the triumphs and defeats of women destined for success.

Theirs are the heartwarming stories culminating in overwhelming and phenomenal victory.

Order information:
$12.00
Website: www.professionalprodigy.com
www.amazon.com
P. O. Box 641, Hillside, IL 60161
Ph: 708.449.8058, fax: 708.449.0001

ABOUT the AUTHORS

Cynthia L. Berry

"A profoundly talented writer, Cynthia wields her pen with captivating stories of struggle, conviction, and revelation. Possessing an unparalleled ability to carry her readers through her soul's uttermost rendering, Cynthia unveils life stories in their truest form."

Alumni of Northwestern University, Cynthia has a B.S. in Psychology and a M.A. in Guidance and Counseling. With a passion for evangelism, her writing reaches beyond the church pews, inspiring individuals to find their purpose. Cynthia is also working on several other books including ***Soul Tied***, to be released Spring 2007 and a collaborative sequel with Ms. Downer entitled ***Women in Power II***.

A native Chicagoan, Cynthia and her family reside just outside of Chicago.

Sheila A. Taylor-Downer

Sheila A. Taylor-Downer is a Life Coach and can eloquently speak to women through the visualization of her words. Sheila A Downer wants to make a difference through her books to let the reading public know that they are not alone. There is a champion of their cause...the cause of escaping into great books.

She is the author to be reckoned with the likes of Bebe Moore Campbell and Toni Morrison. Sheila will succeed in turning around lives, one at a time.

She is working on her 4th release **Motivated by Passion . . . Held Back by Fear**, to be released in the summer of 2007.

